T0365146

THE UNPARDONABLE OBJECTIVE

THE BLACKWELL CHRONICLES

JAMES T. AND CYNTHIA A. RUNYON

WESTBOW
PRESS
A DIVISION OF THOMAS NELSON

WestBow Press books may be ordered through booksellers or by contacting:

WestBow Press
A Division of Thomas Nelson
1663 Liberty Drive
Bloomington, IN 47403
www.westbowpress.com
1-(866) 928-1240

Because of the dynamic nature of the Internet, any Web addresses or links contained in this book may have changed since publication and may no longer be valid. The views expressed in this work are solely those of the author and do not necessarily reflect the views of the publisher, and the publisher hereby disclaims any responsibility for them.

Any people depicted in stock imagery provided by Thinkstock are models, and such images are being used for illustrative purposes only.

Certain stock imagery © Thinkstock.

ISBN: 978-1-4497-1021-7 (sc)
ISBN: 978-1-4497-1020-0 (e)

Library of Congress Control Number: 2010942656

Printed in the United States of America

WestBow Press rev. date: 1/13/2011

PROLOGUE

SUNDAY MORNING, APRIL 12

The man watched through the windows of the sleek Lincoln limousine as the sun began to rise over the cool dew-covered ground. The light bowed its rays around the silver lined clouds to the east filling the morning sky with pink and red hues. Normally, a sunrise with such vibrance would lighten the heart of the single passenger within the long black vehicle, however this morning the heavenly shading added an ominous feel to the drive.

The vehicle left the large marble buildings of Washington just 20 minutes earlier and was now entering the countryside surrounding the nation's capital. With its rolling hills, tall tree lines, and farms peppering the landscape, Virginia was truly a beautiful state.

Any other day, the same drive would take twice, if not three times as long, but on Sunday mornings, the streets and highways were quiet. This is why the man chose to make the weekly trip when he did; minimizing the frustration caused by traffic congestion and road crew delays.

The Lincoln left the monotony of the highway and turned onto a small road that wound its way into the Virginia hills. No longer in his comfort zone of million dollar residences, the passenger entered the small farming community nestled with simple two story, wood sided homes snuggled up to red and white painted barns. Of all of the places in the world he could have purchased for her; here is where she wanted to be. He still didn't understand after all of these years.

Ten more minutes of driving found the limousine on a dirt road that ended at a bricked enclosure sealed with a wrought iron gate. The Lincoln stopped and the chauffer got out and opened the door for the man in the back.

"Thank you, Layton," the passenger said as he stepped from the comfort of the plush limousine.

The cool, wet air of the morning surrounded the man as he found his footing on the grass-covered lawn next to the vehicle. Sunday mornings were never easy, but always necessary, so he closed his eyes for a second to prepare for the task ahead. After preparing himself, he gently grasped the two red roses offered by his driver and walked toward the gate.

The chauffer watched with admiration as his employer passed the car and headed toward the entrance. Many in his position would have moved on years before, but not him. The man in the dark suit forced himself to remember.

Layton knew the tradition well, for he was there seven years ago when the ritual began and had not missed a Sunday with his employer since. He closed the door and stood in a respectful stance next to the vehicle.

Looking inside for over a minute, the tall man stood at the gate before opening it. The creak of the metal partition echoed throughout the mountainside adding to the darkness of the experience. He walked under the ivy covered brick arch and stepped onto the path leading up the gentle rise to the center of the area.

The walls to the square enclosure were about five feet high and 100 feet long. In each corner stood a pink dogwood paired with golden-yellow forsythias. The walk was lined with tulips and daffodils, all stretching to reach the sun's earliest rays.

He paid quite a bit of money to keep the area maintained, and it was obvious that the funds were well spent. In addition to the azaleas lining the walls, and a few well-placed Redbud or flowering cherries, the whole area was covered with a lush layer of grass.

The rise of the path allowed him to look around and see well above the walls of the enclosure, revealing the countryside's rolling hills. He stopped and tried to view the beauty of the land through her eyes. To the east, the sun was bouncing off of the tops of the hills while white fog settled like a calm sea in the valleys. He turned around and noticed an eagle soaring on the morning air.

While those things were beautiful to the man, they were truly magical to her. He remembered times when they would come to this spot and she would talk nonstop about everything from the shape of the clouds to the color of the wild flowers. Often, they would visit just to sit and look at the beauty of the countryside. Though he never much appreciated the breaks when he was younger; she loved it and so he continued to go. In her eyes, everything had beauty and the world was innocent.

The man turned his attention back to the path and headed forward up the gentle incline. Although he had visited this location hundreds of times in the past, this occasion would be different. He traveled the final 25 feet to the top of the rise and ceased his movement where the path ended.

Standing there in silence for what seemed like hours, the man finally moved forward, knelt down and placed a single rose next to each headstone. The headstones were made of black granite and identical except for the left being just a bit larger. The monument on the left was dedicated to his wife, Stephanie. Under her name were the words, "Your love gave me life." To the right, the delicately carved letters formed the word Katherine with the statement below saying, "Your innocence gave me joy." His wife and daughter had been dead for over seven years and his heart still ached.

Standing up, he clasped his hands in front of him and looked at Stephanie's granite marker as it reflected the sun rising in the sky.

"Good morning, darling. The sunrise was beautiful. I wish you could have seen it. The sky was full of pink, red, orange and even some blue. It is just your kind of morning."

He looked over to his daughter's headstone. "Hello sweetie. I sure miss you. I brought you a beautiful rose. There aren't any thorns on it," he thought for a second. "I can just imagine you smelling it and then putting it up in your hair. It would have looked lovely on you."

The words stopped, and a few tears fell down the man's cheeks.

"Oh ladies, how I wish you were here. I would be better this time. I wouldn't take our time for granted." He wiped away his tears.

"We could come here anytime you wanted and have a picnic, or hike through the woods, if you were just here.

I bought all of this land for you," he said gesturing to the countryside. "Everything that you could see in all directions is yours, if you were here." He dropped his head to his chest.

"Darling," he said looking back to his wife's grave. "I have tried hard to make it without you, but it is difficult. I put on a good face, but you would be able to see through it very quickly. My life is dark." He watched the eagle fly overhead.

What freedom he has, he thought, looking up at the majestic bird.

"Oh, if I had that kind of freedom. My heart is so heavy. I know that you wouldn't want that for me, but that's how I feel."

The conversation stopped.

His demeanor changed and he spoke more quietly, "Do you remember me talking to you a while back about a project I was working on? A really big assignment that could change the world?" He paused for a second as if waiting for a response.

"Well, we are just about finished. Today the world will be different because of this work."

Turning away from the hillside memorial, he continued to speak. "Honey I have worked diligently and I believe that I deserve some of its benefits." He stopped.

"Darling, I need to ask for your forgiveness. I have done something for you and Katherine, for us. It is something so great ... and yet so horrific." He dropped his head and turned back toward the headstone.

"I have set things into motion that can't be undone. These things were meant for us but will change the world in such a way that it won't be recognizable. Honey, it will be a better world, one where you won't be taken from me.

Stephanie, I will have you and Katherine with me again. This time it will be better. This time I will keep you close, and you won't leave me again."

He looked up to the sun that was finding its place in the sky. The red and pink hues were disappearing and clouds were taking their place.

Turning his head back toward the tombstones, the man became more determined. "This unpardonable path I have chosen will save us all. I will have you back with me. Ladies, this week I *will* see you again! I love you."

At that, he turned and walked with determination toward the vehicle. The driver had the door opened and waiting for him as the man closed the large irongate to the memorial.

"Back to Washington," he said as he sat on the plush leather seats of the stretch limousine.

"Yes sir."

As the long vehicle turned to leave the area, the man in the back viewed the cemetery one last time.

The man felt hope like he hadn't felt in years. This dark time in his life would be over in just a few days. Because of his sacrifice, everything could be made right.

If everything goes as planned, the next time I am here it will be for a picnic with my dear ones, he thought. The man smiled and the Lincoln drove away leaving a trail of dust.

1 — SUNDAY MORNING, APRIL 12

Dr. Benjamin Keith squinted at the clock, and let his head fall back against the soft, down-filled pillow while listening to Mozart's Requiem. He had been awake most of the night, receiving only sporadic sleep at best. Sunday mornings were a respite from his usual tasks, but this specific Sunday was much different. He had been preparing for it all his life.

As a scientist, or more specifically, a world-renowned physicist, he was accustomed to carrying heavy equations around in his head all day, however, when he hit the pillow it had always been lights out. Last night was different. He had gone to bed with more than just the usual problems.

At about 4 a.m. the man's mind started racing, and it was useless to try to stop it. Always in control of himself, he took great pride in his tremendous self-discipline. His five-foot, ten-inch frame was very athletic from diligently spending 45 minutes per day in aerobic exercise and topping it off with a good amount of weight lifting. Benjamin's body weight never varied from 170 pounds, and he was strict with his diet. Even though in July he would turn 46, most new acquaintances took him to be a decade younger. Constancy was the motto of Dr. Keith, and it suited him well, however, all of his self-discipline could not stop his mind from whirling.

He threw over the comforter, sat up on the side of his cherry sleigh bed and shrugged. *I suppose it's to be expected. I'd have to be God-if he existed-to sleep on the day culminating my life's work*, he thought as the Requiem continued to play. *Isn't it interesting that on a day when my life is truly beginning, I am awakened by Mozart's final masterpiece? Ironic.*

On a normal Sunday morning, this scientist would get out of bed as late as 7:00 a.m. As his wave radio roused him with a pre-selected classical station, he would close his eyes and allow the music to take him to places that were unattainable in the here and now. It was during this special hour of music and reprieve that the great physicist discovered most of his grand theories.

Today he was out of bed within a few minutes of the alarm going off. Mozart had been the initiator of many theories, but at the moment the composer would have to wait. *I've done all the thinking I can stand for one day*, he thought, as he rose to shower. This specially designed bath took him away from the busyness of the city. It's cove-like design covered in natural rock and adorned with plants, allowed him to imagine being in

Maui under a secluded waterfall. This blissful rinse, as he called it, always forced the previous problems of the week to fall from his back, therefore the shower was more therapeutic than hygienic.

Following the wash, he dressed-nicely as always. Ben, as his close friends called him, dressed well for every occasion, wearing slacks and a tie to work even though his field of expertise didn't call for it. More often than not, the strict dressing got in the way of special experiments and fieldwork, but he felt the ensemble allowed him to gain respect and authority by always being the most immaculately dressed person in his lab.

Sundays were never as formal, but he still pulled on his nicely ironed chinos, leather loafers, and a polo shirt before heading to breakfast. As he was getting dressed he began to smell the specialty of the morning. His educated nose couldn't determine what was cooking downstairs, but it smelled delicious.

As the scientist looked in the bathroom mirror and combed his dark brown yet slightly graying hair, he saw a successful man. Dr. Keith was someone who had made his own reality; a person in charge of his destiny. The man he saw in the mirror was a success.

After getting dressed and leaving his bedroom, he walked a little straighter. He carried himself with more dignity because he knew that after today the whole world would be looking at him and revering him for his accomplishments-even if the whole world was represented by only a few scientists and some government representatives. Tomorrow the planet would be different even if no one knew it, and it was all because of his struggle. He would be seen as great because he had worked diligently to be so. He had forged his legacy, and had carved out his own place in history.

Ben would not rush past the accolades he was about to receive just to start the next race or conquer the next mountain. The scientist would milk this moment in time for all it was worth because he had earned it. Doubtless, there would be cushy offerings from universities to be the Dean of their Math or Science division. *I wouldn't accept anything less than MIT or Berkeley,* he thought to himself. Of course, the government would use their limitless resources to attempt to keep him producing for the "national good," but Ben would have to determine if it was for his good. *Who is to say that I can't be a Dean and do a little government work on the side? I could always get the students to do the research and kill two birds with one stone.* The thoughts kept coming as this future Nobel Prize winner walked down the stairs.

Ben loved his townhouse because of the way it was designed and where it was located. A stylish and trendy home was one of the many perks given to him, because he was one of the few people in the world with knowledge in his specialized field. The government needed his expertise so they took special precautions to keep him happy. Limousine rides, expense accounts, high-level clearance, and freedom to make decisions in his lab were nice; however, the townhouse capped it off.

His two thousand five hundred square foot colonial townhouse was small compared to many of the Senators' or Congressmen's residences, but it suited him just fine. He loved that it was over 150 years old and located only a few blocks from the Capital Building.

Living on A Street and having the Supreme Court within view gave Dr. Keith a sense of power and importance. It was exhilarating for him to think of the many life-changing decisions that were made just a few feet from his door.

As he passed the large bay windows with their view of the street on his way downstairs, he was reminded of how content he was with this place. He felt lucky today. Within his view were other beautiful townhouses containing well-educated, important people. On Sundays, he could see neighbors walking their dogs or jogging. It was now early spring and the trees were bursting with cherry blossoms in full bloom. Spring in Washington was truly beautiful. For that matter, so was winter. He took real pleasure in the large snowdrifts that built up under his front steps. If he looked just right he could almost imagine himself 150 years ago when the neighborhood was fresh and new. The horse-drawn carriages would slowly cross his mind's eye, while the street-lamp lighter would walk down this quaint lane snuffing out the flames on the gaslights in the morning. The winter scene, he thought, was always innocent and pure.

He brought himself back to reality as he noted scientifically that the thing he most enjoyed about living on A Street was that there weren't any children on the block. There weren't many lawns or playgrounds in this part of D.C., so the area stayed quiet.

Breakfast was the meal of the day that Dr. Keith looked most forward too. As a scientist in the midst of serious work that took constant focus, he could never be certain that lunch would be on time or even happen at all. When Ben had lunch, it could be anything from a candy bar to a sandwich from a local deli that a personal assistant selected for him. There was the infrequent official business meal with Senators in the Senate dining room being served by a French chef; but that also meant key business was being conducted. Lunch was always digested badly during this vital transfer of information, so he almost preferred the candy bar.

Dinner wasn't any more predictable than lunch. Because Ben had never married, there wasn't any reason for him to get home for dinner at a particular time, so he chose instead to work late most nights, picking something up on the way home, heating up a frozen dinner, or scraping together some leftovers.

Breakfast, however was a treat. Money wasn't scarce for the Doctor so he'd hired a personal chef to prepare breakfast and an occasional lunch to go. The meal could consist of anything from eggs benedict to pancakes and sausage. Each morning it was different and the anticipation was almost better than the meal. *What could that heavenly aroma be,* he reflected? *Seafood? Shrimp? Maybe Lobster? Who knows what he has cooking down there.* His mind started working on this new problem as he stopped in the hall to write a note to himself about the project. He smiled at how the question plagued him.

The Doctor continued down the stairs. After many years, distinguished teaching positions, countless published papers and three years dedicated to this single government project, he had arrived. Dr. Benjamin Keith was about to change the world and forever be remembered for breaking the final frontier. *Just twenty-four hours left. What a day*!

As he entered the living room, his pride shifted from his academic prowess to his eye for interior decorating. Large overstuffed leather chairs resided in the center of the room. Cherry wood bookcases filled with literary classics, of which a few were first editions, covered the walls. The imported Oriental rug topping the hardwood floors and richly colored draperies over the large windows added to the room, but it was the Picasso over the fireplace that drew the eye and centered the space.

Dr. Keith wasn't fond of the Analytic Cubism period Picasso went through late in life, but he had purchased the brownish monochromatic painting with the awkward cubic dancer for well below market-value. This rare find was also a subject of conversation for him at many of the dinner parties he threw, so he could overlook the dislike he had with its style for the benefit it gave him in society.

Dr. Keith walked through the doorway and caught view of the chef. Clark was a tall man who didn't look like he was designed to be a cook. His broad shoulders and low voice made him more like an NFL quarterback than a chef. His muscular physique made it obvious that he exercised daily. All of that aside, he knew his way around a kitchen, so the renowned scientist didn't judge the book by the cover. Clark came on Tuesdays, Thursdays and Sundays, and for the last two months his breakfasts had never been a disappointment.

"Good morning, Clark," said the excited Doctor.

"Good morning, Dr. Keith, how did you sleep?"

"Could have been better, but I can't complain. What's for breakfast?"

With a large grin, the chef said, "Because this is a special day for you, I have made a dish you are going to love, Shrimp Buljol."

Even though Ben wondered how the man knew it was a special day, he wouldn't turn down a meal that smelled so heavenly.

"Thank you, let's eat," said the Doctor with a smile.

As the physicist ate, his day went through his mind. First he would meet with John Hughes, the head of the Senate Intelligence Committee and leading Senator on his project who would reassure him that all was well with the government's end of the project. Next, he would go to the lab to convene with the scientists and technicians to make certain the equipment was ready for its maiden test. Finally, if the tests were successful, he would spend the rest of the day sipping champagne and receiving accolades and praise from some of the most important leaders in Washington.

As he finished his breakfast, Dr. Keith said, "That was delicious. Thank you Clark, you are a wonderful cook and have given me a great start to this very important day." Clark looked over and nodded in gratitude.

Then the Doctor got up from his seat and went into the living room. As he sat down in his recliner, grabbing a few quiet moments to catch up on the world's events before heading out, he noticed a handwritten note that was sitting under his newspaper.

"What's this?"

While Ben was reading the note, Clark quietly walked up beside him, stuck a Glock31 revolver next to his head and pulled the trigger.

"You're out of time, Doctor," the large man said as Dr. Benjamin Keith slumped over in his chair.

Clark took a bite of the doctor's leftover breakfast before leaving, "You're right Keith; I am a good cook."

2 — SUNDAY MORNING, APRIL 12

Clark. It wasn't the best he could come up with, but the name of one of his childhood pets seemed an appropriate alias for the job. Walking casually out the front door of the Doctor's town home, he opened a high-tech phone and waited as it dialed and gained access to a restricted line. His boss was waiting to hear he'd succeeded; the call couldn't wait.

The assassin had been hired with special precautions to ensure anonymity-the high-tech phone being one of them. Every number needed for the job was stored in order of completion of every phase of the project. Opening the phone directly dialed the restricted access number. When the conversation was over and the phone was closed, the number was erased from the equipment's memory. Voice-locked to Clark alone, if he didn't say his name within five seconds of flipping the top, the memory chip would destruct, removing any special functions and thus turning it into an ordinary phone. Even a complete disassembly of the device would prove inconclusive about its initial use.

Clark was known throughout the world as a master at his craft. Initially an operative for the National Security Administration, he had a psychological profile that proved he could carry out an order that 99% of humanity found offensive; yet he felt no remorse or regret. He'd spent twelve years in the Navy and his last four in the special SEAL division. Clark had no family life and no parental ties. As an operative, he was uniquely perfect for his job.

The assassin was alone and could claim all success in life as his own. He hadn't had any help from family, and for all practical purposes, didn't have family.

This man's childhood was not typical, but it had prepared him for the hard world that became his life. When his friends were coming home from school to eat a nice meal around the dinner table, he was working as a sweeper in a sawmill; the same mill from which his father worked. Four hours each night he swept up dust and picked up loose pieces of board. Leaving work tired, dirty, and hungry, he dreaded going home to his drunk and abusive father. His mother was too preoccupied in her own desperate attempt at surviving to quench her little boy's needs.

When Clark's father was 18, his high school team took state due to his talent; therefore he was accepted to college on a baseball scholarship. The

11

summer before he was to leave for college, a drunk driver hit him as he walked home from his final game, shattering his leg along with his dream of a baseball career or even college. He walked with a limp after that and become more bitter and angry with each passing step. The loathsome job at the town mill was his only recourse.

The assassin loved his mother dearly. She wasn't a beautiful woman by the world's standards, and the years of living with an unloving man were apparent. However she was the only thing in his crazy life that made sense, and so she was beautiful to Clark. They would spend many hours in the back bedroom, making up stories of a loving home far away, while Father was getting drunk in the living room watching television. Of all of the outrageous scenarios they dreamed together, the one he liked most was of a father who came home happy each night to see the family he loved gathered around the dinner table. They could dream together and hope together. Unfortunately, it was no more real than the dreams of a fictional character such as Andy Griffith being his dad.

Clark and his mother took special time on Saturday night to prepare for Sunday morning. Mom would press and starch his worn and often too small shirts and pants until they could stand on end. They would read their Bible together and she would prepare Clark for his Bible study at church in the morning.

They weren't the best-dressed or smartest people in the little congregation, but they were probably the only people who wanted to be there. It was a great escape for the few hours they were away from their sad and disappointing life.

Church wasn't a country club to him or his mother; it was where you made right all of the wrong of the world. When nothing made sense, church was a healing time for the two battered souls.

His father never went to church and didn't want any of his hard-earned money going to, as he would say, "Line the walls with more gold." There was always a fight if he thought mom was taking his money and giving it to the church. "If the church needed money," he would add, "God can give it to them."

Life was difficult but manageable in Clark's household. Being the child in a dysfunctional family, Clark knew how to make everything right. He knew how to say the right words or calm down the situation, but life is unpredictable, and so that summer night in July almost made sense.

Just turning twelve, Clark wasn't supposed to be working at all, let alone twelve-hour days in a sawmill. However, the boss liked him and valued his hard work so he broke federal regulation and paid Clark under the table so he could help out his family situation. Clark was working the ten-to-ten shift that week, which was a particularly hard week for his father. The summer weather had kicked in, and the plant could get up to 120 degrees in July and August. The pain in his leg from the accident years earlier seemed to intensify with temperature. The discomfort worsened with every elevated degree until it was unbearable for a man who stood all day in one position.

One night he arrived home to find his father yelling at his mother. Evidently, the washing machine had broken during the day and Father couldn't fix it. They didn't have money to waste and his wife was expecting him to throw what little they had out the window to fix a machine that he said she should have been more careful with. The angry man stormed out and left for his favorite bar.

Several hours later he came home with a vicious intensity that Clark hadn't seen before, and immediately started pushing his mother around. The day was forever clear and vivid; one that Clark would never forget. This scene often flew into his mind on occasion as if it were happening before him.

His mother was getting up from one of the many body blows that she had received. As Clark was running to his mother, his father pushed her one more time. It was during this fall that she hit her head on the edge of the kitchen counter and never regained consciousness.

Clark ran over to try to help, but it was too late. His father didn't quite know what to do. He thought she was acting because she had faked being hurt many times before to get him away, but this was no charade.

The only person that gave him love and helped him work through the difficulties of life was dead in a pool of blood on the floor. Something snapped in Clark. He went into the bedroom and took out his father's shotgun, like he had many times before. This time, however, there was no dreaming up some improbable fantasy that would leave him fatherless; this time he loaded the gun and went back into the living room.

Upon reentering the room, his father was standing in the same position that he was moments earlier with a look of bewilderment on his face. Clark wondered if he was sorry for what he had done. Did he understand the extent of his actions? It didn't matter to the boy, because he aimed the rifle and shot his father in the chest. The man dropped to the ground immediately and Clark was left in the room alone.

When the police arrived, they labeled it a murder-suicide because Clark was too much in shock to speak. The entry wounds on the father looked like he could have shot himself. The gun was positioned in such a way that it looked like it dropped following a self-inflicted shot to the chest. The case was wrapped up quickly and Clark was put into a foster home that night. Because the family didn't have anything but debts, Clark wasn't able to take anything with him when he left.

The young boy spent the next six years in 14 foster homes. Because of the anger from the years of abuse, and the loss of the only person he loved, he was very difficult to control and therefore moved from one foster home to another.

This young man determined to protect himself from the evils his life dealt him. He would never again feel love and would never again go to church. God had abandoned him and didn't protect the one person in his life that he loved; his mother. He turned his back on God. Church was for the weak and mindless who needed a one-hour conscience appeasement to make it through their privileged, meaningless lives. He now knew that his father was right about one thing; you have to make your own comfort and way in this world.

He enlisted in the Navy at age eighteen, an angry young man with everything to prove to no one in particular. Joining the Navy gave Clark the family he'd never had, and he worked his way up the ranks quickly with little effort.

Several years after enlistment, he became a SEAL. It soon became obvious to his commanders that his profile was shaping up for special assignment work. His unique ability to remove all emotion, his hard focus, his iron determination; his profile was like reading the special operators handbook.

Clark's assignments began to involve infiltration, and it came easy to him. His methods of infiltration and information retrieval were unorthodox and always effective. After four years in the SEALs, he was recruited to the NSA.

The agency had dispatched him to Columbia to discover who was supplying heroine to Miami. A new political party had taken over the office of Homeland Security and they wanted to be known as the group with a hard stance toward drug trafficking. Clark figured he was just a pawn in a large game of chess, but wasn't that the story of his life?

Spending six months without even a single lead, Clark finally caught a break. Well-trained in the art of disguise and with a little planning, he forged Italian-Colombian connections, and was personally introduced to the drug lord in less than two weeks.

Manuel Roderiguez was not a typical Columbian drug lord. No greasy black hair and thick mustache as is seen in the movies. Manuel could easily have been a CEO for a major New York bank. As the paper on the walls showed, he'd been educated at Yale and received his MBA from Harvard. He was kind, gracious, and when in Manuel's presence, one felt like a king. Without inside information, Clark would have never guessed that the engaging Mr. Roderiguez sold close to a billion dollars in drugs annually to Miami alone.

After several weeks with Manuel, and having gained all the information the U.S. government needed, Clark was told to remove the drug dealer. He balked. Manuel was likable; he'd treated Clark with respect and had even become a friend; if a drug lord can be a friend.

But Clark finished every job and took pride in his accomplishments, so, the first chance available; he placed a gun to Manuel's head. In terror for his life, the drug lord offered Clark ten million dollars, and with little hesitation, he took it. *Mercenary? If the shoe fits!* The thought didn't even faze him. There was more money on the other side.

Manuel knew talent when he saw it, and Clark had talent. After his relief expired, his brain took over. Realizing Clark's potential, he placed him on the payroll fast. Switching from a low-paid, ultra-secret civil service job, to earning millions in dollars and respect was not a difficult decision. He agreed to help Manuel on a case-by-case basis; one infiltration, one theft, and one murder at a time.

Clark worked several more years before becoming his own independent contractor. Many entities around the world hired him to remove "problems," and for the most part, he enjoyed his work. Yes, there was the unpleasantness of the job itself and the annoying fact that the U.S. government was always after him, but the money and the freedom more than made up for the down side of his particular occupation. An agent with top-secret information and high-level clearance could not go AWOL. It was because of this that he nearly keeled over when his old boss tracked him down to ask for his help.

Six weeks and eight false meetings allowed the assassin to finally trust that the man actually wanted his services and not his life. When they ultimately did meet, and the man told Clark the extent of the mission and the money that he would make, he knew that when the project was over, he could easily retire anywhere in the world.

This time as the phone sounded, Clark knew his old boss would once again be pleased with his work.

"Yes?" came the voice at the other end.

"Breakfast went well, and the kitchen is cleaned and put in order," said Clark while entering his car.

"Fine. Continue on and call me after you're through. I'll have your help waiting."

"I'm leaving now and will be there in twenty minutes." Clark ended the conversation, started his car, and drove from the townhouse.

"Come on honey, we're gonna be late." Hudson Blackwell did not like to be late.

"I will be there in a minute," said his slightly irritated wife. "You only have to get yourself ready for church; I have myself *and* two children to get ready. Not to mention starting lunch, ironing *your* shirt at the last minute and…"

"Alright, just hurry! I don't like being late every Sunday," Hudson replied hoping his words might move her along.

Even though Sara's constant misunderstanding of time was a point of controversy between the two, Hudson desperately loved her. He would continue to be late to every event in life if it meant that he could spend that life with her.

He'd met Sara in High School and loved her at first sight. Hudson wrestled for the team in High School-the Fighting Trojans-and they had a pretty good record. Much of their success was because of Hudson, and he enjoyed the notoriety it gave him. Being right at six feet tall and weighing in at 210 pounds made him one of the larger men on the team, and everyone enjoyed watching the heavy weights wrestle. The smaller guys just didn't draw the crowds.

The night he met Sara, Hudson was on the mat with Jack Johnson. The guy had a reputation for not using deodorant the day of the match and rubbing garlic all over his body so his opponent's nose might force his body to give up without a fight. Hudson didn't give in that easily even though Jack's pungent plan had worked many times before with a roster full of other opponents. As the two men went in and out of locks and holds, Hudson noticed a girl in the stands. He'd never seen her before, so he figured she must have been from the other school. She had golden blond hair, thin Roman features, a beautifully innocent smile and bright wide eyes. For an instant his mouth opened, and his eyes got stuck on the girl of his dreams. It was during that brief period of time that Jack rolled the love-struck wrestler, and Hudson began counting the ceiling lights. After a quick three count, the school's favorite was out and the aromatic opponent was victorious.

It wasn't his best moment on the mat, but after the match he sought out the girl in the stands. Not being the smoothest guy around, he told her bluntly that he'd lost the match because she distracted him. She quickly furrowed her brows and walked off. However, after a few quick corrections to his insensitive statement, he got a date.

Their first date wasn't anything spectacular, the normal pizza and a movie, but it was the beginning of a romance that wouldn't die. Hudson loved Sara's beautiful blue eyes and her short but tight five-foot, four-inch frame. He enjoyed the way that she could speak for hours on whatever seemed to cross her mind. And most of all, he loved *her*. She had a zest for life that he didn't have. She could talk about the beautiful night sky or a simple flower in someone's yard, and seemed to live life to the fullest giving Hudson a new and refreshing outlook. He was hooked from the beginning and would continue to stay that way.

Sara and Hudson dated for several years and were married right out of college. Sara earned an English degree and Hudson a Bachelor's in Electrical Engineering. It wasn't very long after the two were married that Sara became pregnant with the first of their two children. They had a little boy named Michael and a girl named Amy. These children were the joy of Hudson's life and everyone knew it.

Soon after his first degree, the graduate went back for a Master's in Electrical Engineering. Being an ex-wrestler in love with excitement, he worked as a security guard for top sporting events. Getting recommended by each suit he worked under soon gave him the idea that he was good at the occupation of protection. Not long after that realization, came a call from the Secret Service. He was the perfect candidate, tall, great eyesight, a Master's degree and the right psychological profile. He could remain cool and could perform well under any circumstance.

He protected the governor a few times and eventually was called by the Secret Service to guard the President. Several years into this arduous, stressful and travel-laden job, he grew tired of the many hours he had to be away from his Sara and the two children that were growing up without him.

When Senator Hughes called him with a special project, he jumped on it. For three years he enjoyed the comfort of being at home and having a "normal" day job. Of course, the hours were sometimes odd, but it was nothing like flying around the world with the President and being gone for weeks at a time.

"We need to leave now! Sunday School starts in five minutes and we are ten minutes away from the church," Hudson growled out as his little boy sat at his feet needing his shoes tied.

"Honey, you know nobody actually comes on time. Anyway, you married me, so you will have to just put up with me. It's not good to start off the Lord's Day in such a huff," Sara said with a smile as she started down the steps putting the back on her earring.

Looking at his beautiful wife as she approached the bottom step diverted his attention from the time, and Hudson knew she was right. It wasn't good to go to church angry even though his whole world seemed to blow up when he was late. He didn't know if it was the engineering training that made him so exact with time or if it were the years spent guarding the President. It was understood when the President was going to leave at a certain time, he left at exactly that time. Many of the spy movies make jokes of synchronizing watches, but as a Secret Service agent, that is exactly what he did-every day. Time was everything and if you were late, the President's life was at stake.

"Okay, I'm ready," Sara said at the door as if she had been waiting for hours. He grimaced as he finished the knot in his son's shoe. It never failed. Hudson got up thirty minutes later and was ready twenty minutes before Sara, however when she finally came down the stairs he was always working at something as if he were behind. Sara always made it look like she was the one on time.

Hudson knew that his wife was also right in implying that they would be the only ones in their seats ready for Sunday School on time. Indeed, after the ten-minute car ride, and the ten minutes to get into the building and drop their children off in their classes, they were the first couple to arrive besides the teacher. As the teacher began to speak, Hudson mused to himself that this day seemed to repeat itself every Sunday.

They headed into the worship service after class like everyone else, but this was Sara's time to shine. Everybody loved Sara. As she communicated with her mouth and hands, Hudson just stood beside her and smiled. The word quiet described him perfectly, and he enjoyed just watching his beautiful little wife. She stopped to talk to every person she could and always ended up late to worship; walking in from the back during the first congregational song of the morning where Hudson was waiting with an extra hymn book open for her. It was a great ritual and after many years of practice, he still loved to tease her about it.

Hudson enjoyed the sermons. The Pastor truly studied The Word, and it showed on Sunday morning. He would expose a certain passage of scripture in a way that convicted his soul through a deeper understanding of the Bible. His messages did that for others, also. Several of the men would discuss the sermons over coffee at church-sponsored men's breakfasts, and his topics would even come up at non-church related events.

Sara nudged Hudson out of his thoughts and tugged his arm to find his Bible.

"Open your Bibles to John 20:24," began the Pastor. In his early 60's, he was the perfect image of a Pastor. He was wise and had a thorough grasp of the scripture. In his presence many had been moved to "share" with him problems, blessings, and even life stories. He listened quietly and gave biblical answers that meant something. Nothing trite, nothing irresponsible ever escaped his lips.

"In this society one would be considered a fool to buy into something sight unseen. Con men would call these people, "an easy mark." Whereas wisdom in our daily decisions is part of obedience to Christ, one must comprehend the difference between foolishness and faith. Faith must be held without evidence, yet it is by no means foolish. Let's read verse 29 before we pray: 'Then Jesus told him, you must believe because you have seen me. Blessed are those who haven't seen me and believe anyway.'"

Hudson bowed his head then jolted upright again as vibrations at his hip alerted him to a call from work. Nervously fumbling for his cell, he nearly dropped it as he read the tiny screen. His boss! No one ever called him on Sundays; it was his single day away from work. He'd made that clear from the get-go. Scenarios played through his mind as he listened for the pastor to finish praying. *What could be this urgent?*

The pastor finished with an "Amen" and started to speak.

"Honey, I need to take this call, it must be an emergency. I'll be back as soon as I can."

She was worried, but just nodded and patted his back, displaying a close-lipped smile on her face as he squeezed his large frame past her knees.

He found the lobby and pulled out his phone. *Senator Hughes had better have a good reason for this.* These thoughts didn't calm him, for tension edged its way into his shoulders.

Having taken too much time to answer the phone, Hudson had to call the number left on his caller ID back. The phone rang only once before it was picked up. "Senator Hughes office," came the voice.

"Blackwell here, I believe the Senator needs to speak with me." The aid immediately transferred him to the senator's private phone.

"Senator, it's Sunday. You'd better not be calling to give me your golf score."

"Blackwell, this is no time for light-hearted banter. Get yourself over to Dr. Keith's house as quickly as possible. We have a problem, a very large one," said the Senator with a controlled degree of tension in his voice.

"Yes sir, I'll be there in 20 minutes. Anything you can tell me right now?"

"It's Dr. Keith. Meet me there." He hung up cryptically with a decided click, leaving Hudson to think up plans about getting his family home after church. Putting away his phone he maneuvered his way silently through the back door and started the search for willing transportation.

He quickly spotted the Cortens in their usual seats. *At the end of the pew,* he thought gratefully. Leaning over his friend's shoulder, he whispered his request as nonchalantly as possible. Charlie nodded and gave a warm smile.

"We'll even feed 'em if necessary!" It was barely a whisper, but Hudson knew that they would take good care of his family.

"Thanks, my friend!" he whispered back and gave a warm pat on his shoulder. Hudson's relief was obvious to his older friends.

He made his way past the stained glass windows and large doors leading to the front pillars of the church. Once here, it was a quick jog through the parking lot and into his car. Worrying had never been a part of Hudson's life. However, receiving an enigmatic emergency call from the Senator telling him to meet at the home of the scientific genius responsible for a world-changing project on the day before the scheduled trial could not be a good thing.

He could feel his stress levels begin to rise as he fumbled uncharacteristically with his keys; dropping them twice on the way to his car. A hard sigh escaped as he forced himself to be still.

Lord, give me your peace that passes all understanding. You alone are worthy of all my attention. You've said, 'Who by worrying can add a single hour to his life.' Got it, Lord? My faith is in you.

Even though he still had a dark foreboding in his spirit, he knew who controlled the future. Eagerness took over as a wave of determination flushed the fear out of his being.

He found the key to the family mini-van and unlocked the door. His world was about to change, and the feeling of anticipation was palpable. As he drove from the parking lot, the man was infused with peace, confidence, and the unmistakable call of God.

4 — SUNDAY, APRIL 12, LATE MORNING

Cool as a snow cone in December, Clark thought as he marveled at his own ability to pull off such a deed with no effect on his usual routine. Turning left onto A Street, he crossed over to Independence Avenue. Many years before, when he was young and inexperienced he would have been nervous; looking over his shoulder and assuming everyone was going to take retribution upon him. However, that time was in the past.

Success. It's all in the planning.

The "Old West outlaw on the run" feeling had pervaded his mind and attitude before he had gotten a handle on it years earlier. He wasn't Billy the Kid anymore.

I could've taught that amateur a few things about fear, and how to kill it. Of course, neither did he have to watch for young bucks with guns looking to make a name in a shoot out with him.

He receded into a random thought pattern. The Capitol building loomed defiantly in the distance, and he smiled. Irony permeated his Volvo's brand new beige interior. The entire world leaned to hear the words of those in that intimidating building, yet one of those civil servants, elected by the people had hired him. For murder. For deception. For a host of other less-than-tasteful services as well. The highest of elected officials calling upon him because of his. . . uh . . . service record? A low chuckle escaped his throat, and he felt even more untouchable.

As he turned south onto Highway 1, he saw the Washington Monument and Lincoln Memorial. Clark wondered what the first President would have thought about the city that bore his name. Laws are passed to benefit a small minority in the congress. From the buildings of the beautiful metropolis come taxation and oppression. *Wasn't the Boston Tea Party over a three pence tax-tenths of a cent-and currently the average person works through May to pay their annual taxes? Our forefathers are probably rolling around in their graves.*

The leaders of this ivory-covered city publicly claim support for the words "In God We Trust," while privately and with desperate measures find ways to remove the connection of country and God from everything in their path. *Hypocrisy. Pure and simple! Complete hypocrisy. At least dictators are up-front about their desire for unquestioned power, and you always know where they stand.*

Leaving D.C. couldn't happen soon enough. His eyes narrowed as his mind began to seethe with venomous thoughts boiling in his long-neglected, God-starved soul. *There is no other nation on earth where I feel more controlled and restricted than "God Bless America" with its restraining freedom and all-important liberty. It's all a sham to keep the few in power while the many think they are in control.* A dictator's jail felt more comfortable and honest to Clark than American soil any day.

Clark fumed as he passed Arlington National Cemetery. He shook his head to prevent the angry tears from welling up in his eyes. Once again the city was an emblem of propaganda. As a SEAL, he led many top-secret raids. More times than he could count he brought home fewer men than he left with. They were heroes! They died for their country in the worst possible ways and deserved honor and respect in their deaths. Their missions had been top secret and sensitive enough for the U.S. government to deny the men and their assignments and thus efficiently rejected any knowledge of those who allowed them their freedom.

These men would never be posthumously decorated. Their families would not get military support, and of most importance to Clark, they would never be buried in Arlington National Cemetery; the place where heroes rest.

Merging onto the George Washington Memorial Parkway, he headed toward Alexandria. He wiped angrily at the stubborn tears that had slipped his notice. *Man, get control of yourself. You've got a job to do!* He needed to get his head back in the game and focus on the job at hand.

He started a mental checklist of things he'd done to ensure that Dr. Keith's death looked like a suicide, so as to harden his mind against the pain that had throbbed its way into his throat.

He'd taken several steps in preparation for the job. Getting on the rotation schedule of Dr. Keith's cooks wasn't an easy process. Ben had good taste and hired from one of the best catering companies in the city. For Clark to become a chef with them, papers had to be made showing that he graduated from a prestigious cooking school and had worked for the finest restaurants. He'd accomplished the first with a call to the Culinary Institute of America in New York. A few days of research, computer legwork, and paper pushing proved itself when they sent him a newly reprinted diploma "to replace the one burned in the kitchen of Saint Louis' finest eatery."

Documents in hand, he'd had to beef up on his cooking skills. A smile curled up at the corner of his mouth, revealing a roguish grin. Studying books had never been his favorite pastime; hands-on was more his style, so his method of self-improvement took on the same flavor. His smile widened at the memories of elegant places and the women he'd picked up there.

Finding companionship hadn't been a problem for Clark since joining the SEALs. After all, being six-foot-four with a large, well-kept muscular build, bright blue eyes and a mischievous grin made him an immediate attraction. Two weeks of using women for their taste buds had paid off nicely. He'd developed new cooking skills and brushed up on a few other things while he was at it.

The references needed from his last job were simple. They required a few keystrokes to update the templates already on file in his computer and a few phone calls to assistants in other cities. He remembered thinking that most of the places on his reference list were so stuffy and high collar he would never have walked through their doors under his own power.

After monitoring the catering company's calls to his references-assistants in various places-the cookery hired Clark very quickly. Getting into Dr. Keith's kitchen was a little more difficult. However, when the Doctor's normal cook was *randomly* mugged in a parking lot and sent to the hospital with a broken hand and arm; and after a quick romance with the sweet young lady in charge of scheduling, Clark had the job.

The next phase had been easier: the acting segment of the job. He made a fast relationship with Dr. Keith, obtained a key and almost unlimited access to the house. *Who wouldn't trust a cook with great references?* Within a week he had retrieved any information that wasn't yet known about the project Dr. Keith was working on.

Arriving on schedule each day, he earned the scientist's trust and conversation. The guy didn't own a weapon-was scared of them-and told Clark flat out the he had recently become a pacifist and no longer believed that violence was necessary.

Clark purchased a gun and forged papers in the name of Dr. Benjamin Keith. He knew the law. No guns in D.C. But there were also exceptions within the government. Ben now had papers authorizing him as an official "exception" and was given a sweet and overly powered Glock31.

Clark thought about giving the Doc a membership to a rifle range with his name signed in the registry on several different occasions, but, knew Dr. Keith had probably revealed his newfound pacifist philosophy to someone other than his cook. He merely slipped the revolver into an unused drawer in the townhouse and filed the paperwork under "SECURITY" in the Doctor's personal papers.

Next, it was necessary to know a little bit about the Doctor's routine. Most engineers and scientists were very methodical in the way they lived their lives, and Dr. Keith was no exception. Clark picked up on this when he noticed him reading the paper immediately after breakfast and from cover to cover-back to front. It was unusual in its method, but it was still something unique Clark thought he might use. It was, after all, the ideal time to commit suicide-right after reading the morning paper. By killing him immediately after opening the paper to the back, it would appear that he had shot himself after completely reading the news and thus well after the caterer had left.

Reading an entire paper does take time, and the FBI certainly wouldn't know of his unusual reading habit. Not that he was worried about the FBI-his boss would take care of them through whatever means of misdirection he had at his disposal-but his job needed to be as thorough and complete as possible.

Finally, to end the charade, there needed to be a note. Yes, Clark thought it was a little over the top, but the boss had a hand-writing expert craft the message and thought it would be a quick sealer for the case.

Let him read the note. Let his confusion dawn into awareness as his life comes to a close.

Everything went without a hitch that morning. His breakfast was a complete success, even if it never got fully digested, and his little banter with Dr. Keith seemed natural until the moment came.

Pulling the trigger was never difficult. Actually, it was rather fulfilling for Clark, seeming to satisfy some need for vengeance that was never soothed.

When the good doctor lay slumped in his chair, dead eyes wide with horror, Clark had stood for a moment staring at him. For an instant, something like sadness struck deep within him. Dr. Keith had appreciated his cooking. He appreciated him as an honest man with abilities beyond his own. The Doctor spoke with him as an equal and Clark had gotten to know the scientist fairly well. He had learned of Ben's past and family and in return Clark was able to get him up to speed on his life to that point-at least some fabricated information to help solidify his current assignment.

The emotional moment went as quickly as it came. Clark began to scrub the place of fingerprints and any remnants of the chore. Everything had gone as planned.

The assassin was almost through Alexandria before he could mentally set the whole event aside. It was completed. Part A of the job was accomplished. *Now for the final destination of the morning.*

Cox Manufacturing was an ordinary looking building; a typical off-white cinderblock structure with a single glass door leading to a receptionist sitting behind a small desk. A parking lot in the front and a delivery dock in the back completed the disguise. Being decorated up nicely with shrubs and a modest sign on the front bearing the company name finished the faux image.

No one really knew what Cox Manufacturing produced because no one had ever cared to find out. The only way the average person would become interested in the company was if it started to lower their property values. So far Cox Manufacturing had stood the test and seemed to be a nice little company earning its keep on the block.

Clark wondered what those self-absorbed citizens might think about the five-story basement below ground floor with enough Uranium 235 to kill all life within 1000 miles.

He flicked on his right signal and eased into the parking lot. Clark had been in this building at least a dozen times before, usually at night, but was not an employee. He did, however, know everything that went on within it.

After parking his car in the back, he strode up to the rear door and popped open the very normal-looking dead bolt lock. Clark pressed his thumb against the surface and waited for the print analyzer to recognize him. Upon acceptance, the analyzer would send a small current of electricity into his waiting appendage. Clark never got accustomed to submitting himself to an intentional shock.

The electrical current was designed to calculate the resistance within the person's body. Unless Clark had gone through a large body mass change within the previous 24 hours, the second stage of security would allow him through.

After the jolt came a retinal scan. In the center of the back door, about eye level was a large peephole that would check blood vessel alignment. Upon acceptance, the door opened to an inside chamber where a guard stood ready to examine the visitor and ask for the password of the day. The word changed frequently, and today's word was chrysanthemum. *Good thing I don't have to spell it.*

Once Larry the guard-actually a very large, well-trained Army Special Forces sergeant-okayed Clark from the inner chamber he was free to move into the large open area that housed the special equipment and the main apparatus.

Clark gripped the doorknob to the basement and noticed his palms sweating. He was getting a little nervous. Up until this point Clark had been in training, now he was to put that training and all of the courage he possessed to the test. What Dr. Keith was going to do the next day, Clark was going to do in the next few minutes.

As he walked into the large open area, his eyes were drawn to the center about fifty feet below. All employees and rare guests entered at the street level and were immediately ushered up to the metal railing that kept them from falling into the large pit below. Clark pushed the button next to the rail and called the open-air elevator to the top level.

"I've been waiting!" came a shrill voice from the lower level. A white-coated man holding a clipboard was looking up at him from the center of the basement floor. "We don't have all day!"

Clark never liked Dr. Keith's assistant and would've removed him from the situation long ago if he hadn't been essential to his very survival on the mission.

"I'm here, and I'm on time," Clark answered with disgust under his breath.

As the assassin rode down in the open elevator he was still overwhelmed by the sight in front of him. Every inch of the fifty foot high outer walls were covered with computers. It didn't take a programmer to figure out that each mainframe must be necessary to drive the large apparatus in the center of the room. There were two bulky generators in opposite corners of the large rectangular floor. The generators provided immediate and heavy-duty backup when the apparatus was running, so if there were a power failure, the computers would continue to ensure the accuracy so crucial to the function of the mission. The entire space was covered in a rubber-type substance that minimized static electricity.

In the middle of the room was the main piece of equipment. The top-secret function this craft provided had already resulted in the murder of Dr. Keith. Clark knew there would be more casualties before the project was put to rest.

The apparatus looked like a giant pearl cut in half with the top portion suspended telescopically from the lower half. When placed together, the machine was about seven feet in diameter. The base, consisting of four tubes, shot straight up into the mother of pearl exterior of the lower half, supporting it but making it appear delicate and unstable. The cockpit was located directly in the center of the base with two seats and a dashboard from what appeared to have been a U.S. military fighter jet.

The mother of pearl covering wrapped the entire sphere. The machine needed a coating that was hard and could take extreme pressure, yet would also help to reflect the energy bombarding it during the project. After a year of failure the scientists discovered that diamonds-altered through a process of melting and molding-could be conformed to a covering that would provide protection adequate for the function of the craft.

The only part of the machine not contained directly within the sphere was a high-intensity laser cannon. The cannon completed the operation of the apparatus by opening a temporal hole and was Dr. Benjamin Keith's life's work. Fueled by Uranium 235, the activated liquid sapphire laser, given the opportunity, could punch a hole in the moon and keep going. Clark harbored a secret fear of the cannon. *That thing freaks me out every time I see it*, Clark shivered.

"Are you ready?" said the nervous red headed man.

"Let's go."

"Okay. All you are supposed to do is ensure that this works. Dr. Keith isn't here to supervise you so I must be assured that you understand your place in this trial," replied the diminutive assistant with a hint of superiority. "Do not attempt to be a maverick. You are not Chuck Yeager."

Clark nodded curtly. He knew what he was supposed to do, and didn't like being treated like this man's preschooler. *Man, when this project is over . . . it's payback time!*

His toe almost caught on one of the telescopic legs causing him to do a sort of hop-step as he moved toward the craft. Clark swore under his breath. Getting this little man out of his mind right now was imperative to his own safety during this mission.

"If all goes well, this should be the shortest trip of your life."

"Let's get on with it," Clark barked out.

"Okay, I've already programmed the device and will be monitoring your progress the entire time. You just need to push the activation button from the inside each time you are ready to initiate the program."

"Fine." They had been through this a thousand times before. The little man was just having his moment in the sun.

On the wall behind him the clock read 10:26 AM, April 12. Time was everything on this mission-the clock determined success or failure. It received its base time from the Optical clock in Colorado which was always correct. It sure beat the old atomic clock being more than 100,000 times more accurate.

"Climb into the cockpit and we'll start the process at 10:28," squeaked the little man; excitement growing in his voice.

Crunch time! Clark thought with anticipation. The fear he had been fighting the last twenty-four hours transformed into a steady flow of adrenalin. Climbing over the side of the lower half, he sat in the left seat and belted himself in.

With a quick thumbs-up to the technician, the room went dark. A slow, steady hum indicated that the generators had kicked on, and seconds later his eyes adjusted to the lights emanating from the computers all over the room. An ominous feeling overpowered him and for a brief instant he thought he might wretch over the side. Fear rolled up his spine before he got his control back.

The four telescopic shafts within the cockpit began to slowly drop the upper half in place. A loud clamp indicated the locking mechanism had kicked in. Clark's heart was thumping from his stomach to his throat. For a few moments the cockpit was totally silent save the blood pounding in his ears. The sphere was completely dark except for the cockpit lights in front of him. All colors of light-emitting diodes blinked and illuminated the small craft in which he was entombed.

"Ten, nine, eight."

The machine began to hum.

"Seven, six, five," the computer counted down.

A smell started to form in the air that reminded Clark of a blown transformer attached to fluorescent lights.

"Four, three, two."

The laser below came to life and a reddish-yellow aura was reflected out of the four tubes at the base of the machine.

"One."

Clark could see a blue glow from within the sphere caused by the intense electrical power whirling around his body. He felt his body tingle.

"Zero."

The room filled with light from the millions of tendrils covering the sphere. One could almost walk on the electricity that engulfed the room.

From behind the protective glass, the scientist couldn't believe his own eyes. He'd been over equations, simulations and schematics for years, but this was unreal. At the peak of an unbearable brightness, the sphere disappeared, the computers shut down, and the room went dark.

Lights fluttered. The computer's squealing pitch slid to a low hum once again and the entire room was back to normal. After the lights returned, the generators turned themselves off. Everything looked as it did before except for the absence of the craft in the middle of the floor. All the scientist could do was to wait.

Three minutes and 46 seconds later, the generators kicked back on. The lights went out and the computers began to hum like before. The room began to fill with a bluish color and the electricity returned. When the lights within the room were at a blinding level, the craft reappeared.

Once more, all equipment within the room returned to base-line operation.

The scrawny scientist leaped from his chair and ran to the device. The sphere was steaming as he placed his hand on the analyzer on the side of the vehicle to open the vessel. After several seconds of nervous waiting, the sphere released and the steam began to clear. Leaning closer, he stared straight into Clark's eyelids which were fluttering open.

From shock, the scientist fell back as he saw Clark stand and climb out of the sphere-holding the clock from the wall behind him, which read 10:33 AM, April 12.

Were it not for the complete surprise he'd just experienced, the scientist would have been ecstatic. After a few brief but necessary seconds to catch their breaths, both Clark and the scientist looked to the wall where the clock should have been. The timepiece on the wall that matched the one in Clark's hands was now replaced with another.

The assassin had traveled a year into the past removing the original clock. Dr. Keith after an investigation, and not being able to explain its absence, replaced it with another over eleven months ago. Both men knew they were successful.

"Call the boss," Clark said to the excited scientist. "Tell him it works and that I will meet him at 2:00."

"Do you two ladies need a rest? Your backs got to be hurtin'."

"No ma'am, we are fine," Katherine replied.

"Honey, don't ma'am me. I am not that old. My momma was a ma'am." The heavyset black woman continued mumbling and looked around the room at her helpers. She saw Nacadro Escamilla.

"Nacho, get over here and give these ladies a break. It would take five of you to work as hard as these ladies have been working."

Nacho smiled because he knew Miss Nora was big on exaggeration. No one had spent more time at Grace Mission, so he immediately stopped what he was doing and went over to help.

"Can I give you a break?" the young man asked.

Stephanie spoke first, "We are fine."

Katherine affirmed the position, "We're going to finish this painting before we take a break."

"Ladies, I better help or Miss Nora will have my hide. When she says somethin' it goes."

Stephanie bent over with a smile, "Well, you better get to it."

"Nacho, what's your story? How did you end up helping Nora?" she asked.

"Wow, it's been a long time," Nacho began. "I would say that I was one of the first people Miss Nora helped when she got here. I was a street hood just like most of the people that come through the doors." He rolled the brush in the paint and started covering the walls.

"I left home when I was real young. I think I was about twelve. I lived on the streets and was real fast taken into a gang. See, I still have the tattoo," he said raising the sleeve on his shirt.

Katherine looked at it very closely.

"I was a bad guy, and I am still not proud of what I was. I would rob stores, hold up old ladies, take shots at rival gangs, do drugs..." He hesitated for a second. "You name it-I did it."

Stephanie stood there with her mouth agape. She couldn't believe that the kind, gentle man in front of her had such a past.

"Well, one day I was strung out, broke and hungry. I passed this church downtown where Miss Nora had her first mission and was going to rob it. I walked in, took out my gun and told the three people there to give me all of their money." He began to laugh.

"You know what?"

"What?" Katherine said with big wide eyes.

"Miss Nora said no. She told me I wasn't gettin' a dime."

"What did you do?" asked Stephanie.

"I didn't know what to do. I had a gun, people were supposed to do what I said. I was all mixed up. I couldn't believe that this big woman was telling me she wasn't going to give me anything.

Well, I put the gun in her face. I said that I was going to blow her head off if she didn't give me everything she had."

Both ladies were locked into the story.

"You know what she said?" The ladies shook their heads.

"She said that she wasn't scared of my little gun because Jesus was in control of her life." Nacho pointed one finger up and waved it back and forth. "Then she pointed that finger and told me that I better let Jesus have my life or I was going to hell. I couldn't believe it.

She said that she would give me food and help me with a place to stay. She also said she'd find some people to get me clean, but she wasn't going to give me a red cent."

Stephanie hugged her 14-year-old daughter.

Nacho placed the roller back in the paint and did another stripe on the wall. "Then she said, 'Well, what'll it be? Let me tell you about this Jesus and get a good meal, or go to hell?' I put the gun back in my pocket and haven't ever left."

"What a story!" Stephanie cheered. "Have you accepted Jesus?"

"Yeah. That night, Miss Nora told me what God wanted for me, and I've been on his side ever since. It was hard, but she helped me get off of drugs and out of the gang.

I work here 20 hours a week and am working on my diploma. Some day, I hope to go into the ministry and share God's love fulltime to those people on the street who were just like me."

He finished his story and put the brush down.

"When did you get this building we're in," Stephanie queried.

"About three weeks ago. Miss Nora had a mission running out of a Baptist church six blocks away for years. She started needing more and more space. She has a clothes closet, food pantry, and brings in physical and mental health people a lot to look at whoever has trouble. Well, her ministry grew too large and the church couldn't give her any more space.

So when this old deli closed down, she let it out that she would like to have it, and God provided. People from all over sent her money to buy this place."

Nacho pointed around the room, "Miss Nora has helped lots of people. Everybody loves her, so enough money and more came in for her to buy the building. God shows himself mighty everyday; this is just another example."

Nacho leaned in and spoke more quietly, "I have to be honest; it's more dangerous down here than at the church. The gangs tend to run in this area, but this is where she wants to be. She wants to take Christ to the people and that's what we're doing.

How did you ladies get here? You look like you ought to have a house in Trump towers or something like that."

Stephanie spoke up. "Our church does a mission trip to this area every year, and we felt like we should go.

I am so glad that God urged me to. I have learned so much from Miss Nora over the last few days. She's taught me to look at the heart and not the physical appearance."

She looked over at Katherine, "We talk about helping others and sharing God's love. We've given monetarily to help mission projects all over the world. But until you go and see the people's faces and the way God changes them completely, it never changes your heart."

Miss Nora yelled across the room, "Nacho, you're talkin' too much. We're never gonna get this place painted with all your storytelling. Come on over here and help this gentleman. Bring the ladies with you."

"Yes, Miss Nora," he yelled back. "We better go help or we'll be in trouble."

"Thank you for the story," smiled Katherine. "We'll be over in a second."

He returned her smile and walked across the room.

"Honey, this is the real world," Stephanie said pulling her daughter aside. "Most people don't live in Kalorama Heights in D.C. next to ambassadors and statesmen. I am glad that we're here."

"Yes Mom. I didn't know that there were people like this."

"Honey, everyone needs God. The richest and the poorest. Sometimes, we must get out of our comfort zone to make us better missionaries for Christ."

"I wish Daddy went to church with us. Maybe he could come on the next trip?"

"Katherine, your daddy doesn't really want a relationship with Christ. We need to continue praying for him. Maybe God will draw him in soon."

"I'll pray harder," said the young woman with a smile.

They walked over toward Nacho. As they crossed the building, Stephanie looked out the front glass windows and saw a low rider full of young men sitting about half a block down. They were staring at the mission. *Maybe they are in need of help*, she thought, *God please let them know you.*

"I need some help," the young man with Miss Nora said. He was sweating profusely and shaking.

Nacho spoke up, "Sure man, take off your coat and put down your bag. Get comfortable. We can find you something to eat."

"Darlin', you alright? You seem a bit nervous," asked Miss Nora. "You can relax here. God loves you and so do we. Why don't you sit down?"

"I don't want to sit down!" he yelled.

Stephanie pulled Katherine close; nervous over the situation.

"I gotta do this."

"Do what, honey?" asked Nora.

"I gotta do this. It's the only way in. They won't let me in if I don't." The teenager was shaking violently.

Nacho spoke up, "Man, you don't got to do anything. Just relax; let's talk. Let me tell you about Jesus. He loves you."

"They'll respect me if I do it."

Nacho knew what was happening. "Man, they're lying to you. I know. I've been there. Don't do what they told you to do. It'll haunt you the rest of your life."

"I got to!"

The young man stuck his hand in his bag and pulled out what looked to be a small Uzi. He was crying. "I got to do it to show them I'm tough enough."

Nacho yelled, "Stop!" He dove for the gunman.

Nora didn't have enough time to move her large frame, so she was the first to drop when the bullets began flying.

Nacho wrestled the gun away from the young man and threw it across the room. He immediately began helping those bleeding around him.

The lost young man ran from the front door and down the block to men high-fiving him as he jumped into the low rider. Those in the car slowly drove by the front of the building looking at the carnage that had occurred. When the occupants were content with the outcome, the metallic green older model Impala barked its tires and sped away, not to be seen again.

There was chaos in the building as Nacho continued yelling, "Call 911." His heart broke as he went from person to person assessing the damage. In most cases there wasn't anything he could do.

The emergency vehicles took their time getting to the mission. The poorest part of New York didn't seem to be a priority for the authorities. However, when they did arrive, they came in force: there were ambulances, police cars and fire trucks.

The technicians worked without rest for over an hour trying to save some; but for the most part, their efforts were futile. The metallic spurt lasted for only three seconds but in that short period of time six people were sent to Jesus.

Three were regular workers at the shelter. Of course, Miss Nora, one who had shared Christ's love to so many, fell victim to the violence that she fought so hard to stop. And finally, two ladies who had come from Washington to spend a week offering hope in the inner city lost their lives to an ugly part of humanity that they had never seen.

Because of a gang initiation, Nacho became the leader of Grace Mission; that tiny light situated in the middle of a very dark city.

Hudson turned onto A Street feeling a weight in the pit of his stomach. His prayers had eased his fears, but he still felt heavy with concern for the situation he was about to walk into. What had happened to Dr. Keith? What had he heard in the Senator's voice? Replaying the brief conversation over in his mind he realized something was wrong-elusive-but definitely wrong.

Whatever it is-it can't be good. His face was still lined with apprehension when he pulled onto the narrow cherry tree-lined street in front of Dr. Keith's townhouse. There were two police cars, a fire truck, and an ambulance all with their lights blinking, practically blocking the street. Surrounding these vehicles were more than ten dark sedans; most likely the FBI. Dr. Keith's value to the government would require the highest level of investigation of anything involving him. There was no doubt, more people and vehicles were on the way.

Getting out of his minivan-which he'd managed to squeeze between a dark sedan and an ambulance a block down the street-he saw a figure step from the front door of the doctor's townhouse. Hand to brow, the Senator was scanning the bright horizon for a moment before settling his gaze on Hudson. With a brief direction to a uniformed officer, he started in Hudson's direction; the sun behind him radiated a sort of aura that made him look dark and larger than he really was.

Senator John Hughes had been in politics for over twenty years, and had become one of the most influential men in Washington, and maybe the world. His earliest dreams as a child had been of influence and power.

Power. A small word with huge implications. It provided what money could not. Money without power was limited. Power without money-well, was there such a thing?

His beginnings were privileged. Best family name, best schools, and the best friends money could buy. The finest of everything and the ability to get anything he wanted had been instilled in him from his earliest education. Law school had been his first real step toward politics.

At six foot two with only slightly graying hair, the older man looked impressive, even intimidating as he approached Hudson.

"Hudson, I'm relieved that you came so quickly-this being Sunday and all."

Taking a final look around the street, Hudson pulled in a clean breath of morning air so as to take a short rest in the innocence and beauty of the view before the ugliness of the world rushed upon him. "So, what happened," he said as they began moving toward the chaos on the lawn.

"The FBI has been investigating for the last two hours. It appears Dr. Keith committed suicide this morning."

"Not a chance!" he said in disbelief. "Tomorrow was to be the biggest day of his life! The day he'd worked toward for the last fifteen years! There is no way he committed suicide." His hand went to his forehead as he mentally raced through the reasons he could be wrong. After a moment's hesitation he started again.

"A brilliant physicist with no signs of mental illness or distress of any kind doesn't just wake up the day before the most crucial moment in his life and kill himself. It doesn't happen!" Hudson could hear the confusion in his own voice, but he couldn't stop the flood of thoughts pouring from his mouth.

"I've been working with Dr. Keith for almost three years. His passion about tomorrow's big moment was huge! He wouldn't kill himself."

Hudson began to think of other options, "Has anyone considered this to be an assassination or, at the very least, a homicide-maybe a well planned burglary-gone-wrong? Someone could have been searching the place for details about tomorrow's big experiment when Dr. Keith interfered!"

"It does seem odd," said the Senator, "but the FBI investigates assassinations, homicides, and suicides–especially high-profile ones-everyday. They are not exactly inexperienced. I take their word for it. The best agents have been here for hours now and it is their conclusion that the obvious signs of suicide can be trusted as accurate."

"Senator...John, bring me up to speed here. What do we know? I need proof-this does *not* add up!"

The two men navigated their way through the many obstacles, including the bright yellow '**do not cross**' tape from the police department, to the front door of the townhouse. The perimeter of police tape was difficult enough to maneuver around, let alone the reporters, gurney, and medical personnel. FBI agents were still huddled in small clusters on the lawn, discussing and re-discussing, but always shaking their heads in resignation.

Breaking the security perimeter brought no relief from the commotion. The inside of the house was no better than the outside. There must have been at least twenty personnel from all areas of service. Hudson could see men in dark suits all over the room, obviously FBI. The police photographer was still taking photos of the scene, forensics people were packaging up the remaining evidence, and one was still dusting for prints. The police were assigned to guard duty and taking care of the press since the FBI had arrived, but a few of them still lingered indoors, trying to look like a part of the investigation. The coroner and his two assistants were busy unrolling and preparing a body bag for its eventual occupant.

The work of wrapping up the evidence was obviously near completion, but what about the actual investigation into that evidence? How could they conclude "case closed" so quickly? Finally, there were three people around Dr. Keith's body. The agent guessed that one was the city coroner, and the other two were his assistants.

"I was supposed to meet Dr. Keith for coffee in the Capitol dining room this morning around 9:30," said the Senator as he began to tell the story. "We were going to go over all of tomorrow's last minute preparations to ensure that everything went without a hitch. We were also going to celebrate. It has been three long years and we were finally ready to make magic happen. Suffice it to say that Ben didn't make it to brunch and I got worried. You know Ben, he was always conscientious, and on time."

"So he was late and then what did you do?" asked Hudson.

"I called his house, and when I didn't get an answer I came over. This location is just a few blocks from the Capitol, and I was here by 9:50. That's when I found him," said the Senator with remorse.

Hudson walked around the area that appeared to be his living room and began to take in all of the information. Had this been a social call, he would have been very impressed with the beautiful home and all of its unique attributes. However his eyes were quickly drawn to an oversized leather chair that supported a bloody motionless man. He was definitely shot through the right temple. He was slumped over in his chair with his right arm hanging over the side, and a gun was on the floor just below it. His left hand was holding a hand written note, and a blood splattered newspaper was sitting on the table to his left. The kitchen was clean and the only thing out of place was the remainder of Ben's breakfast lying on the dining room table.

"Didn't Ben have breakfast made each morning," asked Hudson.

"Yes and we're checking on the cook now," replied the stately Senator. "The story we've received so far is that everything went fine, and the cook left the house without seeing anything out of the ordinary."

"This just doesn't seem right. Why would a man dress up to kill himself? Why would he quietly eat breakfast, read the paper and then blow his brains out? I know Dr. Keith, and this isn't him. The house is immaculate."

Hudson began to walk upstairs in hopes of an answer to this illogical act. As he entered the doctor's bedroom, once again he was surprised. "His bed is made!" he mumbled to himself. As he entered the bathroom, he noticed everything in its place. "The bathroom is clean and organized," he said to himself.

He walked back downstairs shaking his head and looking at the Senator. "Hudson, a tragedy like this doesn't make sense. I'm just as upset as you are. Ben was a good man and a brilliant scientist. Let's take a break from this scene and get something to drink."

"Thank you, but no sir. I need to go check the lab. Has anyone been over there yet?"

"No, if this is a suicide, then there shouldn't be anything out of the ordinary. Also, I would be the first person called if something was amiss. Go home, Hudson, and we'll meet at the lab in the morning," said the Senator speaking with warmth and concern.

It was getting close to noon, and the on-site investigation was coming to a close. The Coroner had placed the body in a bag and was rolling it out to the wagon. The FBI had apparently gained enough information to warrant ending their work, at least for now. The preliminary information was that Dr. Keith had indeed committed suicide, and unless something was found in forensics, the case would be closed.

Hudson was having trouble putting all of the information together. Why would a man kill himself on the eve of making unparalleled worldwide history? Why would he get all dressed up just to commit suicide? He knew that Ben was rather peculiar, but most geniuses were. Maybe the scientist was overwhelmed with the pressure. Maybe he knew that something was going to go wrong with the trials and couldn't handle the disappointment? Hudson never really did talk to him about his personal life, so maybe something was going on there. But the agent knew something was wrong. All of this was just too convenient and too illogical coming from a man who lived in mathematical theorems and scientific postulates.

After the FBI agents placed the blood-splattered newspaper in a bag with the suicide note, they gathered all of their samples and equipment, and departed.

Right before Hudson left the home, he saw something else that was out of the ordinary. Dr. Keith was left-handed but the fork the scientist used for breakfast was sitting on the right of the plate. If a person was left handed, then the fork should be on the left.

As Hudson bent down to get a closer look, he noticed a greasy smudge on the fork. The agent didn't know what it was, but he knew who could tell him.

Very quietly Hudson put the fork in a plastic bag, then into his pocket and left the house. If all of these investigators weren't going to take the used breakfast utensils, the agent didn't see that there was anything wrong with his temporary acquisition.

"Hudson, go and get some rest. Spend the day with your family. We'll need you a lot in the next few days, so relax. Isn't this a church day for you?"

"Yes sir," answered Hudson.

"Well, get back to church and say a prayer for your friend."

"Thank you, sir."

As Hudson left the house, the scene was much different than when he had entered. The street had lost its innocence, and the air that just a few minutes earlier was clean and clear now seemed heavy and unsustaining.

The agent looked around and many of the cars and emergency vehicles had left. The reporters were gone. Most of the city investigators had moved on to other more pressing cases. There was still crime-scene tape strewn about and a few police officers lingering, but all of that would be there for several more days.

After Hudson got into his minivan and started the engine, he was overwhelmed by a sense that there was something very wrong going on. He couldn't place his finger on it, but had to keep quiet about his personal investigation. His years of training gave him the sense that this was an inside job and that he had better keep any information to himself, until he could discover who was behind this tragic loss.

Hudson pulled a small phone from of his pocket and after a quick inquiry into a number, he made a call to an old friend, "Good morning, Susan, this is Hudson Blackwell, how are you?"

"I, I'm fine, I haven't heard from you in-what is it-six, seven years. Are you still with the Secret Service?"

"No, I've moved on to more exciting things, but I don't have time to reminisce; I need some help. Are you still working for the EPA?"

"Yep, still wear a lab coat each day," Susan replied.

"Great, can I meet you at your lab-preferably within the next few hours? I need you to analyze something for me."

"Sure, I guess. Is there something I need to prepare for? Why all the rush?"

"Susan, this is very important, and I wouldn't have called you if I didn't think you could help, and be trusted. I can bring you up to speed when I get there."

"Give me an hour, and I will meet you at the security desk," said the woman, taken aback by the odd request.

"Thanks Sue, I owe you big for this one," he said as he closed the phone, placed his vehicle in drive, and sped away.

The EPA building was a beautiful ten-story structure. The grounds were meticulously manicured and there were trees lining the parking lot. The edifice was covered in green glass reinforcing the image that the Environmental Protection Agency wanted the public to have of its organization-that of a group that protected the environment. As Hudson pulled into the parking lot, and claimed a space near the front, he spotted his old acquaintance through the front glass doors waiting for him.

Hudson had known Susan McCoy for over ten years. He met her when he was working on a case with the FBI, trying to discover how high levels of arsenic were making their way into the Missouri River. Because the agent was always polite and patient, a friend was made in the technician, and usually his tests were run before all of the other work on her desk.

As the agent got closer, he noticed that Susan still had the shoulder-length auburn hair and kept herself in the gym; it was good to see her again. Hudson wished that this were a social visit, and not one with such darkness attached to it.

"Susan, how are you, it's been too long? Let's walk while we talk," Hudson said with a smile.

"So what have you been doing with your life?" she answered, leading the agent to the elevator.

"Lots of things."

As the two government employees left the atrium and entered the elevator, they quickly came up to speed on each other's lives. Susan learned that Hudson was married and had two children. Hudson listened as Susan told him she was still unattached, but had been dating someone for over a year and hoped he would finally decide to take their relationship to the next step.

They exited the elevator onto the fifth floor and entered through the door in front of them, it was obvious that they were in the right place. There were two nuclear magnetic resonance machines, an atomic absorption machine, an X-Ray crystallograph, and a mass spectrometer. In the corner Hudson saw centrifuges and a wall of chemicals. Before they reached Susan's desk-a bench with a computer-they passed several other instruments, a ventilation hood, walls of glass tubes, beakers, Bunsen burners and condensation towers.

"We don't officially have any tests running currently, but it is regulation that we put on goggles," she said as she handed him a pair from her desk.

Hudson let out a small laugh and put the goggles in place. He thought to himself how funny it was that physicists, chemists, and biologists; highly intellectual people used protective eyewear which made them look so unintelligent.

"Sit down Hudson. Why all the cloak and dagger stuff? What's the big secret?"

"I don't want you to be involved too deeply in what I'm working on but, suffice it to say, I need you to find out what is on this."

Hudson pulled from his pocket the plastic bag containing Dr. Keith's fork.

"I would say it looks like eggs," Susan said with a smirk.

"Sue, I've missed your sense of humor. I think you know that I'm not talking about the food. It's that stain on the end." Hudson showed her a two-centimeter smudge mark on the handle of the fork.

"Well, it looks like an oily residue of some kind. What do you think it is?"

"I really can't tell you."

"I'm not going to tell anyone what you are working on. I'll know what it is eventually. If you can narrow my search, I can have the results much more quickly; possibly within the next few minutes."

"Okay," he said hesitantly, "I think it's gun powder, or possibly gun oil."

"Well that makes my life much easier. I don't normally test for those substances, but I have a book over here that will tell me how to prepare the material so that we can analyze it."

Susan got up, walked to an adjacent wall and picked up a book. She then walked over to several machines and turned them on. Next, she moved over to a wall full of gas cylinders and opened several of them. One was labeled O_2, another was labeled N_2, and yet another was N_2O. He knew that these gasses would be used in the equipment, but was ignorant as to how.

"Hudson, this book shows many different types of gun powders and gun oils. Are you looking for an exact composition or do you just need your suspicions satisfied?"

"Just tell me if I'm right and that's all I need," he answered feeling content that he came to the right person.

"Easy enough. This shouldn't take more than twenty minutes."

As Susan carefully picked up the fork and started toward a counter top full of beakers and test tubes, she noticed something.

"Hudson, it looks like there is a portion of a finger print here. Is that important in your work?"

"A print?" he responded. "That would be the icing on the cake."

In all of the busyness of the morning, Hudson hadn't had any real time to examine the utensil, so this information could make his job much easier.

"Sue, do you have anything we could use to get a copy of the print? That print could be even more important than the substance that contains it," Hudson said with instant excitement.

"Sure, we keep a camera in the lab so that we can photograph anything that comes in. That way if a specimen or substance arrives broken or contaminated, we can catalog it and cover our backs against those who continually seek to blame the lab techs. Let me get it."

As Susan went to get the camera, Hudson examined the fork. Could he really be lucky enough to have the identification of the killer, or was this just Dr. Keith's print? Would the killer have shot the scientist, and then taken a bite of his food? This was too much to comprehend.

It is commonly known that when a gun is fired, the hand firing the gun will have gun powder embedded within it for a few days. Many criminals have been brought to justice with this simple information. It is also known that a well-used gun is going to be oiled. Because it looked like gunpowder and gun oil had been mixed in the print on the fork, it would lead one to believe that the fork was used after the gun had been fired. So Dr. Keith may not have committed suicide. This was the reasoning that Hudson was relying on, and hoping to be true.

Susan came back quickly. "Let's take a lot of pictures, maybe one will come out," she said.

"Thanks Sue, you might solve this case for me," he said as Susan smiled.

Once all of the pictures were taken, Susan got down to business preparing aqueous solutions and calibrating the machines.

After ten minutes, she was ready. "Hudson, looks like the machines are accurate. Time to test your samples."

In one machine, she injected a small amount of the liquid directly into the sample reservoir. In another, she placed a test tube filled with the liquid.

THE UNPARDONABLE OBJECTIVE

In the final instrument she placed a small beaker half filled with the liquid. Evidently, that machine needed more of the substance to test.

"Hudson, each of these instruments is testing for the same thing; they just do it in different ways. This machine is going to bombard the sample with electrons, in order to excite whatever is in there. This CRT will give us a visual analysis of what it found," she said pointing to the screen.

"This second machine will essentially burn up the liquid, and the gas byproduct that is produced will be analyzed. This final instrument is going to look at the liquid and see how the light is refracted through it. Different substances refract light differently and this book will tell us what the results show. If these machines don't give us results, there are other tests we can run. However, it will need to be something very rare or a substance that hasn't been studied before, for these machines to not render a result."

Susan took another few minutes to allow the equipment to test the substance. She then pulled off the printouts from each of the machines and went back to her bench to review the findings.

"Hudson, the machines that we use here in the labs are filled with data from the substances that we routinely check here at the EPA. If we need to analyze mercury levels or find out what byproducts a steel company is pumping into a lake, that's easy because the machines are calibrated to look for those types of things. Very rarely, do we do work for the FBI or crime labs. Therefore, these computers will not give us results showing that there is gunpowder on your sample because these instruments don't normally look for gun powder. Do you understand?"

"Yes, I understand," Hudson said as he shook his head.

"All that being said, let me tell you what we know. Because you were able to tell me what you are looking for, I was able to look up some of the data for gunpowder and gun oil. The information that I pulled off of the machines shows me very large spikes on the graphs when it comes to carbon and nitrogen. Gunpowder has very high levels of nitrogen; that is what makes it so powerful. On the other hand, petroleum based oils are heavy carbon-based chains, and that could line up with why the carbon element within the sample is so high."

"Hudson, if I were to make a guess from this preliminary information, I would say that your assumptions were right." Susan turned her head from the paper toward Hudson, "Please remember that these results are not conclusive. If you want, I could send the rest of the solution over to the FBI labs. Their machines will be ready for this type of test. Or, I could keep testing for the next few days and see if I can narrow in on what you are looking for."

Hudson interjected, "No, Sue you have told me what I need to know. I have a feeling that if this sample got to the FBI, it would be put on the back burner, or would somehow come back with results that don't match what you gave me."

"What are you saying?" Susan replied with confusion. "This would be a simple test for them."

"I'm saying it's not the machines I'm worried about. I need to go. Thank you for your help. You've been great. Why don't you come over to dinner with that non-committed guy of yours and we'll have a cook out. I know you'd get along well with my wife," he said as he started to walk out.

"I would love to. Maybe you can have a talk to that guy of mine and see if you can get him to pop the question."

"Don't worry, I'll set him straight. Thanks Sue, I really owe you." At that, Hudson opened the door and began to leave the lab.

"Hudson, don't forget the chip with your pictures!" she said as she tossed him a memory device. "I hope you catch what you're fishing for."

"Me too," Hudson replied as he placed the chip in his pocket and left the lab.

The first man to ever break the time barrier; Clark smiled. Sunday was one of the quietest days in Washington, so the Metro ride that dropped him off at the Air and Space Museum was peaceful and refreshing. Looking inside the glass front of the massive museum he saw the Wright brothers Flyer, the Bell X1, and the Apollo lunar module. Clark felt great pride in knowing that he was an equal with Orville and Wilbur Wright, Chuck Yeager, and Neil Armstrong. Each of these men had done something grand for themselves and mankind at the risk of losing their own lives, and Clark was now one of them.

Possibly, in the future, they might have the pearlized sphere hanging from the ceiling of the famous museum. There could be a placard placed upon it giving Clark's story-hopefully without the deception and murder. If that reality ever did come to pass, they would need to change the name on the building to the Air, Space and Time Museum. Clark brought himself back to reality and knew that he would never receive credit for the feat he had accomplished. He was just a pawn in someone's hand, and as long as he got paid, he would be fine with that.

He turned into the Hirshhorn Sculpture Garden and admired the bronze sculptures made by world renowned artists. For the most part, the garden remains a well-guarded secret by those working inside of the beltway. Even though its ten foot walls contain beautifully sculpted works of art; contemporary sculpture is an acquired taste and most tourists visiting the town would rather go to see Ford's Theatre, the Lincoln Memorial, or the National Archives than try to interpret what the sculptor was thinking when he placed two metal two-by-fours together and called it Sunset. Therefore its central location in D.C. along with its general obscurity makes the garden a perfect choice for Clark to meet with his boss.

Having reached the secluded spot precisely at two, he found his boss sitting on a bench in the corner.

"Hello, Clark," the man said.

"Afternoon," Clark replied.

"It is good to see you. Sit down and tell me about this morning."

As Clark sat down next to him, he detailed the events of the morning. He told the man about how well the first stage of the assignment went.

"Dr. Keith has been removed from the equation with relative ease. I made it look like a suicide as you asked. I cleaned the room and swept it for prints."

"Are you sure that you cleaned it thoroughly? We can't have clues being left around."

"This is my job and I do it well. There isn't anything to worry about," Clark said with shortness in his voice.

"After our call, I went to the lab and fulfilled the next stage of the assignment. The machine works!" Clark said, hardly containing his excitement over his accomplishment.

"Tell me about that," the man asked with skepticism.

"It was the oddest thing I've ever done." Despite the business-like nature of the meeting, Clark could not keep the excitement from his voice. "For several seconds before the machine was preparing to jump, it felt like the apparatus was a seven foot ball of static electricity. Every cell in my body tingled. I don't know how to explain it. But, just as quickly as it began, it ended. All of the tingling subsided and the machine powered down. The sphere hadn't moved at all, so I thought the test had failed."

"What did you do?"

"I pushed the button to raise the lid on the sphere and jumped out, ready for a fight. I was certain that Keith's assistant had made a mistake, so I was going to let him have a piece of my mind. However, after I finally moved through the steam the machine had produced, I discovered that I was in the room alone."

"What did the room look like?" asked the man, totally absorbed in the story.

"It was completely empty; I was the only one there. It didn't look like it did when I left. It was like the room wasn't finished, having holes on the walls where computers should be, the control center wasn't glassed in and had a lot of the equipment missing. Also there was no security guard; I would guess because there wasn't anything there to guard."

"Interesting," replied the man with a smile.

"Anyway, as I walked around the lab, I realized that either the jump had taken place or the room had been ransacked in just a few seconds. So I got on the elevator, went up to the top level, and walked outside. Thunderstorms were dropping buckets full of rain; something that wasn't happening when I entered the building."

The man nodded in understanding.

Clark continued, "I knew that a storm couldn't pop up from clear skies in ten minutes, so I was convinced that I was successful.

The idea behind the jump was the strangest feeling. I couldn't believe that I had just traveled through time to re-live a portion of the day that had been lost over a year ago. It was a power I'd never experienced."

"Then what happened?" asked the man as he looked around.

"I went back inside, looked at the clock on the wall and confirmed that it was April 12th. Going back down to the bottom level, I pulled a table over to stand on, and removed the clock from the wall. I knew that the clock was non-essential so I wasn't worried about taking it. I put my proof in the passenger seat, reversed the process, and wound up back in this time."

"Great, what a story," the man said with calm collection. "It is time to implement the final stage of our strategy. I purposely up to this point haven't told you the true mission that I'm sending you on. We've been preparing you, through language and culture classes, but have kept your final assignment a secret, in case this day never came."

"I was wondering when you were going to let me know."

"Well, my friend, a new day has been ushered in, and so it's time. You leave tonight."

"Tonight, that is not enough time! I need a break; this has been a seriously exhausting day. Why not tomorrow?" Clark quickly interjected.

"You are ready, and to use an old saying; 'time is of the essence.' If we wait more than a day, then we might not be able to get the sphere out of the lab. There are forces that are going to want to shut this project down without the guidance of the good scientist. It must be tonight!"

"I'm not sure. With notice this short. My fee will have to go up. I don't like moving without an ample amount of planning and preparation."

"Name your price. Money's not a problem."

"I'm going to double my original estimate, I want $20 million. Ten in my account before I leave, and ten when I return."

"Fine. Done. I want you at the lab tonight at 8:00 sharp. I'll have your favorite helper there to ensure that you get to where you're going. I'll also have all of the tools you'll need for your assignment waiting for you. This abstract contains all the information required to perform your duties. Read it well because these few pages may save your life. Do you understand?"

"Yes. Read the book and be in the lab at 8:00," Clark repeated with frustration.

"Good. You might want to rest this afternoon and get a good meal, because tonight you are going into the trenches," the man said with a dark smile.

At that, the boss stood up indicating that the short, but informative conversation was over. Clark also stood, and with a final glance, left the garden.

The boss sat back down and watched Clark head up the steps to the main Mall. As he glanced down at his watch, his eye caught a very unique piece of art. It was entitled *The History of Man* and was composed of roughly hewn metal that looked like the world, animals, people, and various religious symbols. He wondered if that sculpture would look the same after he accomplished his task. He thought to himself that only time would tell.

9 — SUNDAY, APRIL 12, LATE AFTERNOON

As Senator Hughes entered the massive doors to the Senate building he knew that the impromptu meeting would not go well. This committee was filled with differing opinions on the project, and there had been many heated discussions in the short time that the group had been together. Telling the members of this assembly that the genius behind their entire project had killed himself could put the scientific research years behind, or shut it down all together.

Upon entering the meeting chambers, he found all members in their seats, present and accounted for, looking through varying packets, books and papers. Never had everyone been there on time, let alone early. This would be a long afternoon.

"Hello, Senators, thank you for coming on such short notice. I know that each of you had your day planned; I would never have asked you to be here if it hadn't been an emergency." Senator Hughes spoke with calm assuring tones.

"John, skip the formalities and get on with the reason why we're here," said Senator Arlin Dupree.

"Yes, why are we here on Sunday afternoon? I was on the twelfth hole when I got the call," interjected Senator Jack Hooks.

Senator Alison Seagrove remained silent, while Senators Robert Strickland and Bennett Austin were in a heated debate about a bill they were co-authoring. They were attempting to push legislation through the house that would allow lower income families to place their children in a modified schooling program at the age of two; believing this would allow their parents to take on more hours at work. The two men were to bring their bill to the floor during the next Senate session and were still working out all of the kinks.

John Hughes, the chairman, brought the meeting to order.

"Senators, I'm not going to waste your time," he said with caution. "Dr. Benjamin Keith committed suicide this morning around 9:00."

The sudden silence was deafening. Each person in the room sat in their seats with their mouths hanging agape.

"He committed suicide?" said Senator Dupree, incredulously. "What in the world would have driven him to do that?" he added with increasing volume. "This man was supposed to make history tomorrow and he kills himself?"

"Yes Senator, but please remain calm," replied Hughes.

"How can we remain calm?" interjected Seagrove. "This is a terrible tragedy. What drove him to do this?"

Senator Strickland broke into the conversation, "Are we going to have to shut down the project?"

"We can't shut it down! We're too close. This project could change mankind like nothing that has ever been attempted before," said Senator Austin.

"Please, everyone remain calm," said Hughes trying to regain control.

"Don't toy with us John, we have to shut this project down. I didn't like it from the beginning. It's just not right. No one should have that kind of power," yelled Senator Dupree with defiance.

"Senator, we've heard these words before, almost every week. We don't need them repeated again," said Austin as he rose and poured himself a cup of coffee.

"Don't tell me what I can say and can't say. I'm an equal member of this committee, and I'll make myself heard," Dupree shot back at his fellow committee member across the table.

Senator Seagrove spoke with her natural calming tone, "Gentlemen, this is no time for yelling. We need to get to the bottom of this. We must decide what is to be done." Alison Seagrove always had the ability to ease a tense situation.

At 53 years of age, Senator Seagrove's term had begun six months ago, only a year after her husband, a multi-term Senator from Illinois, passed away from a massive heart attack. He had just begun his most recent session in the Senate when he fell over at dinner one night. Because the name Seagrove had such high recognition within the state, his campaign advisors asked Alison to run for his open seat. She did so reluctantly, and won.

Alison Seagrove was sworn into office several months later after a landslide victory, having no background in politics except for being the wife of a well-respected Senator. She was appointed to all of the committees her husband had been a member of; and this special intelligence committee was one of them.

"You're right, Alison, we must decide where to go from here," replied Hughes with a smile.

"Bennett, get me a cup of coffee while you are up. We could be here a while," said Strickland.

"Sure Robert."

"We need to go to the President and tell him that we are shutting this project down. God is telling us that we shouldn't be doing this," said Arlen Dupree.

Arlen Dupree was a very large 60-year-old man; a typical Texan. His ostrich boots and 80x beaver Stetson cowboy hat made it difficult for anyone to miss him, especially in Washington. He stuck out like a sore thumb, and liked it that way.

Senator Dupree was born and raised and had lived most of his life outside of Dallas and made his money the hard way; he'd dug it out of the ground. He went to church each Sunday and gave most of his money to the seminaries, his church or missionary organizations that dominate the Dallas/Fort Worth area. He knew that God had given him the money, and it was his responsibility to help God's work anyway that he could. He also believed God was in control of certain things, and man shouldn't try to help. When he heard about this project, he knew that he had to be involved in order to represent those who see God as God.

"Arlen, don't get all religious on us. Some of us don't ascribe to the same views that you do," stated Strickland.

"Just calm down Arlen, everything's going to be fine, "added Austin.

Senator Robert Strickland was from California and Bennett Austin was from Nevada. They sided together on just about every decision that had to be made. Both men were liberal in their point of view and wanted very much for this project to happen. With a scientific breakthrough like this, they could reverse tragedies that occur, or go back and alter a situation so that it could be changed in their favor. These men saw Dr. Keith's work as the future and worked diligently to be members of the committee. They wanted to be in on the ground floor, so that when the machine became viable, they could help to decide how it would be used.

"Don't patronize me, men. This project is wrong. Man shouldn't have this kind of control, and the death of its leader ought to be a sign to you," yelled Dupree.

"Please, everyone calm down. We are not going to let signs or feelings determine what we do with this project. We need to think logically about what the next step should be," stated Senator Hughes.

"Can David, his assistant, take over?" asked Bennett.

"I don't think so. He is a great technician, and if the machine works he can maintain it. However, he is not the mind behind it. I'm not really sure if he truly understands all of the math and physics involved in such a project," Hughes answered flatly.

Alison broke in, "Are there any scientists in his field doing the same kind of work? There is bound to be somebody at MIT, Caltech, or Berkeley who could come in and finish."

"Possibly, but we could be put years behind!" said John with frustration.

"We shut it down!" said Arlen as he slapped the table.

"I'm with Arlen, this is too important to haphazardly tread into unknown waters," added Seagrove.

Hughes looked down at the table and said, "I'm inclined to side with you. We've lost the light that could take us through the dark tunnel ahead."

"Don't get dramatic John. We ought to at least see if it works before we shut it down."

"You're right, Robert, we ought to go through with the test tomorrow, before we make our decision. Hudson was going to do the test wasn't he? He could still go, and then we could meet back to decide," Senator Austin stated.

John Hughes shook his head and said, "I don't want to put Hudson in that situation. If something went wrong, the only person who could have brought him out of it would have been Ben. No, we need to take some time to regroup. Besides, I think regardless of Ben's death, the Congress would have shut us down anyway."

"What do you mean?" asked Strickland as the room became still.

"Rumors are going around that Congress was going to try to shut us down tomorrow. The economy is slow and the government can't justify the amount of money this top-secret project costs," Hughes answered.

"You're telling me that after years of work and close to a billion dollars spent, that group of religious fanatics might shut us down. There are too many Bible thumpers in that branch of government," yelled Austin.

Seagrove interrupted, "Bennett, be respectful. You may not like their decisions, but at least respect their office."

"Great, the new Senator is lecturing me," Austin barked back.

"Everyone calm down. I really think the Congress was going to shut us down, so this may have worked to our benefit," Hughes said with calm assurance.

"What could possibly be a benefit?" interjected Strickland.

Hughes began again, looking at the committee, "You know that if we are shut down, there is no time to protect the work. Everything that has been gained here will be filed away until another political or economic climate decides to open it up again.

However, if we shut it down because of Dr. Keith's death, it is still essentially opened, and we can take our time to plan what our next steps should be. We could tell the President that we are going to regroup and take time to think through the project. Then, at a later date, we could try to get the work moving again. This way the lab, equipment and research stay intact. If the Congress wins, then it is locked tight, possibly for decades. Dr. Keith's death was a tragedy, but it looks like we can protect his life's work."

"You're making it sound like we're doing something wrong. I won't be part of a deception," stated Senator Dupree.

"We aren't doing anything wrong. The President will be aware of everything that has taken place here today. You have my word," replied Hughes.

The Senators worked for several more hours formulating plans to pause the project so that it could be started again very soon. They discussed interviewing new project leaders and thrashed out tactics to keep the finances flowing during the hopefully short break.

"So we're all agreed. I will call the President in the morning and tell him of our decision. I would ask that you would remain quiet about what has transpired within this room today. I will check in on the lab and the project periodically to ensure that our decisions are respected. I believe that's all. Thank you for coming, and we are adjourned," Hughes said with finality.

The Pastor of Capital Heights Christian church had never seen the parking lot so full. Taking the reigns of the established congregation just four years earlier, the thirty-four-year-old father of three had prayed for a building full of lost souls, but not for the reason that was forced upon him today.

Nathan Miller had been in the pastorate for over ten years before he was called to Capital Heights. Teaching in a small church, going to seminary, and leading a family was tough, but seeing lives changed was worth the effort.

The young man's first church was in the hills of northern Virginia. The building would only hold 40 people, and every one of the 25 that showed up on Sunday mornings was somehow related.

Pleasant Hope church fit the mold of a family chapel to a tee, and it came with an older patriarch whose family had owned the building for hundreds of years. He made all of the decisions: where everyone would sit, when they would have a fellowship, how long the sermon would go, and how many hymns would be sung.

Nathan would later use that church as an example on more than one Sunday morning, and he always said that there was one good thing about his time in the rural countryside; he was never told what to preach. That is, unless his older mentor didn't like the topic, scripture passage used, or points of the sermon: which happened quite often.

During his time at Pleasant Hope, Nathan was often reminded that there was no need to evangelize the community because that building was bought and paid for by family and was to be used for family. If non-family members needed a church, there were plenty of other places they could visit.

For a man who wanted to see God work in powerful ways, it wasn't a surprise when he left after only a year. That experience had seasoned Nathan and better prepared him for his next congregation.

Woodbridge was a small southern suburb of Washington D.C. and would always hold a special place in his family's heart. It was at Woodbridge Church where he met his wife Amy and started a family. In that small suburb, he conducted his first baptism after witnessing his first decision for Christ in a flock he was shepherding. Finally, it was there where he learned how to lead a church to seek God's heart.

For every Pastor there is a congregation that has touched his heart in a way no other group could; Woodbridge was Nathan's magical experience. The people loved him unconditionally and supported his ministry. They desired to reach their community for Christ, and in the five years that he was there, Nathan saw lives changed and the church almost triple in attendance. So, he was surprised when God moved him to Capital Heights.

The young Pastor questioned God for months before he took the new assignment located just a few miles from the Mall in Washington. Why would God move him from a young healthy congregation where the worship space was also the gym and fellowship hall, to a grand building with one of the largest pipe organs, more stained glass, Corinthian columns, and Italian marble than in the Capital Rotunda?

Nathan didn't have any problem with the features within the church; his difficulty was that the people were so proud of them. They would talk for hours about the beauty and expense involved in creating such a cathedral, but would never spare a word about the God who gave his life for them. The place was cold and had the feeling of a mausoleum.

Capital Heights was known throughout the area as being the church to make connections. Many Senators, Congressmen, and Judges attended. In turn, lobbyists, reporters and up-and-coming lawyers also darkened the doors.

There hadn't been a baptism in the church in over three years and the 73-year-old retiring Pastor was known for his eighteen-minute sermons consisting of a few minutes of Bible recitation, a short story, and the reading of a poem. Nathan had no idea how the church got his name and contact information, and wasn't sure why God was punishing him this way, but he took on the challenge.

In his first year at Capital Heights, Nathan would have left for an offer to flip hamburgers for a living, but none came. So instead, he stayed in the fight and eventually began to see some fruit within the congregation. People's hearts were being softened and true ministry was starting to take place. That was why this day was so difficult.

Nathan's assistant Joyce knocked and peeked around the door. "Brother Nathan, it's time to begin."

"Thank you, Joyce. Give me another second."

She smiled and closed the door behind her.

The young pastor looked out the window of his study toward the front of the church and saw a line of limousines waiting to unload their influential patrons. Nathan had preached many times to crowds such as this. Limousines were commonplace at Capital Heights, but not on a Thursday. Today's message would be difficult.

"God, give me the ability to show your love for your people in the next few minutes. Today I am going to need your words more than ever," he prayed as he left the study.

Nathan entered the sanctuary to the sound of the organ playing the old hymn "In the Garden," and took his place on the platform. Normally behind him there would be a choir loft full of singers; today there was empty space. However, there were over a thousand people sitting in front of him ready to pay their respects to the two sweet ladies resting in the mahogany coffins situated in front of the platform.

As he looked out over the congregation, Nathan saw numerous faces that he recognized. Many were members of his church and had toiled in ministry for years with the ladies they were honoring this morning. Some were high-powered leaders within the government.

The pastor didn't know these attendees personally, but had seen their faces on *CNN* or *Fox News*. As he counted this group's heads, he was wondering if a section of the Legislative branch of the government was shut down, because it looked like they were all at Capital Heights that morning.

Scanning to the back, Nathan saw cameramen and a group with laptops sitting in the balcony. The reporters had attacked like wolves when the news came in. After a day of non-stop calls from the press, Joyce turned on the answering machine and let the phones ring.

Finally, the young pastor turned his attention to the front row and saw the family. The row was empty except for one man.

Normally, the pastor leading the funeral would spend time with the family before the event. It was a good opportunity to comfort the relatives and bring them hope for the future. During these visits many old stories were shared helping to build the framework for the sermon offered at the funeral, but not in this case.

Nathan called the man many times and did his best to visit and pray with him during the loss of his wife and daughter. He wanted to help him start the grieving process. Each time, he was quickly dismissed by one of the many secretaries or assistants. He was told in no uncertain terms that he was only needed to lead the funeral.

Through a few calls to fellow church members who had spent time with the man's wife, he learned that her parents had died years earlier and that she had no other siblings. He also heard rumors that the man's parents didn't approve of her; something about her lack of pedigree. That might explain the lack of people on the family row, he thought to himself.

The young pastor had developed a burden for the lone man sitting on the front row once he got to know Stephanie and Katherine, the mother and daughter lying in the coffins before him. He had observed them at church for several months and noticed that they came by themselves. That wasn't abnormal. Many single women came to his church. However, Stephanie praying by herself before each service made her stand out.

Knowing that she would be in the sanctuary by herself, Nathan often spoke to her after she finished her prayer time, and so was brought up to speed on her situation and desire that her husband accept Christ.

Nathan was burdened along with Stephanie about the situation. He wanted to get to know the man and see if he could share Christ with him, so he decided to drop by their house one night. Stephanie and Katherine were very down-to-earth women. He would have never guessed that they lived in one of the most elite and well protected neighborhoods in Washington.

After being turned away from the neighborhood by the many security guards at the gate, he decided that his next attempt to reach the family would be by phone. Nathan called for weeks, and each time Stephanie said that her husband was either in meetings, out of the city, or just not at home.

Following numerous failed attempts, and at the brink of giving up, Nathan finally found the man at home and was invited for a late dinner. Because the pastor's children would need to go to bed, he decided to go alone.

The pastor was not ready for what he would see. Stephanie's home was at least five times bigger than his. He had never been in a house so large. Their mansion was elegant, containing marble, antique wood floors and true crystal chandeliers. The backyard, if that is what one would call it, had a 50-foot long swimming pool with cabana and statues all around. The grounds were meticulously manicured and there were servants to help at every turn.

The dinner was superb and the conversation enthralling. The man shared story after story about his time in government and his part in many pivotal decisions in American politics in the last twenty years. Nathan knew it was a rare opportunity to have dinner with a leader like this; but no matter what laws the elected official helped to pass, they paled in comparison to the life-changing message the young pastor wanted to share.

Dinner ended and the men went into the study, a beautiful room containing walls of books, oriental rugs and dark leather chairs. The man offered Nathan a glass of brandy from a crystal decanter, but the pastor turned him down. They sat down facing each other in high wingback chairs.

"So Nathan, what is it that you would like to talk about?" asked the man while sipping the brandy.

"I just wanted to come by and get to know you. I have spent some time with your wife and daughter and have grown to love and appreciate them. I thought it was time that I met one of the most important people in their lives."

The man smiled and took another sip. The watch weighing down his wrist appeared to be a Presidential Rolex, and the ring on his fourth finger had a diamond that would make Nathan's wife's engagement ring look embarrassingly small, "I love my ladies more than life."

Nathan knew that these words were not part of his public persona. He was speaking from his heart. "I would give everything for them. I'm a very lucky man."

"Yes you are." Nathan stopped for a second. "Have you ever thought of coming to church with them? They have mentioned many times how they would love for you to come."

The man smiled and obviously put back on the facade, "Pastor, let me be totally honest with you. I am a very busy man. Most Sundays I'm working, but even if I weren't, I wouldn't go to church.

But, I am glad that they go to church. I think it's a good outlet for them and it's their way of performing community service."

Nathan interrupted, "I don't believe they think it is just community service."

The man continued on, "Haven't they helped to paint the church? Didn't they help in giving clothing to the needy? I think they said that was a program you started. I also believe that they have worked in your after school tutoring programs."

"Yes, those are some of the ministries that Stephanie and Katherine have helped in."

"I believe that my sweet wife told me that she was thinking about going to New York with a group from your church to help build or restore some type of a mission."

"Yes," Nathan responded.

"Well, all of this sounds like community service to me, and I'm all for it. Most of what I do is to help the general good of the country. I work hard so that those who are less privileged will have fair representation under the law. I am proud that Stephanie is leading Katherine to be civic minded, and if that is how she wants to spend her time, I'm in full support."

Nathan had to speak up. "We do more than community service. We help with physical needs so that we have an opportunity to tell them of their spiritual need. Our goal is to share Jesus and the sacrifice that he made for us."

"Nathan, I respect you and your profession. I think it commendable that you want to better other people's lives. Churches have helped countless people throughout the centuries, and I hope that they continue. But I don't believe in Jesus."

The young pastor could not believe what he was hearing. Stephanie and Katherine were so full of the Lord. How could they live in this home?

The wealthy man continued, "I believe that Jesus was a good man. He offered a great moral code for humanity. There are many religions around the world that say he was a great prophet. Who knows, he could have been the best man to ever walk on earth, but I don't believe that he was God.

Stephanie has been on me for years about this. She was raised in a religious home and I wasn't. I've done very well for myself without all of the spiritual ties."

He stood up next to his chair. "Of course, my wife would like me to go to church with her, but she knows not to pressure me. She is well aware that I have enough stress coming from my job that I don't need any more at home." There was a note of finality, and maybe a hint of warning in his voice.

"Pastor Miller, I want to thank you for coming," he stuck out his hand to offer one last greeting, "It has been a pleasant evening."

"Yes, I've enjoyed our time together," Nathan reluctantly said as he stood.

Holding his brandy glass in one hand and placing the other on Nathan's shoulder, he escorted the young pastor out of the room.

"You guys are doing some great things down at that church. I've heard many positive reports. Tell you what, would $10,000 help your cause?"

"Yes, well… I guess," Nathan was dumbfounded. Was he being paid off?

"Great, I will have a check sent to the church within the week."

The man motioned for one of the house servants to lead the pastor out.

"It has been a great evening, thank you for coming."

He smiled, left the room, and that was the first and last experience with the man currently sitting alone in the front row.

The young pastor still ached over the experience of that night, trying many more times to meet with him, but knew down deep that he would never be face to face with the public servant again. The memories pained the pastor because they reminded him of what a powerful witness the man would have if he just knew the Lord. With his sphere of influence, he could do great and mighty things for God.

The end of the organ solo brought Nathan back to the task currently at hand; standing, he walked to the pulpit. A hush grew over the crowd as he gave one last look over the congregation and began to speak.

The funeral began with prayer, and progressed into the eulogy. Katherine was just a freshman in high school, but was on the honor roll and had been an active part of the youth group at Capital Heights for over three years.

Stephanie was committed to the church and rarely missed a Sunday. What surprised the pastor was all of her civic work. It made sense to the pastor that being the wife of an influential governmental leader would require her to lead out in community service, but it took over two minutes to read through her accomplishments. He was so proud of the unassuming woman and so grieved that the Lord had taken her home so early. The world was losing a precious soul.

Once Nathan finished praising the women for their achievements and offered a few stories of their work within the church, he began his sermon. The minute he heard of the loss of Stephanie and Katherine, the pastor knew that the ladies would have wanted him to preach the best evangelistic message he knew how. Their desire was always that their husband and father know the Lord. So after much prayer and study, he went back to the basics and shared the most recognized verse out of the bible: John 3:16.

In the 20-minute sermon, Nathan shared God's love for humanity. He mentioned over and over that God loved man enough to send his one and only son to earth. His perfect son, that was without fault would die a horrible death, making himself a sacrifice for all of mankind. The pastor went on to explain that eternity in heaven is easy if one just recognizes that he has made mistakes and calls on Jesus to forgive those mistakes.

It was one of the simplest and yet most important sermons that Nathan had ever offered, and throughout the entire message, the man in the front row didn't turn away. He kept his eyes glued on the pastor the whole time.

Lord, be with him. Touch his heart, prayed the pastor several times to himself during his sermon.

When he finished his message and offered a final prayer, Nathan walked down front and stood beside the opened coffins. It was customary for the pastor to greet the family and other mourners as they gave one last goodbye to the departed. This was an awkward tradition that Nathan disliked, but gladly accepted on behalf of Stephanie and Katherine.

The ushers went to the back and started releasing pews one at a time in order for the attendees to make their way through the line. Nathan greeted hundreds of people and watched as they moved to the lone man in the front row. He was always gracious and greeted each person with a smile, if not a warm embrace.

This time of paying respect went on for over 30 minutes without a stop. Speaking to hundreds of people, he never shed a tear. Not at one time did he drop the smile that he put on along with the $2000 suit and $1000 shoes that he was wearing. Nathan could see through the façade, and wished that he were more honest with himself and everyone else.

Finally, the ushers came to the first row. The man slowly walked to the end of the pew and came forward. He went to his daughter's casket first. Inside lay a young girl who appeared to be merely sleeping. There was the feeling that if you could just give her a nudge, she might awaken. He stood there and looked adoringly at his precious child for several minutes before he moved over to his wife's casket.

When he approached the lifeless body, it was the first time in the ceremony that Nathan saw emotion. The man rubbed her face with his hand.

"Darling, I love you. I will miss you more than you know."

After another minute or so, he walked up to the young pastor and looked him in the eyes. The stare was long and full of malice.

He spoke slowly and quietly. "I have lost my wife, the only woman I have ever loved. My true joy, my daughter is lying in a casket just a few feet away."

Nathan's heart was broken for the man. He wanted to speak but knew that it was important at this time just to listen.

He continued, "I have lost everything that I've ever loved and everything that truly loved me. I am very much alone."

He stopped talking for a second, but never broke the eye contact.

"If your God is so full of love, how could he allow this to happen to me? Why would he permit harm to two innocent ladies doing his work?"

The man looked down for a fraction of a second and then regained eye contact. However, this time the look was different. The face was altered. His features were unchanged, but Nathan saw an evil and malice that he had never seen, nor would ever hope to see again. The man was a cauldron of hatred.

The pastor backed up a step.

With a slight growl in his voice and heat coming from his breath, he spoke through gritted teeth, "I hold you and your God responsible for this. I will have my vengeance."

Following his final words, the man straightened his tie and coat, turned, walked up the aisle and out of the building.

As Hudson was driving from the lot of the EPA building, the clock on the radio in his vehicle told him that it was a little past three o'clock in the afternoon; reminding him that he hadn't eaten anything all day and needed to make a call. Pulling the phone from his pocket, he dialed the number, wondering how much he should share with his wife.

"Hello," answered Sara.

"Hi honey, how was church?"

"Where have you been? Why did you have to leave so suddenly?"

"Dr. Keith has been killed."

"Killed," Sara spoke the word softly.

"Well, the papers will say he committed suicide; I believe he was killed."

"That's so...wait. Hudson, why do you see this differently than the press? What do you know?"

"I can't get into it now, but I found some things to make me think there is a government cover-up, and I'm going to get to the bottom of it."

"Please be careful, don't do anything crazy."

"Don't worry, I'll be fine, although I'll be out late tonight. How was church?" he said changing the subject. "How was the Pastor's sermon?"

"It was great as usual. I picked you up a copy of the service. In short, he stressed that the Lord wants us to believe in Him without seeing. That is the greater faith. Thomas couldn't believe in the resurrection and the power of the Lord without placing his fingers into Jesus' hands and side."

"Sounds like a good one. I need to run. I've got several other places to go and stops to make before the day is over. Give the kids my love, and don't expect me in until late."

"Hudson, be careful. If the government is involved like you suspect, there are greater powers at play than you can control."

"I'll be fine, but I do need the prayers. See you tonight."

"I love you and of course will pray for you," said his wife with a tone of concern.

"I love you," said Hudson.

Closing the phone, he picked up a hotdog at a roadside stand and drove over to the FBI crime labs in downtown Washington. Portions of the building never closed, and he hoped that he could get someone to look at his information and give him the name of the person who had been in Dr. Keith's townhouse earlier that day.

Designed in the 1960's version of contemporary, the FBI building was large and took over a square block of expensive downtown Washington D.C. real estate. Its younger style stuck out badly among most of the other government buildings in Washington that were hundreds of years old, and adorned with columns and statues.

The best thing about this building is the basement level three-story car garage; Hudson mused as he parked the vehicle.

The FBI was a fascinating agency. Hudson loved taking his children on the tour they offered through the building. It was a priority at least once a year, and they looked forward to it for weeks. The tour showed the computer methods used to apprehend criminals, and there were excursions through the labs where children can perform hands-on experiments. In the ballistics lab they could watch lab technicians firing weapons. The bullets were recaptured and the distinctive marks on each projectile examined. Many crimes had been solved by analyzing spent rounds.

The most exciting and anticipated portion of the tour came toward the end. The tour guides would lead the on-lookers into the FBI museum, where they found real stories of how the agency captured the most wanted criminals such as Pretty boy Floyd, John Dillinger, and even Al Capone. There were photos of crime scenes, evidence and several real mock-ups. Hudson's children loved this room the most and could spend hours there. The agent wouldn't be going to the museum today; he locked his car and headed up the three flights of stairs to the finger printing lab.

Hudson's clearance allowed him to move easily through the very secure building. However at each different level and section of the structure, he had to hand over his identification badge for scrutiny.

The badge contained a 3-D holographic image of the agent. Depending upon the angle in which it was viewed, one could see all 360 degrees of his body. Also contained on the card was vital information such as his clearance level and any non-visible identifying marks. Finally, the badge contained a data memory device that held every bit of information that could possibly be known about the government agent.

The agent made his way to the fingerprinting lab and spoke with a technician named Peters. Peters was a round, pale man who looked like he and his desk had been sitting there too long. Candy wrappers, half eaten hamburgers and empty soda cans littered the area. However, Peters knew his business. He took the chip Hudson retrieved from his pocket, and began to work.

"I'll download anything that comes up to the liquid crystal display in your car," he said smacking on some pretzels. "If everything goes well, I should have some type of information; the information you are looking for within the next few hours," said Peters with a smile as he took a drink of cola.

"Thanks, the sooner the better," said Hudson as he left the work area.

—

Clark had been resting in his apartment for over an hour before he pulled out the abstract from his briefcase. He didn't appreciate working this way. As an assassin, he was a professional and always took time to know his target. He watched them for weeks before he made his move.

He grunted and shifted his weight on the luxurious sofa. To be ready to leave for an unknown mission in just a few hours was ridiculous. The only reason he had put up with the situation this long was due to the incredible amount of money he would receive for the next target. Yes, his boss had given him Hebrew lessons for over a year. And yes, he had learned obscure customs of a people that had been dead for a millennium, but how all of that information would fit together remained a mystery.

The seasoned professional was nervous and apprehensive. He was required to make sense of everything by eight o'clock tonight. He supposed the $20 million would motivate him to accomplish things differently than he had before.

Clark opened the thin folder and began to read; terror began to race through the man who had not known fear for a very long time.

Scratching his chin, he shut his eyes, "I should've asked for more money!"

—

When Hudson left the FBI building, he headed to the lab, hopefully his final stop before home. If everything looked all right there, he could go home and get a decent night's sleep. While he snaked through the streets of D.C., navigating his way to the George Washington Memorial Parkway, he began to think about the loss of his friend Dr. Keith. He remembered the time when Ben had called him out of the blue about three years ago and asked him to be part of the project. Hudson was never quite sure why he was chosen, but he had a feeling that the previous President had suggested him because of the hard work and dedication he had invested during his stint in the Secret Service.

When the physicists told him that they were looking for a test pilot of sorts, Hudson quickly turned the offer down. There were plenty of Navy pilots that the government could pull from. If they needed someone with even more experience, they could call NASA. Hudson had just left the Secret Service and wanted some type of normalcy in his life, besides, he couldn't fly a plane, a helicopter, or even an ultra-light. However, Dr. Keith calmed his assumptions by telling him that the person they were looking for didn't need any flight training. Any special instruction necessary to the project would be provided. Ben said that they were looking for someone who was cool under pressure, had a deep sense of loyalty to the country, and understood the necessity for secrecy for this project. Finally, Dr. Keith told him he'd been highly recommended and should at least have lunch with him the next day to talk about it. Hudson relented.

During this brief meal, the universe was turned upside down for the agent. He couldn't believe that mankind could attain what had been up to this point "the impossible." The scientist talked with such excitement for over an hour about his work, and his motives seemed noble. He believed that this project could change mankind for the better.

After an hour of discussion, Hudson finally accepted the position for several reasons. First, he was told he could be home almost every night with his family. This was extremely important to the family man; he didn't want a life like he had as a Secret Service agent. The second and most important reason was that Hudson believed this project needed someone with his religious background and fear of God, so as to somehow keep the work on a righteous plane. If this exploration got into the wrong hands, the world could be adversely affected, possibly pulling people away from the Truth. He could not let that happen.

—

Clark read through the abstract several times, still not believing what he was being asked to do. Several times he picked up his phone, ready to quit the project, but the money sounded so appealing.

Although not poor by any standard, the $20 million would allow the assassin to never have to work again, and retire very comfortably anywhere in the world with a life of luxury and indulgence. This one last score would put him on easy street. His shoulders dropped in defeat; he would just have to fight his fear and prepare for the situation ahead of him.

After reading through the few pages for the fourth time, he reluctantly got up and took a shower, hoping he could calm his nerves and focus his thoughts. Stepping into the shower, the warm water relaxed him, but didn't alleviate the doubts circling within his mind. After finishing with a cool rinse, he dressed in his sweat pants and went into the main room of his suite to stretch through a couple of Tai Chi katas. Trying to loosen his muscles and joints for the difficult project ahead, he would need to employ every trick he possessed to prepare for the unbelievable week that was in front of him.

—

Hudson left the Parkway and turned onto Beacon Street. After a few blocks, he saw Cox Manufacturing. The cream colored metal building looked quiet. The fact that there were no cars in the parking lot, and it appeared that there had been no activity during the day, eased his fears that Dr. Keith was murdered because of his work. If someone were to kill the scientist for this project, they would most likely have made an appearance in the lab today.

Parking behind the building, he saw nothing out of place. Hudson walked up to the back door and put himself through the security measures. The back door clicked and opened. Larry stood before him wondering why he wasn't scheduled to be there.

"Hudson, it's good to see you, but I wasn't expecting you. What are you doing here?" asked the large man.

"I just needed to come by and make sure everything was fine. Have you heard that Dr. Keith committed suicide this morning?"

"Yes, it was tragic. But there isn't anything going on here. I would've called if there was a problem."

"I'm not questioning your good work. This trip is for my own peace. I'm going to spend a few minutes in my office, and then I'll be out of your hair."

"Okay, just don't be too long. I'm sure this has been a long day for you, and you need to be with your family."

"Thanks Larry."

Hudson left the outer chamber and walked out onto the upper deck. Looking over the railing, everything seemed right. Hudson called the elevator and rode down. As he walked around the bottom level, once again nothing seemed out of the ordinary. The computers were quietly humming around the walls. The observation room was dark and locked up. Hudson opened up lockers and saw that all of the equipment was in its place and seemed to be unused.

The agent continued to walk around the room and saw only two things that seemed odd. The clock that hung on the wall above the observation room over a year ago, was sitting on a table next to a start-up generator. *Where had that clock come from*, he asked himself? Also, a small circle of water had pooled around the sphere. Had a temperature change within the room caused condensation to form? Perhaps the condensation drain for the air conditioning was overflowing. Maybe there was a flaw in the machine? He made a mental note, shrugged, and moved on.

Finally comfortable with the scene, he went into his office down the hallway off of the main floor. The small room was always in disarray, and he wanted to get everything in order. There was no telling what the next day would hold with the loss of the great scientist, so Hudson spent the next hour or so making sure all of his work was organized and presentable.

—

Clark left his apartment and walked to a chic Italian restaurant around the corner. The apartment purchased by the agency hiring him was located in a trendy part of D.C.; within walking distance of a variety of businesses including a coffee shop, a Mexican restaurant, an Irish style pub, a copy center and a drug store. Clark frequented Papa Luigi's the most often.

While small in comparison to the many chain restaurants that covered the nation, its food was out of this world. Everything was made fresh by third generation Italian immigrants. Of course, you wouldn't eat at Papa Luigi's because you were concerned about your health. Everything was prepared in real butter and was covered with real cheese. Clark loved to eat there. Once inside the restaurant, it looked like any family eatery that might be found near the piazza, in Venice. Presently, Clark would quite literally have killed for a Luigi calzone.

He entered the restaurant and was seated at his special table. As a regular customer, Clark had built up a rapport with the owners, so they treated him as one of their own. It didn't hurt that Clark spoke a good amount of Italian.

The assassin spent the next hour in the restaurant, eating and conversing with the staff. He knew that this would be his last real meal in a restaurant for a while so he wanted to make the most of it. He even ordered a glass of their best red wine to top off the experience.

Close to 7:30, Hudson knew he needed to get home. He'd spent an hour organizing his office and finishing work that he had left unfinished for weeks. Then he'd spent another hour going through the events of the morning and thinking about the death of his friend.

Hudson had tried to share Christ with Dr. Keith many times, but the man just couldn't believe in a God he couldn't see. How odd, when Ben lived and breathed in the unseen. Everything the physicist did was theoretical. From the hypotheses on paper, to the abstract usage of formulas that no one could prove, Ben showed over and over again that he could believe in God if he chose too.

But neither did Dr. Keith believe in evolution or some sort of spontaneous self-organization. He even listed his reasons. First, evolution contradicted the Second Law of Thermodynamics which states that ordered energy inevitably collapses into disorder. He would say, "This immutable law makes it clear that things don't just naturally organize themselves."

Second, Ben had seen the odds tables of the possibility of mutations occurring in just the right order and with the right frequency so as to cause a positive effect on species. These odds were so small that they approached the infinitesimal. To Dr. Keith it was obvious that if a species grew an eye or wing, it wouldn't necessarily provide any advantage for the creature unless the other parts required for the function appeared at the same time. Hudson had heard his Pastor say once that spontaneous generation could be compared to a medieval alchemist producing by chance a silicon microchip; in the absence of a supporting computer technology, the invention would be useless, and would most likely have been thrown away.

With all of the genius the scientist possessed, he couldn't make the leap to believe in a benevolent Creator. This never made sense to Hudson because of the many mathematicians through the ages who had turned to Christ. Each of them finally had to believe that if the most probable of explanations doesn't work-i.e. evolution-then one needs to move to the improbable hypothesis, no matter how it disagrees with normal logic. Another hypothesis that paralleled this closely was Occam's Razor.

A Franciscan monk born in the late 13th century, William of Ockham stated, "*Pluralitas non est ponenda sine neccesitate*" or "plurality should not be posited without necessity." Always take the simplest explanation, or the one with the least degrees of difficulty. It is much easier to believe that God ordered the universe, than to trust that quadrillions of mutations occurred

JAMES T. AND CYNTHIA A. RUNYON

in just the right order so as to make mankind. Ben could not follow that line of reasoning even though he had no hypothesis to offer himself.

Ben and Hudson spoke often about matters of religion. The agent would bring up verses in the book of Romans showing that nature itself declares God's glory. He would also tell him that accepting Christ changed his life for the better.

Hudson even attempted to use logic to influence Ben's decision. He told the physicist that Jesus fulfilled over one hundred Old Testament prophecies about the coming of a Messiah. Yet, Ben was unmoved. Hudson bore the sad knowledge that his friend had left this world and entered into an eternity without God.

At 7:45, Hudson pulled out his phone and stepped into the elevator on his way up to the observation floor. Following a few short rings, his wife answered.

"Hey sweetie, I'm about finished with all I need to do and should be home in 30 minutes. Could you have something for me to eat?"

Sara responded, "Sure, I'll warm up some leftovers. Be safe and I'll see you soon."

Closing the phone, he looked at Larry the security guard, "Good night, see you tomorrow."

"Good night, Hudson."

The agent left the building and drove away.

Clark left Papa Luigi's full and satisfied, and walked back to his apartment. The tall man knew that his boss would have any equipment that he would need for the job so he just picked up his keys, the abstract, and of course, his weapon. He never went anywhere without a gun. Then he headed for the parking garage.

His Volvo made the twenty-five minute drive to Cox Manufacturing effortless. As he pulled up behind the building and parked, Clark sat for a few seconds to focus his thoughts. He could feel his own hesitation; once he entered the building there was no turning back. Pressing down the fear that had worked its way into his throat, he determined to go in with conviction and purpose. A few seconds later, he was at the back door going through the security procedures.

Upon entering and walking over to the observation railing, Clark looked at the ominous sphere. Tonight it held much more importance in Clark's life than it had every other time he had seen it. Tonight that machine would be his lifeboat, and if it failed, Clark knew he would die.

"Come on down," the scientist yelled having arrived just a few minutes earlier. "It's time to go!"

Already, the scientist's frail but impatient form irritated him to the core, but Clark reminded himself one again, that his expertise was required to float his lifeboat. He rode the elevator to the bottom and noticed a calfskin bag that evidently held the equipment that he would need.

"Is this for me?"

"Yes, that should be all the gear that you'll need. I haven't looked through it, but I'm told that you'll know what to do with its contents," answered the red headed man.

Clark opened the bag, took the contents out and placed them on a table. There was a tunic of sorts, a broad blade knife, some sandals, a wig, some rope, a flashlight, ten coins, a few pearls, some energy bars, several maps, and a laser weapon. This final item was the newest and smallest of high-tech guns. It resembled the old Taser, but without the wires. This laser type device could incapacitate its victim in a few seconds. The only down side was that it only had a few shots before it needed charging-and where Clark was going there wouldn't be any place or way to charge.

The assassin put the articles back in the bag and took out the folded abstract from his pocket.

Waving the folder in the air and then placing it on the table he asked, "Do you know where I'm going?"

"I've been given coordinates, but it'll take a few minutes to plug them in and verify trajectories."

—

Hudson was approximately 25 minutes from the lab when he noticed that he had forgotten some of the work that he was going to bring home. It wasn't vital that he finish it that night, but he wanted everything in order in case the project would be put on hold in the next few days. Hudson got off at the next ramp and reentered the highway going back to the lab.

—

The scientist finished inputting the data; the calculations showed that his destination was verified in the computer. Everything was ready for Clark to begin the final stage of his assignment.

"You've been through this before, but didn't change location. It shouldn't be much different than this morning but will take a little more time to complete. We calculate about a one second delay for every hundred years that you travel, and when you change location that also adds time. It will not be instantaneous like it was this morning. Just be prepared for a longer and possibly more bumpy ride."

"Fine. The sooner I leave, the sooner I get back."

Hudson turned into the parking lot and drove to the back. He noticed a dark colored Volvo parked in Dr. Keith's spot. The car was unfamiliar, but the spot it parked in made Hudson shiver. *I might just be getting paranoid,* he thought, however, he strapped on a 9mm Smith and Wesson that he kept under the seat just in case.

The agent cautiously walked to the back door and went through the security measures. But when Larry opened the door for him, Hudson noticed that he looked nervous and skittish.

"Hudson, why are you back? It's getting pretty late."

"I forgot to take some work home. I'll just be a couple minutes."

As Hudson walked over to the rail he saw a strange man sitting in a chair below. As the man looked up, Hudson saw surprise, fear, and anger drifting briefly in turn across the man's face. The agent stood stunned for a fraction of a second as he returned the stranger's look of confusion and fear. Suddenly, the stranger jumped up, found his firearm, aimed and fired before ducking behind the sphere. Catching on quickly to the reality of the situation, Hudson quickly pulled his revolver and held it close before running for cover himself.

"Larry! Larry!" Hudson yelled.

Hudson ducked over by the elevator and watched in horror as Larry pulled his M16 and prepared to fire-he wasn't aiming at the man below, but himself. The ex-secret service agent instinctively fired a shot into Larry's trigger arm, but he'd still managed to get a round off into the elevator before staggering back and loosing his balance. Hudson shot the guard again, this time dropping him to the ground.

Shots rang out from the lower level. Hudson crawled to the other side of the observation point and looked over. He saw the large man looking up in the direction that he had just moved from and David, Dr. Keith's assistant, moving toward him from the lower observation room. David was also carrying a gun.

"Who's up there?" whispered David to Clark.

"I'm not sure," the assassin muttered. "Give me cover, I am going for the sphere."

David began to fire a shot every couple of seconds. Clark picked up his bag, ran for the sphere and jumped in. He pushed the button that lowered the canopy while buckling himself in.

Hudson quickly understood that David wasn't on his side and was a potential co-conspirator in Ben's death. He listened for the clicks signifying a pistol depleted of rounds and quickly popped a couple of shots in the direction of Dr. Keith's assistant. Hudson heard the thud of a limp body and looked over. One shot had caught David in the chest, and it had done its work. The scientist dropped to the ground and the gun slid from his fingers.

Hudson quickly ran for the back stairs hoping to beat the canopy's closing. He didn't want to shoot into the sphere because of the possibility of Uranium leakage. When he finally reached the bottom level and opened the fire door to the lab area, he saw that the sphere was closed and preparing for a jump.

When the sphere closed and the mirrored shield was in place, Clark pushed the activation button on the console and the ten-second timer began to sound. Hudson bolted for the nearest exit.

"Ten, nine, eight."

The machine began to hum as Hudson sped for the observation room.

"Seven, six, five," the computers began to buzz, and the generators were spinning at 100 percent.

"Four, three, two."

The laser came to life and Hudson jumped under the desk in the computer room not having enough time to close the door.

"One."

Hudson felt electricity all around him.

"Zero."

The sphere disappeared in an instant and so did the mysterious man contained within it.

Hudson heard David mumble and so he ran over hoping to help him.

"I was wrong, Hudson. You've got to stop him," he muttered with the painful knowledge of his error.

"Where did he go, what was his mission," asked the shaken up agent?

"I'm sorry, you've got to stop….."

After seeing the man go limp, Hudson knew that the misguided assistant was dead; he got up and took in the scene. While attempting to rationalize what had happened in the last few minutes, his eyes saw a folder lying on a table across the room.

The weary man walked over and picked it up. On the cover were the words, "Unpardonable Objective." Enclosed within the simple folder were just a few pages. As Hudson quickly read through the brief, he was instantly filled with surprise and terror for what the man, who had just left in the sphere, was going to do. Hudson called Senator Hughes.

The phone was answered in a couple rings, "Hello."

"Senator Hughes this is Hudson."

"Where are you?"

"The lab. There has been a shoot-out and several employees are dead."

"What happened, Hudson?"

"I don't have time to tell you now. We need to send up the 71. The sphere has leaped and if we don't find it, the world as we know it could be lost."

12 — SUNDAY NIGHT, APRIL 12

The three most important words in real estate are the same for time travel: location, location, location. When Senator Hughes discovered that the sphere had been taken, he quickly sent the Habu out to search the globe for its temporal signature. Confident that the search had begun, and the three aircraft were encircling the globe, he drove to the lab where Hudson awaited him.

The SR71 Blackbird, code-named "Oxcart" during its development, flew on a tremendous 65,000 lbs of thrust, with a maximum altitude of over 100,000 feet at Mach 3.5 and the ability to fly for over 4,000 miles without refueling. The sleek "hooded" appearance of the Blackbird, earned it the nickname Habu after the dreaded Habu Cobra in Okinawa, Japan.

Dr. Keith had three Habu at his disposal. Each of these aircraft was identical and kept at the ready at Andrew's Air Force Base along with the President's Air Force One and Marine One. The only thing unique about these 71's was the slight bulge on their bellies containing equipment that would search for the temporal signature of the sphere.

Ben had discovered a peculiar side effect of time travel. The physicist postulated that if a machine could be built that would allow someone to travel back in time, eventually it would begin to right itself to its original time; causing a detectable temporal anomaly.

For example, suppose one wanted to see the bombing of Pearl Harbor on December 7th 1941. It would not be as simple as setting the sphere to the correct time. A landing site would need to be very well planned out that would protect the sphere for the next 80 years. Because once the sphere landed in 1941, it would begin to possess time in every instant after that. Therefore it could be detected in 1942 and 1943 et cetera, up to the instant it left.

While the sphere is out of its correct time, it is invisible until activated and takes up no space in any other time once it begins its correction process. Therefore the sphere would not be a problem for societies after the jump because they would not detect it visually or tactically. The problem begins when it is found and used after someone has jumped.

The sphere could have landed very easily in Oahu Hawaii in 1941 and would be quickly detected in the present by the equipment installed in the

Habu. However, a hotel could now occupy the same space as the sphere, making it very difficult for someone to access it in the present with the key, without having to remove the building that is built on top of it. Location is everything for time travel.

When the Senator arrived, he quickly walked over the dead guard at the front door. As he approached the railing and looked down to the floor below, he found Hudson engrossed in a notebook, sitting in a chair next to where the sphere should have been. The Senator saw a body with bright red hair laying a few feet behind and knew instantly that it was David, Dr. Keith's assistant.

"Hudson, what has happened?" asked the Senator in astonishment.

Hudson looked up rather uncertainly and said, "I don't know. I just don't know."

The Senator took the elevator down and quickly pulled up a chair to talk with the tired and confused agent.

"I had a feeling something wasn't right with the scene at Dr. Keith's house this morning. Dr. Keith wouldn't have killed himself, so I came out here looking for something to back up my suspicions."

"Do you really think Ben was murdered? The FBI said that it was a closed case, and the coroner's office backed up their findings."

"I know Senator, but I believe the events of this evening have proven something's going on."

"Tell me what happened."

"I came out tonight and found just about everything as we left it yesterday evening. So, I went to my office. With Dr. Keith's passing, I wanted to ensure all of my work was up to date in case this project was shut down for a while. I also spent quite a while just reflecting on the loss of my friend."

"I knew that you two were very close. He spoke very highly of you, Hudson."

"Thank you. Ben was a good man," Hudson said with reflection.

"Well, I'd left for the evening and was heading home when I discovered that some of the work I had intended to bring with me was not in my car. I'd left it on my desk, so I turned around and came back. When I returned, I noticed an unfamiliar car in Dr. Keith's parking place.

Once through the back door, Larry was surprised to see me. I didn't think much about it initially, but in retrospect, I obviously wasn't supposed to be coming back. He was trying to get me to leave. That's when the world turned upside down. Some man I hadn't seen before started shooting, and then Larry and David got into the action. I pulled my gun and fired at the closest targets. The Lord certainly spared me, or I'd be dead right now.

These men were trying to kill me. I worked with David and Larry for years; and thought they were friends." Hudson rubbing his eyes said, "They tried to kill me."

"I cannot imagine. I thought that they were loyal to the project. Who could have influenced them to do this?" said the Senator in confusion.

"Hudson," he said seeing the papers clutched in his hands, "what do you have in your hand?"

The shaken agent gave the abstract to the Senator. "I believe these papers show what they intend to do. There's a plan, equipment, maps, even an anticipated target. We've got to get the sphere back and stop whoever it was that left in it."

The Senator quickly read it through, and became flushed. "This is impossible, isn't it? Who would want to do something like this, and why?"

"I don't know, but we can't let him try. Once we find the sphere, I'll be ready to jump back and neutralize the threat."

"You are the only person that can make this situation right, Hudson; the only one trained to pilot the machine."

"Well me, and our friend who took it."

"I stand corrected. Go home. I know that I've said that to you several times today, but you really need to go home."

Hudson immediately looked nervous, "I told my wife I would be home over an hour ago. I bet she's worried sick."

"Give her a call and calm her fears, then meet in my office at nine in the morning. We need to formulate a plan to ensure that our "friend" who's lost in time, doesn't complete his mission. The abstract seems to indicate that he will watch his target for several days so we have a little bit of time on our side. We'll need you ready and focused when you go back to stop him."

"Don't worry, Senator."

"Call me John."

"Yes sir, John, don't worry, I'll be prepared for anything he has in mind."

At that, Hudson stood up and left John Hughes with the abstract, the work of cleaning up the lab, and the process of trying to make sense of what had transpired. He knew this was the effort of professionals with connections, possibly in the highest levels of the government, and that if John Hughes were successful in splintering this ring, it could possibly be at the cost of his career or life. People with this much power don't go down easily.

While Hudson was riding the glass elevator to the top level, he looked down at the scene and saw the body of his friend and the pool of blood around him on the basement floor. When the elevator stopped at the top level, he stepped out, suddenly overwhelmed by the lifeless body of his friend Larry. Hudson wondered if these two men knew the Lord. Were they with God right now? He quickly came to the sad awareness that they couldn't have known God and tried to kill him in the way that they did. They were working for a master who tantalized them with power and prestige; an evil leader who used them for his purposes and then took their lives. The agent sorrowfully realized that he would never see these men again; here on earth, or in heaven.

The spiritual load seemed to weigh on the agent even more than the difficulties of the day. How would God see his own actions of the evening? He had worked with these men in very close quarters for years and hadn't witnessed to them. He hadn't even invited them over to his house to get to know them better. So many opportunities to impact their lives with the message of Christ, and he had failed. In a sense, Hudson was just as responsible as those lying on the floor for the events that had taken place over the last few hours. If they had known Christ, and the powerful life that they could have had in him, they wouldn't have been motivated to kill and be part of a conspiracy so evil.

Hudson left the building, passed the unknown dark sedan and entered his car. Closing the door, he began to pray. The tears began slowly, and then came more forcefully until he openly wept against his steering wheel.

"Oh, Lord, I'm sorry. I have had opportunity after opportunity to share your message, and I failed. Please forgive me. I could have averted this outcome if I had been faithful to your command to share your message. Please forgive me."

Hudson sat there for several minutes before he began to feel his heart lighten. He knew that the Lord had forgiven him, even though he hadn't deserved it. He felt humbled, yet refreshed and strengthened.

"Thank you, Lord. I'll never let an opportunity pass by me again."

Feeling better, Hudson left Cox Manufacturing and veering onto the George Washington Parkway, headed toward Washington. The flashing red of his visual phone indicated that he had a message waiting for him.

When he played back the communication, he discovered that the technician from the fingerprint lab had information on his case. He immediately dialed the call-back number and quickly saw the stubby technician on the heads-up display in his car.

"This is Hudson."

"Yes, Agent Blackwell. I thought you might want this information as quickly as possible." The technician put down his box of carryout Chinese food and typed a few commands at a computer console behind him. "I'm downloading all of the information that the FBI has on your man to your current location. My computer says that you are in a car. Would it be alright to send it there?"

"Yes. I can send it to my home later, if need be."

"Fine. You need to be careful with this one. We were able to find out a lot about him, but there is a Code Three restriction on his file. That could only mean that he is special ops; possibly an agent with the CIA or even the NSA. He must have made a big mistake for you to have found a print. These guys usually don't make mistakes."

"Thanks. I'll look through the file and call if I have questions."

"The file is all that I can help you with. You'll need to go deeper than me to find more information on this character. Somebody wants him kept a secret."

"Thanks for your work. Goodnight."

At that, Hudson ended the call, and began to look at the data that was scrolling across the heads-up display in front of him. As he continued his drive toward home, he noticed that this man was military trained and highly decorated, not to mention, possessed the restrictions the technician had spoken of. However, the one thing that stuck out the most in the information before him was his name, Michael Jensen.

13 — SUNDAY NIGHT, APRIL 12

Clark was not as prepared as he would have liked for the turbulent ride in the sphere. In his haste to leave the lab, and the gunfire of the unexpected guest, he hadn't enough time to secure the seat restraints that should have kept him from bumping around inside the cockpit. Partway through the journey, the assassin's head was forced into a support beam rendering him unconscious; causing him to awaken an hour later feeling as if he had been the ball in a rugby match.

The world's first time traveler took a few minutes to calm his nerves and then began to remember the experience that he had just gone through. As the sphere closed, and he'd pushed the execute button on the dash, everything began to change. The outer shell of the sphere became transparent making the world outside of the vehicle visible. The lab instantaneously disappeared and everything around him became a mixture of brown and black.

Recovering from his time of forced sleep, he remembered something that David once said. He explained that if the sphere were relocating itself to another place in addition to another time, it would prioritize the events and get itself to the new location first. David stated that the sphere would take the most direct route to get to its new position. If the machine were moving across town, it would instantaneously move horizontally through whatever was in its way. However, if the sphere were going to another place in the world, the scientists hypothesized that the vehicle would choose the shortest path between the two locations; a corridor through the earth.

This whole line of reasoning was difficult for Clark to understand, but he quickly resolved to accept the facts that were before him. The brown blurry substance enveloping the sphere had to be the layers of strata that he was transported through to get to his present location.

A crooked smile lit his face, "I just moved through the earth. Amazing! It sure was faster than using the airlines."

Once the vehicle found its new location, by design it would then begin its ascent into the past. It was during this period of time travel, and before it found its desired historical mark that Clark was able to watch through the front of the sphere. As his overwhelmed brain tried to take in the action before him, he saw huge rectangular blocks that had to be at least 30 feet long. Some of the blocks were standing upon others and some of them were laying on the floor around him in a haphazard way.

As the sphere reversed through time, the traveler observed the world in front of him as if he were watching an old reel-to-reel movie in reverse. Instead of blocks falling, he saw them rising from the floor. Even though it was very quick, he believes that he witnessed a 30-foot long, multi-ton block rise from the floor at least 70 feet and settle itself at the top of the cavern.

Clark was preparing to open the canopy and leave the vehicle when suddenly; the sphere was violently thrown backward. In that sudden motion, Clark was thrust forward and his world went black.

—

Hudson awakened the next morning to the rich smell of coffee and the memories of unsettling dreams. The agent's imagining couldn't be called a nightmare, but were definitely unnerving due to their dark nature. The loss of Dr. Keith was without doubt an emotional weight, but would it cause visions of a self seeking world devoid of direction and hope? Hudson's subconscious was working overtime, and he prayed it wasn't giving him a taste of his future.

The man very rarely got up earlier than seven, but the events of the previous day gave him fitful sleep at best. He was up at 5:30 before the sun, and into his Bible shortly after that.

Hudson started each day with a personal time of reading in the Bible. He felt it gave him strength and encouragement. This morning was no exception; in fact, today he needed God's word even more than ever before. Turning to the fourth chapter of Philippians, he realized that God was attempting to speak to his heart in a powerful way; today's words seemed to leap off of the page. *"I know both how to be abased, and I know how to abound: every where and in all things I am instructed both to be full and to be hungry, both to abound and to suffer need. I can do all things through Christ which strengthens me."*

After a quick shower, he walked softly down the hallway to go downstairs and have breakfast. Before he left the second floor, he peeked in and looked at his sleeping children. Bobby was all twisted up in his sheets like a mummy, lying on his back sideways off the bed. Amy was snuggled up tight with her stuffed lamb she called Cotton. Her bed was neat and straight, and if she hadn't been sleeping in it, the bed would have looked untouched. Hudson loved his children and seeing them sound asleep, without a worry in the world, made him proud that he was their father. He quickly gave them a kiss, whispered his love, and headed downstairs.

Sara always got up before the sun. She enjoyed sitting out on the screen porch, hearing the birds and reading her Bible. She would say that the morning was the time she spent with God, and if she had to get up before the sun to have quality time with him, she would. This morning, as Hudson opened the back door and interrupted her quiet time, she was softly singing the old hymn, Purer in Heart, O God.

"…Watch Thou my wayward feet, Guide me with counsel sweet; Purer in heart, Help me to be."

"Morning, Honey. Sorry to bother you, but I'm going to need to leave in a few minutes."

"I was just finishing. Do you want something to eat?"

"Maybe something small, my stomach is nervous."

"Come in, I have oatmeal on the stove," she said as she kissed him and walked inside. "How was your sleep?"

"Not good. When I slept, it wasn't for very long."

"I'm sorry," she said with true empathy. "Here. The four tablespoons of brown sugar will boost your blood sugar, if not your nerves," she giggled as she placed it in front of him. "During my prayer time this morning, the Lord gave me a peace about all you have going on. I know that he'll give you strength, and guide your paths. As I was reading through Psalms this morning, the 23rd just stuck out at me. "Though I walk through the valley of the shadow of death, I'll fear no evil: for you're with me; your rod and staff will comfort me.

The Lord already knows what you're going to do, and has prepared the way for you to do it. It's going to be alright."

"I love you. I need to get to the Capitol building," Hudson said as he quickly finished his oatmeal and started to put on his coat.

"I'm praying for you, and I love you, too."

Hudson gave Sara a tender kiss knowing there was a good possibility that there may only be a few opportunities left to do this. He didn't want to forget the moment, or neglect to show her the love that he had for her. The man left the house, backed out of the drive, gave a long look at his wife waving from the front door, and drove downtown.

—

Clark awakened in a daze lying over the controls. As he began to sit up within the sphere, he noticed blood all over the console. He quickly realized that the blood had to be his own.

"How badly am I hurt," he mumbled searching for the wound.

Being a former Navy SEAL, Clark started running through old training techniques to determine his physical state. He began to move his arms and legs; they seemed fine. He pulled up his shirt and looked at his abdominal area; there were no glaring swollen or bloody areas. There might be internal bleeding, but no signs were apparent. He felt around on his lower back, not locating any sore areas; his kidneys were fine. He felt his ribs, and they weren't broken.

Breathing a sigh of relief, he winced in pain realizing there must be a crack or two, but he would survive. After feeling his face, he discovered the source of the blood; a three-inch gash in his forehead that had long since stopped bleeding.

Remembering that he had been unconscious, his thoughts returned to time. The assassin dropped his eyes and looked at his watch to see how long he had been unconscious.

"Almost 20 hours," he barked.

As he said the words, he could feel his heart thumping through his head. The pain was excruciating. Pressing his hand over his temples the assassin knew only time would stop the thumping.

His face contorted into a grimace. He obviously had a concussion and needed to take some time to rest before heading out. Millions of dollars were at stake if he accomplished this final mission, so the ragged man pushed the button that opened the canopy. He would have to work through the pain.

Holding his breath as the cover opened, he waited as air began to rush in. After a few seconds had passed, he trusted the breeze on his face enough to breathe it. The air was a little musty, but it would sustain him. While the canopy continued to rise with a sound that seemed unnatural in this earthy place, he began to totally take in the area around him.

Clark flipped a switch on the dash that turned on the proximity lighting located at the base of the sphere. Looking around, he noticed that the cavern was much larger than he had initially thought. The floor that the sphere was resting upon was at least fifty-by-fifty. Beyond the measured space were boulders, and mammoth blocks all piled and situated in ways that the original builders could never have intended. The ceiling above him was at least seventy feet high. The cavern, appeared through the assassin's eyes to be an old cistern, because of its domed roof, square geometry, and tightly bricked floor.

The large space would have likely collected channeled rain or river water, but from its present state appeared to have been unused for decades, possibly centuries. The assassin was suddenly grateful for he had been given several maps.

One was of the region where he would be tracking his target. It listed the cities where the victim could be found and general information about the people located within those cities. The information at his disposal would allow him to find out whether the people were mostly Jewish, Greek, or Roman, and who their rulers were. The country he would be working in had a turbulent past-or present, depending on his perspective-and he needed to know everything he could about its people to ensure his surviving of the mission. Ignorance could cost him his life, for the leaders within the era that he had traveled to were known to kill people cruelly and without much provocation.

The second map was of the cave in which he was presently located, made by an American archaeologist who knew more about this spot than anyone else in the twenty-first century world. The map was sparse at best and gave more written directions than pictorial location. The map had a rough sketch that showed a small opening on the north end of two fallen, but unbroken thirty-foot blocks. He recognized the spot.

"That's it," he mumbled to himself.

Clark slowly started to rise and exit the sphere. Just standing made his head scream at him to rest. The ache was so strong that he nearly lost his balance as he found the steps attached to the side of the machine. Clark slowly pulled his bag from the cockpit and noticed why the vehicle had been thrown back so violently. Sitting just in front of the sphere was a three foot high, 20-foot long block. Evidently the sphere was located in the space that the block was to fall. When the block naturally fell through time, it claimed its permanent space, thrusting the sphere into the nearest vacant area.

By design, the sphere was supposed to possess time in the twenty-first century, so it was just borrowing space from this time in which Clark found himself. Therefore the vehicle wasn't even scratched by the altercation-not that the assassin could say same thing about his forehead.

American jeans and shirt would most likely mean his death, so Clark slowly opened the bag and began changing into the tunic provided for him.

Not liking the look, he enjoyed the room the tunic afforded him. His stash fit well underneath the garment.

Knowing it would hurt; he pulled a water bottle from his sack, moistened his shirt and began to clean his face. As painful as the cleansing was, walking out of a cave covered in blood would draw just a little too much attention to him; something he couldn't afford. After staining most of the shirt and using all of the water, he was satisfied that he had removed as much blood as possible.

Next, he pulled the wig from the sack. It was imperative that he have this part of the disguise to guarantee the image was complete. Ensuring that his new hair had a tight fit, Clark had to give it a strong tug, which didn't help his already painful gash and throbbing head. After a few expletives, the hair was in place.

The assassin was told to grow a beard over a month ago, but didn't think it was necessary. He liked having a smooth face, and this could have been a potential problem knowing only the young or unmarried went with clean faces. He definitely wasn't young, and by the standards of the time, should have been married at least 15 years earlier, therefore he glued on the last vestige of his costume; a beard.

This wasn't in the planning, but he needed to hide the large gash in his forehead. So finally he tore a portion of his undergarment into strips and formed a long piece of cloth. *I can afford a little plastic surgery later to restore my good looks,* he thought to himself. He braided and knotted the strips until they were in the shape of a very thick rope. Placing its center over his gash, he tied a simple knot in the back. It wasn't perfect, but would have to work.

Removing all of his jewelry; the chain from his neck, and Krugerand coin ring from his hand, and slipping on the sandals, the image was complete. He took the calfskin bag and loaded all of the articles except the flashlight back inside of it. He turned on his light, looked around, took a deep breath, and started to walk through the exit before him.

Almost immediately, his forward movement was brought to a sudden end. To his left and right were 20-foot high walls made of solid limestone. In front of him, the light from his flashlight illuminated a small hole at his right foot and another one located about ten feet up, both being about two feet in diameter.

"What now," he yelled out in frustration.

The reluctant explorer opened the map and instructions given him, and looked at the information. Everything seemed very clear. He was to leave the cavern through an opening between two large fallen blocks, and continue through the breach until he reached the next large cavernous room. As easy as the information sounded, it wasn't possible to follow the commands.

"The map's wrong!" he barked feeling every word through the ache in his head.

Clark knew from the beginning that there was always a chance that the information he possessed, and had learned through months of training, wouldn't be accurate. The Temple Mount had been changing since its inception.

The assassin knew that the first temple was built by Solomon in 950 BC and stood for over 400 years until it was destroyed by the Babylonians in 586. The second temple was completed in 515 BC. Five hundred years later in 15 BC, Herod added onto the site and reinforced the walls, making it a strong military installation. This third temple, called the Herodian temple, was the one existing in this time.

Clark's map was drawn with reference to a temple that was conquered again in 70 AD under Titus. After Muslims entered the city, in 637, they moved or removed the rubble from the previous invasions, so that they could hold their own prayers on the site. Later, a shrine was built, and by 715, the Dome of the Rock was completed. Add to this the many earthquakes and dozens of leaders reinforcing and moving underground structures, therefore his information was wrong.

Dropping his shoulders, and looking at his map, "This map could be as many as 2000 years out of date." The seasoned professional was discouraged.

Getting down on the ground, he shined his flashlight into the small hole at his feet. As far as he could tell, it didn't lead anywhere that his large frame would allow him to go. He couldn't see another opening at the back of the hole; not that there wasn't one. It would be a very tight squeeze if he chose to investigate the small space, so he resigned to look elsewhere.

Pointing his flashlight up, Clark complained, "How am I going to get up there?"

Knowing that he would have a reach of almost nine feet if he jumped; the upper opening was beyond his capabilities. There were plenty of blocks around for him to stand on, but they would weigh 300 pounds or more so he couldn't move them.

Turning around and walking out of the breach, Clark dropped the map and headed back toward the sphere. "The upper hole is not an option; I'll have to find another way out," he said with determination in his voice.

14 — MONDAY MORNING, APRIL 13

One of the great benefits of working in downtown D.C. was the Metro; a subway system like no other. The line was clean, safe and offered door-to-door access to the main downtown buildings.

Hudson exited the subway car with a mass of other commuters going to the nation's seat of power. There were young college men and women, who had to be pages and runners, nicely dressed ladies, who were most likely secretaries and personal assistants, as well as a contingent of important-looking people, possibly Congressional, or Senate seat-holders. Washington was a great city. Anyone-given the right set of circumstances-could stand side by side with their government representatives.

After showing his clearance badge to the many guards and security personnel at each point within the building, the agent finally made his way to the third floor of the Senate wing. Having walked down the hall and passing many doors, he saw the sign for Senator Hughes, and entered the outer chamber of the office suite. The Senator's secretary, Julie, smiled and directed him into the conference room.

Upon entering the room, he quickly felt out of place. At the end of the long table before him was Senator Hughes reading through a pile of papers. Sitting around the table were men and women with different colored uniforms indicating the many branches of the military. These were not low-ranking personnel; Hudson could make out birds, gold leaves, and stars on the lapels and shoulders of the coats, proving their status as the upper echelon of the military. The stone cold faces of the personnel proved that they were not there to socialize.

Sitting among the many uniformed officers was Senator Arlin Dupree. Hudson had never met the man, but knew of him through his outspoken manner and repeated run-ins with the press. Because of his staunch conservative values, the press always asked him for a statement, and then would proceed to blast him later through clever editing.

The press could make God seem wrong through enough camera tricks, he thought to himself.

"Come in Hudson," said Senator Hughes. "We've been expecting you." The Senator stood and walked over to shake Hudson's hand. "As you can see we've been working for quite a while. Several branches of the military are represented here. Over there in that corner is General Denton from the

Army," he said pointing across the table. "He'll help us with the land aspect of this project. Sitting next to him is General Miller. He is with the Air Force and heads up our 71 division. Across the table is Admiral Hopkins. If there is water involved, the Admiral will become very important. Each has aids and advisors. Over there is Senator Arlin Dupree. He's on the Senate committee."

The Senator walked Hudson to a chair located next to his at the end of the table. Once Hudson had taken a seat, minor conversations around the room ceased, and all eyes focused on him.

Senator Arlin Dupree stood up and began the meeting. "Hudson, I know that the last 24 hours have been difficult for you. While at church, you found out that your friend and boss was dead. You then got into a shoot-out at the lab last night, and wake up this morning to a tense meeting with the brass." Hudson nodded slowly and continued to listen. "Hudson, I never liked this project in the first place and I will be glad to see it come to an end," preached Senator Dupree.

"Senator, no commentary! We all know what you think. Your thoughts aren't going to help the situation now," interjected Senator Hughes.

"John, don't tell me what I can say." There was a slight pause in the conversation as the room became quiet. "Hudson, I don't know what else to say other than we need you to get the sphere back."

General Miller broke in, "What the good Senator is asking for is your expertise. You are the only one trained to navigate the sphere back home, and we need you to do just that."

"Where is it?" asked Hudson.

"This morning about 2:00, the 71 division located it at coordinates 31°47'16" N and 35°13'7" E", and at a depth of minus 9.6 meters."

General Denton walked down the table with a map and pointed to the location, "It's right here," he said.

The map the General had placed in front of Hudson was topographical. The agent could recognize the Mediterranean Sea. Below that, he could make out the Sinai Peninsula and Egypt to the West. The place that the General was pointing to appeared to be Israel.

"Hudson, the sphere is located in downtown Jerusalem. To be more specific, we believe it is located in one of the ancient caves below the Temple Mount," said Hughes with strain in his voice.

"Under the Temple Mount?" questioned Hudson.

"Yes, it's about 25 feet below the Wailing Wall," added Admiral Hopkins.

"There is no way we can get in there to get it out!" Hudson said standing to his feet. "Jewish-Muslim relations are too strained. No one will grant the U.S. clearance in there. It is the most holy site in the world for Christians, Muslims, and Jews, so if we scratch a stone trying to get it out, we could have war with one or multiple nations."

"Hudson, relax," interjected Senator Dupree. "Please sit down. I know this looks like a mess but we think we have a solution."

"There is no solution. The Israeli government will never let us in there. And let's suppose that we somehow did get in there to get to the sphere, what about the killer who took it," said Hudson with frustration and fear in his voice.

"What killer?" asked Dupree.

"Michael Jensen. I pulled a print from Dr. Keith's house and had some of my contacts run it. Somehow, an ex-military SEAL knew enough about the sphere to kill its creator, gain access to the lab, pilot it to Israel, and begin a secret mission."

The room immediately began to roar with noise. "No one told me about a killer!" barked General Miller in protest.

Senator Dupree began one of his tirades, "What killer! I was told that Dr. Keith killed himself."

"Everyone calm down!" shouted Senator Hughes. Looking to Hudson, he spoke in a voice that sounded somewhat betrayed, "Hudson, why wasn't I told about this? If you had information, you should have brought it to me, and I would have walked it through the proper channels."

"The crime scene investigation yesterday was a joke," said Hudson standing and pacing. "The FBI was looking at everything except the clues that stood out. It was obvious that there was a cover-up. I didn't want to get you involved until I knew that my assumption was correct."

"Did you say Michael Jensen?" asked Admiral Hopkins.

"Yes, that's what the sheet said. He has a code-three restriction on his file. Evidently, he works for one of you."

"I remember a Sergeant Jensen in the SEALS about seven years ago. He was an excellent soldier and very dedicated to the troop. However, as is so often the case, he was recruited by another branch of the government to do covert work. I don't know what happened to him after that. I can make some calls."

The grumblings began again within the room. "Everyone calm down," repeated John Hughes with audible frustration in his voice. "We don't know for sure that Dr. Keith was killed. We also don't know that Sergeant Jensen or Michael Jensen is the one who took the sphere."

Hudson interrupted, "I'll bet that the abstract I gave you last night will have his fingerprints on it."

"What abstract," Senator Dupree yelled. "No one told me or this group about an abstract." The room began to roar once again with voices.

"I didn't think it was the right time to bring it out. After we solved the problem of the sphere, I was going to tell everyone about it," said Senator Hughes, feeling that he had almost lost control.

"Who gave you the right to make decisions for all of us? Hughes, I'm going to bring this before the entire Senate committee and the President. This is not your show." Arlin Dupree was angry and every one knew it.

Hudson was getting nervous. He knew that this group was going to send him into the thick of this and they didn't even know all of the information. He was quietly saying a prayer asking God to guide this meeting and his future steps. The agent retook his seat.

John Hughes felt himself beginning to turn red. He took a calming breath and spoke once again. "There is more information that we could speak about, but my first concern has been to get the sphere back. We can't let it fall into the wrong hands, and we can't let whomever took it fulfill their mission. I thought it was more important to stay to the task of locating and retrieving the vehicle." Everyone seemed to relax with his explanation. "Let's tell Hudson what we plan to do. This new information-that we will definitely check up on and discuss later-will not change the plan to retrieve the sphere."

General Denton stood and placed a folder in front of the agent. "We need the sphere back. We can all agree on that." Hudson nodded. "You're the only one who can pilot it, so you're going to have to go and get it."

"Hudson, the General's right. We need you. You are the only one who can make this situation right," spoke Hughes with a calm soothing manner. "If we don't go and get the sphere, who knows what will happen? The one and only thing we know for sure is that it involves Israel because of its location. The abstract that you handed me last night spoke of a plan, but is it accurate, or just a plant to throw us off?" Senator Hughes stood and began to walk around the room, "What does this person have in store for Israel? Is he trying to change U.S.-Israeli relations? Is he attempting to destabilize the entire region? Does he want to steal something or start a war? Or is he just on a sight-seeing tour? The only person who can find out is you," Hughes said as he stopped pacing and looked right at the nervous agent.

The room became quiet as they waited for Hudson to respond. He looked around and with all honesty said, "Everyone in this room knows that I'll do my best to protect this nation and the world. Tell me what you want me to do."

For the next twenty minutes, the leaders in the room brought Hudson up to date on the instability within the region, hoping to prepare him for the anti-American sentiment he would receive. They then explained the process involved in getting him to the Temple Mount.

"Once I'm there, how am I going to navigate the tunnels? I've never been to the Temple Mount and don't know the Jewish language. Will I be watching my back for gunfire while navigating through small dimly-lit caverns?"

"We've already thought about that," interrupted General Denton. "There's one man who has made over fifteen expeditions into those caves. He was in the military in his early twenties, but is now a part-time minister and professor at a seminary."

"How is a seminary professor going to help?" Hudson asked incredulously. "I'll need the best military men that you have."

"This professor has good relations with Israel and knows the underground like the back of his hand. He has no family ties and is an archaeologist fluent in ancient languages. Those are the main subjects he teaches at the seminary. As you stated earlier, it will take months to get permits to go under the Ancient City, therefore this operation will not be sanctioned by the Israeli government. This professor is on speaking terms with the Prime Minister, so if there's a problem, he could ease the situation. When you do get to the sphere, you can send him back home and continue with your mission."

Hudson didn't like the idea of having a non-military man in the loop, but from the looks of it, he didn't have a choice. "Where is he? When do I meet him?"

"He's in Louisville Kentucky, at Southern Seminary; a Southern Baptist institution. You have a private flight out at 1:00 and an appointment to meet him at 2:30," said Senator Hughes. "However Hudson, the professor doesn't know anything about this, and won't know why you're there."

"What do you mean? He doesn't know about the mission?"

"No, he doesn't, and he can't. He needs to think that this is a last minute government sponsored research trip. You can't tell him of the danger or that you will be breaking just about every Israeli law that's on the books."

"This isn't right. I can't take a civilian into that kind of danger. I'm sure his ethics wouldn't allow him to do this. There has to be another way."

Senator Dupree spoke up, "Hudson you're right. This is a terrible situation, and I agree with everything that you've said, but this is the only way. We started down this slippery slope when we built a machine that would defeat time, and now we can't stop ourselves. The only way that we can bring this thing back so that it doesn't do any more harm, is to use this innocent bystander for his knowledge and then hope he can make it back out without getting caught."

"So what am I supposed to do? What do I tell him?"

"You tell him that the government needs his help in a dig and we need him to leave tomorrow. Tell him there is a short window of opportunity and that he is the only person who can do it. Make him feel big and important. Tell him that he'll be paid well and will most likely get a book deal out of the information he finds. We don't care what you tell him; just get him on the plane at 8:00 Tuesday morning. Promise him anything, just get him there."

Hudson felt terrible. Sara had told him that the Lord would be clearing his path, but would the Lord lie? Could God want him to use this poor man, a man of God, in this way? This didn't sound like God, but Hudson knew the plan of his enemy. Jensen had to be stopped at all cost.

"Okay, I'll do it," Hudson said reluctantly.

For the next hour, the agent was briefed and given passports, itinerary, where to find equipment, money, maps and a plan to bring Michael Jensen back. Any and every question that Hudson had was answered and given attention. It seemed that the only thing left to do was to begin the mission.

"Oh, yeah, one more question, what is the professor's name?" asked the agent as he was leaving the room.

Senator Hughes, stopped what he was doing, looked up and spoke across the table, "Dr. Todd Myers."

The flight to Standiford Field took a little less than an hour, but to Hudson, it was an eternity. Throughout the flight, his conscience weighted the agent like a millstone around his neck. The Bible made it clear that lying was wrong, and to make the situation worse, he was going to lie or "manipulate" a man of God; a Minister. His actions were supposed to be justified because they were for national security. Hudson could imagine God making a special punishment just for him.

The Falcon, Hudson's private jet, headed for the business area of the airport; a section housing other aircraft such as Learjets, Citations, King Airs, and a couple 737's. Coming to rest next to a Fokker painted in a corporate logo of green and yellow, Hudson saw a man standing next to the entrance of the building. It wasn't hard to see that he was an FBI agent because of the ordinary, well-worn suit and blank stare. Hudson wasn't expecting an escort, but the Washington office most likely sent someone to ensure that he got to the seminary on time.

Hudson retrieved his briefcase from the seat next to him, exited the plane, and walked toward the entrance.

"Are you Agent Blackwell?" said the man as he extended his hand.

"Yes, call me Hudson," as he shook his hand.

"Agent Wilkerson. Mark. The D.C. office phoned our division here in Louisville about an hour ago and asked us to get you to an appointment."

"Okay. I wasn't expecting anyone. I was told that there would be a car waiting, and that I'd drive myself."

"I don't know anything about that. Evidently, they changed their minds. I was told to be here at 2:10. We can call the local office if you'd like and see if we can clarify this."

"No, by the time we worked it out, I'd miss my appointment. This will be fine."

"Do you have any luggage or anything you need help with?"

"No, this is it. Everything I need is in my briefcase. Let's go," replied Hudson heading into the Fixed Base Operator.

The agents headed through the small waiting area of the jet service company, and Hudson was amazed at the luxuries. Normally when the jets landed, there would be limousines waiting to whisk away the person he was assigned to guard, therefore they very rarely went into the building. Hudson didn't know what he had been missing out on. The floors were marble and there were large leather covered chairs in the waiting area. There was a row of Internet connections, monitors in each corner tuned into the news and money channels, and a fine dining area. This waiting area even had a TCBY for those needing a healthy yogurt fix and a Cinnabon for those not concerned with their health.

The men walked through the building seeing well-dressed executives in expensive suits talking on tiny cell phones. There were pilots looking at charts, and even the occasional aircraft maintenance man dressed in his oily coveralls. As Hudson observed this microcosm of society, he thought how exciting must a celebrity's life be. How powerful would a government dignitary feel rubbing elbows with the world's most powerful people? However, he quickly remembered his family at home, and the thought disappeared.

"Do you need to get something to eat or use the facilities?"

"No, I'm fine. I have a 2:30 appointment, and I need to be there."

"The car is right in front of the building," agent Wilkerson said as he pointed to the doors.

The agents exited the building and started for the parking lot. The car they were about to take was easy to spot. It was a dark blue Crown Victoria. Behind the decorative radiator grill were a red and a blue light. Hudson could see the bars of lights in the back window area and the basic black tires with black rims; the government plates topped off the look. He'd spent many hours in a car just like this and always wondered why the government used such transportation. Even his grandmother could spot an unmarked car, obviously the drug dealers and assassins had these vehicles pegged. It seemed that if the FBI wanted to go unnoticed, they would use normal looking cars, maybe even a minivan. Hudson was amused by the thought. However, he wasn't in charge and didn't see the government listening to his ideas any time soon.

Walking over to the passenger door, he noticed that the seat was piled high with folders and papers. "Would it be alright if you rode in back? I have a system up here and it would take me hours to get it back if I moved it. If you really need to be up here, I can do some rearranging."

"No, the back will be fine." As Hudson went to the rear door he noticed that this was a prisoner transport car. It was easy to tell by the center dividing glass and the lack of window and doorknobs on the inside. "Do you transport a lot of prisoners?"

"What?" the man said with a look of confusion.

"This is a transport car. Do you transport prisoners?" Hudson questioned again.

"Oh, yes. Things were a little slow today, so I was the one who got the call to help you."

Hudson opened the back door, placed his briefcase on the seat and crawled in. Mark closed the door behind him and walked around to get in through the drivers door.

"Sure has been a beautiful spring so far," said the tall man as he closed his door.

"Yes, D.C. is blooming with cherry blossoms. This is the most beautiful season in the capital city," said Hudson as he moved to the center of the back seat. Normally he would sit on one side, but a transport vehicle had two sturdy beams running through the back area of each side of the rear seat. These beams were used to lock the prisoner down with handcuffs to ensure that they didn't move around and hurt anyone.

Agent Wilkerson started the car and began to back out of the parking space. "I sure am sorry you have to sit in the back. The agency has been going through cut backs and each man is required to take on more cases. Eventually the criminals are going to rule the streets. The only way I can keep on top of it is to make my car my office."

"It's fine. I guess it's good in a way, because it will allow me to see how the other half lives." Hudson was being pleasant but really didn't like being in the small prison. There was absolutely no way out except through the help of someone from the outside. The glass that separated him from his driver and the glass in the doors and rear window were all bulletproof; often made from Lexan plastic. The seat in front of him and the doors were covered with a Kevlar coating making them bullet proof. The floorboard and the roof were heavily reinforced with metal sheeting meaning that it would take hundreds of rounds of shots to cut through it. One would have to be ready for a war in the back seat to find a way out.

Mark put the car in drive and left the parking lot. As was common with most airports of the size of Louisville International, it was conveniently located near a highway, so the driver veered onto Highway 65 N and headed for Southern Seminary.

Hudson took the next few minutes to open his briefcase and look through the bio he had on Dr. Todd Myers. The information he was given on the professor stated he was 36 years old and five foot eleven inches tall. There was a picture of the man, but it had to be over ten years old. It was most likely a yearbook picture, possibly when he received his Master's degree. The picture showed an average looking man with dark brown hair and dark eyes. He was very trim and looked like he spent some time in the gym. Who knows what he looked like now?

Professors tend to sit a lot and go to fancy lunches. "He's probably 300 pounds and will get himself killed because he's so fat and slow," mumbled Hudson.

As Hudson continued to read through the bio he discovered that Dr. Myers was born in Kansas City, Missouri and had received his Bachelor's in Mechanical Engineering from the University of Kansas.

Why would he go from being an engineer to a preacher? This person was already an enigma, Hudson thought to himself.

After receiving his Bachelor's, he went to work for a construction company and evidently moved up the ladder extremely quickly. Several large public works projects that he had designed were listed among the information, and a few of them Hudson already knew of or had read about. Evidently, at the height of his engineering success, he'd gone back to school.

Dr. Myers moved from K.C. to Fort Worth and went to Southwestern seminary. The information showed he'd received a Master in Theology and a Master in Music.

I'm going into the trenches with a musician. He'll be able to sing to our captors and soothe the savage breast, he thought with a nervous laugh.

"Did you say something?" asked Wilkerson as he looked in the rear view mirror.

"Not really." Hudson continued to read on. Myers became an Assistant Music Minister in Dallas at one of the largest churches in the state, but then moved on to be a Music Minister at a smaller church. He finally got his Ph.D. in Ancient studies at Dallas Seminary.

Now he's starting to be helpful, he thought.

He excelled in Hebrew and had a fascination with archaeology. From the pages that Hudson had in his folder, he learned that Myers had taught at Hebrew University in Jerusalem and had been on over 30 trips around the world to help in various archaeological digs. Some were in Turkey, Iran, Syria, and of course, Israel. Over 20 of the trips were to Jerusalem to work under the Temple Mount.

The last few pages in his folder gave some of the recent accomplishments of the professor. He had written three books on ancient Hebrew; coauthored two books on the processes involved in an archaeological dig; had been at Southern Seminary for the last three years, and was being hounded by universities all over the world to become part of their staff or to offer various lectures on one of his specialized fields.

Hudson discovered two more things about this man, first he was still a Minister of Music and finally, he was very busy in community service.

"This guy's active," Hudson quietly said to himself.

Having put the information back into his briefcase, he said a short prayer asking the Lord to work this situation out in such a way that he would honor him in all that he did. As Hudson opened his eyes, he looked ahead and noticed the Eastern Parkway exit, and knew that it would only be a few more minutes now. However, the driver continued on Highway 65 and passed the exit.

"Mark, we missed the exit."

"What?" asked the agent as he looked in the back mirror.

"We missed the exit. We were supposed to take Eastern Parkway," Hudson said in frustration. He didn't like incompetence and he had to be there at 2:30.

"I know how to get to the seminary."

"I memorized the route while I was in the plane; I thought I would be driving myself. We were supposed to take the last exit."

"Oh, yeah, Eastern Parkway is under construction. It would've taken longer than the northern route. It will only be a few more minutes," said the agent with a smile.

Hudson thought through the map in his mind. He knew that there was a highway that cut through the loop around the city. So, he had to relax and believe that the agent knew the city better than he did; he would have to apologize to Dr. Myers when he arrived late.

As he sat back in the seat preparing for a few more minutes of sight seeing around the city of Louisville, Hudson noticed something under the seat in front of him. Bending over he retrieved a wallet size picture of a very attractive family. There were three children and two parents; it looked like they were in front of a large natural formation, most likely the Grand Canyon. The top right of the picture had a crumpled look as if it had been in a clip; possibly attached to the visor. As he looked at the base of the picture he saw some words obviously added by some type of photo editing software. This must have been a picture sent out to friends and family, possibly for Christmas. The simple words on the face of the picture were: The Wilkersons at the Grand Canyon

As he looked back at the faces on the picture, he immediately noticed that the man driving the vehicle was not in the picture. The father within the picture was a fair-haired man who could stand to lose a few pounds, while the person driving his car and escorting him to this important meeting was trim and muscular. This was not Mark Wilkerson.

Hudson's blood pressure went through the roof. He couldn't shoot his way out with his 9mm; only twenty shots, and his surroundings were bullet proof. He couldn't hurt the driver if he had to. No, Hudson decided the best thing at this point was to get to know the driver.

"Mark, tell me about yourself. Do you have a wife and family?"

"No, never had time. I guess you would say I'm married to my work."

It was about this time that the car passed the 71 E exit. They were still heading north on highway 65. As they passed the exit, they crossed the Ohio River below. The area must have received a good amount of rain because much of the river was white with rapids.

"Mark we passed our last exit. This direction won't get us to the seminary." At the statement, Hudson watched the man's countenance change. He was no longer smiling and happy, but traded that expression for one of determination and focus.

"You aren't going to make it to your destination today," said the man without looking at him.

"Who are you? You obviously aren't Mark Wilkerson. The agent showed the picture to his captor who looked back and nodded.

"No, I'm not Mark Wilkerson," he said flatly. "You must be important. I'm supposed to make two kills today because of you. The first was Agent Wilkerson," he said as he continued to look forward.

"Who was the second?" asked Hudson hoping to find a way out of the situation.

"Was, isn't the right word. It would be better stated, who *is* the second?" said the man with a grin.

"Okay, who *is* the second?"

"You are, Agent Blackwell."

He knew the answer before it was said, but the reality of the words brought action to his thoughts. *God help me*, he prayed to himself. "So where are we going?"

"You'll find out soon enough."

The car continued over the Ohio River and drove a few more miles before it turned west off the highway. It curved down an industrial road and passed several large operating facilities. The first company smelted steel. Hudson could see the sparks through the building. He noticed smelting areas, and a large furnace. Then, they passed a turbine power plant designed to create energy from the Ohio River.

As the vehicle continued on its course, it twisted off the main highway and turned down a small road that was obviously not used very often. "We goin' fishing?" Hudson asked trying to lighten the situation. Predictably, he got no answer.

The driver continued on in silence until he reached an open area adjacent to the Ohio River. Seeing another dark sedan with a man in it brought to life what was going to happen: they were going to dump the car in the river and he was going with it!

"Who's hired you to do this? Can we work this out some other way?"

"Sorry, I've been paid very well to get you out of the picture."

At that, his captor stopped the car, opened the door and got out. Hudson watched him walk over to the other car and come back with a two-by-four.

What do I do, he frantically thought?

The man opened the driver's door, engaged the safety brake, and placed the two by four between the front seat and the accelerator pedal, causing the engine to race. "Have a good ride," said the man before putting the car in drive and releasing the safety brake.

Instantly, the automobile lunged forward and accelerated toward the edge of the river. The rapid velocity closed the driver's door with a thud. The frightened man in the back seat pulled his gun from under his leg where he placed it when he knew of trouble, and started to desperately shoot at the windows. As he turned to fire at the back window, he saw his driver get into the other car and drive off.

The sound of the gun was deafening but it would have been worth the pain had the projectiles destroyed their targets. Each shot fired offered no better results than the last. Hudson's thoughts were a race of panic, reason, and prayer.

The driverless car hit the water and the engine ceased to race. The silence of the engine quickly gave way to the sound of roaring water. The water from the rapidly moving river started to rush in through the dash and front doors.

"God help me!" Hudson cried.

The speed of the river hitting the side of the car caused a huge surge of water over the top. It worked its way from the descended front of the car

THE UNPARDONABLE OBJECTIVE

toward the back. Water began puddling around the agent's feet. Hudson let off a few more shots but quickly understood that the way out of the car would have to come without the gun. Racking his brain for anything to get him out of the car, he suddenly remembered how the trunk was designed.

Except for the bars placed in the back seat to restrain the convicts, there was free passage into the trunk. Hudson started pulling with all of his might at the back seat. He was able to remove sections but the work was slow going. The water was now up to his knees. In a very short time, the vehicle would be filled and Hudson's air supply would be gone. Adding to this predicament was the water temperature. Because it was still early in the year, the water had to be in the 40's; causing him to eventually lose focus and control of his body. He had to get out of the car!

The agent used every bit of strength he possessed to remove the center section of the back seat. Finally he had it out of the way. There was a clear view of the trunk. However, it was difficult for him to squeeze his large body between the two metal bars in the back seat. The water was up to the top of the doors. The car was at an angle with the front pointing down, or he would already be under the water as he headed into the trunk.

The agent finally squeezed his hips through the small area and was doing all he could to keep his nose above the rapidly rising water. If his guess was right, because this car was a newer model, it would have a safety release from the trunk. This was a required addition to every vehicle but had only become mandatory in the last few years. Hudson prayed his theory was correct.

The trunk was totally filled with water as Hudson took his last breath. In the dark he frantically searched the space for a handle or a lever, but came up with nothing. After what seemed like an eternity underwater, with his lungs burning for a cool breath of air, his hand found what seemed to be a t-handle. He pulled the lever and the lock opened. The trunk lid began to rise, as he scrambled to get out. In the time it took him to find the emergency release, the car had sunk under the water approximately three feet and the extreme undercurrent was going to make it difficult to reach the surface before it was too late.

Hudson grabbed his gun in case they would be waiting for him, and pushed off from the trunk as forcefully as he could. The man swam as fast and hard as his body would allow, but it seemed like hours for him to make it to the surface of the roaring river. Eventually he broke through the rough waves and took a large life-saving breath of air.

"Thank you God," he said breathlessly looking to the clear blue sky.

The rapid movement of the water pushed him down the river bank over one hundred feet before he could grab onto the root of a tree and pull his tired and cold frame out. Looking back at the river, the car was nowhere to be seen. If it weren't for the protection of God, Hudson would still be in it.

He rested for a few minutes, made sure that the men weren't waiting for him, and headed back up the road looking for someone to help.

Hamilton Testing Services was a ten-minute walk up the dirt road for Hudson. It was a small steel building with a dirt and rock covered parking lot housing a few cars; none of them new. Except for the painted letters on the door, no one would have known the building was open for business.

Hudson walked through the front door, wet and looking like a whipped puppy. The woman with a few extra pounds sitting behind an old metal desk put down her book and immediately looked at the odd man in her presence.

"Hello, may I help you," she said with a pause, "why are you so wet? It's cold outside. Have you been swimming?" she said with a confused look.

"Yes, as a matter of fact I have."

"Fred, come out here!" she yelled with a strong southern drawl. The name really sounded like 'Frae-yud.'

"What is it, honey, I'm running some... What happened?" said the man wearing goggles, gloves and an apron as he looked at Hudson.

"It's been a morning. May I make a call?" Hudson asked as he walked toward the phone. As he was picking up the receiver, the woman saw the gun in his pants and started backing away. The agent immediately noticed her fear and tried to calm her.

"I work for the government, and I've been in an accident. I'm not going to hurt you and will be out of your way as soon as possible. Here is my identification," he said as he pulled the card from his soaked wallet.

This answer calmed the two who looked like the only excitement they'd seen in the last few years was the cresting of the Ohio River.

Hudson called 911, and during their wait, the Hamiltons were able to find some old clothes and paper towels with which to dry the agent. Before the police arrived, Hudson made a call to the seminary. He was able to talk with Dr. Myers' secretary and work a new appointment time with him around 5:15. He told the nice lady on the phone-most likely a student trying to pay for her schooling-to sincerely apologize for his missing the 2:30 meeting and that if he had to have a police escort to get there by 5:15, he would. The secretary didn't know that he was being serious.

The sudden blare of sirens burst into Hudson's ears, causing his escalating headache to grow in tandem. The tired, if somewhat damp agent ran out front and told the officers to turn off all of the noise. The crime was long over and there was no need for the commotion.

When the authorities finally arrived, they came in force. Because Hudson worked with the government and possessed a high security clearance, he'd become their top priority. This fact did not go unnoticed.

Sally drawled, "Whew! You must be mighty important to cause all this ruckus."

There were four police cars, two FBI cars, a fire truck, the fire chief, a wrecker, and an official from the River patrol. Each came with their lights flashing and their sirens blaring. The Hamiltons commented that they had never had so many vehicles in their parking lot at one time.

The FBI and police immediately began to ask the business owners for any information they knew about the events in question. Mrs. Hamilton remembered two cars going down the road around 2:20 that afternoon. The first was approximately ten minutes before the next. Sally Hamilton took pride in the fact that she remembered the events with such clarity, and that a handful of men were writing down her every word.

Sally's husband ran the business and she took the occasional phone call and wrote the checks at the end of the month. Her position as the owner's wife gave her the freedom to read, or even look out the window all day if she wanted to-and most of the time she wanted to.

Even though Sally's observations were helpful in setting a time frame for the murder attempt, the Hamiltons had little else to offer the investigation. After the police and FBI had asked everything possible, they told Fred and Sally that they might be calling them later if any additional questions came up. The sweet couple agreed to help in whatever manner possible, so the convoy left the small parking lot and drove down the road to where the car had plunged into the river.

The scene looked like a normal fishing hole. It was a sandy-rocky area where people would back their trucks up to the water and spend the day drinking beers and telling stories. Except for Hudson's story, there would have been no indication that anything had occurred there. However, after a helicopter was called in and located the car down the river about 100 yards, everyone got more serious.

The first thing on the FBI's agenda was to take moulage molds of the available tire tracks in the sand. This was a process that started with plaster of paris or some other solid forming compound being poured in the tire track. The compound would form around the shape in the sand and give a three dimensional representation of the tire. Usually the only thing the test accomplished, was to narrow the possibilities of cars used for the crime, but that was a start.

This test was also great for footprints. The depth of the print could give the approximate weight of the individual as well as the size and type of shoes worn. Several prints were located at the scene and subsequently sampled.

It took over an hour for the wrecker to get the car out of the water. Divers had to be called in to hook up the vehicle. Each time the large truck began to winch in the line, the wrecker was dragged toward the River. The car's weight would be more than tripled with water, therefore pulling it from the strong surge of the mighty Ohio River was nearly impossible.

The police called in a larger wrecker designed to pull semis, although it still had trouble keeping its footing, eventually, the winch made some headway. After twenty minutes of slow and methodical pulling, the car was on dry land and the agents started analyzing it for clues.

It was doubtful that anything would ever be discovered in the mud filled car. The authorities would send their best people to work the vehicle over for clues, but Hudson knew it was a lost cause. Even his brief case was a loss. He was glad he'd read through the bio file on the professor during the drive in.

Weary to get to the professor and finish his assignment for the day, Hudson asked one of the local cops to drive him to Southern Seminary. The officer readily agreed, but it was after 4:30 when the car that would take him to his appointment pulled out, and finally left the scene.

Learning his lesson and sitting in the passenger seat, Hudson realized for the first time that he needed to pick up some new clothes. The cover-alls and the worn t-shirt Fred had given him wouldn't make a good impression with Dr. Myers. Missing the first appointment had already placed him on shaky ground with the over-achieving professor.

What would ill-fitting, holey clothes do to my chances, he thought.

As if an answer to his unspoken prayer, a local *Wal-Mart* popped up on the horizon. After 15 minutes in the store, he was dressed nicely in slacks and a shirt.

The agent was dropped off at Southern Seminary a little after five. Hudson was immediately impressed with the beauty of the school. Each structure was made of brick and had a colonial look. There was a courtyard in the center of the seminary and a large beautiful church with a steeple at one end. Had Hudson not gone into work with the government, he could see himself becoming a pastor and learning at a place such as this.

The agent located Norton Hall and walked up the stairs to the second floor. He was right on time, and glad that his second impression with the professor would be one of punctuality and promptness. As he walked to the end of the hall in search of room 216, he heard the playing of a piano and some light singing. It was coming from the room he was supposed to enter. The song was not a hymn; however it was religious in nature.

Hudson stood listening a moment to the inspired love song, wishing his church would include this and other heartfelt and moving music to its worship service. He knocked on the door; the music stopped.

Opening the door, he walked into the beautiful, neatly kept office. The walls were covered with bookshelves filled with books, and an electric piano stood next to the carefully organized wooden desk. As the agent continued in, he saw pictures of a man camping, bungee jumping, skydiving, weight lifting, piloting a plane, and scuba diving. There were pictures of this man in front of some of the most famous places in the world, and one with him receiving a black belt in some type of martial art. These pictures had to be of Dr. Myers.

The young professor walked around the desk, and with a smile thrust his hand out, "Hello, I'm Todd Myers, are you Hudson Blackwell?"

"Yes, sir I am," Hudson said, taken aback from the image of health and fitness before him.

The professor was in perfect shape. His body was lean as though he exercised daily, and the agent even felt calluses on his hands from years of lifting weights. He reminded himself never to judge anyone again. The professor was strong and vibrant, nothing like he had imagined.

"Please sit down," said Dr. Myers as he pointed to some simple leather chairs sitting in front of his desk.

"Thank you." Hudson already liked the man because he didn't seem to be putting on airs.

The professor's office was meant to be used, not just seen and admired. It was simple and understated, and everything was in its place and made sense.

"Are all of these pictures of you?" asked Hudson as he sat down.

"Yes. I ought to be embarrassed. I guess some people have a "me" wall but I may have gone overboard."

"You've accomplished alot."

"God has given us one chance to enjoy all of the great things here, and then we will leave this world and get to spend eternity with him. Heaven will be great, but it will be different, and I can bet that we won't be skydiving, or skiing, because we will be too busy singing praises. I'm just trying to complete my list of things to enjoy before God takes me home," said Dr. Myers as he sat in the chair across from Hudson.

"Now, how may I help you?" said Dr. Myers getting to the point.

"Dr. Myers, I have an opportunity for you."

"Don't call me Doctor, Todd will be fine. May I call you Hudson?"

"Sure. That would be fine. As I was saying, I have an opportunity for you," Hudson cleared his throat and looked everywhere except into the professors staring eyes. Could he pull off this lie?

"I love a good opportunity. What do you have?" said Todd with a smile.

"Well, the government has a dig going on under the Temple Mount and we would like you to head it up."

"What dig, what have you found?" said the man with a puzzling look on his face.

"I can't get into that because it's classified. You would find out once you got there."

"Are you saying that the U.S. government wants me to lead an expedition?"

"Yes. You would be the leader and would get the credit for the findings. You would get all of the publishing rights and the government would pay you a healthy salary in the meantime," Hudson said as he felt God looking down on him in disapproval.

"When is this to take place?"

"We would need to leave tomorrow morning. The discovery is too important to wait."

"Tomorrow! I can't leave tomorrow. I'd need to get clearance from the Deans and I'm teaching a full load. There's no way that I can go tomorrow."

"Dr. Myers, I mean Todd, we must have you. This is too important. You are the only one that can get this done. I know this is short notice, but it's imperative that you go. The government will clear all of the channels for you getting away. All you have to do is go with me at 6:00 in the morning."

"I would be going with *you*? Are you an archaeologist?" said Todd with confusion. The professor didn't recognize his name as a person who ran in his circles. It would seem if the government were this excited they would have pulled well-known people to help with the job.

"Uh, no I'm not an archaeologist," the agent mumbled.

"Are you a diplomat?" Myers asked tentatively, even though he felt that wasn't the case because of Hudson's mismatched clothes and frazzled appearance.

"No. I presently work with the FBI."

"Why would the FBI be working on an archaeology dig? May I see some identification?" Dr. Myers said as he stood and began to walk around the room.

"Yes, here is my I.D. The FBI's involvement is kind of complicated. However, we are involved."

The professor looked at the information and continued to speak. "So, you are asking me to be part of a secret archaeological dig-whatever that could mean–put on by the FBI. You want me to stop everything I'm doing here; the teaching, the book writing and planned activities, and leave with you tomorrow morning to work on something that I won't know about until I get there. Is that right? Is that what you're asking me to do?" He was being very pointed with his demeanor and line of questioning.

"Yes, I guess that's essentially it," Hudson answered, not knowing what the man was thinking.

Dr. Myers walked around the room for a minute or so, obviously in deep thought. His hand was rubbing his chin and he closed his eyes several times. Hudson gave him the silence that he seemed to need.

After what seemed like an eternity, the professor turned around, and with a smirk on his face said, "You're the one."

"What?" Hudson replied in confusion.

"You're the one. God has been preparing me for the last few months for something, and now I know what it is."

Hudson remained silent, praying that the Lord would work this crazy situation out. He knew that God could do it, but didn't know how.

"It's all making sense now," said Dr. Myers as he walked and talked faster. "For the last two weeks, my soul has been troubled. I didn't know why. I've been praying and studying the Word, hoping that the Lord would reveal what he had planned for me, but didn't. He just told me to wait and that he had something very large for me to do. I thought God wanted me to go back into the ministry full-time, or go to the mission field. However, this morning, God gave me a calm feeling. He told me that it would be worked out today. You're it. You're what the Lord has planned for me." He stopped walking and stared back at Hudson. "But, something isn't right."

"I'm sorry, what's not right?" Hudson asked, fearing the answer.

"I'm supposed to work with you, but you aren't being honest. I don't want to call you a liar, but the Lord is telling me that you aren't being honest. What's really going on here?" he said as he sat back in the high-back chair across from Hudson.

Hudson felt like the Lord was drilling right through his heart. He knew that he had lied to the man and if he now told the truth, what would he think of him? Would he still do the mission?

"I've told you what I know," he answered, looking away.

"You aren't telling me everything you know. What's the real mission?" he said as if staring right into the heart of the reluctant agent.

Hudson stood and started to walk around. He took a few seconds to get his thoughts together and began to speak. "Todd, I'm a Christian man, but I've lied to you. We... I, desperately need you to go on this mission, and I was willing to say anything to get you to do it."

"What do you expect of me?"

"Todd, will this remain between us? Your safety and mine will be at risk if you ever reveal to anyone what I'm about to tell you," said Hudson with all seriousness.

"It's our secret."

"The government has been working on a machine that would travel through time. They finally did it, but it was hijacked by an ex-government operative and is now residing under the Temple Mount. From what I've been told, you are the only person who knows those caves well enough to get me in there, so I can apprehend the person who took it and keep him from destroying the time line.

When we go into Israel, it will not be with their permission. We will be renegades, and if we are caught the U.S. government will not acknowledge us or our mission. Once we find the machine, you will need to make your way back to a designated rescue site alone, while I proceed with the case. I give our chances of being successful at 50%. The only thing that is 100% is that if we don't do this, the world as we know it will be changed, and not for the better. My primary concern is not getting the vehicle back. This is where the government is placing its focus; however, if I'm right, the reason why the agent stole the vehicle is what is truly important."

Hudson expected the professor to throw him out of his office as he sat back down and waited for a response. If he saw through his earlier lie, what would he think about a man he has known for only a few minutes, telling him about time travel? There is no way this professor would put his life in harm's way for a crazy story like that.

The professor closed his eyes and leaned his head back, apparently praying. When he opened them, he got a crazy smirk on his face and said, "Now why didn't you tell me that in the first place? Don't you feel better?"

"Yes, I do," he said, with a smile.

"Evidently this is important to the Lord, so it's important to me. I'll do it. It sounds like it could get me killed," he paused, "but it would be worth it to give my life for God's work."

"Thank you," Hudson said with a large amount of relief.

The two men talked for several more hours, discussing many of the logistics that would be involved, and the possible mission the assassin might be on. The idea of what the madman was trying to accomplish terrified Todd, but gave him more trust in the sovereignty of the Lord.

Hudson looked at the clock hanging on the professor's wall and finally realized what time it was. It was after nine, and if he didn't get some rest following the day he had been through, any ability he had to stop a killer would most likely fail.

"Todd, you better get home and try to rest. The morning is going to come very early," Hudson said rubbing his eyes.

"I don't think there's going to be much sleeping with all that you've told me, but I do need to get ready for the trip," replied the professor, starting to stand. "Can I take you anywhere? Do you have a hotel or a place to stay for the night?"

The word hotel triggered something in Hudson's mind. This was the first time since his morning adventure in the river that the agent thought about his safety. He had spent hours talking with the professor in an office structure open to anyone on campus. In his concern to persuade Dr. Myers, the weary man hadn't once thought about those who were working to kill him. They knew where he was to be that morning, so they had to know his agenda for the day. The local police frequencies would have announced hours ago that he didn't die in the submerged car. He now knew that his reserved hotel room was off limits. For that matter, he and Dr. Myers might even now be in grave jeopardy.

Now very awake as adrenaline started to surge through his body, the agent began to look around the room. Dr. Myers noticed the sudden change in Hudson's demeanor.

The professor's office was one of four in an office suite—a small room within a large one. Anyone wanting to get into his place of work would have to enter the main building and the outer workplace where the secretary was stationed. Looking around the room, he noticed that the professor's door was solid oak with no windows. There was one outside window on the back wall but it opened to over a 20-foot drop and had no ledge. Breaking a leg was a good possibility with that kind of fall. He would have to find another way out.

He pulled the revolver he had concealed against his back. Releasing the clip, Hudson realized he only had 4 shots left. *Not enough*, he thought to himself.

Dr. Myers stood and walked around his desk to see what was happening and quickly backed up when he saw the gun.

"What's going on?" asked Todd as he sat back in his seat. "What are you doing?"

"Todd, does this seminary have any type of security?"

"Yes, after nine a professional service is on campus, and all students must show ID to enter the property after dark."

"Do they carry firearms?" replied the agent very quickly.

"What's going on Hudson? Why are you asking these questions?" Todd shot back.

"Do the security people carry guns?" Hudson groaned out with dismissing patience.

He replied with some uncertainty, "Yes, yes I think so."

"Can you get them on the phone?"

"Sure, someone's always at the security office ready to help."

"Call them and try to get a couple men to escort us out. I'm concerned we aren't safe," said the agent with a focus that Todd hadn't seen.

As Todd got on the phone and began to dial the numbers, a new realization of the gravity of this project came upon him. This wasn't a game; it was life or death. While he listened to the line ringing, he began to pray God would direct his path and allow him to fulfill the mission Christ had planned for him.

"Hmm, it isn't answering. No one's picking up. Someone's supposed to be there at all times." He let it ring another three times and then hung up the receiver. "No one answered. I'll try another number. There's always a security guard at the front gate." After dialing the number and hearing the phone ring over 20 times, he looked at Hudson with resignation. "I don't know where they are. There are supposed to be men in those locations after nine."

"We need to leave this building. Where are the exits?" Hudson spoke quickly while putting the gun behind his back and looking out the window again.

"The main exit is in front of the building and then each end of the building has doors that lead out onto the campus."

"Which exit will get us to your car the quickest?"

"East," replied the professor knowing that he needed to give Hudson the shortest answer possible.

"Todd, we may have some people waiting for us outside. I need you to get your keys ready. It'll be a run to your car." Hudson opened the professor's door slightly and looked into the outer office, but didn't see anything out of order. After closing back the door, Hudson said, "Are you ready to go?"

"No, there are things in this office that I'll need for the trip! I have notes and maps of the underground structure," replied Todd anxiously.

"Sorry, but if I'm right, you'll need both hands free to run."

Myers barked back as he moved behind his desk, "I can't get you into the underground without my notes!" He quickly found a file cabinet, opened the third drawer and pulled some papers from a hanging folder. After glancing through the information and making sure they were the ones needed, he stuffed them down his shirt, "Ready to go."

Hudson pulled his gun from his back to his cheek, and opened the door slightly. Looking around, he nodded to the professor, and they both ran into the outer office.

—

Clark found his way back into the large area containing the sphere and began to look around more closely. *There had to be a way out of this large room*, he thought to himself. *If water came in, it had to get out somehow.* As he walked about the corners looking for an exit, he was amazed at the size of the architecture. The cavern was enormous and must have been a monumental undertaking to build. The stones that formed the walls around him had to weigh more than one hundred tons each. *How many men must it have taken to build this place?*

Clark walked the entire circumference of the room and couldn't see any hole large enough to squeeze through. This just didn't make sense. A room this large would require at least a three-foot aqueduct leaving from it. He stopped and thought through the problem once again. As he looked up, he saw the hole in which the water would enter the room. It was approximately 60 feet up and impossible to get to with the equipment he had in his sack.

Almost talking out loud, he mumbled through the problem. Each place he thought should contain an exit came up without one. He would point to one corner expecting from its geometry to find an exit. Each was sealed up tight. He did this to several more places without luck, until he pointed back to the sphere. It was his final option.

The sphere originally came to rest about ten feet from the wall until a block relocated the vehicle and subsequently knocked him out. The vehicle was presently positioned tightly against an outer wall, having been moved over 15 feet. *Could an exit be behind the sphere?* He dropped his sack and came up to the vehicle.

Looking around the back toward the wall, he came up empty. He moved to the front and looked around the machine; once again finding no exit. Finally, he crouched down and looked under the vehicle. A channel, approximately three feet in diameter, began at the base of the vehicle and ran deep into the wall. It would be a tight squeeze, but it was the only way the time traveler saw as a possible exit. This opening would lead him out of the room, but to where?

He walked back over to his sack, picked it up and quickly squeezed his large frame under the vehicle and into the hole. He was sure this wasn't the exit intended for him to use in the mission. Was there a reason for this? Did this lead to an area that would make it difficult for him to leave the Mount? These and many more questions began running through the seasoned veteran's head, but he took a second to calm the thoughts and resolved himself to deal with any threat as it came. This may not be the intended exit, but it was now his only way out. It would have to do.

—

The outer office was empty. The receptionist had gone home hours ago, and any one who wanted to harm the two men hadn't made their way to this room yet. The work area was very plain in decoration. In the center sat a large wooden desk. Sitting against the wall directly in front of that desk were two large leather chairs. A few file cabinets, a picture of a man holding a bible, several plants and a bookshelf completed the room.

Directly in front of Todd and Hudson was the only exit that allowed someone onto the main hall. The door was solid oak and along side the entry was a one-foot wide window. Just above the door was an early 20th century vent window presently tilted in.

Hudson quietly walked over to the door and looked through the side window each way as far as he could.

"Help me move this chair," Hudson whispered to Todd. "I need to see down the hall through that vent window," he said pointing up.

Todd moved without hesitation and scooted the large leather chair. Hudson climbed up and peeked out through each side angle of the window. There were people in the hall, but Hudson couldn't find anyone out of place.

"Do they lock this building down at any time during the night?" asked the agent.

"No, this facility is opened 24 hours. There is a computer lab in the basement where students can literally work all night," replied the professor.

Hudson knew quite a bit about Southern Seminary. It had a long tradition and had been in existence for well over one hundred years. There would be people in their 20's working on a bachelor's degree right next to others in their 60's working on a Ph.D. Because this seminary placed a large emphasis on missions, the possibility of foreign nationals walking the halls was very high. To put it simply, if an assassin was on the hall right now, there would be no way to know it. Everyone he saw carried something: a brief case, backpack or handful of books. *This is the worst possible situation to be in.*

Hudson stepped down from the chair. "There are people in the halls, but I can't see anything out of the ordinary. That doesn't mean that there isn't a potential problem waiting." Dr. Myers stared right at the agent being sure to absorb everything he was saying. "We're going to leave this room and walk down the hall as quickly as possible without drawing attention to ourselves. I'll let you lead since you know where your car is."

Hudson picked up a couple books before leaving the outer office so that he could hide his gun and still keep it accessible. "Are you ready?"

"As ready as I'll ever be," said the professor with some hesitation.

"Then let's go."

At that, Dr. Myers opened the door and began to lead the way down the hall. The agent's Secret Service training came into play as he scanned each end of the hall and every doorway they passed. The vigilant men were making great time and were only approximately 40 feet from the exit when a man opened a door up in front of them and walked with determination toward Dr. Myers.

Hudson was about to push the professor out of the way, when one of the Doctor's hands showed a palm up to the agent.

"Dr. Myers, do you have a few minutes? I'm having trouble with the translation you gave us. You know how particular I am about making the passage say just what it was intended to say."

Every professor had a problem child; one of those people who just wouldn't go away. They would make up troubles just to get time with the professor. Evidently this mid-50's, balding, overweight man was Todd's.

"Sam, we can talk about this later. I have an appointment to get to."

"You see here in this translation," said the short man showing an open book without even hearing the professor, "If I translate this Hebrew line using the Hifil tense, it has this meaning and if I use the Hitpael tense, it has a whole other meaning. Either could work here and I..."

"Sam, I need to go," said the Professor rather abruptly interrupting the pesky student mid-sentence.

Hudson was getting very nervous and Todd could feel the tension in the air. The agent was continually scanning forward and back, and with so many people walking down the hall, his job of ensuring their safety was very difficult.

"Well, we have a test coming up, and I want to do well. Can you give me a hint, or can I walk with you out," replied the student, unfazed.

"Sam, I can't help you right now," barked the professor.

"Well then, when can we meet, since I want this translation to be correct?"

At that point, everything went into slow motion. Hudson continued to scan as two men walked in the doors through which he and the professor were attempting to leave.

"Will you be here tomorrow?" asked the man oblivious to their situation.

These men didn't look like anyone else he had seen at the seminary. Their clothing looked just like everyone else's. Physically they didn't look out of place, except their facial expressions showed hate and malice. Hudson's pastor always said you could recognize a Christian by his eyes. Joy and peace was there; death hid behind the eyes of these men.

The minute Hudson's eyes met those of the men at the end of the hall, they began to place their hands into their jackets and pull something out.

"Can I just spend a couple minutes after class?" continued the wannabe scholar.

"Sam, we'll discuss this tomorrow," the professor barked back and started to walk away toward the gunmen.

"Get down!" Hudson screamed, instantly pushing the professor to the floor. He dropped his books and lifted the gun in his hand.

Simultaneously, both men pulled their weapons from under their jackets and were preparing to fire when Hudson beat them by milliseconds, dropping to the floor and firing off two shots. He hit one of the men, who fell to the marble tile with a hard thud. The second man fired blindly. He hit the wall a few feet to their left and ran into a side corridor.

"Let's go!" Hudson grunted to the professor. We only have a few seconds," as they rapidly got up and ran the opposite way down the hall.

Leaving the passage to exit down the main stairwell, Hudson's last view of the corridor that had held his enemy was poor Sam shrieking and dropping his prized Hebrew homework as he scurried into the room that he had left a minute earlier.

—

Clark worked his way through the narrow, dark passage as quickly as possible. His head was killing him and several times he had to stop moving just to let the pain subside. Not knowing where he was going, he was making good time nonetheless. With one hand holding a flashlight and the other pushing his bag, he snaked his way through the underground labyrinth hoping to find a way out.

While unrelentingly crawling on his belly through the dank underground, he occasionally encountered mice or rats.

"Ouch," he yelled, being bitten from behind. Endeavoring to destroy the creature, he banged his already hurting head on the ceiling of the aqueduct, almost losing consciousness once again.

After pushing about three tenths of a mile through the small dark and rocky tunnel, his tired body and throbbing head got the best of him. He had to rest. The assassin pulled out an energy bar he had hidden away in his shirt pocked, and ate it. He threw the wrapper down the passageway behind him. The time traveler got a quick chuckle as he imagined the archaeologist's face that would find it many centuries from now. What would they say? What if they made this discovery before energy bars and plastic wrappers were invented. *I need to be sure to look in history books when I get back. They'll probably think aliens left it. It could be one of the great mysteries of mankind.* He laughed to himself.

After consuming the quick snack and polluting the tunnel and time line, he turned on his side, and placed his sack underneath his head. He had to take a short nap. Since his flashlight was of the Faraday type, he decided to leave it on during his nap. *Maybe the light will keep the vermin away.*

—

Hudson ran down the main flight of stairs two steps at a time with Dr. Myers following closely behind. Every person on the stairs immediately got out of the way when they saw the agent running down with a gun pointed ahead. The students backed up against the walls or left the stairwell altogether. The two men spanned the distance in record time; Hudson burst out of the main doors first.

"This way," said the professor as he followed through the doors behind him. He made a quick right turn and ran on the grass in front of the colonial styled building. Hudson looked back through the door and saw their pursuer starting down the stairs. He made a desperate shot through the glass doors up at the assailant. It might buy them a few more seconds. The two tired men only had a six second lead and one shot left. *Would it be enough?*

The parking lot for the faculty was to the side of the building, which meant they would have to run half the length of the structure before they could get out of the line of sight of the killer. Dr. Myers was making great time and was almost to the end of the building. Hudson followed as quickly as he could.

"Almost there," yelled the professor. "I'm parked on the end!"

Great, thought Hudson. *Why couldn't he have parked closer?* By this time Todd had rounded the corner and was safe for a few seconds. Hudson made the end of the building just to hear a shot ricochet off of the structure a foot away. His assailant had made it through the front doors and was quickly following them into the parking lot.

Once Hudson got a view of the parking lot and the car on the end, he understood why the professor had parked it as far away as possible. Sitting in the last space on the right, next to the grassy lawn was a 1969 Dodge Charger. Red with black stripes, and it was immaculate. *Wow, what a machine*, thought Hudson as he ran for his life.

The professor was at the driver's door unlocking it when he looked up, "Hudson, watch out!"

The agent ducked around a car in the lot and looked back. He saw the man making a turn around the building, in hot pursuit. Hudson yelled for him to stop but the attacker kept running with his gun aimed at the professor who was almost finished unlocking his door. The agent knew that he only had one shot left, but he had to use it. He hastily aimed his pistol and fired, shooting the man square in the chest.

The pursuer dropped like a charging lion, tumbling several times; his gun skittering across the lot. Hudson immediately took note of where he thought it would be then put his attention back to the man 30 feet away on the asphalt.

Dr. Myers cranked the engine. It wasn't hard to hear a 426 Hemi with glass packs start up. Most likely the entire seminary knew when he started his car. "Let's go," yelled the professor through the lowered window.

"Just a minute," Hudson said quickly. Because he saw no movement out of his pursuer, he slowly came out from behind the car with his gun aimed. He knew he didn't have any rounds left, but his attacker didn't possess that same information. Once he made it to the man, he rolled him over and saw that he wasn't dead, but very close. His shot couldn't have been more accurate: dead center in the chest.

Hudson was broken. His first thoughts weren't anger but sadness. Did this man know God? Had he just sent a man into eternity without knowing Christ? He ripped off his outer shirt and pressed it over the large seeping wound. The man coughed a few times and opened his eyes.

"Who do you work for?" Hudson asked with force. "Why are you after us? Who do you work for?" he repeated.

The man didn't have any strength left but began to whisper. Hudson leaned over him and placed his ear to the bloody man's mouth. "I work…I work for the same…same people…you…you do." The words spoken rocked the world of the highly trained professional. Hudson pulled away. This man worked for the government. *Was this one agency against another? Had someone within the government gone off the reservation? Was there a rogue leader that no one knew anything about?* While all of these questions bombarded the agent's thoughts, he looked down at the man on the ground and watched as the life left his eyes.

He was dead and so was any chance of getting new information. Hudson said a quick prayer, asking the Lord to forgive him for his actions and praying…more hoping that the man had accepted Christ at some time within his life. At that, he left him and walked over to where he thought the gun had come to rest. He found it lying under the back tire of a beat up 76 Chevy Vega. *There sure is a disparity among the salaries of the professors on this campus.* He picked the weapon up and ran over to the professor's Charger.

Presently, people were starting to make their way to the area because of the gunfire and the ruckus in the hall. Hudson gave one more look back at the lonely scene on the lot, and with resignation opened the door and got in. "Let's get out of here, we don't have time to answer the questions from authorities," said Hudson to the man backing the car out of the space.

"Where are we going?" asked the man as he pushed in the clutch and dropped the stick into first gear. The machine barked as it lunged forward.

"Right to the airport."

"I need to go by my house and get some things in order."

"That can't happen. Those who are after us are in the highest levels of government. They know where you live, your habits and even your pet's name. If we go there, we'll be facing another confrontation like this. No, we go to the airport."

"I thought we were leaving in the morning," said Todd as he drove past the main gate heading toward the highway.

"It looks like our itinerary just got moved up eight hours."

At that, the professor turned the classic muscle car south onto highway 64 and headed toward the airport.

Once the two fugitives were established on the highway with the seminary fading behind, Hudson felt safe enough to pull out his cell and make a call. While punching in the numbers, he looked over to the professor who had his eyes fixed on the road and was quietly mumbling to himself. Realizing the professor was praying by the words he was speaking, he closed the phone without initiating the call and laid it in his lap.

"Todd, can we pray together? I know that the last few hours have been rather action-packed to say the least, and if you're anything like me, you're a bit overwhelmed. We need God to give us strength in this task."

"Great idea," he said with a look of gratitude.

With only the street signs passing and the engine lightly humming, Hudson closed his eyes and began to speak. "Dear Lord, we love you. You know that we are attempting to do something bigger than we can handle. We don't know how this will turn out, and we ask that you would give us strength and protection. Lord, we didn't ask for this position or seek this task, but we are willing to perform it. Please guide our steps and in the end, be glorified through our actions. Amen."

"Thanks," said the professor looking relieved. "So much has happened in such a short time. I don't feel prepared or adequate."

"You know God's word better than I do. Philippians 4:13 says, I can do..."

"All things through Christ who gives me strength," reciting the professor with the agent. "That is a verse we're going to have to rely on for the next few days."

"You said it. God's going to be all we have-literally." At that the agent picked up the phone and brought up the number he had entered earlier. This time he pushed the dial button and it quickly connected.

The phone was answered by Senator Hughes. Hudson got right down to the point and brought him up-to-date on the events of the morning, including the river. Then he told the Senator that Dr. Myers would be helping him on the mission, but that they had to leave the seminary fairly quickly because of the shootout and the two dead men left on the campus. In conversation, Hudson warned Senator Hughes of a rogue governmental leader or a mole somewhere.

"Senator, someone knows what we're doing. The man who tried to kill me told me before his death that he worked for the same people that I worked for," said the agent looking from the window.

"Hudson, I can't believe what you're telling me. No one can know about the sphere. It was top-secret and only a small committee and the President know anything about it. He may have been trying to get you off track. I'll do what I can to cover-up the events at the seminary, you just need to be on the plane in the morning."

"Senator, we need to leave right now. If we give them another 12 hours, we may have another run-in. We're on the way to the airport right now. How can you get us out tonight?"

"The plane is on the ground now, but the pilots have their flight plan prepared for the morning." The Senator thought for a second, "I'll call the commander. How long until you reach the airport?"

Hudson lowered his phone and looked over at the professor, "How long to the airport?"

"Around 20 minutes," he said stoically looking through the front glass.

"20 minutes, Senator."

"Hudson, let me go and I'll make the call right now. We'll get you out tonight. Just keep yourself safe. We need that sphere back in one piece and in the good guys' hands."

"We'll do our best."

Hudson ended the call and pushed the first speed dial number. After a short conversation with his wife telling her that he would be gone a few days; he gave his love, closed the phone and placed it in his pocket.

The agent sat for a second just hearing the dull rumble of the tires on the road before turning on the car radio. With the top-of-the-line sound system including a high power amp and graphic equalizer in the Charger, the agent expected loud music to blare, instead a political conversation stuck in his ears.

"With what I've seen out of you, I expected classic rock, not talk radio," said Hudson rather jokingly.

"You just need to catch me on the right day," he retorted with a crooked smile. "I mainly listen to..."

"Stop," Hudson said placing up a hand. "Listen."

"...To repeat. Southern Seminary one of the oldest institutions in Louisville and the first Southern Baptist Seminary has just had a tragedy occur on its campus. It seems that two men, believed to be students..."

"Students?" cried the professor in disbelief.

"...were violently shot while on campus. One man was found on the second floor of a classroom building while the second was found in the teacher's parking lot. Each man's identification showed him to have been a long time student. Neither was found to have a weapon and there seems to be no reason for the gangland style killings. Added to this mystery is the absence of two security guards who neglected to check in at their last watch. Authorities believe that their disappearances are connected to the murders.

They are also searching for a Hebrew professor and an unknown man who were seen running through the halls of the classroom building where the incident took place. They were ultimately seen speeding away. Dr. Todd Myers..."

"That's my name! They think I did it," cried the professor in disbelief.

"...a young but dedicated scholar is sought for questioning. He is known to own a red and black 1969 Charger, the same car reportedly leaving the scene at the time of the killings. If you know of Dr. Todd Myers' whereabouts or have seen a car matching the description, please call the Louisville Police Department immediately. Stay tuned for more information as it becomes available. Now back to..."

At that, Hudson turned the radio off and noticed how the professor's demeanor changed. "Todd, it's going to take time for the Senator to work this out. You're a visible figure on campus and all of the students would've known you. Obviously, the police will be looking for you."

"But I didn't do anything. We need to go back so that I can talk to the police. We can work this out very quickly."

"We don't have that luxury," replied Hudson, rather detached. "Someone wants to detain and keep you from working on this project. They know that you're one of the only people who can get me through the underground to the sphere. One way or another, you will be framed for this. Go back now and you go to jail."

Hudson turned in his seat and looked out the window. "The thing that makes me nervous is how quickly they legitimized the assassins. Somehow they broke into the seminary's database and made them out to be students. Have you seen those men before? They aren't students, are they?"

"I never saw them until tonight. They certainly weren't students."

"Someone also cleaned up the scene," the agent said with some question. "I have one of the men's guns with me right now, but the other man shot at us also. What happened to his gun? Evidently, there was another man on the campus who took the gun and anything incriminating from the two bodies. It would take a group of people behind the scenes to change computer files and give these guys student records. It makes me nervous how smooth and connected this operation is." Hudson got quiet and thought for a few seconds as if trying to put all of the pieces together.

"Hudson, what do you think? What should we do?" asked the driver nervously.

"Get us to the airport; we have a flight to catch." At that the professor slammed down the accelerator, throwing the men back in their seats. The engine roared to life and they speedily disappeared on the long highway.

—

It took 15 minutes to arrive at Standiford field, better known as Louisville International Airport. The last ten minutes of the ride were carried out in silence as both men reflected upon their day and the future lying ahead. "Go right to the Air National Guard entrance," said Hudson breaking the silence.

Todd followed the signs and came to an entrance blocked with several guards carrying machine guns. Directly behind them was a small outbuilding where the gatekeeper stayed.

"How may I help you, sir," asked the young soldier leaning from the window.

Hudson leaned over showing his Level One credentials to the man and told him that they were expected. The soldier made a quick call and immediately opened the gate. A camouflage painted Humvee made its way to the entry and they were asked to follow it to a hangar toward the end of the field. Todd was glad he had the guide because the sun had gone down hours ago and the area in which he was driving was abnormally dark. Very few lights were on, and those that were, glowed at a lower illumination. All around were soldiers with guns drawn and support vehicles speeding off in every direction. It was obvious the military unit was on high alert.

The Kentucky Air National Guard was designated the 123rd Airlift Wing. Its eight squadrons and seven flights carried out everything from administrative, logistical and aerial support to security and medical functions. The wing was created in 1946 and initially flew P-51's. Through the years they had flown everything from F-86 Sabre jets to RF-101 "Voodoo" supersonic reconnaissance aircraft. They were finally given the C-130B Hercules transport aircraft and have been flying it ever since.

However, as the Charger made its way around a large hanger into the open, it wasn't the C-130's that got their attention, it was the extremely large, sleek, well known body style of the aircraft on the ramp that gave the professor a second look. The black aircraft being illuminated with floodlights and surrounded by fuel and maintenance vehicles was definitely out of place.

The professor mumbled, "That's a Concorde."

"Yes," replied Hudson. "In October of 2004, the Concord made its final commercial flight and retired at Filton field in Bristol, England. The aircraft sat there for 18 months when the U.S. bought a couple. They didn't really have a plan for them, so they just sat on this side of the world. Because we always knew that there was a chance we would have to find the sphere quickly, and time was of the essence, the project bought one and brought it up to date. That aircraft you see is a Concorde B. The B has a longer range, is quieter and more stable at slow speeds. The entire leading edge of the aircraft can droop down."

"Yes, adding a greater angle on the wing and making it fly better at slower speeds," interjected Todd. "As a kid I dreamed of flying on the Concorde, but it was only for the wealthy. When their certification was removed, I never thought I'd see one again."

"Well, you still aren't supposed to be seeing it. We painted it black and only fly it at night. The color helps, but it's still difficult to keep this aircraft out of the public eye. We call it Dark Night, and it should get us to Israel in about three hours."

The Humvee escort wound its way around the heavily guarded facility until it drove into a large hangar. Todd stopped the Charger outside of the huge doors until a heavily armed guard motioned him to continue into the building. Once inside, they were asked to step out of the vehicle and take everything necessary for the mission with them. When they had found what they needed, a two-star General entered the open area and came to greet them.

"Hello gentlemen, I'm Major General Thomas Aaron, and I'm in charge of this facility."

Hudson walked up to the officer and shook his hand. "General, I assume you know why we're here. I think you have our ride out front."

"Yes, you men have this base in an uproar. We're in stage three alert to ensure your safety. What're you doin' that demands this kind of emergency?"

"Sir, they didn't tell you?" asked Hudson rather nervously.

"No, they didn't tell me a thing. I don't like throwing the men into this turmoil without a little explanation," he barked with some force.

"I'm sorry, sir. When will the aircraft be ready to leave?" As Hudson said this, a sergeant took the keys from Todd and drove his vehicle to a corner of the hangar.

The General looked rather put out and hesitated before he spoke, "We're busy procuring the last items needed for your trip. Dark Night is ready now. It took every bit of fuel we have on the base to top off the tanks. Currently, the pilots are updating their flight plan because of the new departure time. The base was thrown into chaos 15 minutes ago when we received the call to move you out tonight. We didn't expect to be leaving until daybreak."

As Todd watched his car drive away, Hudson continued to smooth out the situation with the General. "Yes sir, I'm sorry, but if we don't leave now, we may not get to leave."

Todd stood staring at his Charger, noticing a flurry of activity around it. "Sir, what are they doing with my car?" he asked nervously.

"We were told to hide the vehicle on base until you're able to come back and retrieve it. Follow me." At that, the General motioned for them to follow.

Todd gave one more look at his vehicle before he left the area. By the time he had crossed the building the soldiers had thrown a large tarp over the muscle car and surrounded it with various barrels and crates. They then buried the treasure beneath a mountain of parachutes. The vehicle was essentially gone. *I hope this isn't a foreshadowing of what's going to happen to me*, he thought morbidly.

The side room that the two men were taken into was little more than a storage closet, with supplies and tools lining the walls. In the center of the space was a table where three men in green military flight suits were looking over a seemingly haphazard pile of aviation weather charts and flight plans. When the General entered the room, the men stopped what they were doing and braced themselves to attention.

"As you were," he set them at ease with a disarming wave and spoke to the officer in charge, "Colonel, how long before you can man up?"

"Sir, immediately, sir. It was a little tight, but we're ready. We've had to alter our original flight plan and we've been running the numbers to make sure it's going to work. Major Davis has coordinated with Air Traffic Control to get our clearances moved up."

"Outstanding, Colonel. We need you airborne as quickly as possible."

"Yes Sir. The flight engineer is warming her up as we speak," the Colonel said with a nod of quiet confidence. As the two majors hastily folded the charts and stuffed them into a small navigation bag, the Colonel quickly snapped to attention, smartly saluted the General, and headed for the paraloft to don his flight gear.

The General turned to Hudson as the pilots departed and lowered his voice. "Guys, I don't know what you're doing, but we've had some odd supplies enter this building in the last 24 hours. Unpolished precious metals, rubies, pearls, old roman coins. To contrast that, a Taser, climbing gear, passports and visas also came in. What are you up to?"

Hudson looked at Todd, "It looks like they got everything on the emergency list. We'll check it out en route. General, I…" Hudson stopped at mid sentence and began to listen to noise outside the hangar. Sirens were blaring.

Immediately, the phone rang in the office and the General picked it up. After listening to the person on the other end for approximately 20 seconds he spoke to Hudson, "Are you in some kind of trouble?"

"What are they saying?"

"We have a mess of police at the front gate and they want me to hand you over to them."

"You need to stall them. General, your orders are to get us on that plane, is that right?" Hudson said ushered with confidence.

"Yes, those are my orders."

"Then get us in the air now!"

The General looked at him curiously for a second and then spoke forcefully into the phone receiver. "I don't care what they say, they can't enter a military installation without a call from the Pentagon. Stall them!" He smashed the receiver into its cradle with a muttered complaint.

The General quickly strode to the door and summoned his aide. "Bill, run and tell the crew that they don't have twenty minutes. That plane needs to be in the air in ten." The Major immediately scampered off. The General turned and looked at the ragged men in front of him. "It looks like you have had quite an adventure today already. Can I get you something to drink before we get you on the plane?"

Hudson spoke up first, "What I need most is some rest."

Todd quickly followed, "I need a restroom."

The General pointed to the corner where a bathroom was located and Todd found the room. He needed the small room more for an emotional break from the situation than a physical release. Once in the space, he looked in the mirror and questioned what he was involved in. The day had started so easily, and through the natural or supernatural course of events, he'd met an agent who told him that time travel was possible, had two men try to kill him-who in turn lost their lives-and now was wanted by the police for capital murder. The man he saw in the mirror looked much older than his 36 years. His doubt-filled eyes were surrounded by bags that didn't exist hours earlier.

The Hebrew professor turned on the water and splashed his face several times. The cool wash wouldn't remove the events of the day, but it did make him feel more alive. *God give me strength*, he thought. *This mission hasn't even started yet and I'm doubtful of my abilities.*

In his lifetime, he had never doubted himself before. Anything he'd wanted to attain, he'd succeeded. Any goal he sought after, he'd accomplished. He knew that this experience would be bigger than anything he could accomplish. This wasn't simply an earthly goal; this mission could only be accomplished through Christ's strength. God was going to grow and stretch him through this experience, but was he malleable enough to handle it?

He left the bathroom to see Hudson and the General talking in a corner. Hudson had evidently told the officer about the mission. The seasoned veteran looked like he was told more than he could handle because he stood in front of the agent with his mouth agape. When Todd came up to them, it took the General several seconds to snap out of his trance and acknowledge his presence.

"Are you men…men ready…ready to get on the aircraft?" he asked, somewhat dazed.

Hudson looked at Todd and they were both in agreement, "Let's go."

They walked into the hangar and noticed that the sound of the sirens was much broader now. The poor men at the front gate must be going through a mess. They hopped onto a Humvee and drove out to the beautiful, yet menacing aircraft on the tarmac. At any other time in Todd's life, the possibility of taking a ride on the Concorde would have left him breathless with excitement. This time he was breathless with the realization that it may be the last plane ride he would ever take. As their vehicle began to slow, preparing to stop next to the stairs, the General received a call on his cell.

Because the General listened without saying a word for over 10 seconds, Hudson knew that they were going to have trouble getting the vehicle off of the ground.

"Continue to hold them. Do not let them enter this base! Do you understand Corporal? Do not open the gate! I will be there in two minutes." He closed the phone and looked at the driver as the large transport vehicle came to a stop next to the stairs. "Get up there and bring me Colonel Taylor."

The young guardsman ran up the stairs and quickly had the Colonel at his side. As they walked to where the General was sitting, he began to speak, "Colonel, you need to get this plane off of the ground. I imagine that right now, the airport has revoked your clearance and will do all that they can to keep you from leaving this facility. You must get this plane in the air and allow these men to accomplish their mission."

"General, we can't break military or FAA rules. You know that we must follow the rules of this airport. We aren't on a military base, this is a civilian airport."

"I know. But local government doesn't know what is at stake here. We have the right to surpass any rule during a wartime situation, and Colonel, our lives as we know it are in jeopardy. This is a war like none other. No matter what happens, you must get this aircraft in the air. That's an order!"

The Colonel looked nervous, "Yes sir." At that he ran back up the stairs and rapidly continued his preflight.

The General got out of the vehicle and so did the two men. "Agent, Professor, I wish you Godspeed. Everything that was requested is on the plane waiting for you. I pray that your mission is successful for all of our sakes."

He shook their hands and then hopped back on the Humvee as they sped toward the front gate where the area was aglow with red lights from police cars. Waiting at the top of the stairs was a Lt. Colonel who pulled them in and closed the side door on the aircraft.

As they looked around, they didn't see a Concorde designed to transport passengers, but a flying computer lab. The seats were removed and replaced with workstations. Todd could see four distinct work areas complete with desk, chair and computer equipment. All of the passenger windows had been removed, in order to reduce drag and possibly increase the airspeed by 50-60 knots.

The men were ushered into observation seats located at the front. This aircraft, even though it had been upgraded with a completely glass cockpit in contrast to the many gauges the original Concordes were equipped with, still required three pilots to fly it. The pilot and copilot were obviously at the front of the plane. Seated directly behind the copilot was the flight engineer, and behind him were the observation seats. Because this was a military aircraft there was no need for cockpit doors, so the two men were seated right in the middle of all the action.

Once Hudson and Todd took their seats, they heard the sound and felt the vibration of the large Rolls Royce Olympus 593 Turbojet engines come to life. Shortly after the engines showed normal readings, the pilot sought taxi clearance from the tower. "Louisville Ground, Military 1 with ATIS Victor ready to taxi from Guard ramp requesting three-five right."

The controller came back immediately, "Military 1, hold position and shut down. There are some city officials needing to speak with you. Expect them within three minutes."

The three pilots looked at each other and Colonel Taylor spoke, "General Aaron told me this would happen. He said we're to go."

"Military 1, did you copy, over?" barked the loudspeaker overhead.

"We could lose our ratings and be put in jail," said the copilot.

"I was told this is of paramount importance. We go-now get ready to move this vehicle out. Let's see how well I can bluff," said the pilot.

"Military 1 cleared to taxi to three-five right."

"Negative, Military 1, hold your position. You are not cleared to taxi!" yelled the air traffic controller.

The almost invisible jet began to move. Because the guard base was located at the south end of the field, the plane would not have to go far to get into position for takeoff. Occasionally, a UPS aircraft would arrive, but other than that, the airport was almost totally shut down after nine because of the lack of commercial flights scheduled. The seasoned pilots would have to hope the runways were clear for the next few minutes.

As the long sleek aircraft started moving and turning to get into position, everyone aboard was able to see the tangle of law enforcement vehicles at the military gate. "It looks like you've angered a hornets nest?" the pilot interjected over his shoulder.

"It would take too long to explain," replied Hudson. At that, the pilot returned to the business of checking switches and gauges as the copilot hurried through the taxi and takeoff checklists.

Within 30 seconds, the mammoth aircraft was in the run-up area and ready to turn on the runway for immediate takeoff. The control tower continued trying to dissuade the pilots from following their course of action. "Military 1, you are not cleared onto the taxiway or runway three-five. Move the aircraft immediately to the nearest ramp area and prepare to be boarded."

Hudson could tell that the pilot was nervous by his perspiration and elevated breathing but followed the orders given him. "Jack," said the pilot to the copilot, "get ready for 80 percent on the engines."

The copilot placed his hands on the four throttle levers and waited for his next command.

"Louisville Tower, Military 1 is entering runway three-five right and will be transferring to military command once in-flight."

"Military 1 you are not cleared! Do not enter runway three-five right!"

Within a few seconds of that command, everyone aboard Dark Night saw red and blue lights entering at the end of the field. They were over two miles away but would be coming quickly. "Guys it looks like they're going to try to stop us," uttered the pilot with a determined voice.

"Colonel, you've to get us to our destination. You can't imagine the repercussions," yelled Hudson. Todd was sitting back in his seat with wide anxious eyes as he slowly tightened his seatbelt. He was a thrill seeker, but didn't defy authority, or have a death wish.

The pilot made a quick look to his left out the window to ensure that no other aircraft was on final, and then glanced over to his copilot, "Jack this isn't how we're supposed to get this beast in the air, but… full power."

Immediately, the copilot pushed the throttles to 100 percent. The pilot had the aircraft situated on the taxiway but would have to turn the large jet and prepare for takeoff at the same time. On the speaker overhead, the control tower continued to bark out instructions and make threats, as the copilot began to read through takeoff checklists. At the end of the field, the red and blue lights were getting larger and more threatening.

Jet engines are not like normal combustion engines. When the throttles are pushed forward on a small prop plane, the engine immediately reacts and there is no lag time. However, jet engines take time to get up to speed. The pilot was using this knowledge to finish his turn onto the runway-which looked more like a freeway with all of the cars approaching.

"25 knots," said the copilot. The engines were taking their time to get up to speed. "40 knots." The police cars continued to get closer. "70 knots," said the copilot with some hesitation. The turbojet engines were beginning to come to life. "90 knots." The buildings were moving by at a faster rate. "110 knots." The police cars were bearing down and getting too close for comfort.

Todd was subconsciously pushing himself back in his seat as if that would get him farther from the oncoming vehicles.

"130 knots." The aircraft was about to take flight. "150 knots, V$_r$!" the copilot announced, commanding the pilot to rotate for takeoff pitch. Immediately the pilot pulled back the yoke and the front end of the plane started to come off of the ground. "160 knots." It seemed like the back wheels would never leave the earth. The police cars were on them and the end of the runway was coming up fast. A couple of drivers had parked their cars on the runway while they ran for their lives away from the looming aircraft. Several swerved out of the way, almost being run over by the main gear that had not yet left the ground.

Finally, the main gear was airborne. "Gear up," yelled the pilot. The copilot immediately moved the lever. After several seconds he announced, "Gear up and locked. 200 knots."

"Right turn to 100 degrees, raise the nose to 20 degrees," spoke the pilot as calmly as if he had done this a hundred times before and being chased by police wasn't any sort of abnormal experience. After the aircraft was on an easterly direction, he asked for the nose to be brought up to cruising angle. Once in position, forward visibility was at a minimum.

"Continue to flight level five-zero-zero and increase to mach 2.75 as soon as we're level," said the pilot. The copilot immediately began to push buttons into the computer and the horror of the past few minutes was behind them.

The pilot turned in his seat, removed his headset, and looked at the passengers, "Well men, it looks like we made it. I hope this mission is worth the effort, because we're in really big trouble when we get back."

Hudson looked at him and with all seriousness said, "The world is at stake."

"There's a small galley with some refreshments behind you, other than that, just relax and leave the driving to us. We'll have you on the ground in about three hours."

"Thank you, Colonel. Time is of the essence."

19 — TUESDAY MORNING, APRIL 14

Clark awakened slowly to the sight of nothing; the tunnel he occupied was pitch black, and his flashlight must have gone out hours earlier because it didn't have a hint of power left in it. As he became more conscious, he realized his head still hurt to the touch but didn't throb like it did when he began his nap.

The groggy man started shaking the flashlight and after 20 seconds it was glowing brightly again. The tunnel hadn't changed. As he aimed the light in front and behind, he saw the same thing-darkness. *I was hoping this was all a bad dream; evidently not*, he thought with resignation.

After looking at his watch and realizing he had been asleep another five hours, he cursed himself. There was no time for another delay! Even though he essentially had all the time in the universe at his disposal, he needed to finish this project and get on with living the good life. He would fight the urges to take naps in the future and do what he could to get into a normal stakeout pattern.

Placing the watch back in the bag, he began to move again. His knees were sore and his back ached from crawling so long on the rocky floor, but there had to be an end to this tunnel. He once again got his pattern down very quickly. The large man pushed the bag in front of him an arms length, pulled himself with his right arm and pushed forward with his knees while steadying himself and shining the light ahead of him with his left arm. He continued the pattern for a hundred feet or so until his arms got tired and knees began to ache. Once his appendages returned to some form of normalcy, he began again.

Approximately three hours into this trek he started to see light. It didn't look like anything at first, just an area that wasn't as black as before. He pushed through the tunnel with renewed strength to determine that he truly was seeing illumination ahead and wasn't going blind from the glare of the flashlight. With this new hope, the bricks began to speed by on either side. Once within 100 feet of the exit he turned off the light and started to slow his pace. There was a room at the end of his trek, although very dimly lit. The assassin could tell that there was something blocking the exit; possibly a box of some kind or perhaps hay.

Once his eyes began to adjust to the light he observed movement on the other side; people were in the room. He also heard sounds; unnerving sounds. No real words of any kind, just a low and mournful type of noise that sent chills up his spine. The sounds combined with a new smell in the air, made him nervous. The scent was not one of a dank and musty unused tunnel, but one more putrid and decayed; *could it be rotting flesh?*

As he approached the opening, he moved as slowly and quietly as possible. The assassin stopped pushing his bag and left it behind. Inching toward the exit, he noticed that the gap was blocked by a crate. It didn't look like it was very heavy and could be pushed out of the way.

Looking through the inch opening around the box, the man could see parts of the room. Not everything was visible, but the small line of sight allowed him to see enough to make sense out of the scene before him.

Backing away from the hole, he tried to get a grip on the situation he found himself in. It now made total sense why there was such a stench and awful sound coming from the dimly lit room. His tunnel ended at a Roman dungeon.

—

When the supersonic jet was safely in the air, both Todd and Hudson fell into a deep sleep. Hudson was awakened a couple of hours later by a terrifying nightmare. Normally the agent had uneventful slumber, and rarely ever dreamed or remembered his dreams, but this was different. He was soaking wet from sweat, his heart was racing, and couldn't remember ever being so terrified by something that wasn't real.

The vision was of a dark and awful place, one where people thought of nothing but their gain and desires. Death and hate were everywhere. There was no peace or hope and the sun never shined. In the dream, he was attempting to protect his family from those who were trying to kill them because they were the last vestige of good in a lost and dying world.

It took the agent several minutes to calm down and realize that what he went through wasn't real; at least not yet. The world did have hope, and the sun did shine, even though it was dark outside of the aircraft. Once he felt like himself again, he tapped the pilot on the shoulder and asked him where they were. He was told they were presently in Algerian airspace and would be on the ground in less than an hour.

"Colonel, I was told there would be a bag waiting for me, do you know where it is?"

"Yes, I believe that is yours right there," he said pointing to a large black duffle bag sitting ten feet farther aft. The carrier was about three feet long and appeared to be packed to the brim.

The agent unbuckled his seatbelt, left his chair and went over to the duffle. After opening it, he found passports, visas, diplomatic immunity cards, cash, and charge cards for both of them. Also within the bag was gear for climbing and repelling. There were flashlights, energy bars, several bottles of water and some handheld weapons: several nine-millimeter pistols, a Bowie-type knife and a laser weapon. As he looked deeper he found 1st century clothing, a glue-on beard and some sandals. Once he was at the end of the bag, he revealed some old coins that looked new, different types of raw metals, some precious jewels, pearls, and a card with transliterated phrases and coordinates to program into the sphere to get it back to where it belongs. It looked like he had everything he needed. As he was about to zip the bag back up, he noticed that Todd had awakened and was looking over his shoulder.

"Do you have a miracle in that bag?" asked Todd standing over him, "because we're going to need it."

"No, no miracles," he said with a smile. "Why, what's on your mind?"

"I don't see any way to get into the underground. There are only a few digs in the area this time of year, and permits to work anywhere in Israel take months-if not years to get approved. No one knows that we're coming, and all of my contacts at Hebrew University will be too busy preparing students for finals to spend any time greasing wheels with the government to allow me into any sight on the Mount."

Hudson zipped his bag and looked up at the professor, "Todd, do you believe that God wants you here?" The weary man nodded. "Do you understand the importance of what we're trying to do?"

"Of course," he said rather quietly.

"Do you think God wants that madman to accomplish his goals?"

With the large Rolls Royce engines humming outside, and the aircraft moving at over 1900 miles per hour, the professor sat back down in the observation chair. "No."

"Well then, it looks like God's going to have to work all of those things out for us. Here's how I see it: if he doesn't work it out, and we're killed, that would be better than being on this planet if we fail." At that, they both got back into their chairs and rode the rest of the flight out in silence.

As Clark lay against the constricting rock tunnel wall, he tried to assess his circumstances. His first thought was to get out of there and return to one of the side passages he had ignored earlier. This thought left as quickly as it came.

Because the tunnel was fairly narrow, there was no way he could turn around. He would have to back himself hundreds of feet before he could move into a side passage. Then there was no assurance that he would find a different outcome than he had before him. The dungeon was his only way out.

There were several bits of information he could deduce from just looking through the small opening. For one, he knew that any person in that room with any life left in them would begin to make a lot of noise when he attempted to move the crate, leave the tunnel, and enter the room. In addition to that, anyone not chained down in some way, might attempt to leave through the tunnel in which he came. There was the possibility they might try to overpower him for anything that could help to give them an edge the next time the guards came. He was strong and in much better physical health than these men, but the last thing he needed was to fight off an entire dungeon full of desperate prisoners.

The final problem he could see looking through the small opening was that this room appeared to be a close cousin to the room he had left hours before. There were almost certainly many of these underground vaults in the complex, all connected by a series of underground tunnels. *Was this the best way out?*

The moaning and suffering coming from the room just a few feet away made him want out of his present situation even more, however this was not a time to make rash decisions. He would have to plan his escape carefully. One wrong move could ensure a permanent stay in the room before him. So, he decided to observe for a while longer to see any patterns that might arise and help him out of his situation.

—

Dark Night entered Israeli airspace around 5:30 a.m. and was on the ground at Lod Airbase, the heavy transport squadron side of Ben Gurion International, at 5:42, just before sunrise.

The sleek black aircraft was immediately guided over to a large hangar that was open and ready to house the supersonic turbojet. The Concorde was designed with a moveable nose so that the pilots could see the ground on takeoffs and landings. However, even with the nose at its lowest angle of 12.5 degrees, it was a struggle to see what was going on right in front of the aircraft. However, the highly trained pilots eased the jet into the hangar without difficulty and began reading through checklists to shut it down until the vehicle was needed again.

The flight engineer rose and went to the passenger door to open it. The agent and professor looked at each other, "Are you ready?" asked Hudson.

"As ready as I'll ever be," said Todd as he stretched.

Waiting for the ramp stairs to meet up with the side of the aircraft, the agent looked out into the open space of the huge building and noticed the hangar doors closing. Simultaneously, large fans on the ceiling began to kick on; pulling the heat from the room that would be created from the hot Rolls Royce engines.

While they waited to depart the aircraft, Hudson noticed a handful of highly decorated Israeli military men standing on the floor in front of him. There were at least a dozen soldiers in fatigues with M-16's encircling the aircraft.

If they had this many men inside the building with guns, how many did they have outside?

An American looking gentleman stood in the crowded hangar looking out of place in his blue suit and red tie. He had to be a U.S. representative; possibly the ambassador to Israel. Hudson thought through the possibilities but knew that he would find out soon enough.

—

Clark waited. After watching the dark room for several hours, he knew he didn't have the entire picture of what occurred in that area over the course of a day, but thought he had enough information to ensure he would make it out of the dungeon alive without becoming one of its residents.

Through his time of surveillance he'd noticed that the guards only came in once and that was to feed the prisoners. The two soldiers who crossed his view to dish out the food were each armed with a short sword. It was obvious from their body language that they didn't want to be there so they were out of the room in less than two minutes. Because he couldn't see the entire space, he didn't know if there was another person protecting the door to ensure that no one overpowered the guards and tried to leave. If he were in charge, there would be another person on the door.

There must be another guard.

The next thing he noticed was that no one moved the whole time he peeked through the small hole; not a single person crossed his view except the soldiers. If this room were like the one in which he began his trek, it was large and had plenty of space to move around in without crossing his limited line of sight; but the odds were low that he had missed any movement. Somebody should have walked by his lookout, that is, unless the prisoners were locked down. His line of sight didn't allow him to see everyone, but he had heard the screams and moans and heard what sounded like chains rattling around. The most dangerous criminals would have been locked down, but was everyone? By the several conversations he'd heard going on, along with the moans, coughs and cries, he assumed the room to contain around 20 men. Either those in the room were shackled and couldn't move, or they didn't have enough energy or desire to get up. Whatever the case, he wasn't concerned with the prisoners; their threat was a manageable one.

As he thought through the situation, he realized that there were several other problems before him. First, it would be best to leave at night because of the ease of finding places to hide, however he didn't know what time of day it was. During the day they could spot him and send men on horses after him. He possessed some 20th century technology, but couldn't take these soldiers for granted. They were highly trained and could kill him quickly if he was caught off guard.

The second problem was that he didn't know how far underground the dungeon was or where the exit would lead him. What if the way out was a set of tunnels to other dungeons? It would be an obvious disadvantage to be locked in an underground labyrinth of tunnels filled with guards. He had to assume the best; the exit led to the surface.

The assassin moved backward in the tunnel to his bag and pulled out the large knife and laser weapon. That was all he could hold and hoped all that he needed. He threw the bag over his shoulder and snaked the 20 feet back toward the entrance of the room trying to focus his thoughts. As he lay on his stomach with his eyes closed, he took in several deep breaths, letting the air out slowly and with purpose. After repeating this process several times he was ready.

"It seems like there ought to be an easier way to make 20 million dollars," he mumbled to himself. Moving toward the crate blocking his way, he was ready to enter the unknown.

—

Hudson started down the long flight of metal stairs with Todd following closely behind. Even before they were at the base of the steps, the man in the blue suit walked forward to greet them.

"Hello gentlemen, I'm Agent Thomas James, NSA and I'll be escorting you to the Old City," said the man rather flatly. "Do you have any more gear? Anything that I can help you with?"

Todd shook his hand and said no. Hudson affirmed the same, carrying the bag over his shoulder. "If you're ready, then we'll go," the NSA agent stated as he turned around and started to leave. The two men followed without delay. Both thought it was rather awkward to pass the high-ranking Israeli soldiers and not say anything. The officers stood in a straight line looking at the two men who were about to break into the underground of one of the holiest sites in the world.

What had the soldiers been told about the two unassuming men leaving the hangar? Had the government pulled in a big favor or placed diplomatic pressure to get the aircraft housed and the men off of the airbase without going through customs.

Agent James led them away from the hangar to a brand new Mercedes S-class parked among the military vehicles. He opened the trunk and motioned for Hudson to place his bag inside; declining the officer, he kept the bag with him. The NSA agent closed the trunk and pushed the hand unit to unlock the doors; Todd taking the back and Hudson moving into the passenger's seat.

It had been less than 24 hours since Hudson's experience with the last agent sent to pick him up and take him to an appointment. So he didn't trust this man yet and was going to do all he could to protect Todd, himself, and his ability to stop the madman who was 2000 years in the past.

As he closed the car door, Hudson noticed that its weight was unusual for a standard-market passenger car. He hadn't been in too many cars this expensive, but he knew an armored car when he felt one. The glass had a dark tint to it, which was typical of bullet proof glass. This lightweight transparent armor could take direct rounds from a .357 magnum and still hold up. The roof, doors, hood, and floorboard were likely reinforced with flexible, multi-layered, ballistic nylon armor and the tires were "run flats" requiring total destruction to slow the car's progress in a dangerous situation. To complete the package, the engine and power train were modified to accommodate the added ton of armor to the vehicle.

As the silky black Mercedes left the parking lot, Agent James looked over at Hudson, "Agent Blackwell, I was'nt made aware of your arrival until just over three hours ago. Needless to say, I've been busy ever since. I was told to find a way for you to get into the underground of the Holy City. That's not easily accomplished, especially in three hours."

He paused and looked both ways as he moved the vehicle out into traffic. "I wasn't told what you plan on doing, just that you needed access. So, I've been in touch with the U.S. Ambassador. He had me contact several professors at Hebrew University and they connected me with a couple expeditions currently running in and around the Old City."

The agent stopped talking as he made his last turn out of the airport facility onto Highway One; the main thoroughfare from Tel Aviv to Jerusalem. Once the luxurious automobile was up to cruising speed he continued. "After a large donation to the cause of their choice, I was able to get you onto each site as observers. I told them that you were researchers with our government and were sent to investigate new dig techniques. I had to make something up on short notice; that was the best I could come up with. After I offered them money, you could have been anyone and they would've let you in."

Hudson looked back at Todd with a smile, reminding the Professor of God's provision. He beamed back in agreement.

"As I said, there are two archaeological digs presently in process. The first is taking place at the First Century Street on the southern side of the Temple. The second is a dig going on just northeast of the temple in the Pool of Bethesda."

Todd pulled himself forward from the back and stuck his head between the two front seats. "Hudson, we need the First Century Street entrance. I know that site. It's led by Ronald Williams out of Baylor. They discovered an opening in the southern wall a few years ago just below the level of the street. That's how we need to get in, the Bethesda dig won't help us."

"Have you been through that opening before?" Hudson asked looking over his shoulder.

"Yes, that's how I got to the underground location the last time. It isn't a well known route, but I can get us back there again," replied the professor rather excitedly.

Hudson looked over at the agent attempting to maneuver the car around a construction crew, "Well, Agent James, take us to the street site. We don't have any time to waste."

The two men sat back and started planning their next moves. Todd began to look through the papers he had carried with him from his office. He read through his notes and started retracing the route in his head.

Hudson stared out the window at the rugged landscape. *Israel truly is a beautiful country,* he thought to himself.

He had been here several times before as a Secret Service Agent for the President, and knew that in 130 miles, the country could go from parched desert to lush, green hills. There was something very special about this area of the world knowing that Jesus had walked the land several thousand years before. He had to refocus. It was only 35 minutes to Jerusalem and he had to be on his best game when he got there.

—

Clark moved toward the crate, placed his weapons next to the opening, and located a couple footholds in the rock tunnel. He then placed his shoulder next to the box, finally positioning his right hand through the small opening so he could pull from the outside lip of the tunnel. All at once he pulled his body and pushed the box. It moved slowly and made a loud creak as it scraped against the rock floor. He gave all of the energy he had to the task, and eventually the crate moved at a faster rate, even though he still couldn't squeeze through the opening. By this time his legs were fully extended. He needed to find a couple new footholds and quickly.

Just a few seconds into the movement of the crate, the entire dungeon went silent. No one made a sound. Clark found a new leverage position on the side wall and gave one last push. The crate moved another foot; he picked up the knife and laser weapon then squeezed through the hole into the room.

Jumping into the area, he backed against the wall next to the opening. As he held the weapon in one hand and knife in the other, he was amazed at what appeared before his eyes. This assassin had been in many unsavory places in the world such as Iran, Chechnya, and Rwanda, and had seen death in its worst light. He had extracted information from people in such a way that they were often unrecognizable by the end of the process, but nothing could prepare him for the site before him.

The men that lay around the walls could barely be considered human. Several had the remnants of a tunic, but most were naked and lying in their own waste. All of the prisoners were attached to the wall by either chains or ropes, not that those ties were needed or necessary. These men didn't have the energy to walk-let alone break through the large door at the end of the chamber.

There couldn't be a person in the room that weighed more than 100 pounds and their pale color and sunken eyes showed that these men didn't have much time left to live. Many within eyesight had large open gashes. One man had lost an arm to what must have been an animal attack from the way the flesh was ripped from the body. Almost every man with open wounds had maggots wiggling around in the oozing mass, and it was evident that many were dead and had been that way for a while.

The room had a stench that could not be believed. It wasn't hard to understand why the soldiers were in and out as quickly as possible.

The men strapped to the floor and walls were the outcasts of society and were destined to die for their crimes. *What could these men have done to deserve this*, he thought? *Can anything be worth this kind of brutal punishment?*

He let down his guard while he took in the sad estate, but just in that instant one of the prisoners began to yell. *"Ahzraynee, ahzraynee."* Clark had been studying Hebrew and even though the dialect was quite different, he understood 'help me' when he heard it. *"Ahzraynee, ahzraynee!"* It started coming from all over the room. One yelled *"ahzraynoo"*–help us, one started yelling, *"havsheeaynee"*–save me, while another began repeating, *"havsheeah lahnoo"*–save us. Some just whispered the words because of their weakened estate. A few tried to stand, while others reached out as if begging to be released or screaming for a reprieve from their tortuous condition.

The sound became deafening and Clark knew he had a problem. The dungeon, which was almost totally silent before, was now full of noise. The guards would be coming soon!

Looking around the expanse, he found no place to hide. There were no nooks or partitions, just one big open room. He immediately ran over to the door and stood next to the hinges hoping the guards would be looking forward at all of the commotion and not doing a sight check behind the door before they ran in. *"Ahzraynee, ahzraynee!"* The sound was at a pinnacle. He knew that events were going to move very quickly now. *"Havsheeah lahnoo!"*

Giving one last feeble attempt to save their lives, there was nothing the assassin could do to stop them from crying out; he just readied his weapons for a fight and pressed tightly against the wall. *"Ahzraynoo!"* The cries would not stop. Amid the yells and pleadings he started to hear commotion on the other side of the door. It sounded like several men running down stairs. Amid the footfalls he heard clanging metal; the soldiers were armed and would be fuming when they got to the door.

The assassin looked around the room. They were pleading with their eyes. Please help us, they were saying. Clark felt something very different about these people. He had been around hardened criminals plenty of times and could see death and hate in the eyes of those who deserved to be in a place like this, yet these men didn't have that look. Considering himself a good judge of character, Clark wasn't sure what to do with his conflicting feelings. Evidently the Roman leaders knew how to break a man so that the look of hardened anger disappeared.

The solders were getting closer. "*Phimothaytee kristianous! Phimothaytee kristianous!*" they yelled. The soldiers were yelling for the Jesus followers to be quiet. "*Phimothaytee kristianous!*"

Were all of these men Christians, he thought? *Christians in the first century were taught to respect authority and follow the law. Didn't the Bible say something about rendering unto Caesar what was Caesar's? These men had to have committed more of a crime than just following Jesus.*

"*Phimothaytee kristianous!*"

Clark remembered his history and how the Christians were persecuted for their beliefs by many Roman emperors. Even though this highly trained assassin didn't have the same belief system, he didn't think it was right for a man to be treated like a subhuman because of faith in a false god. "*Phimothaytee kristianous!*" The soldiers were at the door. Clark wanted to free all of these men but knew he couldn't; he had a mission to accomplish.

He heard two soldiers at the door, each yelling. Clark didn't know what they were saying, but he had a guess that if these men spoke English, each of these words would be no longer than four letters. "*Phimothaytee kristianous!*"

They banged on the door and stuck their spears through the opening as a type of threat. When the noise in the dungeon didn't stop, they got their keys out and opened the lock.

Clark was pressed as tightly against the wall as possible with his knife in one hand and laser weapon in the other. After several seconds of listening to the guards removing the locking apparatus from the outside of the door, the assassin felt the large gate start to move.

Once the door was open, one soldier immediately went in and saw that the crate that held their extra chains had been moved. He bolted straight to the new opening while the second soldier walked only a few feet into the room. Clark took this opportunity to come up from behind. He put one arm around the man's head and drew his knife the opposite direction across his throat with the other. The man drew his hands up to his neck, but to no avail, for within a few seconds he was on the floor with the life pouring from him.

The soldier now ten feet in front of him heard the fall and turned to confront his partner's attacker. Without hesitation he drew his sword and was ready for battle. Clark aimed the laser weapon at the man's legs and fired. An intense burn caused the man to fall to the floor and drop his weapon. Clark could see the confusion in his eyes. He knew the soldier was asking himself how he could have been hurt by a man ten feet away without a spear or sword. The fallen soldier probably thought that the man in front of him was a god; and right now, Clark might as well have been. He had the man's fate in his hands. With a smile on his face, the assassin walked over and picked up the fallen sword and plunged it through the breastplate covering the man's chest, sinking it deeply into his heart. The soldier shook, mystified, for several seconds and then went still.

The room was quiet. All of the yelling and begging had ceased and there wasn't a sound to be heard. Clark looked out the door and it was clear. No more soldiers could be heard, but that could change in an instant.

He looked back at the men in the room. "You poor fools," he said as if lecturing them. "You sad misguided souls. If you hadn't put your faith in a man named Jesus, you wouldn't be here right now," Clark said with frustration and disappointment.

Turning and walking back to the body of the first soldier, he pulled the sword from the man's belt and threw it over to the closest prisoner. "You need to learn to make your own way in this life and stop putting your faith in others. If you want out, get yourself out."

After leaving the room, he took a moment to regain his focus. It looked as if the stairs outside the door led directly to an exit on the surface. He knew that there would be another man, possibly two waiting at the top so he moved slowly. The limestone staircase had a slight clockwise turn, so he kept his back to the right side as he moved up. The assassin had his laser weapon aimed up the stairway and bloody knife at his side.

Once he had ascended approximately 60 steps he saw the first glimpse of an exit. It was a rough iron gate added on to an existing tunnel. Only one soldier was at the entrance and appeared to be looking out on a common mall area. The assassin observed people walking by with baskets and animals. This might be a market.

He moved up the stairs as quietly as possible until he was within five feet of the gate. Carefully aiming, he hit the man in the back with a shot from the laser. The soldier began to drop but Clark ran up and grabbed him from behind, holding him in position by a strap attached to his armor. The man wasn't necessarily large, possibly five foot eight, but with the added weight of the armor, he felt like he weighed a ton. The assassin hastily moved him toward the opening of the gate by switching his weight from one hand to another through the bars.

When the soldiers ran down to check out the uproar they had left the main exterior gate unlocked. Obviously, they thought that they would be right back up.

What a lucky break, thought the assassin. He pulled the man's body inside the tunnel. Wiping his bloody knife and hand on the man's tunic, Clark took the guard's sword and threw his body as far down the stairs as possible, then hid the weapon, knife and sword in his bag.

He looked out onto the mall and heard no alarming sounds or movements. Everything seemed to be normal. People were walking by and talking normally; they obviously hadn't seen or heard the events of the last few minutes.

Clark opened the door and walked through the gate as smoothly and unassumingly as possible. Gently pushing the door back in place, he made his way from the mall looking like any other first century citizen. Taking a deep breath, he smiled and began the hunt that would accomplish his mission and make him very wealthy.

After 20 minutes of uneventful driving, the black Mercedes encountered highway obstructions, traffic and smog. Highway One had turned into Jaffa Road and was beginning to wind its way through the western part of the city of Jerusalem.

Even though Hudson had been to this metropolis several times before, he was always surprised when he saw such urban sprawl. Jerusalem was a contemporary city and had all of the modern conveniences that could be found in any western metropolitan area. There were five star hotels, office buildings, aircraft flying overhead, and billboards. It also had all of the problems of any western city, traffic being one.

What made this city unique was the abundance of sites of worship. Within a three-mile radius of the Old City, over 50 places of worship could be found. The denominations represented ranged from Greek Orthodox, Dominican and Franciscan Monasteries to Scottish temples and an abundance of mosques. Every religion that traced its roots back to Abraham wanted a piece of land in the area—and most had at least enough to put a building on.

Continuing into Jerusalem, the traffic on the six lane highway, slowed as they got closer to the Old City. An occasional accident or influx of vehicles coming onto the highway from ramps on either side of the thoroughfare made the trip twice as long. Hudson looked out the passenger window at the urban sprawl and saw steeples, spires, and minarets pointing to the heavens along with microwave, radio and cell phone towers. This city fascinated him.

Todd broke the silence as he once again pulled himself up between the seats, "Hudson, look out there, you can begin to see the Dome of the Rock." Hudson had seen it even before the professor mentioned it. "That dome wasn't initially gold colored," he continued. "When they designed it in 691 it had a lead covering and it stayed like that until 1965 when it was recovered with a gold-colored covering. In 93, because of rust, it was recovered once again, this time in real gold."

"You'd be a great tour guide," Hudson said with a laugh.

"I love this city. I've been here more than ten times for digs, seminars, and touring with students on study programs and each time I'm awed by all that's occurred here." Todd pointed out the right side of the car, "Just ten miles that way, in Bethlehem, Christ was born. He healed the lame man at the pools of Bethesda within the Old City walls. He raised Lazarus from the dead just south of here.

If you look straight ahead, at eleven o clock and about five miles," he said pointing through the front glass, "Christ sweat drops of blood and was then arrested. That's the present site of the Church of All Nations. Just a few miles ahead, Christ gave his life and rose from the dead. All of that and more happened here in this small highly fought over city. It's almost surreal."

"It's hard to believe so many peoples lives have been changed because of events that have taken place here," said Hudson looking through the front glass.

Todd's excitement was visible and his words came quickly. "That Temple Mount," he said pointing to the now clearly visible Old City, "is the most highly contested spot by the three major religions of the world. In Judaism, that area is the location of the first and second temple in Jerusalem and they believe will be the third and final temple when their Messiah comes. Therefore it's the holiest site in Judaism.

It's also the third holiest site in Islam. There are two Muslim shrines in the Old City, you can almost see them," he said pointing, "The Dome of the Rock and Al-Aqsa Mosque.

The Bible makes it clear in Psalm 122 that we're to pray for the peace of Jerusalem. Because of that, Christians all over the world keep their eyes and thoughts on this small city. It's hard to believe that over half of the world's population has an interest in that one square mile of land," he said starting to sit back in his seat.

"Gentlemen, we'll be there within the next few minutes," said Agent James, "because you need to get started, I'm going to drop you off at the Dung Gate and then you can make your way down to the First Century Street. That area tends to have a lot of tourists so pay your way through the gate and work your way down to the excavation."

Jaffa Road had turned into Hebron Road, and the Mercedes was paralleling the great walls of the Old City. On their southerly course, they passed the Jaffa Gate and the Citadel. Because the tour buses were lined up letting off their cargo of senior citizens, the trek slowed to a crawl as they tried to pass on the right.

"Do you men need anything before I let you off? Have you eaten?" said the driver.

Hudson spoke first, "I ate a little something on the plane."

"I'm fine, I'm really not hungry," said Todd rather nervously.

The thoroughfare offered several options, and the driver took the left turn onto Al-Salam Road. They were passing the Zion Gate, which marked the division between the Armenian quarter and the Jewish quarter.

Todd was sitting on the passenger side but pointing out the left window. "Just up that street are David's Tomb and the Last Supper Room. Both are crusader spots but they are interesting to visit."

"Crusader spots?" queried Hudson.

"Yes, if you ever take a tour over here, be sure to take it with someone who is educated in the area," remarked Todd with confidence. "For example, there is a church very close to here that has a big granite block outside. It's believed to be the spot where Jesus stepped up to get on the donkey he would ride into Jerusalem on Palm Sunday. A simple tour guide would tell you that as if it were fact. However, a true historian would claim that to be a crusader spot."

Hudson still looked confused.

"In 1095 Pope Urban II said some powerful words. He spoke ex-cathedra that the Muslims had taken Jerusalem and he urged many Christians to go on crusade to try to take it back. It was a terrible time in history and lasted for over 200 years. Countless thousands were killed and tortured over the premise that Christ loved them and people wonder why we don't have better relations with the Muslims today," he said rather facetiously.

Todd was teaching as if he were in class, "Many sites were invented during those centuries to ensure excitement and support from the people sponsoring the 'war of the cross' or crusades.

This is the time in history when the spear of Jesus, pieces of Jesus' cross, sections of his crown of thorns, and so on were found. Some even thought they discovered the Holy Grail.

Most of the relics were taken back to the knight's hometowns so that people could see them for a price. It was like a traveling sideshow and all that ended up happening was that the church fleeced more money from the backs of the already penniless and often indentured people."

Hudson listened with fascination.

"So, just as no one can prove that a piece of wood is from Jesus' cross, neither can they prove that he got up on a donkey on a two square-foot spot of earth. They are both crusader inventions, and there are many more sites like that around."

"That's amazing. I never knew any of that," said Hudson with astonishment.

The NSA agent was beginning to maneuver the high priced sedan to the right of the road so that he could drop the men off.

Todd continued, "Did you know that the Dung Gate gets its name because it's the spot where the city's trash was taken out?"

The car stopped to let the men out.

"Look at that architecture; it's from the Ottoman times. You can tell it from the rock work over the top of … Hudson, look on top of that wall!"

Hudson immediately ducked down so that he could see out through the driver's window. The agent looked as well.

"I've been here plenty of times and have never seen a soldier with a rocket launcher; let alone pointing it at anyone."

Hudson spotted the sniper and yelled, "Get down!" Everyone got as far as possible from the drivers side and huddled to the floor. A flash of light sparked out of the corner of Hudson's eye and the car was rocked by an explosion that could have been heard for miles.

The weapon impacted the street, just below the driver's door, but the explosion was sufficient to thrust the left side of the car into the air more than three feet. The sudden change in direction caused everyone to surge left, throwing the driver's head into the blast-resistant glass. The agent's blood splattered throughout the vehicle. Once the car reached its apex, gravity pulled everyone to the right.

The airborne side of the car started to return to the earth, and in that millisecond, Hudson looked through the driver's glass and eyed the man on the wall. All of the soldiers and tourists were heading for cover. Several senior citizens on walkers had fallen to the street and didn't have the capacity to seek refuge, but one man stood motionless. He was dressed as an Israeli military soldier and stood in place just observing the show in front of him.

Hudson desperately wanted out of the vehicle to even the score.

The car made it back to earth with such a thud that it bottomed out the shocks on the left side of the car. At that point, everyone was thrown left and Agent James once more slammed his head into the glass.

Hudson had pulled his bag close when he sensed the initial threat. He now had a nine-millimeter weapon out and ready for action. The man on the wall started to walk away when sirens began blaring. Military were running in from all areas of the Old City.

"Todd, are you alright?" Hudson yelled.

"Yeah, I'm alright. My ears are ringing, but I'll be fine."

"Agent James are you alright," Hudson said as he looked out the window at the people continuing to run all around. There was no answer. "Agent," he said as he drew his attention to the driver. A helpless feeling ran through his body. He quickly placed two fingers on the man's neck trying to feel a pulse in his carotid artery, but felt nothing.

"Todd, let's get out of here."

"How is he? The agent's not conscious. We can't leave him here like this," he said almost knowing what Hudson would say next.

"The agent's dead," Hudson said looking into the back seat. "We need to get out of here in the confusion or we are going to be interrogated by the government. Open the door and get out!" Hudson commanded.

Because the Mercedes was so well designed and heavily armored, the doors on the vehicle opened without difficulty. As the men hastily exited the car, ran around the front and started for the Dung Gate, they were able to see the damage. The machine looked like it had been through a collision with another vehicle rather than taking a hit from a military weapon. The left side was crumpled up and the tires were flat, but everything else looked fine. It was bittersweet.

Hudson knew the armor had saved their lives, but that same protection killed Agent James. If common safety glass had been there rather than bullet resistant glass, the man would have still been alive because the glass would have given way upon impact instead of acting like a plate of steel.

As they ran across the street to the entrance of the Old City, Hudson gave one more look at the top of the wall. His eyes met those of the man who had tried to kill them. He was slowly walking away and talking on a two-way radio.

Those who were working against them now knew they had made it out of the vehicle alive and were probably aware of where they were headed. The seasoned agent prayed there wasn't a contingent waiting for them at the First Century Street opening. "God please help us," he said as they ran through the gate.

Hudson's plan of escaping in the frenzy worked out well. No one was yelling after them. They just looked like everyone else trying to get away from the danger area. The police who normally guarded the Dung Gate were running toward the bombed car to help, so Todd and Hudson easily made it into the Old City and down toward the excavation area without interference.

"Todd, get us to the site. I don't think we have much time," Hudson yelled as they ran through the mass of people.

"The main gate's over here," Todd said as he ran ahead and to the right. They both jumped a turnstile and started down a long set of stairs.

The area around First Century Street was an open excavation pit. There were always digs going on, but it was primarily a tourist area. In this large expanse could be found ritual baths, a grand staircase, and the famed Double Gate where Paul and many of the disciples would have entered the Holy City. A large percentage of the site contained first century ruins; houses and businesses, and the famed street where Jesus could have walked.

Twenty-first century civilizations tear down out-of-date structures and then build upon the clean site. In biblical times, they used what they could and built over what they couldn't. Therefore, the area in which Todd and Hudson were heading was over 50 feet below street level due to the many civilizations that just built over what was already there.

Hudson scanned the scene as they continued down the long flight of stairs. He felt very uncomfortable. Looking around, he observed too many areas where snipers could hide to take them out. He also noticed that the entire upper level had a railing where anyone could overlook the ancient ruins. If his enemy was bold enough, he could just lean over the railing and start shooting.

He remembered his training and cringed. The most important thing any warrior could do was to get to the high ground-he was seeking the low. The situation couldn't be any worse.

"The excavation's right up here. We've got to make the right turn around the building and then it's at the end of the wall," Todd yelled.

"Don't turn the corner," barked Hudson, starting to lag behind because of the weight of the bag he was carrying.

"What?" replied the professor still running but trying to look back.

Once the professor cleared the end of the building and was beginning to make the turn onto the ancient street, Hudson heard a shot and Todd toppled to the ground. This is what Hudson had feared-there were men waiting for them somewhere around the opening.

Hudson noticed that the professor was starting to get up so he dropped his bag to increase his speed and ran toward his partner. Pulling him up without even slowing, they both dove for ruins that were on the other side of the street.

The First Century Street was sandwiched between a 60-foot wall and first century ruins. Most of the remains were in the form of short three-foot walls, which the men were presently hiding behind.

"Are you alright?" Hudson said looking over the professor. The large bloody area on Todd's right arm confirmed that he had taken a hit.

"I've been shot … but I'll survive," he said. The pain etched in the lines of his eyes told the truth.

Hudson looked over the arm and knew that he would have to dig the bullet out, but there was no time now. He took his belt off and cinched it tight around the man's arm. "This will stop the bleeding; open it up every five minutes or so to ensure that your arm gets enough circulation." Todd didn't look too excited about the idea.

The agent had to find out where the attacker was, so he walked into the ruins a few more feet and looked over the area through any opening he could find. He could only see one gunman, but he was guarding the spot in which they needed to enter.

Why is this place so quiet? There are no tourists or students excavating, he thought.

The seasoned agent knew that there would be more men coming, so he needed to act quickly.

He crawled over to Todd who was doing well under the circumstances. "We need to work our way through these ruins and get closer to the underground opening. Can you crawl?"

"I don't have much of a choice, do I?"

They started to work their way through the ruins; Hudson making quick time with Todd dragging behind. He had the wounded arm tucked up underneath him, wincing with every movement while trying to crawl with the other arm. Hudson was proud of the man and wished they would make it out of this adventure alive so that he could get to know him better.

Every few feet Hudson would look out at the gunmen through an opening he encountered in the ruins, and each time he saw the man in the same place with his pistol ready, scanning the excavation area for movement.

Why hadn't he tried to come after them? He knew that both men were in the ruins and that one was wounded. *We should be easy targets,* he thought, yet the man stayed in the same place. This confirmed in Hudson's mind that he was waiting for backup and had to protect the opening.

Hudson waited for a few seconds until Todd caught up. "You going to make it?"

"I'll make it," he grunted as he stopped and sat against a rock wall. "What are we going to do? You don't have the bag, so we don't have any weapons."

"You're only half right; I left the bag, but have a pistol still under my shirt." He pulled it out. "We need to get closer to the opening. If we can move a few walls closer, I'll be in position to take a shot."

"I know a short cut, follow me." Todd started to move ahead of Hudson through several restored buildings. It was obvious that he had been here many times before.

Hudson got worried. Blood was seeping from Todd's wound, covering his sleeve and hand in dark red. The professor wasn't wincing as much when he moved, but that wasn't necessarily a good thing. He was running on adrenaline, and eventually his body would catch up; this pace could only be kept up for a short time more.

Todd came to a stop and sat again. He was breathing heavily for a man in such athletic shape. The loss of blood was taking its toll. What Hudson was going to do next wasn't going to help it.

"We need to loosen the tourniquet," said Hudson. Opening the belt, the professor grunted in pain and the arm regained color once again. In that few seconds, more blood oozed out of the wound. The flow had slowed, but was still steady. He needed to keep the arm restricted for a while until he could figure out what to do with the bullet lodged inside.

Grunting, Todd spoke, "This is as close as we can get without being out in the open. We should be at his right side. He won't be expecting us this close."

"You wait here," he said as he found a few golf ball sized rocks on the ground.

Hudson threw both stones very quickly in succession. One was tossed right at the man with the gun where the other was thrown about ten feet in front of him. The gunmen immediately shot in the direction from which he thought the rocks were thrown. He didn't know exactly where they originated but was aiming within 15 feet of the men's present position.

Rolling out onto what appeared to be an old street between ancient houses, Hudson aimed and shot once. He missed and scrambled behind a wall. At this point, the gunmen knew his exact location and dumped several rounds into the wall protecting him. Hudson crawled about ten feet to his right, peeked around the corner and took another shot, again missing. This time he moved as far left as possible hoping that the assassin was expecting him to move the other direction. When he had an opening, he looked out and took a shot, this time hitting the man in the stomach. The guard went down dropping his gun and clutching at the bullet wound in his abdomen.

Hurrying, Hudson ran back to where Todd was resting. Pulling him up gently, they ran for the opening. "Todd, get in the entrance, I need to go back and get the bag."

Hudson began to run down the First Century Street toward the spot where he had dropped the bag, leaving Todd on his own. He suddenly saw Arab-looking men dressed in plain clothes. They looked like the man he shot who was presently lying on the street, and they were pulling guns from their jackets and preparing to fire. He reversed direction toward the professor, and with his gun aimed behind him, fired off four shots. This stopped the men in the tracks and forced them around the corner of the building. "We have company, get in the entrance!"

The men were discharging shots at random around the corner, and Hudson let out a couple more shots at the edge of the ancient facade. The gun stopped firing and began to click. He was out of rounds, and everyone knew it.

The agent was within a few feet of the man he had shot just seconds earlier; dropping his gun, Hudson picked up the one lying on the ground. There was movement coming from the man so he knew that he hadn't killed him. Continuing to run, he turned back once more to empty the remaining rounds at his attackers still stationed at the edge of the wall.

He dropped the gun and dove into the underground entrance. Todd was waiting inside the excavation area but couldn't move because of the sight in front of him. The seminary professor was standing in front of a pile of seven people who were heaped on top of each other just ten feet inside the entrance. Some were bound and gagged, while others were not. The youngest in the pile couldn't be more than 20. Each one was shot in the head.

The mangled heap of human debris sickened the professional agent. His heart was breaking as he looked at the vacant eyes staring back at him. Todd was beginning to throw up off to the side. His eyes began to tear up, and the sadness on his face couldn't be described.

"Why? How could anyone do this?" sobbed the professor.

"They had to make sure that we didn't get in here, so they killed everyone entering this area," Hudson replied with agony and anger.

Two shots soared through the hole like lighting bolts and bounced off the wall next to them. Both men jumped and got refocused.

"Which way to the cavern?" yelled Hudson.

"It's through a hole over there," he said pointing and starting in that direction. "We'll need to do some crawling."

"Let's go, we only have a few seconds before they're here."

Todd got down as quickly as he could with a bleeding arm and started to push his body through the small opening on the ground. Hudson followed behind. It was taking longer than expected for the professor to work his way into the tunnel because of the use of only one arm. The pressure put on the other arm made the pain almost unbearable. Hudson entered the hole as soon as he could and pulled his feet up hoping that the men entering the opening wouldn't locate him.

The agent knew that if the men were aware of the location of the sphere, they wouldn't be expending so many resources to stop him from getting to it. Their group would just commandeer it or move it to another location. No, they needed to keep everyone out of the area so they would have time to search for it.

The travelers heard men speaking Arabic behind them. Their attackers were very close but didn't know in which direction they fled. Once inside the initial entrance, the excavation site had many openings and tunnels from which to choose and they weren't sure where to start. Hudson couldn't speak Arabic but the common sounds of frustration and confusion were universal.

Todd led them quietly through the tunnel taking the first left available. They didn't have flashlights and the area was totally black, but Todd seemed to know where he was, so they continued on. After making the turn, the professor bumped his wounded arm on a fallen stone and caught his breath in a loud hiss.

The two Arabic men stopped their grumbling and became totally silent. Todd was doing his best to control the pain but let out another small gasp. The men zeroed in on their tunnel and shot a few rounds down the opening hoping to hit one of its occupants. The sound from the gunshots was deafening but their attempt to cause damage was futile.

They moved through the tunnel as quickly as possible. Hudson pushing the professor's feet to help him along more quickly. Todd giving it his all but occasionally let out a grunt or groan. They made a few more turns then saw a faint light coming from behind them. The attackers had grabbed a flashlight from one of the dead student researchers and were following them closely. Soon they would overtake the agent and professor.

"How much farther?" whispered Hudson studying Todd's swaying form.

"I'm working from memory. Getting very weak. Light headed. I may be taking us to the nearest McDonalds," he breathlessly said with a strained chuckle. "If I'm right, it should be up here just a bit farther."

They made several more turns and occasionally felt as if they were doubling back. At one point, they had to stand up and climb into another set of tunnels. Hudson helped Todd as gingerly as he could, but the wounded man was getting slower each minute and his breathing was becoming labored.

It was obvious that the attackers had made some wrong turns because they hadn't caught up yet, but the sounds echoing through the tunnels indicated that they were still on the trail.

"The cavern should be at the next turn," said Todd out of breath.

As he was speaking, they saw a faint glow ahead. Hudson knew they had found the sphere. After pushing the last few yards, they came to the end of the tunnel. It was sitting about four feet above the ground of the cavern they were entering. Todd pulled himself through the edge of the tunnel and fell the four feet to the limestone floor, not having enough energy to marvel at the time machine in front of him.

Hudson followed behind, but was able to use both arms to get himself down. He immediately looked over his partner. Todd was lying on his back with his eyes closed. Hudson once again released the tourniquet and the arm regained color. The hole had stopped bleeding, so he left the restriction off.

Running over to the sphere, Hudson found it glowing with several lights on. The radiance was a physical affect of the sphere being in a state of flux. Dr. Keith said that the bluish tint might occur if the vehicle traveled out of its correct time. The forward lights were on. Because the sphere was powered by nuclear energy, they could literally run the lights for thousands of years and not diminish its capabilities or power supply.

Hudson placed his hand over a square located on the passenger side of the sphere. Once the vehicle recognized his bio-data, the canopy raised. Looking at the dash, he noticed blood covering the gauges.

Evidently, the assassin had some type of accident in the vehicle, not that he was worried about that now. The agent scraped the dried blood away well enough to view the time frame listed on the display. The numbers proved that the vehicle's last trip ended in the first century.

He needed to take it back to that time, so he reentered the same year into the display. Because the sphere was dependent upon the earth's axis, a specific date could not be entered. He could choose a year but the sphere could not be moved from the month and day. It was connected to where the earth presently sat in its trajectory around the sun. The best option available to the agent was to get the sphere back in time one day behind the killer's arrival, unless he wanted to wait 364 days before he leaped.

The trained pilot wished that there were more flexibility in selecting time periods, and that it was possible to just return the vehicle two days before all of this happened and make it right before it occurred, but that wasn't possible. Hudson prayed that he could pick up the assassin's trail quickly enough to stop him.

"Well, I did my part and got you here ... now get back and stop that crazed man before he destroys the world. I'll be fine. I still have a few tricks up my sleeve," Todd breathlessly whispered.

Looking at the man lying on the floor, Hudson knew their attackers would be coming through the opening within the next few moments. They would beat and torture Todd for information before they ultimately killed him.

Hudson smiled wearily. He trusted and respected the man who had done everything possible to secure the success of the mission. He'd never leave him here to die at their hands.

The highly trained agent must, for the first time in his career, go against the orders of leaving the professor. Todd might slow his pace on the other side and even get him caught, but he knew God was telling him to take Todd along. The Lord was telling him that he still needed the wounded man and Todd certainly needed him.

He ran back over to his sluggish partner on the floor, "Let's go."

"What do you mean? I'm staying here," he said with a cough.

Pulling him up to sitting position, "Nope, you're going with me. I can't leave you here to die, so my only choice is to take you."

"You can't do that. I'll just slow you down."

Hudson was pulling him to his feet, "Yep, you're slowing me down now. Give me some help," the agent said jokingly. "We don't have much time and I'd rather not have to drag you."

Todd was on his feet with an arm around Hudson's neck. The two men were making their way to the vehicle. "I better get some combat pay for this," said Todd weakly.

Hudson replied back with a smirk, "You have to get shot twice before you get combat pay."

They were a few feet from the sphere. "Well, then you can keep your money," he painfully laughed.

Todd was starting to climb in the vehicle when both men heard noises coming from the tunnel they left moments earlier. Their attackers had found them and were approaching quickly.

"Hurry! Move over to the drivers side," barked Hudson.

Todd did his best, and Hudson began to climb into the sphere while pushing the professor with all of his might.

The attackers saw the two future time-travelers and started yelling and pointing their weapons while dropping to the cavern floor. Hudson had to stall or they wouldn't have a chance.

"Todd, close your eyes and ears. Close them tight!" At that, Hudson pushed several buttons on the console placing his hands over his ears and burying his head in the seat behind him. The men were yelling, obviously telling them not to touch anything on the console.

Within two seconds, the sphere emitted a low quick burst of sound that vibrated the limestone walls around them. There was a good chance that the entire Old City heard the rumble beneath their feet. Simultaneously with the sound came a light. This beam was so bright that even Todd and Hudson, who had prepared for it by closing their eyes and sheltering their faces, had their pupils close so fiercely that when they finally opened their eyes, they couldn't see for several seconds.

Once his senses returned to normal, Hudson saw and heard the attackers writhing in agony on the floor. They looked as if they were blind and were still holding their ears. There was a good chance that their eardrums had burst. They would never see or hear again and most likely would never make it out of the cavern.

"What was that," Todd said almost yelling because his ears were ringing.

"I put the sphere through a quick test cycle. The entire vehicle is powered up but because it doesn't leap through time, the energy is displaced to the atmosphere."

Getting out of the sphere and walking over to the men, Hudson grabbed their weapons and flashlights. They kept their hands over their ears, and tried to stop the blood that was now pouring from their auditory canals, therefore they gave him no fight as he rifled through their pockets and wallets.

What an awful way to die: deaf, blind and with no hope or comfort.

The agent said a quick prayer for the men asking for God's mercy on their souls. Todd watched the scene and prayed with him.

Looking through one man's wallet, he found nothing as he started back toward the sphere. However, as he looked through the next man's personal affects, he found a piece of paper. After looking it over, he wadded it up, and put it in his pocket.

Hudson stowed the weapons and flashlights in an area under the seat and stepped back into the sphere, belting himself in.

"What did you find?" asked Todd.

"A telephone number with a D.C. area code. One I have dialed before," he said sadly. "Buckle up, we've a long way to go."

Todd curiously looked over at him for a second. Hudson was shaken by the newly found information, but seemed more determined than ever. The wounded passenger went back to buckling himself up.

Hudson pushed the button and the canopy began to lower. It mated with the lower half and gave off a hissing of pressure. Turning on the dome lighting and looking over at the professor, the agent said, "Are you ready?"

Looking his partner in the eyes, he reaffirmed, "Let's do this!"

Both men turned their heads forward and pressed them tightly against the seats. Pushing the activation button and following a ten second count down, the sphere was gone.

21 — TUESDAY AFTERNOON, APRIL 14

Clark made his way through the bustling market being pushed and cajoled by merchants selling everything from fabric to doves. The assassin had been in Israel several times on assignment, however, the ancient metropolis looked very much different than when he last visited, or rather, *would* visit over 2000 years from now.

The first thing that struck him was the unfinished Temple Mount. All around the future holy site there were people working, building walls and firming up the ground, but it was by no means anywhere near completion. Clark knew that in the year he was presently stationed, Herod the Great would have been excavating the site for at least 20 years; he'd expect more of it to be finished by now. A section of the high wall surrounding the future Temple Mount was in place, but other areas had yet to be started. Piles of rubble were littered about and large earthen ramps were built at strategic locations to help the workers maneuver large limestone blocks to the elevated level.

Clark continued his trek through the corridors of the busy town. The Old City was 2000 years newer than he had last seen it, and it showed. As he looked around, he found the area better kept than the city he remembered. The walls were smoother and the blocks in the street less worn and more tightly seamed. The walls weren't strewn with souvenir peddlers trying to pawn off olive wood crucifixes, Jerusalem shot glasses, T-shirts talking about a relative who visited and only gave a stupid shirt, or plastic replicas of the Old City.

Looking to the sky, he noticed that the air was cleaner, and the ambient noise from a million people driving their cars through greater Jerusalem was absent as well. It was quiet. Except for the conversations going on in the street and the occasional bleating of a goat or braying of a donkey there was no city noise–there was plenty of smell, but no noise.

The assassin noticed he was getting stares and not a few head turns; he didn't look like the people he was passing in the narrow street. They gave him glances and side looks as they walked by. He was light skinned. They were dark. He had blue eyes when they had dark brown, almost black eyes.

His facial features also separated him from the people walking in the streets. He looked almost Roman with high cheekbones and narrow pointed nose but was dressed in a tunic and mantle, as a Jewish man would be.

Something Clark never thought of in preparation for the trip was his size. The assassin was six-foot-four and weighed 230 pounds, whereas the men in the streets were an average of five-foot-three and only around 140 pounds. Even the few Roman soldiers he passed were not that large, possibly five-foot-nine at best. Clark quickly started walking more bent over, lowering his overall height and doing what he could to lower his head covering so as to hide more of his facial features.

As he continued his trek through the rock paved streets, he began to pick up on what the crowds were muttering. Everyone was abuzz about something that had recently happened. They weren't speaking just about the weather or their crops but were truly excited about an event that had taken place. This excitement was visible in every transaction occurring and every greeting taking place.

Clark tried to listen, but couldn't understand everything that was being said. He had taken several months of submersion training in Hebrew, but could only make out a few words. He would need to keep his mouth shut to not appear out of place; not that he wasn't already.

The large man continued walking until he came to a busy crossroad. Looking left, he saw no exit, but when he panned right there was a large double gate about four blocks away, so he immediately started in that direction.

Clark needed to leave the city and get his bearings. The time travel had left him unfocused; something he couldn't be in his line of work. He also needed to find food and a place to rest in order to start fresh on the trail in the morning.

From the sun setting behind him, Clark knew the route he was following to be easterly in direction. This path took him nearer the construction area that would be the future home of the Dome of the Rock and Al-Aqsa Mosque.

The corridor that might help him melt into the crowds was much wider and appeared to be a major thoroughfare through the Old City. There were more merchants selling and possible customers bartering than he'd seen on the side streets thus far.

As he made his way up the slight incline that would take him through the double gate, he noticed something odd about this street. Over the many blocks he had walked through the ancient site, Clark hadn't seen a tidy street. Each was littered with broken pottery, muddy areas, wastewater and dung from the many animals that were dragged through the roads. *Someone needs to invent a garbage can for these people*, he thought in disgust.

While the assassin continued his bent-over walk and kept his head low, the change in this particular street was apparent. This specific area had greenery scattered over the piled up refuse: palm leaves. As far as he could see and even through the gate ahead of him, palm leaves were covering the rocky streets and were piled up in the corners. Many of the leaves that looked to have been picked no more than several days earlier were now fading, broken and soiled from being trampled and sitting in wastewater.

Stopping for several seconds to ponder the relevance to his mission, he suddenly heard shouts, and gave a quick glance behind to see a Roman soldier yelling and running toward him. The assassin picked up his pace and stuck his hand in his bag to locate the long knife he had placed there an hour earlier.

The soldier was pointed with his voice and running at a full clip. The people around Clark were moving to the walls and away from the area as quickly as possible. The assassin continued his forward progression and was very much alone in the middle of the lane. He had the knife out of its sheath and tightly palmed when he heard the soldier yell once again, now just feet away.

Starting to turn and confront his attacker, the young Roman soldier brushed by, shoving Clark to one side. He was apprehending an older Jewish man who had a loaf of bread poorly hidden beneath his tunic.

"*Lowacalty, lowacalty,*" the assassin heard the old man say. Clark understood the Hebrew phrase mainly through context. The thin, frail man was saying that he hadn't eaten.

"*Lee lechem leh acall,*" Give me bread to eat, the old man cried.

Clark's heart was racing as he stuffed the highly honed knife back in its scabbard. He gave the aged man another look as the soldier had him subserviently pressed to the ground beneath him.

How could that old man do anything to earn bread? He could barely walk, let alone tend for himself. Where is his family? Why isn't anyone taking care of him, he thought to himself?

Clark moved down the lane, his last look at the scene was of the soldier dragging the old man, now sobbing, away from the area. He was most likely taking him to a dungeon like the assassin had been in just an hour before.

The old man will be dead inside a week, he shook his head soberly and continued forward toward the gate.

Within a block of the opening, it finally came to his mind where he had seen the opening before. This double gate was the walled up Golden or Beautiful Gate on the east wall of the Old City. In Clark's time it had been sealed up for over 13 centuries, now he walked through it unhindered.

The opening was a good thirty feet high and just as wide. The assassin walked under the arched ceiling, gaining an appreciation for the true magnitude of the fortification. The Old City was designed with walls over ten feet thick.

The Golden Gate was the primary entrance and exit on the east side of the city and allowed those going to Jericho, Bethany and Gethsemane the most direct access. Once Clark was through the large opening, he walked off to the side and took in the panoramic view before him.

Due east, was the Kidron Valley and beyond that, up the hill, was Gethsemane. As he looked off onto the horizon he could see the Dead Sea about eight miles ahead. Panning northeast he could make out the area where Jericho was located, and finally, due south about three miles, he saw Herod's palace, the Herodium.

Clark liked Herod the Great. It wasn't just that he liked him; he respected him. Herod was a man's man. If someone said it couldn't be done, Herod went about making it happen.

Clark looked south and smiled. *I wish I had time to pay Herod a visit, we would probably get along well*, he mused.

The assassin looked back over his shoulder through the Golden Gate and observed the final remnants of the sun as it went below the western walls. Around him, the temperature was dropping and his stomach was growling. These sensations brought him back to his new reality; he needed a place to stay and some food to eat.

Most likely, he would be commandeering these necessities, so he couldn't stay in the Old City. The Temple area had a large number of Roman soldiers posted within its walls. Gethsemane was the nearest town and was less than a mile east of his present location; he would stay there for the night.

Clark made his way east through the Kidron Valley and back up the other side to the small town of Gethsemane. Once he was completely out of the valley and up the hill, he turned back and looked at the Old City. The sun had set, and all that was left on the horizon was a bit of orange glow reflecting off of the tall limestone walls. Looking at the small town, he saw torches lighted in the streets and people leaving through each of the gates. What was a bustling town a few hours earlier had become virtually unoccupied. The assassin spotted a few highly decorated men ambling through the ancient streets and believed them to be priests or religious leaders, otherwise, the town was closed for the night.

Clark turned back toward the tiny town of Gethsemane. Actually, small was an understatement. A first century town in Israel was usually comprised of 10 to 15 homes arranged around a centrally shared courtyard. The neighbors used the courtyard to fellowship and share chores, making each town a quiet and tightly knit group. They didn't contain malls, convenience stores, recreation facilities or fast food restaurants–for that matter, not even a real market. If they didn't work together each day, there wouldn't be food at night.

While walking past the first of the houses in the square, he took in its design. It looked to be a small two-room rock structure. The owners must have found the building materials in the valley below because the rocks appeared to be identical to the ones he had just passed. The roof was flat and was supported by large beams that stretched the length of the building and protruded through both the front and back. On top was a light covering of thatch. Clark looked around the town square and saw several people sleeping out on their roofs to get away from the heat locked up within their houses.

There weren't many entrances into these buildings. Each had a front door about four feet high and two feet wide, which consisted of simple planks nailed together. He assumed that there was an identical back door leading into the communal courtyard. There were a few windows, but he would have trouble fitting his large frame through them. Each dwelling had a chimney, and all were still smoking from the dinners that were made just an hour ago. Clark could smell some kind of boiled fish coming from one of the buildings reminding him of his need for food.

The assassin kept walking. He came upon a large garden, more like an olive grove, and pulled a few of the ripe fruits from the trees. After eating several, he decided that olives were great in a pimento loaf or martini but didn't count as sustenance. He continued on.

After Clark had circumnavigated the entire village, he determined that his best possibility was to try to enter a house where the owners were on the roof asleep. He could get some food and leave before they discovered there was an uninvited guest.

He located a dwelling on the northeast corner of the square, where a man, woman and young boy appeared to be sleeping on the roof. Peering through the side window he couldn't see any lights on within the dwelling, and assuming there weren't any more family members moving about below, he approached the front door. A wooden beam across the inside of the opening blocked the door from being moved, but because there was a gap between two of the front slats, he was able to pick up a stick and quickly slip it through and raise the small makeshift lock. The door opened easily.

Once inside, he quietly closed the door and moved farther into the dwelling, bumping his head on a beam as he went. Clark let out a slew of curse words under his breath. He would have to walk hunched over due to the height of the ceiling being only about six feet.

To his left was a chimney which contained a large pot hanging from a hook. Off to his right, he saw another room that appeared to be some sort of stable. He heard a few chickens and a donkey moving about.

Did these people keep their animals inside at night, he thought? *No wonder it stinks so badly.*

The entire building stood on a dirt floor that was neatly kept, but dirt nonetheless. Toward the back of the room was a ladder shooting up through a hole in the roof. The assassin would have to stay clear of that area to ensure that the family didn't come down and discover him.

Clark noticed that the chimney didn't ventilate well causing the room to be extremely warm and smoky. *Maybe the smoke keeps the fleas to a minimum in this barn they call a home.* Except for a broom, some clay pots, rudimentary farming utensils hanging on one wall, a small wooden table and various pieces of cloth, the room was very empty. *Good thing I'm not a thief, because there isn't anything to steal*, he thought.

The assassin went back over to the pot hanging under the chimney and surveyed its contents. After dipping his fingers in the remnants, he believed the pot contained a type of chicken stew, with onions, garlic, and almost too much salt. Clark wasn't accustomed to that much salt on a meal but was so hungry he didn't care.

The ravenous man ate everything from the pot and then went looking for more. He discovered a small lump of cheese protected in a cloth just a few feet away on a shelf. It must have been a type of goat cheese, not that he cared because he almost swallowed the piece whole. Also on that same shelf were a few oranges, more olives, some dates and a small bowl full of raw vegetables.

Clark ate everything and was beginning to feel a bit better when he saw a wineskin hanging across the room. From the visible bulge on its side, it appeared to be full, so he started toward it when his leg bumped the table on the way.

He couldn't believe that he had made such a novice mistake. The sound wasn't loud but it was out of the ordinary, and caused a rustling on the roof. Someone was awakened and moving toward the opening. Clark had slipped-up and knew that he could make it out the front door, but was concerned that the inhabitants would see him and form a posse' to hunt him down. The backdoor was even worse than the front because it opened onto the communal courtyard. There would be no way out of that situation. The trained professional would have to deal with this state of affairs head-on.

Running through the opening that led into the stable, he backed up against the wall adjacent to the door. Clark pulled the knife from its sheath and held it against his chest. As he looked around the corner, he saw a man coming down the ladder. The owner of the house looked to be in his 20's, about five foot six and one hundred and forty pounds.

The assassin watched as the man walked toward the table. He picked up the cloth that held the cheese, and also noticed the empty shelf that once contained their food. He headed straight for the stable area, assuming that the animals had gotten into their rations.

Clark quickly moved forward along the wall toward the other stable opening. The minute the young man entered the doorway, Clark thrust the long knife up under his ribs and into his heart. The Jewish man stared wide-eyed at his attacker and only made a small guttural sound before he dropped to the floor.

The assassin could not focus on the ladder while he moved along the stable's inner wall. During that short period, the wife must have come down, because she was standing just three feet from the doorway, staring at the man killing her husband. There was sheer terror in her eyes and her hands were shaking while they covered her gaping mouth. She started to scream and run back toward the ladder.

"*Hilacoo, Yacov, hilacoo.*" She was telling her son Jacob to run.

Clark quickly covered the ground between them and thrust the already bloody knife between her shoulder blades as she started up the ladder. Falling to the floor, she caused dirt to billow through the air around them. The assassin looked up through the opening and saw a boy around nine looking down at his lifeless mother's body on the floor.

In that short moment, Clark thought of his mother. He remembered the night she was taken from him, and felt the loss and sadness again as if they were fresh emotions. The anger boiled anew for the man who had taken her from him.

The assassin knew exactly how the young boy felt. He couldn't speak the language, was separated from the boy by 2000 years and a continent, but was aware of everything that he was thinking and going through as he looked down through the roof's opening. Clark knew it would be better to just take the boy's life and end the years of grief ahead, but could hear movement coming from houses on either side and had to leave.

Looking up at the boy one more time, he placed the knife back in the bag and left through the front door out into the cold night, running as fast as he could toward the north. When he was approximately 100 yards from the house, he started to hear screaming and wailing behind him; others had discovered his most recent work.

Maybe, if he kept his fingers crossed, he could finish this mission tomorrow and get back to his own place and time. Clark kept running.

The travelers went through a much smoother ride than the man who went before them. Because the sphere was taking its riders back to a point in history and not trans-locating, the transition was fairly uneventful. During the short hop, they were able to see their pained attackers disappear and were also able to view changes within the large room as they occurred.

Todd kept his eyes on passage that allowed them into the room and watched as a large block fell in front of the hole. In the future they were able to remove that block and allow for easy access; however that wouldn't happen for more than 2000 years and the professor wasn't sure if it would still be a viable exit.

After a preprogrammed amount of time, the canopy on the steaming vehicle opened. By way of proximity lighting, the men were able to see the room, only now they were viewing how it looked 2000 years earlier; there were a few new obstacles.

"Are you alright? How do you feel?" asked Hudson to his weary passenger.

"Are we there? Did we make it into the past?"

Hudson pointed to the console, "The console tells me that we are back in the first century. The only way to be certain is to go up top and see what the world looks like. How do you feel?"

"Weak." He looked at his arm, "My arm isn't bleeding much, but it hurts. My hand is beginning to go numb."

Hudson knew Todd was putting up a good front and that his arm had to hurt. He also knew that the professor was almost certainly afraid because of the lack of hospitals in first century Jerusalem. The agent had gone through plenty of first aid classes and was shown techniques on sealing wounds, but never thought he would have to use the knowledge. The information he had learned and forgotten needed to come back to him within the next few hours.

Getting out of the vehicle, Hudson retrieved the flashlights and weapons, and looked around. "You up to finding a way out of here? It looks like our entrance won't be our exit."

"I noticed that," he said with a wince as he worked his way out of the sphere. "Is there any gap behind that block? Can we move it?"

Walking over to the blocked opening, he saw a slight crack behind it, but not enough to get a man through. "This block weighs several tons and there's no way around it." He then walked over to an opening behind several blocks and saw a small hole at his feet and one about nine feet up. "Todd, what about this? Will either of these get us out?"

Todd walked over and examined the openings. "This lower space will tie up to underground caverns. Not a way out. The upper space might meet up with the channel we took to get in here. It seems to be heading toward the blocked opening and might be our way out. It's worth a try. Give me a flashlight and push me up."

Hudson did as he was told and cupped his hands. Todd put a foot in the human stirrup and was pushed into the hole. The professor let out a loud cry when he had to pull his way into the aperture. Any movement from his bad arm offered excruciating pain.

Todd stopped for a second to regain his strength. With his feet still dangling from the opening, Hudson got nervous.

"Are you alright?" the agent asked.

"Yeah, I'll be fine. Remind me why I came with you-this is a lot less fun than I thought it would be," he said with a low chuckle.

"People can't say no to my magnetic personality."

"You can guarantee that next time I'll say no," he shot back as the tunnel echoed around him. "I think this opening will lead us to the tunnel that got us here. Give me a second."

The professor was gone about five minutes when he came back to the opening facing the other direction. "This'll lead us out. This hole is just a fissure in the wall. It is most likely a design flaw that opened during an earthquake at some point in history. You ready to leave?"

"I have everything that we were able to bring."

Todd gave a concerned look as he peered down through the opening, "Hudson, we don't have anything."

"What do you mean?"

"What are we going to do once we get topside. We don't look like them. I should be able to converse with them on a basic level, but we don't have any period clothing or money. We don't have anything to barter with, and I'm nothing but a millstone around your neck. I'll slow you down." He thought for a second and spoke much slower, "I'm just about spent and don't have any reserves left. I'm getting weaker by the minute."

The agent looked up and spoke deliberately, "We're going to have to rely on God to provide."

"You can say that, Hudson, but this is not the world that we came from. These people will see us as the enemy." The professor was frustrated with his partner's simplistic answer.

"If God can supply a coin through the mouth of a fish for his disciples to pay their taxes, or use a few fish and some bread to feed thousands. If he can allow a disciple to walk on water or heal people. If God can bring someone back from the dead, I know that he can get us through this. If God wants us to stop this madman, then he will give us the resources to do it. This isn't too big for him!"

The professor looked saddened, "Hudson, I've been in God's work all my life and as I look back on it, I've never really had to rely on him. In my classes, I teach the great truths of God to students every day. I tell them of the miracles our Lord did and how God was there for those who cried out to him. I've preached many times on God's provision and have been with people in the hospital and on their deathbed. In each situation I told them how God would get them through, but I've never needed God's miraculous work in my own life.

I've never been sick. No one in my family has ever died or had troubles. We were always middle class and made good money. I worked hard and put myself through college, seminary, grad and post grad school. If I needed something, I took care of it. If there was a goal in my life, I met it through hard work."

A realization hit the professor like a punch in the stomach, "I've never needed God and because of that I've never had to trust him for anything. I've never asked him to show himself in a mighty way because I provided everything I needed. I'm a hypocrite."

Hudson watched as the educated seminary professor was broken before God. He thought it was very interesting that God would use a tunnel 50 feet below the Old City 2000 years in the past to shake the man up.

"Hudson, I'm scared. I don't think I know how to trust God. I don't know if my faith is strong enough."

Hudson looked at his partner who just a day earlier was strong, confident and in charge of his destiny, and now was no more than a child uncertain of his next steps. The agent was by no means a theologian but had been in enough situations to learn that God would provide for his children in the big and small things; the only requirement being an unshakeable amount of faith.

"Todd, God may have chosen you to go through this to make you a stronger disciple for him. You know Proverbs 3:5-6, 'Trust in the Lord with all your heart and don't depend on your own understanding. Seek his will in everything and he'll guide your path.'"

"I've translated it from at least three different languages, but I've never had to use it."

"Well, now's the time," Hudson said as he looked up at his friend. "If there's ever been a point in your life to trust God, this is it.

Let's pray." Both men closed their eyes in the large, dark underground space, aglow with only the aura of the sphere.

Hudson spoke reverently, "Dear Lord, we love and thank you for providing so well and getting us to this point. Lord, you've heard our concerns and know our hearts. We want to do your will but are weak. Lord, strengthen and give us a faith for your work that's unshakeable. Allow us to rely on you, and through the process, make us better followers and powerful missionaries for the cause of Christ.

Lord, you know that we aren't prepared for what we're going to go through. We've lost our equipment and Todd's been shot. Please provide for us miraculously and do as your word says; direct our paths. We love you, Lord. Amen."

Todd looked down at the agent with a smile, "You ready to go?"

"Let's get out of here, we've work to do."

"Grab my arm." The professor dropped down his good arm. "I can't really pull you up because of my bad arm but you can climb up my arm until you reach the edge of the opening."

"That'd give you too much pain. Let me look for another way."

"Hudson, it's the only way. We don't have any rope and you can't move any of those blocks around you. Just grab on."

The agent pulled himself up as quickly as possible but the pain was almost blinding for the professor. To stop from slipping through the hole due to the weight of the 210-pound man, Todd had to hold himself steady with his injured arm. He was able to get the agent up and pull back into the hole enough to allow him in, but then had to sit for several minutes to get a reprieve from the pain.

Hudson shined the flashlight and noticed that the professor's wound was bleeding again. The blood ran down his arm and was dripping onto the limestone floor. "Can you make it?"

"Just give me another minute."

Hudson sat for a second and said another prayer. Todd couldn't lose much more blood without passing out or going into shock. They had to get to a place where they could remove the bullet and allow him to rest for a day. "God please provide," he whispered.

"I'm ready now. Hudson, can you take my flashlight? I can't hold it and pull myself with only one arm. Just keep it shining forward and I'll do my best to find a way out," he said looking tired.

Hudson took the flashlight and followed the professor as they slowly made their way through the labyrinth. The two men moved much slower than when they had entered the tunnels. At many points within the trek Todd had to stop and get a breath, or just rest his arm. On several occasions, the professor turned the wrong direction causing the men to have to back out of their present tunnel; often more than 25 feet. However, he always found his way back to the main channel.

After an hour of crawling on their hands and knees and more than ten rest stops, the professor came to what appeared to be the end. He stopped, looked over the area and backed up. "I think we've made it," he said as he rolled onto his side and looked back at Hudson.

"We're in a storm drain channel. The rain that falls is collected and sent to several drain sites, of which this is one. It then goes into the underground cisterns. From the state of this entrance, it doesn't seem to have been used in many years, possibly centuries.

It's likely that when the businesses and homes were added to this area, the channel caused periodic flooding, so they rerouted the water and closed off the hole. I can see spots of light through the rocks so they aren't piled that deep, but I'm not sure what you want to do." He said all this breathlessly and was almost mumbling toward the end.

"You know where we are with reference to the Old City and how they worked and lived. What do you think we're going to encounter on the other side of the rocks?" Hudson asked in a pointed whisper.

"On the other side of those rocks is the First Century Street. As we get out, a very large and straight wall will be on our left. On our right side we should find many houses and some businesses. Do you think the day and time are the same?" he whispered with his eyes shut.

"Yes, if everything went right, it should be Tuesday, April 14th," he looked down at his watch, "around nine in the evening."

Todd continued, "These people put in twelve to fourteen hour days. Many are farmers and will be preparing for the harvest. Some are merchants, and the rest work on the many government projects Herod has mandated. At the very beginning of the first century, Herod would be working on the Temple Mount area, his palace the Herodium, or laying miles of road for his armies to walk on.

I can't think of any significant religious festivals going. Sabbath is toward the end of the week and there shouldn't be any activity at the temple. It should be pretty well closed down for business." He thought for a second, "Everyone should be asleep or close to it."

"What about the Romans. What would they be up to?" he continued.

Todd was almost unconscious. The blood had run down his arm and was soaking his shirt and pants. Hudson tied another tourniquet, hoping to save as much of the life-saving liquid as possible.

Hudson shook Todd, "What about the Romans?"

"Yeah ... Um... Ok," he mumbled. "This is a Jewish area and they left the Jews to themselves." He muttered on, "The Romans believed in syncretism, where all governing bodies could work together under one central governmental umbrella. They left the Jews to their governing body, the Sanhedrin, and except for death penalty cases, would stay out of the way. We shouldn't see any Roman soldiers, but might run into some Jewish Priests or Temple guards under the command of Caiaphas. The Temple guards will look very much like the Roman soldiers but will have a different chest covering."

Todd stopped for a second to regain his thoughts. "Most of the information we have about this time and place is from the Bible and Josephus. The rest of what we know is from archaeology. I can't tell you for sure what we'll encounter."

Hudson took the information in and said, "Let me climb over you."

The agent did his best to push past the injured man. It was a very tight squeeze but was able to move to the front. Once there, he removed a few of the rocks and was able to make out through the dim light the bustling area that would be an archaeological dig several thousand years from now.

The street was smooth and flat, not like the one dug up in the future. The houses were solid and complete. There were cloth awnings, wooden doors and oil lamps glowing through the windows. As the agent looked around, he couldn't see any human movement. There were several donkeys tied to the buildings and occasionally a chicken or goat would walk by, but for the most part, the town was asleep.

He gave one more pan of the area through the small opening and then started removing the rocks as quickly as possible. He started pushing from the top and was moving the mass of debris fairly quickly. Most didn't weigh more than 30 pounds and moved with ease; however a couple of the larger stones took more effort. When he thought he could get his large frame through the newly formed opening, he called back to his partner.

"Todd, let's go," he whispered. "Todd!" His partner was unconscious.

He knew it was dangerous but he pushed himself out through the hole, turned around on the outside and went back in headfirst so that he could pull the man if necessary. Once back inside, he grabbed the flashlight and shined it in the face of his partner. The man was very pale.

Hudson slapped the man lightly on the cheeks, "Todd, wake up, we're almost there."

The professor mumbled a bit but wasn't making much sense.

"Todd, help me. I need to get you out of here. I'm going to pull, but I need you to help with your legs. Wake up!" He gave a few more slaps and then started pulling. The professor was beginning to stir slightly but was of little help. Hudson was on his own.

The agent pulled with all his might and got to the opening once again. He knew this was a dangerous undertaking because he couldn't turn around and see what was on the other side of the hole. All he could do was trust God.

Backing out of the opening, Hudson pulled the professor with all the strength he could muster. Because his clothing would rip under the pressure, he began pulling him from his good arm. He knew he might easily dislocate the shoulder if he wasn't careful, but he couldn't pull him from his injured arm. It was a chance he had to take.

Hudson was now completely out of the tunnel and gave a quick look around. He didn't see anyone, but that could change at any moment. He stretched back in the opening and pulled Todd once again. His arm and head were now out of the breach; another good tug and he would be out.

Hudson got into a squat position, bent over and pulled him up from behind his shoulders. He must have rubbed his injury on the outer edge of the wall because Todd let out a shriek of pain. The agent continued pulling until he was free from the underground labyrinth.

The sound had awakened people in the area. Suddenly lamps were being lit and the agent could hear movement down several of the side streets.

The professor was awake but extremely weak.

"Todd, help me, we need to leave this area."

"I can hardly move," he mumbled. "I don't have any strength."

"Well, give me all you've got. I'll do the rest."

Hudson knew they had to hurry because his partner wouldn't make it much longer. The professor was white as a sheet and going in and out of consciousness. The agent got him to his feet and wrapped the professor's good arm over his shoulder. Putting his own arm around the weak man's back, he started to carry him through the same area in which the professor was shot just hours earlier.

The agent didn't have any idea where he was going, but prayed the Lord would direct his path. He started to hear movement from behind. Not certain, he believed the noise to be a block away, so he picked up his pace. All of a sudden men began yelling in his direction. Uncertain as to what they were saying, he could guess that they wanted him to stop. He dragged Todd with all his might.

By this time the professor was entirely dead weight and wasn't any help as they fled the locals who were rapidly closing the gap between them. Hudson turned a corner and moved deeper into the neighborhood, hoping he could lose them in a side street or find a place to hide.

Hudson kept up the pace, dragging his partner whose head was now totally slumped forward. The highly trained agent became fearful and discouraged, not seeing any way out of the situation. There was no place to hide and he didn't know his way out of the area. By himself he would have a good chance, but carrying an extra 200 pounds too? The mob was getting closer by the minute. "God help me," he cried.

Hudson pulled the gun he had stashed under his shirt. Maybe he could scare the men away with the sound of the futuristic weapon. No, he knew that he might get those people to run but the sound would wake up everyone else. Besides, he didn't want to hurt anyone. These people were innocent and just trying to protect their families from a potential threat. He would be doing the same thing in their situation, but had to make it to safety, his mission was too important to be stopped now. Through the many fleeting thoughts going through his mind, he resolved to kill his pursuers if it came down to protecting his friend and his mission.

The agent turned another corner that ran parallel with a row of houses and the outskirts of the Ancient City. His escape was getting slower and slower. He drew closer to the houses that were on his left hoping that the shadows cast by the moonlit buildings would offer more cover. The crowd was closing.

"God please help us. They'll be on us in less than a minute if you don't miraculously intervene. God, we need you," Hudson cried with an anguish only felt in true desperation.

He pulled his friend a few more steps. Suddenly, he placed his foot in a small hole, turning his ankle and causing him to roll to the side. The weight and momentum of the unconscious professor drove both men through the front door of the small rock-walled home.

The plain dwelling had a cloth covering over the doorway that offered no resistance as they tumbled. They fell into a mass at least three feet into the home.

Hudson instantly got up and looked at his friend. He turned Todd over on his back and felt for a pulse. It was very weak and his arm was still bleeding even though he had a tourniquet slowing the flow.

Hudson saw movement behind him and noticed a young woman who appeared to be in her upper 20's sitting on her knees before a small oil lamp. It appeared from her demeanor that she had been praying. Her dark olive colored eyes were wide with surprise. Interestingly, he saw no fear or malice in them.

Hearing the crowd as they walked through the street, Hudson looked to the covered doorway. The angry citizens knew that they were in the right area to find the intruders, but from the sound of their voices were perplexed that they hadn't discovered them yet.

He looked back over to the woman who was beginning to stand and was prepared to stop her from alerting the crowd of their whereabouts. Her small five-foot-two inch frame would be easy to subdue, but just as he was about to grab her, she gave him a warm smile and walked over to the professor. She knew that the men in the streets were after the people in her front room, and with a small scream she could have the two men in prison within minutes, but that wasn't her intention.

She bent down over the unconscious man and looked at his arm. The graceful woman saw the large amount of blood but seemed perplexed as to why it was coming out. Normally this amount of blood came from the slash of a sword but the only visible opening was the size of a finger nail. She also seemed confused by the look of his clothing.

Todd was wearing a short sleeve button-up navy colored polo, a pair of tan chinos, a leather belt, dark blue socks, and a pair of trendy leather shoes. How would Hudson explain this to her? She had never seen shoes like that. The fabric was so smooth and colors so rich that only a Roman ruler could own it. The buttons alone would be perplexing. Even though they had been used ornamentally since 2000 BC, they wouldn't be functional for clothing for another 1300 years from their present time.

While looking over his arm, she came down to his hand and saw his graduate ring. On the blue stone in the center was a gold cross. She looked up at Hudson with dismay. The cross for her meant death. Criminals were hung on crosses to die. Why would anyone want to carry around the picture of death? She immediately backed away from the unconscious man.

Hudson walked over and bent down next to her. He spoke in as warm a voice as possible, "It is alright. We aren't going to hurt you." He pointed to his friends arm, "We need your help."

Hudson knew that she couldn't understand anything he was saying, but hoped his tone would allow her to relax. She looked at him for several seconds, got up and walked into the other room of the house.

The agent was very worried. Had she left through a back door, only to arrive again with men carrying swords? Hudson was out of options. If God didn't provide, he knew that he wouldn't make it back to his family and would die in this century.

When she did return, she was carrying a bowl full of water and a handful of loose cloths. "Thank you, Lord. You are Jehovah Jireh, my Provider," he said with a smile.

She looked at him, "*Yihove Yiuhreh?*" She spoke as if it were a question.

"Yes, Jehovah," he answered her with his hands in the air.

She smiled and began to clean the wounded area. Gently wiping the new and old blood away took several bowls full of water. Once it was clean, she thought that the work was completed and began to place a bandage over the gash when Hudson had to stop her.

This was the time he had dreaded for several hours. The agent picked up a small rock he found in a corner of the room and showed it to her. He then pressed it against his arm hoping to show her that there was something buried deep within the muscle. After he repeated the motion several times, and pointed at Todd's wound, she understood what he was trying to say, got a nervous look and backed away once again.

Hudson had several knives in the bag he was given, but that was left a few blocks over on a street 2000 years in the future. He didn't have anything that could remove the projectile. The agent stood up and began searching the small home. When he entered the kitchen area, he found a simple knife around four inches long. He wasn't sure, but it looked to be made from bronze. When he couldn't find anything else, he went back to his friend lying on the floor.

The reluctant surgeon got down on his knees next to the woman and examined Todd's wound. Knowing what he was about to do, she put a hand briefly on his then walked toward the door. Not hearing anyone on the street in front of her house, she walked outside. After a minute or so, she came back in and gave a smile to the agent meaning that the street was empty. Then she went across the room and came back with a small piece of leather. Gently lifting Todd's head and placing it in her lap, the woman opened his mouth and positioned the leather between his teeth. She cradled the unconscious man with all of her strength as if knowing that the intrusion into his arm might revive him in a violent way.

Hudson closed his eyes and prayed, "Dear Lord, guide my hand. I don't know what I'm doing and need your guidance. Lord, Todd's life is in your hands, I guess as it always was."

He bent down, placed his knee on the man's arm and thrust the knife into the wound about an inch and a half. Once it was in, he moved it to each side just slightly. Todd was thrashing about even though he wasn't conscious. The small woman was holding him with all of her might.

Hudson turned on the flashlight he had kept in his back pocket and looked in the wound. The bullet was visible at the base of the opening. Once again, the woman's eyes got huge. The technology in the agent's hand was millennia from being invented. He had no idea what she was thinking and right now didn't have the time to be concerned.

As he looked over the area, he found little bleeding, which helped with the operation, but meant that Todd didn't have much blood left to lose. He stuck the knife under the piece of metal and pried it out. It hadn't hit the bone, but had severed what appeared to be an artery toward the back of the arm; explaining the large amount of bleeding.

Once the bullet was out, Hudson went over to the fireplace and stuck the knife in the embers that were left from a fire burning hours earlier. After several minutes, he pulled it out and went back to his friend. Wiping the wounded area once more, he poured a clean bowl of water in and around the opening and sanitized the knife as well as possible.

Looking at the woman once more, she was ready for the final step and drew the man once again to her chest. Hudson then closed the wound as tightly as possible with one hand and pressed the red-hot knife against it with the other. The professor screamed out once and then went limp.

After several seconds, he pulled the blade away revealing the cauterized wound. The agent placed his fingers under Todd's wrist and still felt a pulse. His friend was alive and it was up to God to keep him that way.

The two moved the professor to what appeared to be the woman's bed. It was a small cot made of tightly woven hay placed in the corner. They positioned him there, covered him with a blanket and left him to rest. Then they sat down entirely drained from the ordeal.

Hudson looked at the olive skinned woman and pointed to himself, "Hudson." He slapped his chest several times, "Hudson." He then pointed to her.

She gently pointed to herself and said, "Aaliyah."

The night was dreadfully long for Clark. After leaving the tiny town of Gethsemane, he ran north for over a mile before taking a break. During his short respite, he heard through the clear night air, a group heading in his direction. It was expected that the murdered family's neighbors would seek retribution-an eye for an eye-so he employed a few techniques learned during his time in the SEAL's, and the posse lost the scent very quickly. Heading southwest back into the Kidron Valley, he searched once again for a place to rest for the night.

After wandering for over an hour through the dark valley, he discovered a rocky overhang about a quarter of a mile from the Golden Gate. In the future it was Zacharia's Tomb and its depth proved to be good protection from the elements.

The assassin gathered some rocks as a barricade and started a small fire at the edge of his shelter but it didn't keep him warm in the cold night air. Adding wood to his fire every few hours made the night long and restless for the seasoned veteran. Just as soon as his body would begin a sleep cycle, the fire would start to burn out causing him to get cold, wake up and put more wood on the fire. This sequence occurred at least six times. Sleep never came.

Morning found Clark stiff, cold and hungry. The temperature must have dipped into the low 30's, for as he looked around from his elevated perch, he saw the morning sun sparkling off the frost that was covering every surface throughout the valley.

Clark had been through many situations in the past and had slept outside on countless occasions but he hated cold weather. The rain forest with all of the bugs was better than a cold night lying on a rock. If the mission lasted for more than a day, he would be staying in someone's house even if it meant another adventure like the night before.

These people can't be too important to the time line. Losing a few here and there won't hurt, he thought as he scratched the fake beard and looked over the Old City. The prop was holding on but would only be useful for another day or so. Hopefully, that would be all he would need.

The sun had risen just 30 minutes earlier, but already the town was coming to life. The doors were opening and merchants were taking their places hanging up their wares. Looking over the countryside, the man could see people approaching from all directions to barter for the necessities of the day.

The assassin stretched out some of the soreness in his back. "I ought to get paid more for this," he grumbled.

As difficult as the previous seven hours had been, the sleepless night offered a small benefit in that it allowed him time to process the information picked up in his short walk through town. Several things still didn't seem right; the first being the exciting chatter of the people in the streets.

He looked down on the semi-walled city and wondered what had occurred in the town days earlier.

Had some ruler, or possibly a King visited? Clark thought through the history lessons he was forced through in preparation for the mission and nothing was mentioned about a visit from a high-powered leader.

Jerusalem was under Roman control, and if a Roman ruler came through, it wouldn't get the people excited, in fact, it might possibly cause Jewish riots. They hated their captors and certainly wouldn't celebrate them.

The second thing he couldn't get out of his mind was the street littered with palm leaves. The assassin couldn't remember any ritual or ceremony that the Jewish people had in the spring involving palm leaves. Around September or October they would celebrate the Feast of Tabernacles which required palm leaves, but that was months away. Why would there be palm leaves now?

A disturbing memory pulled at the back of his mind as if he knew the answer to his questions. He had felt it while he was walking through the small town the day before.

Clark thought about the question as he looked over the city. It hit him.

"This can't be right," he said as he sat down on a large rock. His eyes got wide. "I'm not supposed to be here now!" he yelled angrily.

The assassin was told that he would be in Jerusalem well before this time period. He was years late, and the new time frame he found himself in would complicate his mission exponentially. Clark thought for a second about getting to the sphere and going a few years farther back in time, but decided it was too great a risk. He barely made it out from the underground in one piece the first time; there was no way he would jeopardize his neck again for people who botched his mission in the first place. No, he would complete his assignment at this time in history and hope that it would be sufficient for the future.

Clark realized with total clarity where to find his mark. The man stood up, grabbed his satchel and headed across the small valley back into the city. His target was waiting on the other side of those walls.

Hudson awakened once again in a cold sweat. He had experienced the same nightmare on the plane. The world he saw was the same as before: dark, lonely, and devoid of hope and love. However, this time he wasn't protecting his family from evil; he was protecting humanity.

The agent found himself in a dark apocalyptic world with the backdrop of a volcano spewing smoke, soot, ash and lava up into the atmosphere. In front of him was evil of every kind. People with mangled bodies and distorted faces lined up as far as the eye could see. Holding various types of weapons, they were determined to get past him.

Behind were millions of people, but they weren't an army. They were innocent civilians unaware of the evil about to strike. They were of every race, creed, and gender, and were all oblivious to the threat.

In his dream, Hudson tried to warn the masses of the impending doom, but they were so content in their lives that they dismissed him carelessly. He pleaded with them to help fight. He begged them to take up weapons and defend the world, but they wouldn't. The agent awakened with the realization that he was desperately alone.

"Sara," he called out, expecting to turn over to his wife. He would kiss her and let her cuddle him back to sleep. However, the nightmare didn't stop with his sleep, it continued into the waking hours for he was not in his soft bed but was lying on a dirt floor in the corner of a small rock house. He was still in the first century.

Aaliyah must have heard his call, because she was walking across the room toward him. She was a lovely and graceful woman; a beautiful lady, even by futuristic standards. Hudson wondered where her husband was.

Normal Jewish women had rounded features, darker skin and dark brown hair. Aaliyah didn't fit the mold. She had more Roman features, with high cheekbones and a pointed nose. Her eyes were dark, possibly hazel colored, but her hair was golden brown accenting her olive skin. The lady was a paradox.

Bringing a small clay cup filled with water, she offered it to the worn man. He gladly drank it and got up. The room was small so he crossed it quickly and sat next to his sleeping friend. Hudson pressed his hand to

Todd's forehead and felt warmth but no apparent fever, so the man was still alive.

Aaliyah sat on the other side of the professor, and showed the agent his wound. There were no signs of infection. His arm had an awful burn, but it wasn't bleeding and looked to be healing. The battered area was covered in what appeared to be olive oil and some type of plant extract, possibly hyssop.

Hudson looked at the lovely young woman and could tell that she had been up all night attending to his friend. Around the bed were clay pots, pieces of cloth and various corked jars. The man's hair was oiled and brushed back, his face was clean, and he smelled fresh. His wounded partner looked as though he had been to a spa. Hudson suppressed a chuckle at the thought.

She had removed all unnecessary clothing; his shoes, pants and shirt, and piled them up in the corner, leaving him covered in a multicolored blanket; the kind one would receive at a wedding. Hudson looked around the room and couldn't see anything as nice hanging anywhere else within the modest home. Aaliyah was giving Todd her best, and all that she had. How could Hudson repay her?

The agent bent over his friend with Aaliyah watching and said a quick prayer. "Thank you Jesus for healing my friend…"

"*Yaysoo*?" She asked.

"Yes, Jesus," he said and looked up.

The attractive young woman jumped up from her seat with a smile that lit up the day. She ran about talking a mile a minute. Hudson watched but didn't know what was going on. She would raise her hands to the air and then put them together as if she were praying, all the while talking nonstop.

Hudson stood up from the bed, "I don't know what you are saying," he said while raising his hands palms up and shrugging his shoulders. "I can't understand."

A voice came from behind them. "She's saying that she has seen Jesus."

When Aaliyah heard Todd speaking she ran back to his side.

Hudson turned around and hugged his friend. Todd was awake, weak, but awake.

"Hey man, you're hurting me," mumbled Todd to his overly excited friend.

"You're alive. We weren't sure you were going to make it there for a while."

"I can't go anywhere yet. You wouldn't make it out of here without me," he said weakly with a smile. "What in the world did you do to my arm? It hurts more now than when I got shot."

"Can you move it?" Hudson asked.

Todd moved his arm a few inches and wiggled his fingers. "Yeah, but I don't want to, it hurts too much."

"Great, you aren't going to lose it. Now every time you look at that arm, you'll remember me."

"I don't think I'll ever forget you, no matter what you did to my arm."

Hudson got serious. "Did you say that she has seen Jesus?"

"Yep!" he said with more strength. "I missed some of the words. She's speaking Aramaic, and I'm pretty rusty there, but I got the idea that she's seen him and he's still in the area."

Todd looked at Aaliyah and spoke to her for several minutes. Occasionally she would shrug her shoulders as if she didn't understand. But from the amount of discourse between the two, they were able to comprehend each other fairly well. Hudson could tell that Todd was enjoying the conversation and feeling a kinship with their benefactor.

After what seemed an eternity, both Todd and Aaliyah looked up at the agent.

"She says that Jesus has been in the city for several days. It's kind of odd but from her explanation, the real-the first-Palm Sunday just occurred. Jesus actually rode into Jerusalem a couple days ago. Can you believe that? She says that the town was in a party mode and believed that their King had come. Wow."

Todd stopped for a second just to think about the words that he was saying.

He continued, "Aaliyah went on to give insight into Jesus' character. She's passionate about how Jesus made her feel. He made her believe that she has worth. While speaking to the crowd, Jesus made everyone think that he was speaking just to them. She was and still is excited about his coming.

This is amazing. She said Jesus has been seen arguing with some of the religious leaders, debating the chief priests, and protesting financial transactions within the temple. She says he's been really busy and has shaken up quite a few people around here."

Hudson listened to his friend wide-eyed. How could this be? His savior was within a mile of their present location, and with the reference point of Palm Sunday, the agent knew that Jesus would be crucified in two days.

Can I stop them from putting Jesus on the cross, were Hudson's first thoughts.

He knew the timeline and could warn Jesus of their intent. Maybe he could divert the soldiers and keep them from his savior. The agent came back to his senses. He remembered the words in Isaiah where it says that it pleased the Lord to bruise Jesus so that he could make his soul an offering for sin. If he didn't sacrifice himself, he wouldn't, couldn't be his savior.

It was Jesus' purpose to die, and nothing that Hudson could do would stop that. The world needed a savior in order for man to have an opportunity to spend eternity with God in heaven. Hudson regained his focus.

"Where does she think Jesus will be today?" Hudson asked with determination.

Todd grimaced as Aaliyah cleaned his wound. He conversed with her for several minutes and then looked back.

"It sounds like Jesus has been arguing with the leaders for several days and should continue the discourse for at least for another day or so. She believes that he will be in the middle of the city. In the future we call it Solomon's Porch."

"How do I get there? The sun's already up, and I might be too late," Hudson shot back while pointing to the window.

"If all of the drawings and models I've seen are accurate, we are on the south end in what is called the Lower City. You need to go west along the wall until you find Robinson's Arch. It's a large set of steps leading up the southwest corner of the wall. It should take you right to the agora or open area. That should be Solomon's Porch.

You should find merchants, tradesmen and plenty of priests and leaders. It'll be a well-populated area. If Jesus is going to be anywhere he'll be there.

Hudson, you can't go," he warned trying to sit himself upright.

Aaliyah pushed him back to the cot.

"You'll be dead in five minutes walking around in those clothes."

"I have to get in the city." Hudson wasn't going to take no for an answer.

"Give me a second," Todd said to Hudson as he grabbed Aaliyah's hand.

They spoke for several more minutes. At one point within the conversation, the woman shed several tears and walked into another part of the house.

"I think we can get you fixed up," Todd said fairly somberly to the agent.

Aaliyah walked back in the room with her head lowered carrying some cloth draped over her arm. She offered the fabric to Hudson.

Todd continued, "I asked her if she had something for you to wear. She doesn't know what's going on but understands that we don't look like what we should. I might bring her up to date while you're gone."

"Do what you think is best."

"I found out that she was married a short time but her husband was killed in a construction accident at one of Herod's sites over a year ago. He didn't have any living relatives to support her so she's been very much alone and almost an outcast since the disaster. The tunic and mantle that she's offering were her husband's."

Hudson was humbled by her generosity and thanked the young woman as he bent over and took the garments.

He looked back at Todd, "How do I put these on?"

"I can't help you there," he said with a laugh. "They didn't teach me in seminary how to tie a tunic." He spoke to Aaliyah.

She had a surprised look on her face, but quickly replied back to the wounded man.

"She'll help you. Strip down to your boxers, and she'll teach you to tie it."

Hudson removed every piece of clothing possible to allow for the new garment and still keep his modesty. Then she draped, pulled and knotted the cloth into a wearable article of clothing and after five minutes he was transformed into a first century construction worker.

"My skirt is a little short," Hudson joked.

Todd got very serious with his friend. "Hudson, you don't look like them. You are taller, lighter, and have the wrong features. When you're out, don't talk or look at anyone. You need to keep in the shadows as much as possible. If you have a run-in with a Roman or Temple guard, you'll be in a mess."

The agent picked up a gun and hid it under his outer garment. "I pray it doesn't come to that."

Aaliyah came across the room with a small sack. Hudson opened it and found some bread, cheese, a couple of boiled eggs and several types of vegetables. Once again he was taken aback by her hospitality. If the roles were reversed, would he have been as kind to her as she was to him?

"Todd, would you ask Aaliyah why she helped us?"

The professor spoke to the woman who was standing next to the oven bringing out another loaf of bread. The conversation was quick and to the point, then she went back to work.

Todd looked up at his partner with a surprised smile. "She says that God told her very clearly during her prayer time last night to help anyone that came to her door. When we fell through her entry, she said that she considered that to be in the category of someone coming to her door."

Hudson laughed out loud.

"It looks like God's providing," said the wounded man with a sparkle in his eyes.

Hudson smiled, "It sure does."

"Be careful," Todd said with concern.

Hudson smiled, turned around, and left through the front door.

Clark made his way back to the large Golden Gate. The assassin guessed the time to be about 7:30 in the morning and already, the tiny town was bustling with business.

When he had arrived in town the previous day, Clark had done his best to stick to the bustling streets and avoid more official areas like the one within the town's elevated geographical center. Today, however, he would go into the lion's den and find the man he had come so far to kill.

—

Hudson moved the cloth covering Aaliyah's doorway and left through the opening. Just a short time earlier he was dragging his friend through these small streets, now he was attempting to stop a madman from doing the unspeakable.

Once outside, the agent took in the locale. The morning was clear and the rolling hills to the south dipped and sloped all the way to the horizon. Hudson thought that Israel was much more beautiful in the past than during his time. The land was lush and green and except for fields full of grain, was covered with trees of all sizes. There were no highways, buildings, cars, or city noise, just small villages dotting the countryside.

Aaliyah lived on the last street before open land began. Her house was sandwiched between two others, and if one weren't specifically looking for it, the little entry most likely would be lost among the others. The opening was small and hidden in the shadows of the awnings of the other houses. Hudson could see where her home was to have a sunshade, but the brace had broken and evidently wasn't repaired.

Much of the home's exterior was in need of a man's touch. The wood in the doorframe needed to be replaced. Many of the blocks making up the front of her house needed to be newly mortared, and the agent guessed that the reason her house was the only one without a formal door was that somehow it had fallen off and wasn't replaced.

Hudson knew that men and women were designed for different things and had certain roles in this century. The women had responsibilities such as caring for the children, preparing the meals, sewing and weaving, and other home centered tasks. The men worked in the fields, bartered for goods and led the family as the spiritual leader. The agent guessed that home repair was also part of that male responsibility.

It was against custom for a woman to break gender roles, and since Aaliyah was alone, her home would go into disrepair until a man generously helped, or the elders removed her from the village.

Hudson sent a little prayer heavenward. "Lord be with this generous woman and provide for her miraculously."

The agent turned right and headed along the west end of the massive wall. He was a good 250 feet from its base, yet it was still a massive work of engineering. The blocks extending at least five stories into the sky were menacing to the small towns around it.

The agent kept his head low and covered by the cloth he was wearing. Todd's warnings had him nervous and he wanted to do all he could to keep from being seen. As he was walking parallel to the wall, he found a small tied off portion of grain evidently dropped by someone on their way to the city. It was about three feet long and possibly a foot in diameter. The agent quickly picked it up and slung it over his shoulder. The light weight wouldn't be a problem and the large size might offer more covering as he headed into the city.

About two blocks ahead, Hudson found the staircase Todd had described. It was enormous. The flight of stairs was a southwest entry onto the Temple Mount and had steps at least 40 feet in length. The staircase paralleled the western wall and ascended for about 50 feet until it made a 90-degree turn east before reaching the top.

Hudson's eyes continued on and noticed dozens of columns at least another 50 feet in height above the wall encompassing the full length of the southern edge. These columns had to be the boundary of the Royal Stoa. The agent wasn't a historian but knew that the religious, legislative and judicial body of the Jews-the Sanhedrin-would do their business there. The time traveler was once again awakened to the danger he was in, and pulled his head covering a few inches further down.

Hudson covered the distance to the stairs fairly quickly and began his ascent to the top. The steps were steeper than he was accustomed to, and the height between each step was slightly larger than his staircase at home.

He climbed the almost five stories in a little over a minute and found himself looking down the colonnade of the Royal Stoa. Hudson had learned in a class at his church, that Josephus, a historian from this period, said that this Stoa deserves to be mentioned more than any under the sun. The agent had the same feeling.

The columns seemed to go on forever and supported a roof over the entire distance. Off to each side of the open area were enclosed buildings and open teaching rooms. Hudson knew that any business with the priests took place there. He also remembered that in a little less than 40 years, the Romans would destroy this area sending the columns over the wall into the housing edition below where Aaliyah made her home.

He was suddenly taken aback with the thought that Judas could be within his sight at that very moment bartering for Jesus' life. The beauty was immediately diminished in the man's eyes.

Hudson looked around and saw plenty of highly ornamented men who must have been religious leaders. There were a number of different types of garments, some more adorned than others, but each category of religious leader could cause the agent more harm that he could handle.

In addition to the various priests and leaders, soldiers were paired up every fifty feet or so along the colonnade. They were most likely Temple Guards and were heavily armed. Hudson needed to keep his distance if he were to keep his head.

The agent looked left and found the large open area that Todd called Solomon's Porch. He continued in that direction with the help of the masses pushing in around him.

"The Porch," as it was so quaintly called, was far from a simple porch. The open-air marketplace encompassed at least six city blocks. It was bordered by columns and walls at least 50 feet in height, and at the top of the columns was a covered roof walkway that could be accessed by officials and guards. The streets were made of solid blocks of limestone, and the entire area was immaculate.

As Hudson continued out from under the Royal Stoa into the open market place, his eyes were drawn to the center of the enclosed area. Within the heart of Solomon's Porch was another walled region. It covered about a city block, and at its core was a large enclosed building. Hudson was over a block away and even at that distance; the building dwarfed the 50-foot columns around him.

That must be the Tabernacle of Israel, he thought to himself. He continued closer.

The huge majestic building took in one-third of the enclosure and was covered in white granite. The front of the structure was smooth with four large columns and a 30-foot door; plated in gold. As Hudson looked up he saw more gold in the form of an ornamental decoration along the front and top of the structure. While he was gazing on the beauty of the edifice, the sun reflected off of the gold with such intensity that Hudson had to look away to keep from damaging his eyes.

The building was beautiful and so important to history. Within those walls, the Sanhedrin mediated cases involving everything from loss of property to personal injury. It was also within those walls that one day a year, on the Day of Atonement, the Chief Priest would make amends for the transgressions of the people by sacrificing animals to God.

Hudson smiled. He knew something none of them knew; something that would both frighten and anger those same priests. Within those walls, a fifteen foot square curtain would be torn from top to bottom in a little less than two days when Christ died on a cross and made it possible for man to access God without sin, and without a priest.

The agent knew that the curtain sheltered the Holy of Holies, which contained the Ark of the Covenant. Since God kept his earthly residence within that room, only the Chief Priest could enter and make atonement for the people of Israel.

Christ would be the perfect sacrifice, abolishing the sacrificial system and allowing anyone the opportunity to commune with God. Hudson could not believe that he was in this historic place at this time. He just wished that he could be a fly on the wall when the curtain tore so that he could witness the expressions on the faces of the priests.

Continuing on, he pushed his way through the large and busy open area. It was only around eight in the morning and the porch was already full of people moving from place to place. He worked his way toward the front steps of the Tabernacle hoping to find the man he was seeking.

—

Clark progressed under the large arch and into the walled city. Once inside the fortified barrier, he had several options. He could continue straight and find his way back into the lower city, or could turn left with the mass of people and head up the stairs into the unknown. Knowing that if his mark were in town he would be on the Mount area, Clark veered left.

The staircase was massive and Clark counted a minimum of 75 other people rising up the steps around him. With the many natives pressing in, his progress was slowed, however after several minutes, and traversing almost five flights of steps, he came to the end of the climb.

The top opened onto a large area with thousands of people moving from place to place. Right in front of him was a smaller walled city within the walled city. At the front was a gate, and in the center was a golden crowned building. The assassin assumed that what he was seeing was the main temple, so he headed straight toward its front gate hoping to finish his mission quickly and get out of this town and this time.

Considering himself a night owl, Clark was rarely up this early. He didn't like mornings, and his last few nights hadn't been that great. It was only nine in the morning, but the sun was rising and beginning to heat the rock slab streets. The day was going to be warm and the quicker he finished his mission, the faster he would get home.

The assassin moved closer to the steps leading into the walled temple when he viewed through the crowd, three, possibly four highly decorated men. These bearded figures with guard escorts were most likely priests and were surrounding one lone man.

He looked intently, but Clark couldn't make out the center man's face. People were passing back and forth before him, and the crowd was tightening around the debate, so he never got a clear view of the agitator.

The assassin couldn't hear what was going on from where he was, but knew by the priests' body language and expressions on their faces that they were not happy. Clark could read people like a book and these men easily showed surprise, disgust, and anger at the words coming from the lone man.

The surprise for Clark was that even as angry as the priests were, the crowd was in agreement with the message coming from the apparent rabble-rouser. The assassin believed the supportive multitude to be the only thing keeping the ranting man from being hauled off to jail by the temple guards. The priests couldn't risk a riot by taking away someone whom the people approved of. Clark could see something in the leader's eyes; they would get this man in the end. He moved closer.

—

Hudson paralleled the southern wall of the Tabernacle until he came to the east end. When the agent rounded the corner he saw a crowd comprised of over 200 people. The multitude seemed to be enthralled by something happening on the front steps. With his head dropped low, he moved in closer, hoping to see what was taking place.

Shifting to a better vantage point, Hudson saw four priests debating a single man at the front gate of the Tabernacle. By their raised voices and flamboyant gestures, it was easy to see that they were not in agreement with the man. The agent only had an occasional view of an arm or piece of the debater's clothing due to the group moving in and around him, so he inched closer to the steps.

Once he found his new position, Hudson looked up once more and caught a view of the man causing the disagreements. He was not that tall, possibly five-foot-five. His beard and shoulder length hair were dark brown, almost black; but nothing out of the ordinary. His skin was darker than the men he was debating with; possibly from spending a significant amount of time in the sun.

As the man moved his arms around trying to solidify a point, it was obvious that the agitator was very fit and somewhat muscular. The garments he wore were plain and without insignia, showing that he was not wealthy or part of the government or religious leadership.

Hudson was about to move to a new position when the man who had the attention of so many turned around and looked him in the eye. It was only a short glance, possibly a second in length, but it was enough to shake the agent to his knees.

There was nothing special about the man's eyes. They were large and round like every other Jewish person, however it was the way they looked at him that moved Hudson. Those eyes saw all the way to his soul.

In that short one-second glance, the debater revealed all of Hudson's strengths and weaknesses. He made him feel at once that he could climb the highest mountain and then not possess the strength to stand. In that one second, Hudson felt joy and hope like he had never felt before.

In Sunday School, when Hudson was very young, he remembered seeing pictures of a man with long golden brown hair, blue eyes and Roman features. This person was usually in a beautiful white robe wearing new sandals. Hudson saw many versions of the man over the years. Occasionally he was sitting with a child on his knee, while other times he would be fishing in a boat. Some pictures had the man knocking on the door of a house, whereas the one he remembered most was just of the man's head looking off into the distance.

No matter what the man was doing in the picture, one thing held true; he was always strikingly handsome. At no time did he look dirty or less than the perfect version of the European male with a good tan.

Hudson looked at the man causing such difficulty for the priests. This person bore no resemblance to the man in the pictures. The man before him was dark with rounded facial features. He wore an old garment and had dirty feet and old sandals as if he walked great distances. However, the agent knew without a doubt that the man in front of him was the one the church pictures tried to portray.

This man was not handsome by earthly standards. He was very plain and basic in form and didn't appear to have two cents to rub together, but Hudson thought he was the most beautiful creature he had ever seen. Hudson knew this man, or was it that this man knew him?

It was for him that Hudson came 2000 years into the past to protect. It was because of his promise that the agent had turned his life over to him when he was a young boy. Finally, this man would die on a cross in less than two days for the salvation of mankind. Hudson had found the person he was looking for-Jesus Christ.

Hudson stood in the crowd not believing what he was seeing. His Lord who had died on a cross more than 2000 years before was standing in front of him arguing with the religious leaders of Jerusalem. The God of the universe who came in human form to offer himself as a sacrifice for mankind was just 15 feet away. The man was awed and humbled that God had allowed him to experience this incredible moment.

As a child, the agent would often think through people in history he would want to visit if time travel were possible. He always thought that it would be an exhilarating experience to visit Independence Hall when the Declaration of Independence was signed. Did John Hancock endorse everything that way or was his name written that large to bring attention to his allegiance? What about going to Ford's Theatre the night Lincoln was shot?

Moving farther back in history, Hudson always wished he could meet Isaac Newton or spend time with Constantine. And of course there were the biblical narratives. Who wouldn't want to be there when Moses split the Red Sea or Jonah was swallowed by the whale.

When the agent played this simple child's game, there were always people and places in time that he would want to see, but his Lord, in the Holy Land, was never one of them. He thought that it was sacrilegious to even imagine watching Jesus in the garden or viewing him on the cross; and yet here he was.

The feeling that Hudson was going through was almost surreal. He needed to refocus, bring himself back to this reality, and work on the mission with which he was entrusted.

The agent willed his eyes from Jesus and started to look around the crowd. He knew the savior's disciples would be in the mass supporting their master, so he continued scanning the multitude. After a cursory search there were at least seven men he thought would be good candidates for followers of Jesus. They were trying to keep a low profile and weren't part of the crowd as a whole, but were situated off to the side next to the altercation. Could one of those men be Peter, another John? Hudson could hardly curb his excitement.

Continuing the search for the other five disciples, the seasoned agent located a man that looked out of place. His clothing was of the right color but seemed new and fresh compared to everyone else's. The weave didn't seem to match the textiles used in the clothing people were wearing around him. Also, his sandals were new and to top it off, he was a foot taller than everyone else. Possibly the man was wealthy, but as the agent looked more closely there were other things out of place.

The color of his beard didn't seem right. The man had a European look and was well tanned, but the dark brown beard didn't seem to fit. The beard was also too well trimmed. The man's cheeks and neck were fairly smooth proving that they had been shaved recently, something only the Romans would do. Hudson moved a few feet closer and was able to make out that he had blue eyes and a fresh scar on his forehead.

The agent began to put his hand under his outer garment and secure his weapon when the man looked back. The initial look was a sporadic glance that ended with him turning back to watch Jesus on the steps. But then a look of Déjà vu covered his face and his head snapped back. The wide eyed stare was one of surprise. Hudson could see that the man was puzzled by his presence. Then with a smile, he clasped his hands out in front of him and laughed out loud. The laugh was gentle but deep and unnerving.

The agent knew the criminal mind and quickly realized that this expression of amusement was not caused by something funny. It had more of the feeling of children on a schoolyard starting a game of chase. In his crazy way, the man was welcoming Hudson to the deadly, possibly world-changing game he began when he entered the ancient world.

Hudson was caught off balance by the reaction. He had taken part in plenty of investigations and had captured scores of criminals, but going against a madman with so much confidence in a world he didn't understand made the agent doubt his abilities. He grasped the gun under his mantle more tightly and walked up to the man he had come 2000 years to apprehend.

"Hello Michael," Hudson said in a whisper standing face to face.

With a smile he shot back, "We have met before, haven't we? Was it at the lab site?" He replied in normal voice as if unconcerned whether the people around heard the difference in dialect. "You were the one shooting everyone if I remember. I would love to know how you got here."

The agent was stern-faced, continuing to hold his weapon. "I'll tell you on the way out, Michael. I'm taking you back."

"No, no, no! I'm having too much fun. Not too many people get a vacation like this. Just look around," Clark said while gesturing with his hand, "the air is clean, the water is unpolluted, and there are so many interesting people to meet."

Hudson was undeterred, "You will be coming back with me."

"Now how do you propose to take me back," Clark moved closer to Hudson. "I'm not ready to go. I still have several loose ends to tie up before my vacation here is over."

Hudson still in a whisper answered, "I know that you killed Dr. Keith and I know what you plan to do here in Israel. I won't let that happen. If I can't take you back peacefully, I'll kill you before I allow you to complete your mission."

"Such strong words. We haven't even met yet. What is your name?"

"Hudson Blackwell."

"Blackwell, hmmm. Such a dark name for being an angel sent to save the day. Tell you what Blackwell, if you leave right now, I'll let you live. If I succeed in my mission, things will be so different that when you go back, no one but you and I will know that you failed. It may hurt your ego a bit, but you'll live through it."

Hudson gritted his teeth, "Right now I'm holding a gun, I suggest you turn around and head back out that exit…," he said pointing.

Clark cut him off, "You and I both know that you won't shoot that thing. You have no authority here. We're among the barbarians and have to play by their rules. If you make a commotion in this holy area, the guards will have you in one of their little prisons faster than you can spell 'Help' in Greek letters.

"No," he said with a big smile, "you're in a hard place. You want to stop me but don't know how." The assassin crossed his arms and continued watching the debate in front of him.

Clark was right. What could Hudson do? If he tried to take the man by force guards would come. If he shot the man, he could possibly make it out in the commotion but there was still a good chance that he wouldn't. Any awkward behavior would land him in prison; a place that he would most likely never get out of. Once again, God would have to work it out.

"Do you see that man over there?" Clark said pointing to Jesus. "How could he have made such an impact?"

Hudson was now aware that Clark had identified Jesus.

"Just look at him. Can you believe it?" Clark said with bewilderment. "He's a small little man. Physically insignificant. I could snap his neck like a twig. How could he cause so much trouble 2000 years from now?"

"What are you talking about? What trouble has he caused? He came into this world not to condemn it, but so that through him it might be saved," he said paraphrasing a verse in the Bible. "That man is our salvation."

Clark almost growled as he came eye to eye with Hudson, "That man has saved no one. His life is, and was a huge lie, and I'm going to reveal that to the entire world," he raged as spittle came from his mouth.

"All his memory did was offer people a false hope. It allowed a corporation called 'the church' to take over lives and finances. The church has total control. It can control any entity because it controls the people.

Well, it doesn't control me. The church says that Jesus offers hope. Hope!" The man was getting more and more agitated.

"Where was the church or that man during anything in my life? Where was that man when my father killed my mother? Where was that man when I was alone and going from one foster home to another? I had to make my own hope.

The church states that I can go to heaven through that small little insignificant man. If he can't do something as simple as comfort a little boy who lost his world, there's no way that he can get me to heaven."

Hudson watched Clark through his rants and saw tears welling up in his eyes. Something awful had happened in his past. The psychological baggage would make him much more dangerous.

"I'm sorry about what happened to you Michael, but Jesus loves you and…"

Clark pushed Hudson back with force. He was now angrier than ever. "Don't patronize me. I don't need or want your pity.

That man doesn't even know I'm alive, let alone love me. Don't you think that if he were king of the universe," Clark said as he raised his hands exaggeratingly to the sky, "he would try to stop me?

Shouldn't he know that I just came back in a time machine to kill him? You would think that he'd be interested in that. And yet there he is, grumbling with some old men on steps to a temple that venerates a god that doesn't exist.

No, he's not god, just a little man who somehow got the world's attention. I won't let him do it again."

"Michael, you will be stopped."

"What does it matter to you?" the assassin said with strength. "He's going to die in another day or so anyway. What's the problem if I help him along?"

"Jesus came to sacrificially give his life. It cannot be taken from him," Hudson answered without hesitation.

The crowd was thickening around them to see the argument on the Tabernacle steps.

"Prove to me that he's more than a man! You see him there, what's divine about him?"

"The only proof that I have is how he's changed my life," Hudson said pointing. "I'm a better man; a man with a purpose and a hope of eternity in heaven. He is God, and I will protect him with all of my ability."

Clark dismissed his answer. "If I strangle him, do you think people will be wearing ropes around their necks, or have a Jesus figure on their wall being hung from a noose? What if I slit his throat; I can see everyone in the future having a small knife pendant on their necklace. It's kind of funny don't you think?" Clark chuckled then turned serious.

"Such emphasis put on a cross. A couple pieces of wood and all humanity bows down to it."

Hudson fired back in defense, "We don't worship the wood, but the man who died on that wood. He became the perfect sacrifice because he knew that we couldn't make amends before God for our sin. What's important is not how he died, but that he died and then rose again."

"Does that man look like he could rise from the grave?"

"He does rise from the grave. Three days after he's crucified. There were many witnesses and most of his disciples, men in the crowd among us, went to their graves being tortured and tested without recanting that fact."

Clark had talked long enough, "It sounds to me like the soldiers messed up and didn't kill him after all. He somehow went into a coma or something. That'll not happen this time.

After I kill Jesus, I'll dismember him, cut him into tiny little pieces, and then burn the body. There will be no walking out of the grave."

Hudson could feel the man's hate churning the pit of his stomach. He couldn't believe someone would think of doing such horrific acts, let alone doing them to his savior.

Clark put his hand under his outer garment and grabbed for something. Hudson noticed this and pulled the gun that he had been holding closer to the surface.

"Michael, I'll not let you kill Jesus."

"You don't have a choice. Before tomorrow night, I will have killed your so-called Lord. And by the way, if you call me Michael again I'll gut you as well. He died years ago, the name is Clark."

The second Clark finished his last word he punched Hudson in the face and threw a bag of coins into the air; a bag stolen from a merchant on the way into the city.

The punch was so hard that the agent fell to the ground. All around him gold coins sprinkled onto the ancient limestone walk like morning rain. Instantaneously the crowd lost their interest in the ongoing debate and turned to grab as much of the free money as possible. It was as if they were chickens pecking after the last piece of grain.

Hudson was on his back and locked in. He fought to get away from the people grabbing for coins that had fallen on and around him, but it was difficult. Each time he attempted to get up, someone would move to a better vantage point jostling him again to the ground. Following several attempts, and a few arduous seconds, he was standing and endeavoring to leave the gold hungry pack.

Pushing out as the group scrounged around his knees; he finally broke free of the melee and was able to look around. Clark was gone. He had blended into the crowd and was heading for one of the exits.

Hudson ran for the closest exit, but didn't see the assassin. He ran north up along the wall, dodging merchants and clusters of people to the next gate out of the city, but still didn't see Clark. He had lost him.

Feeling defeated, the agent walked back to where he had been earlier. All of the money was gone and so was the crowd that had piled in around him. Looking up to the steps he noticed that the priests had left and Jesus was talking to the men Hudson had determined to be the disciples.

Before his encounter with Clark he would have been ecstatic to see Jesus talking with his followers, now he just felt lost. Why hadn't he just shot the man when he had the chance?

In his attempt to talk the madman out of the objective he had come 2000 years to complete, the agent lost him. He had years of training and yet lost his suspect.

How could he protect Jesus? His Savior had to go before Pilate tomorrow night and die on a cross the following morning. What an awful task he was given. He had to ensure that Jesus died. Hudson had to keep a man from killing Jesus long enough for Jesus to die at the appointed time.

The man's whole world seemed upside down. Hudson looked over at Jesus once more, and as he did, the savior looked back. The glance was full of compassion and love. Jesus' look of knowing told Hudson to be at peace. The agent felt the Holy Spirit within him and was filled with assurance.

Hudson smiled. Jesus went back about his business, but the agent was revived. It would work out for God's glory in the end. God was sovereign. His will would be accomplished, but Hudson still felt he had a purpose in the first century.

The agent needed to get back to Todd and Aaliyah. Jesus was safe for the moment because Clark would take time to regroup. He would strike at Jesus away from the crowds; possibly at night, so Hudson had a few hours to rest and learn from the professor. He started for the Robinson Arch.

Pulling his hood farther down over his head, Hudson felt his cheek. It was sore. Nothing was broken but there would be no way he would let the assassin sucker punch him again. Next time he would be ready.

It was a close call, but throwing the coins in the air was worth a try, and seemed to work. The melee around his opponent reminded the man of when he was a boy and would throw pellets into a fish hatchery. Every fish in the lake would crowd in trying to get a piece.

Clark thought to himself. *It looks like people aren't much smarter than fish. It only takes one small act to control them.*

His words had a double meaning. Clark had become who he was through hard work and determination, not because some insignificant Jew died on a cross. In the assassin's mind, Jesus wasn't smart enough to stay away from the Roman guards and had made the wrong people mad. *Jesus died because he was stupid and careless; no other reason.*

Pushing the emotional turmoil deeper, he ran even harder. His hope was that Blackwell would think he left through the nearest exit, which was the Golden Gate, when he actually departed through one of the farthest gates. The thought process must have been valid because he ran west along the Tabernacle wall unhindered until he found Warren's Gate.

Warren's gate was small, if not the smallest gate on the Temple Mount. Being situated in the center of the Western Wall just north of Wilson's Arch and directly behind the Tabernacle, it offered more cover for the assassin.

Only a few people took Warren's Gate because of the ease and size of Wilson's Arch. However, the exit was a stroke of luck for the man needing to leave the temple compound unnoticed. He was able to slip into the crowd that was forming a bottleneck around the relatively small opening.

After another five minutes or so of looking over his shoulder, Clark finally relaxed and made his way through old town Jerusalem. The community was small, but not as little as the towns around the massive complex. The settlement seemed to cover the area outside of the western and southern walls. If the entire city compound were placed on a grid, it may have covered a square mile.

Clark needed to get out of the city. He needed to regroup and think about his options. Until this point in the mission he'd thought he was alone, but now he knew that someone was out there trying to stop him. The assassin had been told about Blackwell in his orientation but never dreamed he would be playing a game of cat and mouse with him.

As Clark looked for a quick exit from the city, he reflected on the information he knew about the man who had just confronted him. Aware that Blackwell was a pilot trained on the sphere and an ex-Secret Service agent, he'd also learned that he was chosen for the original project because he was dedicated and heroic in nature.

He would put others before himself, he thought with a mingling of interest and disgust.

Looking south, Clark viewed open countryside. Believing it to be the quickest and shortest way out of town, he headed that direction. While he turned down a side street, he got a bit nervous. He knew that the most dangerous enemy was one that didn't worry about his own well-being. Through his conversation, it was obvious that the agent was religious and had accepted the man Jesus as his savior. This being true, Blackwell believed that upon his death, he would be in heaven with God.

So, as Clark passed women sewing and cleaning, and stables full of donkeys and goats, he summed up his opponent. While crossing streets where those with deformities sat at the corners begging for food, and priests made their way to the walled city, he grew more and more concerned. Blackwell would give his life without regret to stop his mission. The assassin began to feel sick to his stomach.

After carrying out hundreds of missions in the past, Clark had never encountered a foe with such moral determination. The man had targeted leaders of countries. He had assassinated drug dealers, CEO's, wealthy landowners and drunken boyfriends. All of his targets were corrupt in one way or another and would sway depending upon the pressure. None had been the threat that Blackwell would prove to be.

The agent believed that what he was doing was noble and right, and in his mind, he knew that he was saving the world. A man with that type of mission would give everything to complete it, including his life. Clark needed to be on his best game or this would be his last.

The assassin took in the area every minute or so to ensure that he wasn't being followed. While walking south he looked over the roofs of the small buildings to his left and viewed the walled fortress. It was an amazing feat of engineering. He had been all over the world and could only think of a few places such as Egypt and China where this type of architecture could be found.

He continued his scan more southerly down the wall and saw the grand staircase of the Robinson arch. It was mammoth in size and at the present time had hundreds of commuters on it. Every type of person was there, from those who looked to be in their teens to old white-bearded men. There were crippled men hunched over their canes to very tall men.

Clark looked again. He noticed one man that seemed to be out of place.

"Can it be that easy?" he mumbled to himself.

Running up past a few houses to gain a forward view, he kept his eye on the man in question. The peasant was hugging the outside of the staircase and seemed to be tall, but bent over with his face covered. Clark ran south several more blocks.

Looking up, he gained his answer. The man was clean shaven, wearing a brown tunic and doing everything possible to keep a low profile.

"How can I be so lucky?" he said out loud with no concern for who overheard.

—

Hudson left Solomon's Porch with a sore cheek and disappointment over his inability to apprehend Michael; or as he was corrected, Clark. Despite the confidence his spirit received at Jesus' look, he felt like he had disappointed his Lord and the world as a whole. He had never felt so sad.

As he left the temple complex and traveled through Robinson's arch, he walked bent over because he felt the weight of the world on his shoulders. If he didn't succeed in eliminating the assassin, the "best" thing that could possibly happen would be the time line would be altered by anyone they encountered.

Hudson's mind raced. It was conceivable that just bumping into someone could change all of history. He could be slowing someone's progress by taking the position they would have taken if he were not there. Thus they would be slower to get home and would encounter other variables they weren't destined to encounter if they were on the correct time line. This tragedy of errors would follow through to the birth of yet another Hitler, or George Washington's birth never taking place.

His thoughts continued. *If that is the best possibility, the worst would be that Jesus is prematurely killed.*

These thoughts caused him to panic. Looking around, he noticed the outside area of the staircase was used less frequently than the center, so he moved there to encounter the fewest number of people.

What if Jesus didn't die on the cross? What if the madman did what he said he would do and totally destroyed the savior's body? What would the world look like? Hudson's dreams began to come back to him.

206

He now knew why he was having such nightmares. His subconscious had been dealing with the situation before he was ready to cope with it. The agent's visions were of a world without Christ; one totally devoid of hope and love.

In a world where Christ doesn't die on a cross, there would be no expectation of the hereafter, no anticipation of heaven or seeing God. This would force everyone to get what he or she could in the few years they spent on earth. Man would fight, pillage, steal, maim and kill to ensure that he had the material possessions he desired. There would be no contentment, trust, joy, or love.

A world without Christ would be anarchy, placing man against man where only the strongest would survive. A world without Christ would make man selfish, arrogant and proud. There would be no moral compass and the ethical code would be dependent upon who was in power. A world without Christ would literally be hell on earth.

Hudson felt like he was going to vomit. Never had he experienced so much pressure, and never were the stakes so high. He stopped and looked over the side of the stairs at the city below and felt like the prophet Jeremiah when he wept over the city of Jerusalem. *You people are so lost*, he thought with desperation. *You have the most beautiful jewel sitting in your midst and tomorrow night you will discard him as though he were trash.*

Hudson whispered to the ancient town below with tears in his eyes, "Why won't you defend him? Why won't you help me? Jesus came to give you life, and yet you murder him. You are no better than the madman desperate for Jesus' life."

Suddenly, he felt God speaking to him. The words came painfully, but were necessary. The Lord was saying that he was no better than those to whom he was preaching.

Hudson had lived a good life, and by most men's standards was clean and upright. However, in comparison to Jesus, the agent was no better than a filthy rag. God didn't want good, he wanted perfect; that was why he sent Jesus.

In his lifetime, Hudson had lied, cheated, broken many of God's laws and turned his back on the one who had created him more times than he could count. Because of those errors, there was no way that he could get to heaven. God was perfect and needed everything around him to be perfect.

God saw the chasm between his own perfection and his people's sin and sent Jesus to be a pure sacrifice so that all who call on Jesus' name would have the opportunity to spend eternity with God in heaven.

Yes, Clark had come 2000 years into the past to kill Jesus. And if he failed, then within 36 hours, many in this city would ignorantly hang Jesus up on a cross. But Hudson was no better, for he was symbolically one of the people in the crowd who would be chanting "crucify him, crucify him."

Overcome with emotion, the agent looked to the heavens.

"Why am I here?" he whispered with tears in his eyes. "I'm weak and inadequate."

As if a cool rain fell from the skies, Hudson felt God's strength and provision envelope him, and suddenly a verse came to his mind. The agent remembered second Corinthians 12:9 where it says that God's grace is sufficient and his strength is made perfect in our weakness.

The agent bowed his head and closed his eyes on the bustling steps, "Dear Lord, thank you for walking with me. Thank you for being the strength in my weakness. Lord, please forgive me for my arrogance; I am the worst of sinners." Hudson stopped for a second and thought about the truth in his words.

"You know that I'm afraid and don't feel adequate, but I'm going to trust and follow your direction."

Opening his eyes, the agent looked at the city again with a clear vision and renewed energy. He felt fifty pounds lighter because the weight of the world was taken from his back.

Hudson continued down the stairs toward Aaliyah's house. He would rest, check on Todd's condition, and then resume his hunt for the madman.

The walk to Aaliyah's house took another five minutes. Upon his arrival, Hudson found the people within the small dwelling busy with activity. Todd's arm had a fresh bandage, and he was dressed in first century garb. The room had been rearranged to better accommodate the extra men and something was cooking in the fireplace.

After observing the differences in the room, he also saw changes in his friends. Aaliyah was aglow, and was talking a mile a minute with a smile that would brighten any situation. Her mannerisms were more exaggerated and her level of activity was much higher.

Hudson could also tell that she had spent some time on her appearance. Instead of the brown tattered garment she was wearing earlier, now she had on something that looked much newer. The cloth was still brown, but had hints of blue and green in the fabric. She had also pulled back her hair and was keeping it in place with a metal clip.

The agent knew that the loneliness had been very hard on the beautiful young woman. It was easy to see that she was very extraverted and loved being with people. He and Todd had come through time to apprehend a criminal, but might end up giving hope to a first century outcast in the process.

The agent also looked at his partner. The man was out of bed–which he shouldn't have been–and was hanging on Aaliyah's every word. He looked strong and if his bandaged arm weren't visible, the agent wouldn't know that anything had happened to him.

Hudson couldn't close the door to alert them of his arrival because there wasn't one, so he just cleared his throat and all activity in the room ceased. Aaliyah turned toward him, backed up a couple steps and lowered her head in a more subservient position. Todd put a big smile on his face and started toward his friend.

"Hudson, it looks like you made it! They didn't throw you in jail or kill you or anything," he said jokingly with apparent relief, "even though it looks like someone didn't necessarily like your face." Todd grabbed Hudson's chin and turned it from side to side looking at his newly acquired bruise and swelling.

"What happened? Did you find him?"

Aaliyah saw the bruise and brought over a wet rag. She cleaned his face as Hudson started to speak.

"Yeah, I saw him. I don't think that he's too pleased I'm here."

Todd jumped in, "Well, I'd bet not. Did you get into a fight?"

Hudson sat on a small stool, "No, not necessarily. Only one punch was thrown and it wasn't by me. He surprised me to get away. I should've been more prepared."

Aaliyah went back to cooking and Todd sat next to Hudson.

The agent went on for the next ten minutes telling Todd about the events of the morning. He relayed to the professor of his experience with Jesus and how it was surreal to see his savior debating with religious leaders. He also told Todd about his conversation with the assassin and of the physical assault.

The professor listened without saying a word. Only after Hudson completely finished did he speak up.

"Hudson, how are we going to get this guy? He knows just as well as we do that there's no way we can forcibly take him anywhere. As soon as we try, the Roman or Temple guards will come down on us and release him. How are we going to get him to the sphere? We can't drag him through those tunnels. We have a big problem here."

"I know what you're saying. I've already thought through this. Nothing about this whole mission is easy."

Todd smiled, "It looks like God's going to have to work it out."

Hudson smiled back, "Those are wise words." He sat for a second, "Todd, this man is intelligent and takes this case personally. Something happened in his childhood that has turned him against Jesus."

Hudson leaned back against the wall and rubbed his eyes, "He's going to fulfill his mission to kill Jesus before tomorrow night, or die trying. Even though someone sent him here to do this terrible thing, I think he'd have gladly come on his own given the opportunity.

The agent leaned forward and looked the professor in the eyes. "He's a dangerous adversary."

Staying out of sight and blending into the crowds, Clark followed his opponent. The agent traveled through several streets, crossed a few alleys and finally disappeared through a small cloth covered doorway in the center of a row of houses. The area was perfect for surveillance because it was situated at the outskirts of the city.

The assassin looked around and as he panned north saw an outcropping of rocks about two tenths of a mile away. The stony formation was at a higher elevation and would allow Clark uninterrupted visibility of the doorway.

Normally, the assassin would continue on with his mission and only deal with threats as they came. However this opponent was serious and had to be neutralized. There had to be a crack in the agent's armor, however small, and Clark was willing to spend a little time in the sun watching the doorway to find it.

Snatching a refreshing drink from a water pot sitting in front of a barn, Clark headed off for the cliffs. The assassin would lay low and watch the building for the next few hours. His enemy would be removed at sundown.

—

"So what happened around here while I was out getting punched?" Hudson asked while he yawned.

"It's been a great morning," Todd spoke up.

"Aaliyah put an herbal compress on my arm and it is feeling better. It still hurts like nothing I've experienced, but I think I'm going to make it," He said showing the wound.

"She also gave me some type of tea and it has improved my energy level. I feel weak, but am getting stronger by the second."

"What did she use? That information would be great in the future," asked Hudson.

"I'm not sure. I tried to ask but she couldn't explain it in a way that I would understand.

I've studied Biblical Hebrew and Aramaic. I can do a good job of understanding the big picture, but specific words of this time that may not be in the Bible I won't know."

"That makes sense," Hudson mumbled as he leaned against the wall.

"Have you told her who we are or why we're here?"

Todd stood up and started walking.

"I tried to bring her up on everything that's going on. I first told her that we were from the future."

Hudson jumped in, "What did she say?"

"She didn't understand at first. I didn't know the word for future so I had to use examples that would allow her to understand the idea."

"What example?" the agent asked.

"Well, I used the example of reaping. The farmer goes out to sow the grain into his field and knows that in time it will grow, and he will have to go and reap it. The time hasn't come yet, but he still knows that it will. I told her that we were like the wheat that hasn't grown yet."

Hudson got a weird look on his face.

"Yeah, I know it was a stretch, but after about ten minutes of trying to explain, her eyes got as wide as dinner plates and I knew then that she understood what I was saying.

She was very nervous at first but calmed down after I reaffirmed her that we were trying to help her and the world. I went on to tell her that we were like Roman or Temple guards trying to seize a murderer before he kills again."

"Were you able to tell her who we were protecting?"

Todd continued with great excitement, "Yes, I told her all about Jesus. The most difficulty I had at that point was to change her viewpoint of what Jesus was," the professor hesitated for a second, "or I guess, is trying to do.

She is just like everyone else in Jerusalem. She believes that Jesus is here as an earthly king to stop the oppression and to free her people, the Jews. It was very disappointing for her to know that he wasn't going to do that. She was extremely upset. However, when I explained what Jesus was actually here to do, her attitude changed."

"What did you tell her?" Hudson asked showing his excitement for the story.

Todd had a big smile; "I just built up the case for Jesus. I first went through and tried to prove that he was her predicted and coming Messiah."

"Did you quote Old Testament passages?"

"You know it. I quoted Jeremiah 23 where it says that Jesus will be a descendant of David. I then moved onto the book of Micah where it says that he will be born in Bethlehem. Then to Isaiah seven where it says he'll be born of a virgin. I told her the book of Malachi said that Jesus would be preceded by a forerunner who was proven to be John the Baptist.

You know, she knew of John and had seen him preach. This is so exciting. I have been studying this information all of my life and to really be around people who have experienced this is unfathomable.

Let me get back on track."

"No, take your time. This is great," Hudson said.

Todd started pointing the fingers on his right hand, "I went through the verses predicting Jesus' triumphal entry, how he would speak in parables, how he would be meek and mild and loved by infants, et cetera, et cetera, et cetera.

I went through every Old Testament verse that I could think of to build the case, and then I came to what will happen this week."

Hudson's eyes were wide. "It's hard to imagine that Christ will die Friday afternoon, unless Clark gets to him first."

"It's amazing."

Aaliyah brought Hudson some water in a clay cup.

"Thank you," the agent said slowly.

"I then moved on to Zechariah eleven where it says that Jesus will be betrayed for 30 pieces of silver and Zechariah thirteen where it states that a close friend will turn him in.

Aaliyah got visibly upset. She couldn't believe that one of Jesus' followers would turn against him.

I told her that Judas was most likely with the priests right now working out the deal."

Hudson spoke up, "I can bet that she was confused. Jesus' followers had been with him for years and seen him do great and mighty things; and then to turn him in…"

"That was it exactly. But what really got her were the Isaiah passages. They state that Jesus will be spat on, scourged, struck, hated and crucified. I told her that Zechariah even states that Jesus will be crucified with spikes.

She began to cry. For a while here in Jerusalem, everyone thought that Jesus was to be their earthly king. For me to tell her that Jesus dies in two days was pretty tough for her to swallow."

"Didn't you tell her about his rising?"

"I'm getting to that, just hold on."

Hudson laughed.

"I told her that the good part was going to come on Sunday. Because Jesus is God and sinless, the grave could not hold him. He conquers death!" Todd raised his hand up to illustrate it.

The professor pulled over a stool and sat right in front of Hudson, "I then went back to Isaiah 53:5 and tried to bring it all together. That's the verse that says he was pierced for our iniquities and crushed for our transgressions. It goes on to say that the punishment we deserved, he took and through his scourging, we're healed."

Hudson nodded because he knew the verse very well.

"I told her that Jesus was the last and perfect sacrifice. The High Priest has been sacrificing a perfect lamb on the Day of Atonement to cover the sins of the Jewish nation. However, with Jesus' act, that would not be necessary. Jesus was her salvation and essentially, *ca*me to set the Jewish people free, and anyone else who will call on his name."

"It sounds like you had a better morning than I did," Hudson said with a smile.

"I don't know, you got to see Jesus," Todd said enviously.

"True. So how did it end up? Does she believe in Christ?" Hudson asked.

"I wanted to give her some time to take in what I told her. Her whole world has been turned upside down."

"That's an understatement," Hudson responded.

"Last night two men fell through her front door; one of them bleeding. After we invade her house, we then tell her that we've come from the future to stop a guy from killing her future earthly king. We then go on to inform her that her earthly king isn't really an earthly king but a heavenly king who would be proven to be the predicted Messiah. That Messiah would die a horrible death two days from now, just to be raised again on Sunday.

You also told her that her whole religious system would be turned upside down, and that her priests are crooks. I can imagine that she has a lot to think about," Hudson said with a yawn.

"Well, I said it as nicely as I could."

"Yeah, I'm sure you did," mumbled Hudson as he closed his eyes.

"I'm going to let you rest a while. You've already had more than a full day."

Todd walked over to the fireplace and began helping Aaliyah with dinner.

Clark spent the hot, dry afternoon watching the doorway of the first century dwelling. In the hours of surveillance, he observed tired dusty men with tools in hand coming in from the fields.

These people appeared to be well into their 50's but the assassin knew that most likely the workers were no older than 30. *This ancient lifestyle ages a man before his years*, he thought with a chuckle.

In addition to seeing men returning home, his vantage point upon the rocky outcropping allowed him to witness a donkey running from its master, several women slaughtering chickens for their evening meal, general mundane Jewish life, and vulture type birds flying over his head.

"I'm not dying today birds, so move on," Clark said waving his fist in the air. "If I had my shotgun, you'd be my meal." He enjoyed the thought.

With the many mundane scenes that the parched assassin witnessed from his desert hideaway, not a single movement came from the house in question. No one went in, and no one came out.

At one point, after spending several hours watching the front, he progressed north along the upper edge of the crevasse and thought his time would be better spent viewing the rear of the dwelling. However, no movement came from that exit either.

Becoming irritated and sitting up in confusion, "I know I saw him go in," he said to himself.

"There's no way I missed him leaving.

And on top of that, someone else has to live there. He didn't get on the Internet and reserve that cozy, little, rustic Israeli hideaway.

Why hasn't anyone come out?" The hours in the sun without food or drink caused the highly trained assassin to doubt his observational skills.

"No, I know what I've seen," he became extremely angry.

"That worthless piece of twenty-first century trash has caused me to waste hours of time in the sun watching for him when I could've completed my mission. After the sun drops below the horizon, I'll head down there and slowly gut whoever's in that comfy little cottage."

The professional returned to his original position and continued his surveillance with renewed strength and excitement.

"Hey buddy, time to wake up," said Todd while he shook Hudson's shoulder.

The agent immediately jumped. When he looked around, the stony misshapen walls came into view. Then he saw the crude wooden stools and smelled the smoky, poorly ventilated room; his waking nightmare continued. However, being conscious was much preferred to being back in the dream he was experiencing prior to waking.

The night visions were just like the others, but on this occasion he wasn't fighting off the evil around him; the evil had won. His family had been taken. The world was utterly lost and totally devoid of hope.

Hudson rubbed his eyes and looked around again.

"Hudson, you alright?" asked Todd.

"Yeah, give me a second."

The final part of his dream was coming into view. The experience was so real he ached. The agent felt like such a failure and had let his family down. He had let himself down, and now there was no hope for mankind.

Hudson leaned back against the wall and remembered the few seconds just before he awakened. It was the worst part of the entire experience.

The agent was tied to a cross and sitting directly in front of him in a royal looking chair was Clark. He had a knife in his hand and a crooked smile on his face.

"So how do you feel?" the regal figure queried.

"What do you mean?" Hudson forced out the words between pained breaths.

"You couldn't save the world," he said as he gestured in front of him.

"I did my best. I used all of the abilities I had," he cried.

"Your abilities are worthless!" Clark said forcing a finger in the crucified man's face.

"Do you see what your best got you, and everyone else? Your best was an utter failure. You couldn't even save your own family. You couldn't save yourself, and most of all, your best couldn't save humanity."

"I know," Hudson yelled between sobs, "I'm inadequate." His tears flowed like rain from the sky as he dropped his head to his chest.

"You should've never tried to resist me. You were doomed from the start. And now because of your failure, I condemn you to death."

"Oh God, help me," Hudson yelled. "Lord, I need you!"

"Stop your noise," yelled the man scraping his thumb over the edge of a knife, "I crucified your Jesus," he said sarcastically, "on that same tree. He's dead. He couldn't help you."

Hudson was utterly beaten and knew that there was no way out.

Clark's smirk became more evil as he raised his knife and thrust it into Hudson's heart.

"Hey, man, you alright?" Todd said bending down next to his friend. "It's time for dinner."

"Yeah, just had a bad dream."

"Well, this experience would do that to anyone. Come on over. Aaliyah's made a great dinner. Authentically first century."

Hudson smiled, "What else would she make? I can bet a burger and fries are out."

"Hey buddy, she's very poor and has cooked her best for us."

"I'm sorry, we are blessed that she's taken us in. What's for dinner?"

The two men walked a few feet over to a table filled with different foods. Aaliyah was working very hard and obviously loving every minute of it. It was clear that she had not had guests for a while and was making the most of the experience.

Todd pointed to the various delicacies sitting in clay bowls on the short table.

"As you can see we have baked bread, cheese, a variety of vegetables and she went overboard and cooked lamb as the main course. Hudson, lamb is only cooked on special occasions."

"We'll repay her somehow for her kindness."

"We need to do something. She's also poured us some wine to drink and there are grapes and figs for desert."

Hudson looked at Aaliyah and said, "Thank you."

The young woman glanced over at Todd and very nervously said, "Yoo wehcum."

Smiling, the agent looked at his partner and said, "Did she say your welcome?"

"We've been talking all afternoon. I taught her some English, not that she'll need it for a while. The English language doesn't really begin for over 800 years."

"That ability probably won't help her on her resume'," chuckled Hudson as he looked back at Aaliyah.

"Good English," he said tapping his mouth.

She beamed while gesturing for the men to be seated.

Todd thought it was necessary to do some teaching, "Hudson, they don't sit in chairs. It's proper to eat while lying on the floor. Traditionally, men would lie on their left side and eat with their right hand."

"Why's that?"

"First, left handedness was thought to be evil. Second, they don't have toilet paper. You pretty much cleaned yourself with your left hand. Since the right hand stayed clean, you ate with it."

"They don't use corn husks or something?" the agent said with a scrunched nose.

"Tell you what, we'll save the husks for you," laughed Todd.

Both men chuckled while moving to the floor.

Once the men had taken their place, Aaliyah moved back and started to work in the kitchen.

"Isn't she going to eat with us?" Hudson asked.

"The women were not on an equal basis with the men. It's not customary for her to do so," Todd said responding to the question.

"Aaliyah, come," said Hudson gesturing to the floor.

She placed her palm toward the men and backed away.

Todd got up and brought her over to the table. "Please sit," he said while pointing to her area of the table.

She reluctantly sat down with her hands in her lap.

"Hudson, would you bless this meal?"

"I'd love to."

Hudson reached his hands out so that they could pray more as a family. This was his custom at home so he carried it over to his first century friends.

Aaliyah was slow to grab the men's hands but eventually connected the circle.

"Dear Lord, thank you for this meal. Thank you for your provision in growing the animals and the crops. Thank you for Aaliyah and her hospitality. Lord, we ask that you care for and provide for this precious lady. God, your word says that you care for the least of your people, please care for her.

Dear Lord, please order our steps and actions so that we'll do what you would have us do. Thank you for loving and dying for us. We say all of this in your precious son's name, Jesus, Amen."

They dropped hands, and the agent looked over at the professor.

"So how does this work? Do we just get food and start eating, or is it handed out to us? I don't want to make a mistake and start a world war."

"Traditionally, there would be a male host that would start off the process. Aaliyah is not going to take that role, so I'll eat first. I've spent the most time with our new friend and I think that she would be comfortable with me taking on that privilege.

We just dip from the center bowls. You pull out what you need and eat it with your hands."

Everyone began eating.

Hudson coughed, "This meat is very spicy. It's good, but spicy. I haven't tasted this flavor before."

"Aaliyah used all kinds of spices. The meat is salt cured, so that will be a lot of it. I also saw her use garlic, onions, and raw mustard. I'm not sure, but it might be the cumin or coriander."

Hudson nodded.

It was obvious that Aaliyah had never fed men the size of her guests, since the food ran out very quickly with both Hudson and Todd easily downing second and thirds.

With friends sitting around the table and the men catching up on the day, the meal gave a sense of normalcy to the craziness of the situation and put everyone in a more relaxed mood.

—

Clark had been on the cliff long enough! With the sun dropping below the horizon, and the canopy of stars shining brighter each minute, the assassin got giddy with anticipation. He wagered that the villagers would be getting to sleep early so as to beat the heat of noonday, so if he was going make a move, it had better be now.

He opened the bag he had been carrying since arriving in the desert city. It was replete with all of the equipment he would need for the mission; however, his primary concerns were the weapons available.

The man couldn't believe that he wasn't supplied with conventional handguns.

"Like I care whether I destroy the timeline. Just give me a 9mm and let me do my job," he muttered angrily.

Looking in the bag, Clark located several large knives and the wireless Taser. He eyed the piece of equipment. Everything appeared to be functional except for its battery level.

Because it hadn't been charged in several days, the power level was only about half of its potential. He had one good shot left and it most likely wouldn't kill, but might incapacitate his enemy long enough to finish him by hand.

The assassin strapped one knife to his chest, and carried the other blade and Taser in his hands under the long sleeves of the mantle. Leaving the bag behind, he began his way toward the lonely village.

"Blackwell, let's have some fun."

⸻

"So what did you learn about our host today?" Hudson asked taking another bite.

"I believe that Aaliyah's 29. They don't really keep up with birthdays like we do but she thinks she's gone through 29 seasonal cycles."

Because of his excitement, the professor became more animated in the telling of her story. "She's an extremely intelligent woman and can read Greek, something very few women could do in this time."

"How did she learn?" Hudson said pulling the last piece of meat from the bowl.

"I believe that she's the daughter of a woman who was forced to work in Herod's household: her mother was raped. Aaliyah was very closed mouth about it. However, that explains why she doesn't look fully Jewish. She has Roman features and is more petite than most truly Israeli women."

Both men looked at the fair skinned woman.

"Because she was raised among the wealthy, she picked things up by proximity. She evidently taught herself to read."

"Amazing."

"She also told me that her marriage was very short. It was arranged by her father who just tried to get rid of her. Because she was obviously a mixed race, her father took anyone who would marry her.

Normally, women of this time period could decline the new suitor if they chose. It didn't happen very often, but in principle they had the opportunity. That wasn't afforded to Aaliyah. Her father said that if she didn't marry, she was out on her own; which really meant death; she would've been an outcast. She didn't love him, but was forced to marry him. I guess it was preferable to death."

Hudson was mesmerized by the story.

"She said that he was killed in an accident shortly after their wedding. They didn't have any children and he left her with nothing. That was close to five years ago."

"How does she make it? Does she work?" Hudson questioned.

"She takes in cleaning and sewing in exchange for food and occasional help. Aaliyah also gleans the fields like we see in the biblical passages of the book of Ruth."

The young woman got up and started cleaning up the plates. There was hardly a scrap left, so she poured the few remaining crumbs into one bowl and took them outside for the dogs to lick them clean.

Both men got up and stretched.

Todd looked his friend in the eyes, "Hudson, this lady has really touched my heart. She's so innocent and honest."

The professor walked toward the door, "Even though her life has been indescribably more difficult than mine, she doesn't know of the evils that are out there. She implicitly understands that God's going to work it out."

"That is something we all should know."

The men heard a noise outside and both looked to the door.

Hudson whispered, "What was that?"

"I heard it too, it sounded like grunting," he said quietly with determination in his voice.

Hudson instantly pulled his gun and Todd found a staff in the corner used for corralling sheep. They leaped for the door. Their forward motion was halted when Aaliyah came back through the cloth door.

The fragile woman was smothered by the large frame of the man they had been chasing through time. With her head only coming to his chest, one of his arms held what looked to be a bowie type knife pressed against her long and graceful neck. His other arm was pointing forward and held a wireless Taser; a weapon Hudson knew very well.

Once the uninvited guest was completely inside and the door flap fell behind him, the room became completely silent.

Clark had his Taser pointed at Hudson. The agent was in an offensive stance with both hands on the 9 mm pointed at Clark. Todd pointed his staff in a forward posture looking for any weakness in the assassin's position. Poor Aaliyah was trembling with fear because of the large knife pressed against her neck.

After seconds that seemed like an eternity, Clark finally broke the silence.

"What have we here? What a sweet little home." He turned his head and looked at the scared woman, "I love what you've done with the place."

"Michael, let her go," barked Hudson.

"You call me Michael again, and I kill you all."

Todd spoke up, "Is this the guy we're looking for?"

Clark looked over at the man he had not seen yet, "Who's this? Does it take two of you to get one of me? I feel really important." A false lightness edged his words.

"Let...her...go," said Todd, the words dripping from his gritted teeth.

"I will not let... her... go," he said while pressing the knife tighter to her neck.

"Aaahh," squealed Aaliyah.

The blood slowly moving down her neck proved that Clark had broken the skin.

"I'm going to make this real easy. You put down your weapons, and I won't snap her neck. That's a fairly simple command."

Todd looked over at Hudson.

"You know we can't do that. This mission is bigger than any one person. If you kill her, I'll kill you," growled Hudson while moving closer with his gun.

"Stop your movement. You know that I'll kill her."

"Leave her alone. She's totally innocent here," pleaded Todd.

"Innocent people die every day; now drop your weapons."

Todd had been sizing up the staff he grabbed from the wall. It was fairly straight and well balanced. Because he had been in Tae Kwon Do since his teenage years, he had earned a 5th degree Dan black belt and had spent countless hours learning to use a staff as a weapon. The equipment that he practiced with was much lighter and perfectly balanced, but he knew given the chance, he could take the large man down.

Aaliyah was breathing very quickly and beginning to cry. Todd's heart was breaking. He had never felt so much hatred for anyone as he did the man holding his innocent Aaliyah.

"Let her go," both men yelled almost simultaneously.

"Drop your weapons," Clark said again while pushing Aaliyah around like a rag doll. "You have three seconds, and then I kill her."

Both men moved closer.

"One."

"Todd, I have him."

"I can take him," mumbled Todd.

"She's going to die. Two!" Clark's voice wavered as he looked back and forth at the men.

"I can take him," yelled Todd. Instantaneously he jammed the end of the staff into the man's right arm hitting a pressure point and causing Clark to drop the knife. The large man lurched several inches to the left and fired at Hudson.

In the milliseconds it took for the electricity to run through Hudson's body, he fired his 9mm, grazing the large man on the cheek and falling violently to the floor in convulsions.

After the bullet tore across his face, Clark dropped the woman and felt for possible damages. She quickly ran behind the professor as the much smaller man lit into his opponent.

In the many years that Todd had studied the multitude of defense techniques, he had never actually used them to their full potential. Yes, occasionally he would spar with friends, but all of the punches and kicks were pulled so that his opponent was never hurt.

This was much different. Todd knew that he was defending himself, his friend writhing on the floor, the woman behind him and the world as a whole. He had to win this match or everyone would die.

Todd started pummeling the large man with his staff. It was obvious very quickly that Clark was also trained in martial arts, for every staff blow Todd gave, the man quickly offered a counter.

Clark tried several times to fire the Taser at his new opponent; however the battery was totally depleted, so he threw it at him and continued the fight.

Todd knew he would need to drop the staff because he didn't have the space to use it properly. As he dropped it, he also gave the man a roundhouse to the head. The force knocked Clark sideways, but he regained his balance and came back with a few reverse punches and an uppercut strike. Todd blocked each offensive movement and came back with another.

Each man was throwing hook punches, middle punches, knee strikes, thrashing kicks, and ax kicks while performing the best blocks to counter the actions. They were well matched. Only through the mistake of one was the other going to win.

The room was a mess, as one man would fall against the wall and the other fall against furniture. What little earthly possessions, Aaliyah would be totally destitute after the fight-as if she wasn't already.

The men kept punching and kicking.

Hudson was beginning to come to his senses. The weapon had not killed him but forced a pain through his body he would not quickly forget. He was in no shape to help his friend even though he wanted to.

After several more minutes of fighting, Clark reached under his outer garment and pulled out his second knife. Todd should have expected it, but didn't. The professor had no weapon. He had learned to knife fight and knew that he could hold the man off a while, but without a weapon of his own, the war was about to be over.

He looked around for anything that could help his situation. His staff was several feet away and not accessible in time. Hudson's 9mm was not within reach. If he lost this fight, he determined that he would go out with glory.

Clark was not expecting the offensive onslaught from the smaller man. Expecting the knife to stop the battle, his opponent's onslaught took him off guard.

Punch after punch was thrown in tandem with kick after kick. Even with the knife, Clark did not have an advantage. He was nicking the man and had cut his arms up fairly well, but it wasn't slowing the oncoming battle.

Eventually, Clark gave a large push to the professor with all of his remaining strength and got Todd off balance enough that he had an open view of his side. The assassin lurched forward to thrust in the blade…

Thud!

Hudson and Todd both looked up to find the large man lying on the ground unconscious. Standing over his collapsed form was the petite woman barely weighing 100 pounds. She stood with shards of pottery at her feet watching an angry red mound form on the assassin's head. The woman wore a look of satisfaction that quickly faded into dismay as she began to cry uncontrollably.

Todd ran over to Aaliyah and hugged her small frame into his heaving chest. They stood there motionless for over a minute until the sounds of a crowd outside brought them back to the reality they now had to deal with.

She ran through the door and calmed the growing mass. They had heard all of the noise and wanted to know how they could help. Aaliyah was outside about 30 seconds when the crowd started to disperse and she came back in.

Hudson went over to Clark and placed his knee in the man's back until Todd could find something to bind him with. The professor found leather straps and tied his arms behind him, but knew he couldn't get a knot tight enough to make it permanently secure.

"We'll have to watch him around the clock," said Hudson rubbing his temples hoping to soothe the extreme ache between his eyes.

Todd nodded.

When Aaliyah returned, the professor pulled her to his side and examined the damage to her neck. Her graceful form had taken some damage but would heal quickly with the herbs she had used on him earlier that day. He offered her another embrace into which she gladly melted.

Hudson observed the hold and became nervous. It was obvious that there was an attraction moving beyond friendship between the two, and the agent wasn't sure what to do. He hoped that his worries were premature, but knew he couldn't leave Todd in the first century and there was no possibility of bringing Aaliyah back with them to the twenty-first century. Maybe they were just drawn together because of the extreme stress of the last few days; possibly a Florence Nightingale type syndrome.

He needed to break the emotion of the moment.

"How did she get rid of the crowd?"

Todd looked up and relayed the question. After a short discourse, Todd began laughing.

"What did she say?" asked Hudson.

"Boy it hurts to laugh. My ribs hurt, my jaw hurts. I don't think there's a place on my body that doesn't hurt."

Aaliyah looked Todd over and went to get some wet rags.

"By the way, thanks. We would all be dead without you. Where did you learn to fight like that?" asked Hudson.

"At the seminary. Some of those preachers are tough."

Their laughter eased the tension still lingering in the room.

"So really, what did she say to them; the crowd outside?"

"Oh yeah, she told them that a donkey got loose in the house."

"Only in first century Israel could you get away with an answer like that and it make sense." Hudson laughed.

"What are we going to do with him," Todd said as he pointed to the unconscious man on the floor.

Hudson sat up against the wall with his knees to his chest. "I'm not sure. We could start to move him. We could possibly find a cart and carry him in it. But there's no way we can drag him through those tunnels. He has to be conscious for that."

Todd spoke up. "Come on, we talked about this before. This man's not going to go back with us. You know that, don't you?" Todd stopped to let the words sink in.

"He's just as determined in his mission as we are. He's going to fight us with his last breath and most likely get us killed trying."

"I know," Hudson said with resignation.

"Why don't we take turns watching him and work out a plan in the morning."

"That sounds like the best option. I slept the afternoon, so I'll take the first watch."

"Okay."

Aaliyah started working on Todd's wounds. He had cuts covering his arms and some on his chest that were fairly deep. Because of the recent activity, his original gunshot wound began bleeding again too. She gently cleaned and anointed the wounds with oil and natural remedies.

On several instances during the triage, the two would look into each other's eyes and shyly smile as if they were teenagers in love.

Hudson watched his new friends as they spoke without saying a word. They had a connection that time, culture, and language could not separate; the mission had just become more complicated.

29 — THURSDAY MORNING, APRIL 16

The night seemed like an eternity. Hudson vigilantly watched the dangerous criminal for over six hours before asking his associate to reciprocate. The professor was glad to give his partner a break but up to that point had been talking with Aaliyah, therefore wasn't much more rested than the man he was relieving.

The day had been long. It started out with a punch in the jaw and ended with what felt like electro-shock therapy. His face hurt and body ached, therefore when Hudson hit the floor, sleep was quick to follow.

The agent returned to the same point of the turbulent dream he was experiencing a few hours earlier, but this time while his body was hanging on the cross, his spirit was somehow floating above it. From his ethereal vantage point, he could see the four corners of the earth and in no direction was there light. All of creation was dark except for the action taking place below him.

There, Clark was on his throne reveling in the cheers of millions, for he was the victor. The assassin had killed the so-called savior and behind the kingly figure hung the body of the man who had tried to stop him in his quest.

The surreal sight of Hudson's own body added intensity to the already realistic nightmare. He saw the jagged knife thrust deep into his heart and the blood that flowed down his motionless form to the ground; Hudson had to look away. Evil had won and hope was banished.

The agent cried out to the heavens, "How could you let this happen?"

Even though he wasn't part of the scene, just an observer, the millions still laughed at the question.

Instantaneously, Hudson was forced back into the lifeless remains on the cross and awakened to the steamy breath of his captor, Clark.

"You asked how God could let this happen?" He turned and in a sickly sweet voice spoke so everyone could hear the humorous question, "He asks how this could happen!" The man walked around on the platform repeating the question. He laughed with a wickedness that could only be found in the pit of hell.

Clark shouted it, "He asks how this could happen!"

Hudson was utterly alone.

227

The kingly figure turned on a dime and placed his face within an inch of Hudson's then positioned his hand on the knife presently driven deep into the agent's chest.

With a forced whisper he spat, "This could happen because your God does not exist! You've failed and I'm the victor." With force, he thrust the knife deeper into Hudson's chest. The pain forced him out of the dream, back into consciousness, and up to a sitting position.

The agent gave a small grunt.

"Are you alright?" Todd asked, fairly startled.

Aaliyah brought the shaken agent a cup of water.

"Thank you," muttered Hudson. "I'm fine," he said rubbing his hands over his face. "How's our prisoner?" he said feeling like he had been through much worse than an electrical shock.

"I think he's coming around."

Hudson walked over to the man and shook him. Clark began to grumble and started to open his eyes.

"Here he comes," affirmed Todd.

Aaliyah moved behind Todd, her protector.

Clark fully opened his eyes and realized the situation he was in. He started to wrestle with the straps tying his arms behind him.

Hudson pulled his weapon and began to speak. "Michael, you need to relax."

"I said don't call me Michael," he growled.

"I'm sorry; you like to be called Clark."

"So, did the little lady hit me in the head with something? You know that's how it always works, the great ones are inevitably taken out by those they least expect." He formed an evil grin. "Didn't they get Wild Bill that way?"

"I appreciate the history lesson, but we've more important things to discuss."

Clark sat up and moved against the wall. "And what would that be?"

"We need to get back to our time."

"I still have some things I need to do here. You know, see the pyramids, and kill Jesus, stuff like that."

He looked up at Hudson who was still visibly shaken from his dream.

Todd looked out the window. "Hudson, the sun's up. It's going to be tough to move him in the daylight."

"Clark, are you going to go peacefully or is Aaliyah going to have to hit you on the head again?"

He growled. "The next time I enter the sphere it'll be after I've accomplished my mission and killed the three of you."

Hudson looked to his partner, "Todd, what would the townspeople do if they saw us dragging a bound and gagged man?"

"In this area there aren't many guards, so they police themselves. I believe they would chase us down. For one thing, he looks like them and we don't."

"We can take care of that right now," Hudson spoke with conviction.

The agent walked over to the assassin and gave a tug on the costume beard applied to his face.

"Get away from me!" Clark yelled while struggling against Hudson's effort and his restraints.

"Calm down, buddy," said Todd as he held the large man down.

"Get your hands off of me or I'll kill you the next time I get a chance," barked Clark at the professor.

The facial hair came free, leaving the man's face red and raw. Hudson then pulled off his wig.

"Now we're on a level playing field," Hudson said with the hair in his hand.

The tension in the air frightened Aaliyah. She trusted her protectors but feared their actions were enraging the man who had pressed a knife to her neck just a few hours earlier. She quickly left the area and began breakfast.

Hudson backed against the wall facing Clark and folded his arms. It was obvious he was trying to work out what to do about getting the man back to the sphere.

Todd looked over, "Hudson, all we have to do is hold him another day and then the window for his mission will be over."

Clark looked up curiously at the statement.

"I hadn't thought of that," replied the agent relieved to have a solution.

The professor walked toward Hudson and continued. "If we can just keep him locked up until around midnight," he said gesturing toward Clark, "then Jesus will have been apprehended by the priests. He'll be untouchable."

"Couldn't he get to Jesus when he's carrying his cross through town?"

"Boy, it's doubtful. The streets will be lined with Roman soldiers. Jesus will possibly have three or four soldiers assigned just to him."

Todd looked over at the man on the floor, "If he wants a suicide mission, I guess he could try to kill Jesus on the Via Dolorosa, but Clark looks like he has some life left in him. I'd also bet there's going to be some big money to spend back in our time if he's successful. No, he has to get him before tonight or Jesus will be too isolated."

"You're right." Hudson paced the floor for close to a minute before he spoke again. "Let's just sit it out today and maybe we can move him tonight."

"Sounds like a plan," affirmed the professor. "Let's eat."

Todd walked over to the fireplace and asked Aaliyah what they were having for breakfast. She told him that she had some cheese and fresh baked bread. The two men suddenly realized how hungry they were and sat on the ground around the short table.

After a short prayer thanking the Lord for His provision, protection and for delivering Clark into their hands, they began to eat. Several minutes into the meal, Clark spoke up.

"What about me? I'm hungry, too," he barked.

"Even a prisoner gets a meal," smiled Todd.

"I guess so. I'll check his restraints while I'm there," Hudson said begrudgingly.

The agent pulled out a gun and handed it to Todd saying, "Watch him."

Hudson walked over to the captive. Placing a piece of bread in Clark's mouth, he leaned over to check that his hands were still securely tied.

"He's loose!" yelled Hudson.

Todd jumped up to ready his weapon but was too late.

The assassin threw a handful of dirt toward the professor, covering his eyes and temporarily blinding him. Remembering Aaliyah's last position, Todd backed up toward her. She grabbed onto him and pulled them into a corner of the room where they would only have to worry about a forward attack.

Clark continued his arm's smooth motion allowing his fist to land directly in the center of Hudson's face. The agent was hit hard enough to break his nose and cause immediate bleeding. The assassin jumped up and kicked Hudson in the chest driving him breathless to the floor.

Hudson rolled back several feet and did his best to prepare for the next barrage of blows.

Todd was beginning to clear his eyes of the foreign matter and started seeing the outline of the men in the room, but didn't trust a shot on a blurry image. He needed a couple more seconds.

The assassin wagered that he would be pressing his luck if he spent any more time in the dwelling, even though he wanted to kill everyone in the room. He looked over at the professor and knew that very shortly his sight would come back and the bullets would begin flying. He was also aware that Hudson was ready to get back on his feet.

By retreating, the criminal would have the opportunity to fight another day so he ran out the front door of the house. Hudson ran after him but quickly realized that he wouldn't be able to catch the escaped convict with his immense bleeding. He was back in the house within 20 seconds.

The agent was furious and stormed back through the door of the house. "How could I have let him go? What a stupid move," he said sounding as if his nose were close-pinned shut.

Aaliyah came over with a rag and a bowl of water in an attempt to stop the blood that was pouring from Hudson's face.

"He got us both. We messed up."

Hudson grunted as Aaliyah pressed around on his nose.

She spoke to Todd and he relayed the information to Hudson.

"She says your nose is broken. If you get hit there again before it heals, it could kill you."

"Aaah! That hurts," he said as she probed his face.

"Hudson, she can set that. She told me that she's helped soldiers after coming home from war. It's going to hurt, but you need to let her do it."

Hudson backed against the wall of the small dwelling. "I'm ready."

Todd spoke to the young woman.

She knew what she had to do. Bending down over the bloody man, she placed one hand on his forehead and with the other pulled the nose straight. Hudson whimpered and then relaxed.

After several minutes, Todd broke the silence. "Well, if there's a good side, we know where he's going next."

"Where's that?" Hudson said with his eyes shut. Every word physically hurt.

"The Upper Room."

"Todd, we know where Jesus will be tonight, but where's he now?"

"I've been thinking that through and can't remember anything stating what Jesus did on his last day before the Lord's Supper. The Bible doesn't speak on the issue and it's just conjecture or tradition past that."

"Give me your best guess," said Hudson with his head against the wall and fingers squeezing the bridge of his nose.

"He has to be in the Upper Room by sundown which is around six, so he can't be far. I'd guess he would be no more than a couple miles from that spot.

Now Jesus is fully God so he can do just about anything. However, because he's also fully man and knows what he's going to go through in the next 24 hours, I'd guess he would avoid the crowds."

"Why?" Hudson said sounding miserable.

"I think he's going to be lying low. He's been on Solomon's Porch debating with the priests for the last several days, so he won't spend his last few hours doing that. If I were in the same situation, I'd spend my remaining time with close friends saying goodbyes."

"That makes sense. Whom would he have visited?"

"Even as recently as last Saturday he was with Mary, Martha and Lazarus. The Bible makes them out to be some of his closest friends. I would think he went there."

"Where did they live?"

"Bethany. About two miles southeast."

"Well, that's where we need to go."

"Hudson, Aaliyah doesn't know Mary and Martha," he said. "She's heard of Lazarus and the miracle of Jesus raising him from the dead. She was pretty excited about that. But, she can't help us find their home."

"Well, we need to give Bethany a shot. It would sure be quicker to phone over there," he said with a chuckle and his nose still in the air.

He continued, "If Jesus is there, and Clark finds out, that would be an easy place for him to strike."

"I'm with you," thrusting out an arm to help Hudson from the floor. "I have the weapons," he said showing the guns.

The large man slowly rose from the floor and put the guns beneath his undergarment, "Let's go."

After a brief conversation with Aaliyah, Todd picked up the staff he had used the night before and the two men left the house.

—

Clark ran until he reached the main road and then headed north into the busyness of the city. It was obvious that his attempt to remove Blackwell was poorly planned and badly executed; he should have studied his opponent better. The assassin expected someone to be living in the house but was surprised to find out that the government agent had brought a partner; one that was very well trained in martial arts.

The renegade walked by rows of houses and found some dried meat hanging from a hook. Quickly glancing about, he grabbed the snack and continued north past the Temple Mount.

Finding a shady place next to the massive walls of the Holy City, the assassin sat down and pulled pieces from the foot long cut of meat. While eating, he thought about his next move.

He knew as well as his previous captors that there were only a few hours left to kill Jesus. He wasn't aware of the timeline when he first entered Israel but listening to the ninja of the house, it was obvious that Jesus would be apprehended after dark, and crucified tomorrow.

His initial training for the mission had taught him that on Jesus' last free day; he would offer a Last Supper for his disciples in an Upper Room and then go to the Garden of Gethsemane to pray.

Clark remembered the maps of Jerusalem that he'd memorized as part of his training and generally knew where the Upper Room would be located. However, if he were familiar with that general piece of information, so were the two men on his trail.

The assassin smiled. "Blackwell, I have you and the ninja right where I want you." He said out loud and chuckled as he tore another shred of meat and devoured it ruthlessly. There was an advantage to having the pursuers know where he would be because he also in turn knew of their future location.

The man was unaffected as people on the street looked over questioningly while passing. Clark had just moved from defense to offense and had a Hail Mary play that would win him the game. He waved at the curious onlookers.

—

The two men arrived in Bethany just 40 minutes after leaving Aaliyah's house. The small walled community had a central gate with a handful of older men sitting near its opening. They appeared to be doing what older men do; talking about old times and the weather.

"Hudson, this is great!" Todd said in a whisper. "Those men are the elders of the city. Because of their wisdom and experience, they are like the Governor, Mayor, State Supreme Court Judge and Councilmen all rolled into one. If someone has a problem, they bring it to those men who then arbitrate it. It seemed to work out well for the time."

Hudson nodded.

The town was much like any first century Israeli community. It consisted of a dozen small houses, some of which were connected forming a square with a courtyard in the middle. Several homes were larger and had attached barns full of sheep, goats, mules, and a number of chickens pecking at the ground.

The men walked through the dusty streets looking for obvious signs of Jesus: crowds, excitement, or a dozen men hanging around with nothing to do, but found nothing. When they came upon a young girl, Todd began to speak with her.

"It looks as though they were here earlier," Todd said to his partner, "but she says they left a while ago. They were evidently heading to Jerusalem."

"We did our best," replied the agent.

Todd began speaking to the girl once again, and then turned to Hudson.

"Hey man, this is the chance of a thousand lifetimes. She says that Mary and Martha's house is just up the street. Want to go and see it?"

"Just a couple minutes and we head back," the agent said reluctantly.

They walked several blocks and found the house that the girl said belonged to the famous friends of Jesus. The time travelers couldn't believe that they were within a few feet of where Jesus had been just hours earlier.

Todd continued in the same direction a few feet further and saw the hillside past the houses.

"Hudson, come look at this."

The man complied and looked at the rocky mound behind the houses.

"Do you see something interesting about that area?" Todd said pointing.

"Not necessarily."

"That's a cemetery. See the large round rocks placed every three meters or so?"

"Yes."

"They cover tombs. What struck my eye is that one isn't covering the hole next to it."

"Okay?" he said as a question.

"Hudson, these people didn't just keep their graves open. They were always closed unless they were preparing for a burial. I would bet that was Lazarus' grave," he said pointing. "He was raised maybe a week ago. He would have been buried near the home, preferably in some type of hillside. I'll bet that's where Lazarus was raised from the grave.

Can you see the picture?" he said turning back to his friend. "Jesus would have been standing three or four feet from the opening," he said pointing back to the spot.

"I'm getting goose bumps. They would have rolled the rock away and he would have said, 'Lazarus, come forth.' Everyone around would have heard the dead man moving inside, and Lazarus would have walked from the grave as if nothing ever happened.

I can't believe I'm here...now!"

Hudson gave a determined look, "We must get back. It's about an hour and a half until sundown where Jesus is back on the grid with a recorded agenda. It's vital that we get to the Upper Room before Clark does."

Just a small sliver of sun remained in the sky, casting a red hue across the heavens as Todd and Hudson returned to Aaliyah's residence. Even though the sky was still full of light, the professor could see more stars than were possible to count. The atmosphere, undefiled by industrial pollution was another rare treat for the seminary professor and outdoorsman.

Todd had been chasing accomplishments all of his life. He possessed flight instructor, jump, and scuba certifications. He was a professional in martial arts, had an earned Ph.D. and was an accomplished author and archaeologist; but none of these activities gave him any joy. The experience junkie would finish one project just to start another, and never feel fulfilled.

This unbelievable experience was teaching him that life was to be cherished and lived to the fullest. Jesus Christ came to earth so that he-Todd-could have life and have it more abundantly. It took a 2000-year jump into the past to teach the professor this simple lesson; he was determined to be a different man when and if he returned home.

Because of the time it took the men to trek the four mile round trip, they were pressed when they returned. Upon entering their patroness's small home, they saw a large amount of food ready and waiting on the table.

Hudson, "We don't have time for this. We have to find the Upper Room."

"I know, but I'm starved. We've been shot, punched, kicked, cut up, and to add to that, just finished a four-mile hike. We need to eat; this could be a long night," Todd said sitting next to the table.

The three held hands as Hudson prayed and Todd interpreted. Aaliyah was just beginning to understand what Jesus would go through for her. She hadn't yet accepted Christ in her heart but enjoyed the time of prayer. She enjoyed the company most of all.

The time that the men were in her home, meant that she wasn't alone. Aaliyah had been by herself as a social outcast for years, so this short respite from the harshness of life was a literal lifesaver for the young woman. She would go through a tradition she didn't understand to have the touch of another human being.

After the "Amen," everyone began to eat.

Hudson pulled off a piece of bread, dipped it into the stew and looked over at his partner. "Do you know where the Upper Room is?"

"I know where the twenty-first century Upper Room is, and I hope that'll help us with the real one."

"Why wouldn't they be the same?"

"It's that old crusader thing again," said Todd looking over at Hudson.

"The Franciscan Upper Room that tourists from our time visit was made around the 14th century. What makes it awkward is that is has a mihrab or niche in one of the walls. That was added around the 16th century so that the Muslims who took it over would know which way to pray toward Mecca."

The professor broke off two pieces of bread and tore off a chunk of cheese to place between them. He continued his lecture.

"Hudson, it's almost impossible to know exactly where 2000 year old events occurred. We have to trust sites that have churches on them. The Emperor Hadrian in the 3rd century said during one of his visits that most of Jerusalem was destroyed except for a few churches, one of which was believed to be the spot for the Upper Room. However, in the 5th century, no one knew where Jesus conducted the Last Supper. The site was forgotten.

In the 7th century the Persians came through and destroyed all of the churches. However, 600 years later, the Franciscan Monks built a church on the spot they believed to be where Jesus performed the memorable ordinance. Then the Turks ransacked the place in the 16th century leaving Arabic writing that's still visible in our century.

What we know for sure is that Jesus performed his Last Supper in either an extra room or a meeting room above someone's house."

Todd looked over at Aaliyah who had been watching the men intently during the dialogue. He questioned her on the subject.

After several minutes, the professor looked over at Hudson once again. "She says there are several buildings that might fit the qualifications. One is northeast and one is west."

"Which one is it?"

"I went through and told her about the biblical passage. Both testimonies from Mark and Luke say that a man will be going to get water and that the disciples are to follow him and speak with the owner of the house that he enters. This implies that the owner is wealthy because he has servants getting water. The Bible also says that the man will offer them a fully furnished room for their meal.

She believes that the house to our west is the best fit. It's the largest and the owner would have enough money to have an extra room that's completely furnished. She added that the owner has people in quite often.

From her description, the area fits with where the Crusader Upper Room is currently located."

"She sure is informative." Hudson said as he stuffed down several more bites and retrieved his gun from under his outer garment. Pulling out the clip, he counted the remaining rounds.

"How many?" Todd questioned.

"Only two."

"What about the other gun?"

Hudson responded, "It's empty."

After replacing the weapon, he said, "Are you ready?"

"I think so," Todd said, tearing a final piece of bread and standing.

The professor walked around to the fireplace where Aaliyah was beginning to clean up. After he spoke to her for a few seconds, she placed her hand on his face and began to speak.

"*Baruch ata ha-Shem Elohaynu melech ha-olam ha-gomel lechayavim tovov shegemalani kol tov.*"

He touched her face and started to leave.

Hudson was confused. "What was that all about?" he said heading for the door.

Todd picked up his staff. "I just told her that after tonight, all of the problems would be over."

"What did she say?"

"She offered up a traditional Jewish blessing. She said, 'Blessed are You, Lord, our God, King of the Universe, who bestows good things on the unworthy, and has bestowed on me every goodness.'"

"Better words could not have been said," Hudson replied as the men left the house.

Todd and Hudson ran as fast as their first century sandals would allow. After covering a distance of approximately a quarter of a mile, the professor started to slow down and look around.

The men were located on the south end of the wall, a little less than a quarter of a mile from its western end. The professor turned around in a circle looking at all of the multilevel mismatched dwellings.

"Where is it?" asked Hudson.

"Give me a second," he whispered back. "In the first century, the government didn't set standards for home building. So, some houses may have seven or eight foot ceilings whereas others might have six. A two-story house may look like a tall one-story."

He paused with a sigh of frustration.

"I don't see it."

"Oh Lord, let us find it," Hudson prayed.

Todd looked at the corner of the ancient wall and tried to think of where the contemporary Upper Room was with reference to it. He closed his eyes in the middle of the ancient dirt street and focused on the picture in his mind.

Following a few seconds of silence, the professor opened his eyes and said, "We're too close to the wall."

Todd turned around and began to walk south. The men passed house after house. Even though each looked basically the same, being made of clay mortar, sandstones, and wooden timbers coming through the outer edge of the roof; they were all unique.

Hudson had been in the Ancient City for several days but hadn't noticed the disparity between houses until Todd brought it up. Buildings sitting right next to each other could vary by several feet in roof height. Some houses were long and narrow while others were short and wide. As they were walking south he noticed that one house might have a side window where the next would not.

Looking up to the southeast, Todd started to run. The two men rounded the corner of a row of dwellings and found the opening to a courtyard. In the center of the courtyard formed by four straight house rows, stood a large two-story building.

The residence was formed out of the same rock and timbers as every other house. It had the same sandstone color, but was uncharacteristically long for the first century; approximately 70 feet in length and possibly 30 feet deep. The building was a full two stories tall and had a doorway centered along the length of the structure.

The courtyard was immaculately manicured. The ground was smooth and the few trees were neatly trimmed.

The men looked at each other expectantly and Todd broke the silence, "That has to be it."

Hudson looked up and saw a row of windows on the second floor. There was obvious movement coming from within the room, but Hudson wondered who was forming the shadows on the walls and ceiling.

"I need to see in those windows," Hudson mumbled.

He looked around the courtyard and found a large tree that he thought, with Todd's help, would allow him visual access to the second floor.

"Come with me," the agent whispered.

The men ran around the eastern row of houses that formed the courtyard and found access to the large tree. Todd helped the sizeable man up, and Hudson climbed onto a limb leaning into the courtyard. Still not able to see, he continued farther up the large sycamore until he had a clear view of the room.

While looking through the windows, the agent saw a room full of men. Each person varied in size and age and no one was saying a word. They all seemed to be focused on one person who was not visble to Hudson from his position.

After moving to another limb, he knew that they were in the right place. The man he had seen on Solomon's porch, who had touched his heart without saying a word, and would die on a cross in twelve hours was sitting right in front of him going through his last supper.

Once, on assignment, Hudson had personally seen the most famous painting of the Last Supper in the convent of Santa Maria della Grazie in Milan. Leonardo Da Vinci's interpretation had the men sitting on stools along one side of a long table with Jesus in the center. They ate from pewter plates, were in a beautiful Corinthian style room that overlooked the Jerusalem countryside and had on their most colorful Sunday best. However, man's best ability could not paint the real beauty of the scene.

The room was nice, but simple. No Corinthian fluting lined the edge of the ceiling, no wood-trimmed windows overlooking rolling hills. The table was approximately a foot from the ground and square in shape. These men could never afford clothes with the many colors found in the world-famous painting, but donned simple tan and brown tunics and mantles.

They did not eat from individual plates but pulled their food from center wooden trays. Because this was the Passover, the meal consisted of hard boiled eggs, roasted lamb, and matzah bread. The agent could also see some type of greens, a bowl of herbs-most likely bitter herbs, and a bowl full of chopped fruit which was probably haroset.

Jesus did sit at the head of the table which was situated on one of the corners. From that position, the Savior had everyone's attention as he taught what was to come and how they were to continue.

"What's going on? Are we in the right place?" Todd whispered while standing at the base of the tree.

Hudson looked at the scene once more trying to memorize every nuance his eyes could take in. When he felt there wasn't another sight his mind could absorb, he whispered down to his partner.

"I'm coming down," Hudson said while pointing to the ground.

Todd helped Hudson the last few feet down the trunk of the large tree.

"Are we in the right place?"

"Yes, this is it. It's unbelieveable. I'll tell you all about it later. However now we need to circle the building and see if there are any other ways in. Also, look for potential hiding spots or other openings into the compound. You head left and I'll head right. Let's meet on the other side of the square. And Todd, be thorough and careful. Clark could be here right now," Hudson said with a focus in his eyes.

The men separated and each went a different direction. After three minutes the men reconnected behind a bush next to the wall of a house and compared notes.

"Hudson, all of the buildings are connected on my side. Except for the main entrance into the compound, there's no other way into the courtyard.

I only saw the one entrance into the house, the front door. Of course, there are many windows that someone could go through."

Todd pointed, "Just up the street there's a park-like area that we could hide out in. I guess Clark could hide there also." He stopped for a second.

"Man, I didn't see anyone waiting around and there aren't too many places for someone to hide."

Hudson responded, "I saw the same type things. There's another center door in the back of the house, but that was the only one I saw. The big problem we have is that every one of these houses encircling the Upper Room has a back door leading onto the courtyard. Clark could have commandeered any of these homes and be waiting for his time to strike.

While I was up in the tree, I noticed several large bushes sitting on one end of the main house. If we can hide behind them, we'll be able to separately watch each entrance and spot Clark when he comes.

"Sounds good, let's go."

The men ran back to the main opening of the courtyard and looked around the perimeter. Hudson couldn't see anyone else and looked for possible places around the outer wall that Clark could hide. After he felt that the area was safe, they quietly ran for the bushes.

Hudson took his position behind the farthest bush next to the house. He believed that Clark would try to make his entrance through the back, mainly because that's what he would do in the same situation. Todd followed closely, taking his position next to the bush toward the front of the house. The men huddled down ready for a long night.

The time travelers watched the entrances diligently without moving. They heard the occasional noise and would search to find its origin, but inevitably found it had come from a bird or mischievous squirrel.

The men on the second floor eventually broke their silence and began to talk and occasionally laugh. Todd thought to himself during the long ordeal that it would have been great to know Jesus the man. He always thought that Jesus would have had a great sense of humor; a man full of a joy that could be seen through his countenance and observations of the world. The laughter coming from the men upstairs helped to solidify his thoughts.

Looking to the sky, Hudson saw a canvas of stars pressed against a dark blue background. Because he'd spent years in the Boy Scouts, he could fairly easily tell the time. The agent remembered taking his position next to the house around 8:15 and by looking again at the star orientation, noted that they had been in their spots for over two hours. Something was wrong and Hudson moved over to his partner for the first time during the stakeout.

Hudson whispered, "What's wrong?"

"I have the same feeling. Where's Clark?" he said in hushed tones. "It sounds like the men upstairs are about ready to go and nothing's happened.

Clark knows where this place is?" he questioned knowing the answer.

"Of course. He knows everything that we know, if not more. The guy has been trained extensively for this mission."

"So then where is he?"

Hudson sat for a second. "Let's think this through. Clark knows that tonight is his last opportunity to get Jesus. It's common knowledge that

Jesus performs the Last Supper in the Upper Room and then goes to the Garden of Gethsemane to pray before he's arrested.

He'll have been taught where the Upper Room is and where to find the garden, so why isn't he here?"

Todd spoke up, "Maybe he's putting all of his eggs in one basket and plans on getting Jesus in the garden."

"Possibly, but I'd bet against it. This mission is too important to only make one attempt on Jesus' life. If he misses in the garden he's sunk.

He has to know that we're going to be anywhere that Jesus is, whether here or in the garden. However, later in the garden, there'll also be priests and soldiers."

Todd jumped in. "Jesus will break off to pray by himself at some point; if I were him, that's where I'd strike."

"Yeah, me too, except we'll still be there. It's dangerous enough to attempt this without knowing there'll be two body guards on Jesus the whole time."

Hudson leaned against the wall of the house, hearing the men above and thinking through the situation.

After a minute of silence, Hudson leaned forward with a face showing sudden awareness and deep concern.

"Todd, we know that Clark's aware of our presence here. It's obvious that we're going to try to stop him."

"Of course."

"He also knows that we'd follow Jesus to the garden."

"I'm with you."

"What if Clark's planning his big strike like you said earlier, when Jesus prays, but is attempting to remove us from the equation. That'd put him alone with the Savior long enough to get away unseen."

"How's he going to get rid of us? It's two against one and we know where he's going to be."

"Todd, what if he's using this time to divide and draw us off?"

"What do you mean? We're here. Jesus is above us, and right now very safe," he said confused.

Hudson looked to the ground, grimaced, and squeezed his temples with this desperate prayer, "How could I have not thought this through? Oh Lord, please let me be wrong."

He stood up, "Todd, we have one weakness in our armor, and I pray that the madman hasn't found it."

"What's our weakness?"

"Aaliyah!"

The reality of the situation fell upon the professor like a ton of bricks. The two men ran as fast as they could from the courtyard without any concern for who saw them.

The two concerned men ran as fast as possible toward Aaliyah's small dwelling. The streets on the southern side of the Holy City were virtually empty of traffic, and except for the random chicken pecking at the ground or dog walking by, there were no obstructions to slow their progress.

Hudson's worry grew as he got closer. *Please Lord, don't let me be right,* he thought to himself. *How could I have made such a mistake?*

Such mistakes had happened regularly since he had been in Israel. At the recollection of each obvious error, his gut twisted. Up to this point, each blunder had involved only him, and only his life was at stake. That knowledge, even though unacceptable, softened the beatings he continually gave himself. This slip-up was different; it could cost Aaliyah her life.

The agent continued his sprint as he drew a weapon from the shoulder holster under his tunic, while the professor kept up with the larger man foot for foot. Todd had to run faster due to his smaller stature, but the thought of someone hurting his Aaliyah surged adrenaline through his body at a rate that would allow him to run at top speed for hours.

As the men passed the Zion gate and inched closer to the Dung gate, the professor began to think about the gentle woman who had taken them in. He began to pray. *God, how can I have feelings for a woman who died 2000 years before I was born? Lord, you know that this isn't possible, and yet I think I love her. Please let her be safe. Lord, take care of her.*

The beauty of the night and the majesty of the Holy City could not get Todd's mind away from the possible situation ahead. He thrust the staff into the other hand and pressed forward.

The five-minute run felt like it had taken hours when they finally came into view of the small row of houses. Hudson thrust out his hand after they entered the alley next to the dwelling to stop Todd from running to the front.

"What are you doing? Let's get in there," whispered Todd, out of breath.

"Just a second," Hudson said while holding his index finger to his lips.

With his gun pointed forward, the agent crept nearer the building looking around the corner and casing the front of the structure. Thoroughly scanning the area, nothing seemed out of place, and he could hear no voices. Everything was quiet.

Waving Todd forward, the men moved around the corner. The professor had his staff pointed forward ready to strike while Hudson focused on the doorway. Scanning the open countryside, he searched each possible hiding place as they inched their way onward.

Once the two men arrived at Aaliyah's doorway, Hudson moved on past and pressed his back against the side door jam; Todd forcing himself against the opposite side. The agent positioned his ear next to the opening but couldn't discern sounds within the structure because of the wind noise between the buildings.

The moon's reflection lit the street well enough for the professor to make out Hudson mouthing the words, "On three." The agent held up three fingers. Todd knew the plan.

Hudson showed one finger and readied his weapon as Todd tightened the grip on his staff.

A second finger went up and both heart rates jumped exponentially.

Hudson looked Todd directly in the eyes and raised three fingers. Instantaneously, the agent ran through Aaliyah's makeshift door with the professor following closely behind. They entered a nightmare they weren't prepared for.

Aaliyah was sobbing quietly and standing in the center of the room with her hands tied behind her back and mouth gagged. Hudson couldn't see under her garment but guessed that her feet were tied also.

From the woman's neck hung a covered clay water pot that seemed to want to pull her forward. Surrounding the young woman who had obviously been beaten was a perimeter made from her tables and chairs turned on their sides.

Hudson stopped his movement and noticed why the elaborate setup was necessary; inside the makeshift perimeter were at least half of a dozen snakes. All of the reptiles looked to be of the same type because of their identical brownish gray coloring and dark brown chevrons detailing the entire extent of their backs. Each was approximately two and a half to three feet in length and were all coiled in a separate spot within the bordered area.

"Hello gentlemen, I was about to leave," said a voice from the darkness.

Within a millisecond, Hudson had his gun aimed at the shadowy figure while Todd was ready to strike with his staff.

246

"Blackwell, I wouldn't shoot. You're going to need every single bullet to help your little friend over there," he said pointing at Aaliyah.

The terrified woman started moaning through her gagged mouth.

Clark stepped from the shadows dressed as a first century Roman soldier. He wore a tunic and skirt. His chest was covered with a breastplate and his wrists and ankles were covered with guards. A feathered helmet and cape completed the outfit.

"That's a Captain of the Guards uniform," yelled Todd.

"He won't need it anymore," Clark said in a menacing bass voice, turning a bloody short sword in his hand.

Todd was about to jump at the assassin when he showed his other hand that had been kept behind him until now. The bag was squirming and moving.

"Oh Lord, please help us," said Todd as he began to speak to Aaliyah.

She was crying and pleading with her eyes. Her moans became louder.

"Don't speak to her!" growled Clark. "Silence!" he barked while pointing to the small woman.

"What do you want?" asked Hudson.

"Don't think that you can give me anything. I already have what I want. I have you tied up trying to save that little nothing over there," he said while pointing to Aaliyah, "while I go and finish my mission. I will kill Jesus tonight!" he smiled wickedly.

Todd ran at the large man in the intimidating outfit but stopped when Clark thrust the writhing bag in front of him.

"I wasn't sure that you'd make it back tonight. I placed all of my wagers on the bet that you would wonder why I wasn't at the Upper Room.

I knew that you thought of yourself as a hero," he said to Hudson. "Even though she means nothing to history, if you thought she was in danger, you'd try to help."

Hudson was fuming and aimed the gun between Clark's eyes.

Clark continued, this time looking at Todd. "And you, you have a thing going on with her, don't you? It's probably breaking you up inside to not kill me in front of her so you can look like the man who saves the day. If you killed me, she'd probably give you all of her undying affection."

Clark sent a smirk toward Todd, "Hey buddy, I may be helping you out in this situation."

Todd had never felt so much hate.

"It looks like my bet paid off, you guys made it back, and now I have Jesus alone in the garden by himself," the assassin said with a laugh.

Todd inched over and started talking to Aaliyah again.

"I said, don't talk to her. She has enough to worry about."

Clark walked over toward the crude border and looked at the terrified woman. "You know, so far it's been pretty boring."

Hudson mocked Clark, "Where did those cuts on your arms come from?"

"Yeah, she's a spicy one. I'll never be the same. The marks will be something that we can remember each other by."

Aaliyah screeched when he got close.

Todd spoke to her reassuringly.

Clark continued, "Yeah, I'd have expected one of those snakes to have gotten her by now. She's fairly cool under pressure. She hasn't moved an inch," he stopped his speech for a second.

"But the weight around her neck isn't getting any lighter. I'd bet that her back is really starting to ache."

Todd felt so lost. His innocent beauty has been through so much because of their intrusion, and now they might not be able to get her out of this situation.

Hudson whispered over to his partner, "Do you know what kind of snakes those are?"

"No."

"I'll tell ya' guys, it wasn't easy to find these reptiles, but if you press people the right way, they become very helpful."

"What kind of snakes are they?" yelled Hudson.

"It wouldn't be any fun if I told you, now would it? Besides, there isn't any antivenin in the first century. Let's just say that if you are bitten by one of them, you might have 12 hours-if you did everything right.

And your yelling isn't going to bring anyone. The first thing I did before coming to see your sweet friend was to neutralize any possible opposition. You should've expected me to be very thorough."

Clark moved closer to the perimeter with his bag in front of him. "Guys it's been fun.

I'd bet that you started your trek here when the men were leaving the Upper Room. So I don't have much time before I meet with Jesus."

"I can't let you go," said Hudson inching forward with the gun.

"You can and you will." Clark reached over and put his hand on the top of the jar that was hanging from Aaliyah's neck.

He looked directly into Hudson's eyes, "This is going to be fun Blackwell."

Instantly he pulled the top from the jar and threw both that and the bag at the agent as the assassin ran for the front doorway. Aaliyah let out intermittent moans and yells at the top of her voice through her gag, and the bag that was aimed at Hudson hit the floor and let out another half dozen snakes of all shapes and colors.

Todd was able to hit Clark with his staff before he left the building but his armor protected him from the blow. Hudson jumped from the area with the snakes and shot at the doorway, but could not chase after the assailant. He had too many problems of his own.

Aaliyah was screaming. Crying and wailing loudly as possible with the gag in her mouth. Something in that jar had unnerved her and she was beginning to upset the snakes coiled around her.

Hudson yelled over at his partner as he moved away from a large snake. "What's in that jar?"

"I don't know, it's too deep for me to see into," said Todd as he started striking every snake possible with his staff.

Hudson picked up jars and pots and started to smash them on anything moving. They killed quite a few reptiles very quickly but hadn't even started to deal with the situation Aaliyah was in.

If Hudson were right about the man they were chasing, the snakes they were presently fighting were harmless. Clark would have put the most dangerous reptiles in with Aaliyah.

After several minutes, the men had either chased out or killed the bag full of snakes aimed at keeping them distracted. That left the square with the screaming woman in the middle.

The perimeter was about five feet on a side, which kept the men from getting to Aaliyah without the possibility of falling into the square.

Todd continued speaking to Aaliyah, but it didn't calm her cries. She was becoming more and more unpredictable by the second. She would try to hop from the square if they didn't do something.

Todd looked over at Hudson, "What if we just remove a table and see if the snakes try to leave.

"Good plan."

Todd removed the table closest to the door and several snakes began to make their way from the square. Each one that left, Todd would strike with the staff. The two men were chasing off the deadly snakes as quickly as they left the perimeter. The ones that wouldn't leave forced the men to improvise and throw anything left in the room to move the reptiles from their position next to Aaliyah.

One by one, they coaxed the reptiles away from Aaliyah and out of the house. Yet, the woman didn't stop screaming. Her eyes were even wider than before.

When all of the snakes were taken care of, Todd pulled the jar from around her neck and looked inside. He threw the jar out of shock and instinct. It was now obvious why she was so frightened, for in the bottom of the container was a severed head; most likely from the Captain of the Guards. He ran over and covered the remains of the fallen soldier.

Hudson untied her hands but she continued to remain very still and moan. Todd removed the gag and she immediately began to frantically cry and plead with him.

"Oh, no. Hudson, get back." He moved back and Todd pulled up Aaliyah's skirt a foot and saw why she hadn't calmed down.

Both men looked at each other.

Under her garment was the largest of the snakes in the fenced area. It had wrapped itself around her tied legs and looked very angry at the intruders uncovering its hiding place. It was not going to be easy to remove.

Aaliyah began to shake.

"Tell her to relax," whispered Hudson.

Todd tried to calm her, but it wasn't helping. The events of the evening had taken Aaliyah to her breaking point and within a few seconds she was going to collapse.

"Hudson, you get its' attention, and I'll try to grab it around the neck from behind."

"What are you talking about? That snake is deadly."

"It's all that we can do."

Hudson took Todd's staff, and standing behind the terrified woman, began to move it in front of the coiled snake. Aaliyah's trembling was beginning to upset the dangerous reptile.

Gently moving in front of the woman, he raised her skirt to her knees with one hand and with the other, slowly reached for the snake's neck. Todd was within inches of the angry predator when the woman began shaking so violently that she stumbled.

Todd, with lightning reflexes, grabbed the snake, but not until after it had bitten Aaliyah on the calf. He threw the snake toward the door, and it slithered into the night.

Aaliyah fainted and both men dropped to their knees to help.

"Let's get her over to the bed," said Todd.

Gently picking her light frame up in his arms, Todd moved her over to the bed. Raising her skirt high enough to see the bite, the men untied her legs and looked at the wound on her calf. Their worst fears were true; two holes accentuated the place where the snake had punctured her skin.

Hudson tore a long strip of cloth from his tunic's edge and tied it tight around her leg just under the knee as Todd ran for water.

"Clark said we have twelve hours," Hudson muttered in a determined voice as he headed for the doorway.

"Where are you going?" said Todd returning with rags and water.

"After him! He's still after Jesus. If our Lord doesn't make it to the cross, it won't matter what happens to the rest of us. He also has to tell us who sent him on this mission and what kind of snake bit Aaliyah."

Hudson stopped and looked at his partner, "She won't die; you have my promise."

The agent ran from the house.

After leaving the snake pit, Clark sped toward the area he knew to be the Garden of Gethsemane. Normally such a short jog would have been a mere warm-up for the distance runner, but, carrying around 35 pounds in armor and running in sandals made the trek more difficult.

The assassin reached the olive grove in a little more than fifteen minutes. His initial thoughts were those of concern because of his uncertainty as to where Jesus would be. However, after ten minutes of searching, he heard a group of men climbing the hillside toward his position and knew that he was in the right place.

Clark melted into the trees and watched the men's progress. Just a few minutes from completing his mission, he could almost smell the T-Bone steak waiting for him in the twenty-first century.

—

Located due east of the Ancient City, the Garden of Gethsemane stood on a hillside above the Kidron Valley possibly a half of a mile from the Temple Mount and a mile and a half from the Upper Room. Hudson had visited the garden several times while guarding the President, however, in each of those instances he was in a motorcade being lead by Israeli dignitaries who either knew where they were going or followed the well placed signs along the route. Tonight was different.

Hudson ran through Jerusalem in the dark, hoping to make his way to the area he remembered from the twenty-first century. Using the light of the moon, he navigated the narrow paths between the houses on the south side of the Mount, stumbling over every rock and bump in his path. The weary man continued despite the cuts and bruises from the obstacles in his way.

It wasn't the sudden instances of hitting the ground that were bothering the seasoned agent for he had been through much worse many times before. In the years he spent in the Secret Service he had experienced many close calls and learned to cope well with pressure; this time there was no coping. With all of his training, talent and abilities, he was not equipped for this mission. For the first time in Hudson's life, he wasn't prepared. Without God's help he didn't have the strength or energy to complete his task.

While running to the garden, Hudson had time to truly think about the outcomes that were possible if God didn't work. Each result scared him more than the one before; every one reminding him of his inability and God's sufficiency.

Hudson thought through the best of the possibilities; the one where he captured Clark allowing Jesus to complete his life's mission, saved Aaliyah, and returned with Todd safely to the twenty-first century to resume the lives they had before the assignment. The agent was no MIT statistician, but knew that the odds of all of those things going just that way were more astronomical than anything he could calculate. *Lord, please work this out,* he thought as he left the populated area south of the Holy City and entered the Kidron Valley.

Every option after the 'Happily Ever After' ending involved someone losing his or her life. Jesus dying was the worst of the possibilities because that essentially meant that everyone on earth would be lost without a Savior. Then of course, the next 'best' option-if there was such a thing-was where Aaliyah died.

Hudson's insides began to ache. The young woman had been so kind and trusting toward the time travelers and so far all they had brought her was danger, and possibly death within twelve hours. To add more pressure, how could he look his partner in the face if she died from his mistake? Hudson had never experienced that type of failure before and was going to give his all to ensure that it didn't happen now. *Oh Lord, please protect her.*

The agent ran parallel to the eastern wall until he lined up with the Golden Gate. Turning to the right, he began a run up the hill, leaving the valley and starting the last quarter of a mile to the garden.

The thoughts ran through the agent's mind as fast as his feet were carrying him to the final segment of the mission. Hudson had been on many operations and always knew there was a chance that he could be killed, and in the past was always able to remove all personal thoughts and focus on the task. That was not the case this time. In a very few minutes, he would be confronting the assassin one on one, and unless God intervened, one of them would die.

No matter how he tried to delude himself, Hudson knew that Clark was not going to go back to the twenty-first century with him. Even if the madman failed in his mission of killing Jesus, he couldn't be left to his own design in an innocent time with no restraints. Without control, he might just start killing people to see how he could destroy the timeline of the future. No, Clark would have to be stopped, and the only way to do that was to kill him.

Hudson tumbled over several rocks on the hill face toward the garden, but continued in the ascent. *Lord, let me be your vessel. I don't know how this is going to end, but let me glorify you in my actions.*

As the agent pulled himself up from the ground once again, he looked the hillside over and thought he heard a group of men's voices. He pressed on.

Upon reaching the top, he saw Jesus and his entourage entering the garden and promptly hid himself behind a stone shelf. When Hudson looked back over his shoulder, it was easy to understand why his Lord would choose this place to pray. It was situated among beautiful fruit trees, had rocky knolls for seclusion and overlooked the Ancient City. In Hudson's time, the Church of All Nations-or Basilica of the Agony-would occupy this place. Even though a beautiful structure, it paled in comparison to the natural beauty of the rustic garden.

The garden was not like one would see on a farm in rural America. Two thousand years from now, heavy machinery would till the earth producing beautiful straight lines for planting. Here, the area looked to have planted itself. The trunks of the trees were generally ten feet apart but there was no real plan to the area. Hudson would have to stay close to the men to ensure that he didn't lose them in the region replete with hills and rocky outcroppings.

Looking over at the group of men making their way into the garden, the agent believed he could move undetected. He started to leave his secluded spot to follow the disciples until he saw a shimmer of light. It radiated from a location around 60 feet to the south of Jesus' present position. He returned to his hiding place and kept his eyes on the area.

Remaining motionless for over a minute, Hudson saw the glimmer once again. The agent made out the form. It was a man wearing a breastplate, shin guards and a hat, all made of brass; a Roman Soldier. Clark.

Hudson sat watching the man closely. Obviously aware of Jesus' position, the man dressed as the Captain of the Guards was slowly following the disciples through the thick dense garden, hoping to find a place to strike. The agent was on the offensive.

Clark hid in a dense grove of olive trees once he heard Jesus and his disciples approaching. The required readings told him that Peter carried a sword, and there was a good probability that several others carried various types of blades. The man wasn't sure from the biblical readings if they carried the weapons to protect Jesus or used them for various trades like cleaning fish or repairing nets.

Knowing that he was quite adept at swordplay, and with his newly acquired armor, Clark could easily overtake several. Though confident in his own abilities, he didn't know the skill of Jesus' men. There would be little benefit to completing his mission then dying from blood loss due to a stray sword to the arm or leg. He would stick with the initial plan: kill Jesus as he went off by himself to pray.

Clark watched the group enter the garden and kept low until he thought the men were far enough ahead that he could start to follow. Because of the noise his armor was making with the closely knit trees, he decided to work his way to the edge of the grove and follow the men from there.

With no one else around, and Blackwell still locked down with reptiles, the trained assassin moved in closer behind his mark.

—

Hudson watched as Jesus and his disciples disappeared into the dense olive grove. Seeing Clark following behind, he left the safety and protection of the rocky shelf in which he was hiding and quietly moved to follow the group; keeping a distance of about 75 feet.

Following a five-minute walk, Jesus and the disciples stopped their progression and sat down for a while. Hudson was amazed at all of the talking coming from the disciples. They had just experienced a final supper and Passover with their Lord and weren't in a somber mood. The men weren't laughing, but the agent would have expected a more reverent frame of mind. It was obvious that Jesus' followers didn't understand what he was about to go through in the next 12 hours. Hudson now appreciated Jesus' continual disappointment with the men; they would have to mature before they could take over his ministry.

Keeping his eyes on Jesus, the assassin recessed into the trees, waiting for his opportunity. Hudson began to creep toward his enemy, but stopped his forward movement and huddled behind the nearest tree when he saw Jesus stand.

Jesus spoke to his disciples for several minutes then took three of them with him as he moved approximately 30 feet farther northwest. Remembering the passage in Matthew saying that he would take Peter,

James and John with him to pray, Hudson assumed these were the men following now.

Knowing Clark was ready to strike, the agent moved closer to the mock soldier and pulled his weapon. The highly trained marksman had a clear shot of the back of the assassin's head and could easily kill him, ending the mission; but doing so didn't feel right.

Everything in Hudson's being was against taking a life, but he wanted to kill Clark. He wanted to protect his Savior, and gain vengeance for the way the madman had hurt so many in this timeline, yet something wasn't right. The action he was about to take was not what God wanted for him or for Clark.

He re-aimed at his target, and with all of his might wanted to pull the trigger. He couldn't. The Lord, even though presently praying, was telling him not to kill Clark; God had another plan for the man intent on murdering his son.

Lord, what am I to do, he prayed while staring at the assassin, *I want your biblical story to be unchanged. I don't want to go back to my century and read in your Bible of a man who tried to kill you before you were arrested. Lord, tell me what to do.*

Instantly, God's presence and guidance flooded him. Hudson knew that he wasn't to kill Clark, but, was free to keep him from getting any closer to Jesus while he was praying. The agent freed his hands by replacing the weapon in its makeshift holster against his chest and prepared for his next move.

Feeling adrenaline surging through his veins, it was difficult to remain motionless, but Hudson sat pensively for close to ten minutes. Clark did not move, not an inch. He remained in a crouched position with no signs of leaving.

What is going on, thought Hudson, *why isn't he moving?*

Hudson's attentions were drawn back to the circle of men. Jesus had reentered the disciple's prayer area and was pushing on the men trying to awaken them. He was not angry, but had a more disappointed sound in his voice. It was clear that they were to be awake praying rather than sleeping. Getting the disciples back on their knees, Jesus left again to pray.

Clark remained motionless through the whole ordeal. He just watched the situation quietly from a distance.

Hudson slowly moved ten feet closer. Finding a position behind a large rock and keeping his eyes on the madman, he prepared to fight when the time came.

Why isn't he moving? This is the perfect time to get Jesus.

Then Hudson remembered God's word. Jesus goes off to pray three times and only on the third entrance is he arrested.

Clark must be waiting until after the Lord's second wake-up call to strike. The followers will be the most tired and will fall into the deepest level of sleep. This will allow him the most freedom to attack Jesus unnoticed.

Hudson's attention was drawn once again to the group of men before him. Jesus had come back into the camp, expecting his disciples to be praying and finding them asleep. The Lord went through the same process of waking the men and then headed back to his secluded spot.

Clark began to move. It was slow, but perceptible. Working his way from tree to tree, he moved toward the praying Savior. Hudson followed closely behind. It took all of the agent's restraint to keep from grabbing his gun, but knew that God didn't want him to use it. He would go into the fight unarmed; no matter what the outcome.

The highly trained agent followed stealthily for several minutes. He trailed Clark for close to 30 feet before his focus was redirected to the sight of a man illuminated by the moonlight.

The man was on his knees with his hands reaching to the sky. Tears ran down his face as he pleaded with the heavens. The sight of Jesus grieving for lost humanity showed Hudson how much his Lord truly loved him.

Jesus, in that small clearing, was asking that the suffering he was about to go through be taken away. Yet knew it was his destiny to save humanity. Hudson saw a man resolute in mission and determined to fulfill his father's wish.

The agent's attentions were redirected when he noticed Clark pulling something from his waist. The object gleaming in the moonlight was the sword the madman was preparing to use against Jesus.

Knowing there was no more time to wait; Hudson picked up a rock and ran at the assassin with all the speed he could produce. It took about four seconds for the agent to span the distance. Just a split second before Hudson collided with the heavily armed man; Clark looked to his left but didn't have enough time to react. He was banged in the helmet with the rock and knocked to the ground with the force of a freight train.

The men rolled close to ten feet upon hitting the ground. Clark dropped his sword and lost his helmet during the fall. Their present position placed them out of the reach of the praying Jesus, which pleased Hudson, but meant he was one on one with a man who would very quickly understand that his plan was blown.

Clark regained his senses and pounced on Hudson. He straddled the agent, throwing as many blows toward his enemy's face as possible. Hudson did his best to defer them, and thrust his knee up, hitting the groin of the angry man on top of him. The intense pain caused Clark to fall to his side, freeing the man trapped below.

Hudson jumped to his feet and waited as Clark endured several difficult seconds of pain.

"You aren't going to stop me," Clark groaned out the words.

The two men collided once again with Hudson falling to his back. This time he grabbed onto Clark's shield, forcing the assassin into a Judo roll. As the agent rolled onto his back, he kicked Clark under the leg increasing the momentum of Clark's forward movement forcing the assassin down so quickly that he continued to roll over Hudson. Still holding onto the shield, Hudson rolled onto the angry man, ending in a straddling position on top of him.

Now Hudson was throwing the punches, just trying to stop Clark long enough for Jesus to be arrested. He performed several choke maneuvers, all of which Clark broke fairly quickly.

Clark pulled Hudson to one side and then the other trying to get out from under his weight. Each time the agent would counteract the force. The assassin continued the pulling long enough that he eventually moved Hudson off balance far enough to roll away.

Knowing the madman was free, Hudson jumped on him once again. The men tumbled ten feet; one on top of the other, until out of the corner of his eye, Hudson noticed a small rocky ledge. He forced the fight to the rim and threw the crazed man over.

Hitting the ground hard, four feet below, it took several seconds for Clark to get up. Hudson watched the man from the short cliff but noticed movement from behind Clark's position. A crowd was marching through the grove. Many had torches and they were being led by a contingent of soldiers and priests.

Oh no, they're here to arrest Jesus, thought Hudson.

He backed away from the edge, deeper into the olive grove and found a wild area in which to hide, his eyes never moving from Clark.

The assassin was now standing, looking at Hudson's position. He saw the man hiding in the bushes and was about to run toward Jesus' last location when he was grabbed from behind. A contingent of soldiers surrounded him with swords, and pointed at the insignia pounded into the breastplate he presently wore.

The men knew he was not the one for whom the breastplate was dedicated. They peppered him with question after question as the crowd, remaining soldiers, and priests continued their forward progression toward Jesus' position.

After five minutes of unanswered questions, the angry soldiers arrested Clark and dragged him off toward the Golden Gate of the Holy City.

"Help me Blackwell!" he screamed. "Get me out. I don't belong in this time. Get me out!"

The words stopped as a soldier knocked Clark unconscious with the handle of his sword.

Hudson looked over his shoulder and watched Judas' betrayal of Jesus to the religious leaders. The macabre scene had a deep sense of evil attached to it, and Hudson had to look away. All around he could feel a sickening dark coating of the devil's wicked glee. Surely, Satan thought he had finally won his war with God. Turning his head back, Hudson caught a last glimpse of Clark being dragged into the Ancient City.

He had kept the madman from Jesus, but Aaliyah's life was still at stake and he desperately needed information from the man being arrested. Hudson left his secure position and began running; he needed Todd's help.

Hudson entered the dwelling to find the room filled with people; a few were men, though most were women bustling around or praying. The agent made his way through the small staring crowd to Aaliyah's bed where he found his partner gently stroking the head of the unconscious woman with a damp cloth.

Todd felt responsible for what had happened to his innocent Aaliyah, and even though caressing her forehead did not help her present state, it was therapeutic for the professor's wounded conscience and broken heart. He stopped and stood when he saw Hudson arrive.

"How is she?" asked Hudson.

"She's going to die if we don't help," he said as he looked at her with a grave expression. "When you left, she told me to run to her neighbors to get help. I went to the houses on either side and found that Clark's word was good. He killed the neighbors, Hudson-just ran them through with his sword," Todd said with tears clouding his eyes.

Hudson's mouth was agape.

The professor continued. "Then I went down further and found an older woman in her bed. Her name is Ophrah," he said while pointing to a short, gray-haired lady near the fireplace, "she went to get everyone else. It looks as though Aaliyah is very well liked by the women in the community."

"Can they help her?" said Hudson fearing the answer.

"No, not really," replied Todd grabbing the agent's arm. "They know of the snake that bit Aaliyah but call it something like 'black garden death.' I think it's a tie-in to the snake in the Adam and Eve story, but I'm not sure.

They can slow the poison's progression by treating the wound with different types of herbs, but are certain that if there isn't a miracle, she will die in the next day or so."

Hudson had his hands on his hips, "How long has she been unconscious?"

"She went under just a few minutes ago. She was encouraging me the entire time that she was awake. Can you imagine that? She's the one that was bitten, we caused it, and she was telling me that she didn't hold us responsible and thanked us for the way we fought for her."

Todd began to cry while Hudson pulled him into a hug.

"She's going to be alright."

"How can you say that?"

"I don't know, I just feel that God had this thing all worked out before we got here," said Hudson as he pulled away from his partner.

"What happened on your end," said Todd wiping his eyes.

"I'll tell you about it later. Where would they take a Roman prisoner?"

"What do you mean, Jesus was a Jewish prisoner and most likely taken before the Great Beth Din or Great Sanhedrin?"

"No, Jesus has already been taken. The problem is, so has Clark. He was arrested by Roman guards. It's a long story, but we need to get to Clark and try to get him out of there."

Todd's face went stone cold. "Hudson, there'll be no getting him out of there. They'll put him in their highest level of containment. That stolen Captain's outfit will put him before an immediate trial and then'll probably get him executed; if he lives through the torture."

"Well, we have to do something," yelled Hudson as the room went silent and everyone stared.

Regaining his composure and moving back a few feet, he continued, "We still need to know who put him up to this and what kind of snake bit Aaliyah. If Clark dies here, then I guess he will have received what he deserves, but he has to give us the information."

Todd sat down for a second and rubbed his chin with his fingers. Looking up at Hudson he started to speak. "I've never really studied first century Roman law, but I'd guess that they would take Clark to the Judgment Hall or Tower of Antonio."

"Do you know where it is?"

"Yes, it's where Jesus will be in a few hours," said the professor standing and walking over to Ophrah. After a few words with the matriarch, he went over and touched Aaliyah's soft cheek.

Speaking gently, "Lord, be with this woman. Please don't let her die."

A tear fell from his cheek onto her neck. Gently wiping it away, he turned and headed for the door.

"Let's go," he said as the men left the dwelling to enter the cold air of the worst night in Israel's history.

Clark regained consciousness to the sight of a large soldier dousing him with water. His clothes, armor, and various knives were gone, leaving his naked body chained to the wall of a dark and musty stone walled room. The prison was similar to the one he had broken out of several days prior. This time, there were no gadgets or the element of surprise to help him. The assassin was in a situation that he knew he couldn't get out of.

While the soldiers peppered him with questions about the uniform, Clark tried to explain in his best Greek that he had found the uniform in a field and put it on to warm himself from the night. The obviously false story wasn't going to sway the angry group of men.

Following several hours of questions and repeated beatings to every accessible part of his body, a final kick to the assassin's head returned him to the last place of comfort; unconsciousness.

—

The men ran up the stairs of the Robinson Arch and encountered a large crowd gathered on the southwest section of Solomon's Porch.

Out of breath, Todd whispered to his partner, "These people are here because of Jesus; there's no other reason for them to be out this late," he said continuing to walk. "I'd bet that Jesus' first trial with Annas is over, and he's well into his second with Caiaphas and the Sanhedrin court. The crowd's waiting to hear the verdict. Follow me," he said pointing north.

The men ran across Solomon's porch and past the Temple to the northwest corner of the Mount. The Tower of Antonio was a large columned structure added to the upper wall of the sacred enclosed area. Known as the place where Roman politics occurred in Jerusalem, its peak soared over 30 feet higher than the walls.

"If Clark isn't here, we won't be able to find him," whispered Todd.

Discovering a set of steps to the upper level of the wall, Todd and Hudson ascended the stairs to find an open courtyard with a group of people assembled. Sitting on one side of the court were nobly dressed men and women talking with each other.

"Hudson, these people weren't given much notice about this gathering. They aren't dressed in their proper regalia, and would never meet in the middle of the night for court. Something's happened."

Walking farther into the official meeting place, they looked to the opposite side of the square and found public seating. A quick scan of the crowd found there to be over 30 in attendance. Hudson was amazed that even in the first century, people came out to see tragedy; even in the middle of the night.

Human nature just doesn't change, he thought.

Finding seats toward the back, the men took their positions and waited for the drama to unfold.

—

Clark awakened once again to the aggression of soldiers. This time he wasn't in a jail, he was being dragged through a tunnel. The men assigned to him were pulling him face down by the arms causing his knees and the tops of his feet to be bloody and damaged. The assassin quickly regained his footing, and though sore and battered, kept pace with the soldiers through the tunnel. Though he had no idea where he was going, he was up and would do his best to find a way out of his situation.

—

"Look over there," whispered Todd, "there's light coming from that tunnel."

All within the gallery turned their heads toward the passageway at the same time the professor finished his statement. Although the light within the open courtyard was dim, being only lit by oil lamps, the time travelers knew the naked, beaten, and battered man.

"Clark," muttered Hudson.

"Hudson, I was afraid of this," he whispered. "For this group to come together in the middle of the night there has to be an important case. Treason or sedition. Possibly something like killing a ranking official."

The prisoner's hands were locked together and tied over his head to a beam placed in the ground about 20 feet in front of the judicial council. A young boy brought a rolled scroll to a man sitting alone. When a hush settled over the crowd, he read aloud the charges.

Todd listened to the full reading before he relayed the information to Hudson. "If my Greek isn't too rusty, it looks like Clark is charged with the slaughtering of one of their high ranking soldiers, impersonating a government official, the killing of a family in Gethsemane—I don't know what that one's about—and just general malfeasance against the state. They didn't mention anything about Aaliyah's neighbors. They'll probably discover that tomorrow."

A court official stood and questioned Clark. The assassin's Greek was very weak so even if he were innocent, there would be no way for him to communicate it.

"He's trying to say that he found the armor and didn't kill anyone," said Todd into Hudson's ear.

The prisoner was interrogated for ten minutes more before the man sat down and gestured to the committee. Hudson hadn't ever been in a Roman court, but knew those on the other side of the courtyard were deliberating Clark's fate. They came to a decision in a few short minutes. Another man stood to hand out his sentence.

The crowd became deathly still as they heard the destiny of the man hanging from the pole in front of them.

The professor listened to every word and dropped his jaw. "Oh no!" he said very slowly.

"What is it? What's happening?" questioned the agent.

Todd turned to look his partner in the face, "Clark's been sentenced to death."

Simultaneously a large soldier with a cat of nine tails started toward the prisoner.

"He's going to get 20 lashes and then be crucified tomorrow morning," finished Todd.

Clark, from his hanging position began to scream in English. "Let me go! I didn't do it!"

Everyone around, even the official compliment, began to mutter because of their inability to understand the strange language. However, Todd and Hudson knew what he was saying. He was pleading for the mercy he never gave anyone else in life.

The assassin did all he could to bend around the pole, but because he was tied so high, there was no getting away from the man who was about to inflict the worst pain that could be imagined.

The soldier lined up, "No, let me go," screamed Clark.

"God help me," he yelled.

The solder swung the cat. "Aaaahhh!"

He swung again, ripping skin with the pieces of metal and glass attached to the end of each leather strip.

Todd and Hudson sat speechless at the barbarism before their eyes.

With each blow, more of the man's back and sides were ripped away.

Clark screamed over and over again, but there was no end to the soldier's cruelty. It was obvious that the military man took the loss of his friend personally and performed his task with not a little enjoyment.

"Aaaahhh! Help me! God help me!"

The large man swung again.

"Todd, they're going to kill him. He'll never make it to his crucifixion."

"No, these guys know what they're doing," Todd whispered. "If a soldier botches the job and kills a prisoner before his sentence is fulfilled, the soldier will take his place. Sadly enough, Clark's going to experience all of the pain he's been sentenced."

The prisoner was hanging by his hands with no strength left to stand. He still yelled but with less energy. Clark, who was a perfect physical specimen, was now turned to a bloody, mangled pulp. His back, side, thighs, and stomach were changed into something akin to ground beef.

"Eighteen," counted Todd.

"How can they do this?" begged Hudson.

"They're masters at breaking a man. Clark will understand the errors he has made," said Todd sadly, turning back to the action.

"Nineteen," mumbled Hudson.

The soldier stopped for several seconds to dry the perspiration from his hand, then retook his stance. The inflictor's face gave the clear impression that he was going to make this last strike the most painful yet.

Cocking his arm back, the soldier let the nine tails fly, almost wrapping them around the body of the nearly lifeless man before him. Once the sharp edges found their mark, he gave one great pull on the leather, almost removing one side of the already mangled man.

Hudson had never heard such a pained and desperate cry. As the assassin yelled from the depths of his soul, the agent grieved with him. Clark had performed some horrific acts throughout his lifetime, but if they wanted to kill him, then, kill him.

Don't put him through this type of torture. No one deserves this.

Following the twentieth blow, a two-wheeled cart, somewhat akin to a large wheelbarrow, was rolled out through the tunnel by several soldiers. The prisoner's hands were loosened from their tied position and his limp body fell to the ground. Two soldiers came to pick him up. Clark tried to resist them with the last bit of strength he had left, but only earned a swift kick in his bloody side by the man who had inflicted the pain upon him. Clark didn't resist again.

His body was thrown on the cart like a sack of potatoes and rolled away. The dignitaries stood, left the room and the trial was over. The whole process took only 40 minutes. Justice was served.

Standing, Hudson asked, "Now what do we do? We'll never get to him. Todd, I'm so sorry for getting you into this. I'm sorry for getting Aaliyah hurt..." His hands raked through his dirt matted hair.

"Don't lose hope yet," Todd interrupted. "Normally, the condemned have to walk through the streets to the place of their execution. If they can't walk, then they'll be dragged, but this is a public exhibition. Rome is trying to dissuade others from following their example."

The men left the gathering and found their way back to Solomon's Porch, running face to face into an approaching crowd. The people were carrying torches and yelling, while soldiers were attempting to keep the angry mob away from a man they were transporting to another location; most likely the Tower of Antonio.

As Todd and Hudson moved away from the large group, they were able to see the prisoner who was drawing so much attention.

Todd whispered to his partner, "Evidently Jesus has finished his third trial before the entire Jewish leadership and is being taken before Pilate. He'll probably be tried in the same room we just left."

The men stared at the scene.

Watching Jesus, the time travelers could not believe how ghastly the man already looked. Their Lord had been beaten and tortured, completed three trials, and this was just the beginning. In the next three hours, Jesus would be forced to endure three more trials, multiples beatings and a scourging and mocking unfit a human; let alone the Savior of the world.

Todd continued, "Hudson, would you go through all of that pain and humiliation for the people in that crowd?" he said not taking his eyes from Jesus. "They hate him, yet he's going to gladly die for them. And for Clark, you, me, and the world."

"No, man, I wouldn't. Jesus loves us enough to go through all of that. I can't fathom his love. Much less his sacrifice.

Do you want to follow the crowd into the Tower?" asked Hudson.

"No, we know how it comes out. I can't stomach anymore pain for the moment." He looked over at Hudson, "I want to get back to Aaliyah, and I'll bet that Miss Ophrah will know which street the prisoners will be dragged through.

We must rest, because in just a few hours we'll take in sights that our fragile twenty-first century sensibilities won't know how to comprehend."

They started their trek toward Aaliyah's house.

Todd and Hudson were tired, sore, hungry, bruised, battered and hoping for good news; but none was to come. Aaliyah was in no better condition upon their returning. Her breathing was strained and her leg swollen.

"Hudson, we don't have much more time. There'll come a point when, even with the best medical help, she'll not recover," Todd's words were spoken as a whisper while he caressed Aaliyah's face.

"Yeah, I know. Did Ophrah have any information about where criminals are taken to be crucified?" Hudson said bringing another wet cloth from the bucket in the corner.

"She didn't understand why I'd want to go there, but yes, she knew. It's in the same place where they'll crucify Jesus. She was able to tell me that they usually start marching the criminals around mid morning and then hang them up shortly after that."

"Where are they going to be?" Hudson asked.

"Ophrah said that the street is north of the Temple Mount; the Via Dolorosa, even though it isn't called that yet. They march up to a point just north of the northern city walls. The crucifixion itself is going to be in the area of where the Church of the Holy Sepulcher rests in the twenty-first century. Don't worry, I know where everything is," he said with sadness in his voice, holding Aaliyah's small hand in his.

Placing his hand on Todd's shoulder he asked, "My friend, are you going to make it? I'm worried about you."

"Hudson, I'm a survivor. This trip has emotionally weakened me more than I could've imagined. In the last few days I've been accused of murder, traveled halfway around the world, had a car and driver blown out from under me and seen more murdered people than I could've ever imagined, while breaking into one of the holiest sites in the world. That's just the twenty-first century stuff. Then I traveled through time, almost died from a bullet wound, had multiple fights with a madman, witnessed a first century flogging, and have the woman I think I love, get bitten by a snake that should have come after me." Todd looked up at Hudson and finished. "To top it all off, I get to look forward to a good old-fashioned crucifixion where I'll probably see my Lord in the group and then have the possibility of losing my dear Aaliyah.

Sorry Hudson, but I'm really tired," he said with bags under his eyes.

"Buddy, I'm with you." Hudson bent down next to his partner and hugged him fiercely. "I feel exactly what you feel, but God will get us to the end. Just a few more hours and this nightmare will be over."

Hudson walked outside, leaving his partner to grieve in his own way. Looking up into the clear night sky, the agent could see the hint of red on the horizon. Knowing there was no chance of sleeping; Hudson just sat down against the outer wall of the simple dwelling and watched the day begin. The sun was following its destined course, but did it know that its life giving rays were signaling the death of the Savior of the world?

Clark screamed after every breath, until he had no energy or voice left; then he just whimpered and cried. The cold rock floor supporting his naked and abused body just intensified the pain, which was already indescribable.

The assassin knew from his training that he should try to keep moving. He was feeling pain now, but if his damaged areas started to dry out and clot, the pain would be exponentially worse than he had yet experienced; there was nothing left within him to move his body. He had no strength. He had no desire; and worse yet, he had no will.

It was that fact that grieved and pained the trained professional the most. The Romans had broken his will. Clark had more training than a legion of soldiers, and yet he knew down deep that he wasn't going to make it out of his situation. Even though better educated and larger than his captors, he had no strength to resist their intent. The assassin was going to die in the next few hours for his crimes.

The hours of pain and isolation forced Clark to be honest about his life. He was not a good man. Nothing in his existence benefited anyone but himself. Of course, he had known this for some time, but the taking of the next job, accumulating more money and possessions, and having countless liaisons with women that wouldn't last through the next morning had made his lack of worth easy to suppress.

The broken and bloody man lying on the floor was greedy, self serving, a murderer, and would leave no legacy, other than death and destruction.

"What am I? Why did I let this happen?" he mumbled through the pain and tears. His thoughts returned to the only one who ever truly loved him, "Momma, where are you? Why did you have to leave me?" he sobbed with his face against the floor, repeating the phrases over and over. "Momma, where are you? Why did you have to leave me?"

Clark cried for a long time until he screamed, "Oh God, what do I do? What do I do?"

The cell became silent as the man sentenced to death, thought about the words coming from his mouth. "What do I do? What do I do? Momma, what should I do, I don't want to go this way. I don't want to die knowing that I was a disgrace to you. Why aren't you here?"

The man remembered a young boy playing with his mother in a back bedroom. Sitting next to the child laying in bed, the lady was reading from a book. The memories were beginning to come alive. She was reading from a Bible.

Clark began remembering some of the things his mother would say. "Michael, no matter what happens in the world, you can always rely on God... Son, God loves you and died for you... Trust God and he'll be there with you in the difficult times."

The assassin began to sob once again. "God, where are you? If you love me, where are you?"

Instantly, Clark's whole world came full circle. He finally realized what he was attempting to do. The mission he was on suddenly made sense; he was trying to kill the only man who could give him peace; the only one who loved him enough to die for him."

He yelled the words, "Oh God, I'm sorry. Jesus I'm sorry. I was so wrong. I am so wrong."

These are the phrases Clark repeated over and over again through the cold, dark, and lonely night.

—

Hudson watched the sun as it fought to clear the horizon. Its orange and red hues gave an ominous feeling to the beginning of the day.

Red skies in morning, sailors take warning...no truer statement has ever been said, thought the man. He knew the outcome of the next few hours. *Jesus dies today, what a thought.* With resignation, the agent rose from his spot against the wall, stretched, and went inside to find his partner.

Looking over the group of people praying, cooking, and sleeping, Hudson walked straight to Todd. He found the man kneeling over Aaliyah's bed in a prayerful posture. One of the lifeless woman's hands was cupped between his, and the professor was praying from the depths of his soul. With every word, his body shook as if he were trying to move the heavens from his spot within the tiny house.

Touching his partner on the shoulder, and speaking in a quiet voice, Hudson reminded him, "Todd, the sun's up, it's time to go."

After a few seconds, Todd looked up with tears in his eyes, "I know."

"Did you get any rest?" Hudson said bringing over a glass of water.

"No, I've been praying the whole time," he said, rising from his position and caressing the pale woman's face. You ready to go?" he said to Hudson before he turned and spoke to Ophrah.

"I told Ophrah that we had to leave. She's going to watch Aaliyah for us," said the professor looking over at the woman on the bed one last time. "Let's go."

The Via Dolorosa was already well congested when the men arrived close to 20 minutes later. Hudson and Todd knew they weren't late, but by the anticipation within the crowd, felt that the festivities would be starting very soon.

Hudson yelled over the noise of the crowd, "This is like a carnival atmosphere. The only things missing are the clowns," he said as a young boy sitting on his father's shoulders looked over at him. The agent retreated back several feet into the crowd.

Todd covered his mouth so that others wouldn't hear, "These people don't have much else in their lives. They don't have movies, television, football games or other ways to invest their time. Israel doesn't even have gladiator fights, so sadly enough, the only avenue left to break the mundane are these death marches. That's why you see so many children at these occasions," the professor said pointing to the boy looking at Hudson.

The agent couldn't imagine ever bringing his children to something as morbid and debase as this, he even screened the cartoons they watched. "Don't they know that this can hurt their children?" he replied really looking at his partner for the first time in several days.

Todd had aged. His beard had grown in, covering his face and neck. His hair wasn't combed or even washed. His eyes sunken and bloodshot had dark black rings encircling them. The man's energy level was down, and because of all of the beatings he had taken, he looked like each movement was a struggle. The agent couldn't remember the last time he saw his partner smile.

I have to get us back to our time, he thought as Todd responded.

"Hudson, we can't superimpose our twenty-first century pleasantries upon them. This is a different people in a different time. Yes, this is a break from their normal and ordinary," he said as the crowd's noise began to rise, "but these parents don't want their children doing what these men did to have to make this march. They'll take their kids home and explain what this event was all about, hoping to dissuade them from ever breaking the law. The Romans have these marches, not to entertain the public but to show the consequences of bad actions.

If we were to take some of these people forward to our time, they'd be appalled at the sexually suggestive scenes in our primetime shows." The mass of people got even louder and more anxious. Todd had to raise his voice and move closer to Hudson's ear. "These people would never abandon their family into nursing homes, or complain that the government hadn't provided well enough for them. Most importantly, they wouldn't understand the amount of time we spend on ourselves and not in church worshipping God."

The agent understood what his partner was trying to say.

"My friend, we all have problems. We still execute people, just don't march them through the streets first. Understand that we are very much like these people, and in many ways worse. We're all broken, flawed and need a Savior," Todd said pointing down the narrow street. "Something's happening."

Both men looked east and saw movement. "I think we found the right place."

The crowd's noise came to a fever pitch as Hudson pulled in the sight before him. At the beginning of the parade, was a fully dressed soldier riding a horse. He was clearing the street so that the attractions behind had room to progress.

The agent could see at least four soldiers and two criminals following behind. Each soldier was holding onto a rope that was attached to one arm of a prisoner. The beaten and battered men were doing their best to walk, but if they fell, the brawny soldiers would drag them without losing a step.

"Is he there?" yelled Todd.

"I can't tell yet," replied the agent anxiously.

The crowd was yelling epithets and curses at the men, as the soldiers did all they could to keep the masses at bay. Many within the gathering threw old fruit or rotten eggs at the dead men walking; adding to the humiliation of the already excruciating march.

"You are standing head and shoulders over these people, what do you see?" Todd asked with frustration.

"Give me a second, they're almost within view," he barked, pushing himself forward through the crowd.

Both men shoved their way forward until they were face to face with the entourage. The criminal being dragged before them wasn't Clark, but they looked father east up the street.

"Is that him?" asked Hudson with uncertainty.

"That's him." Todd replied with finality.

The man who was once a pinnacle of strength and determination was now transformed into a shivering and cowering remnant of a human being. If it weren't for the short hair and new beard, the time travelers wouldn't have recognized him.

Clark was giving his best effort to walk, but because of the crowd intervention and weakness due to blood loss, he fell every tenth step or so; forcing the soldiers to drag him. The sad man would fight his way back to his feet, and the process would begin again.

When Clark came within ten feet of their position, the men began to yell, "Clark, Clark. What type of snake bit the woman? Who sent you? Clark, tell us, we need to know. Clark…"

The prisoner sent a vacant glance briefly in their direction; his thoughts on his own situation.

"We have to follow him," yelled Hudson. "How do we get through this crowd?"

"We will have to go to the crucifixion site. Golgotha. I know where it is," Todd said turning to go.

"Wait, look!" said Hudson with sadness.

Fifty feet up the road, the men saw a sight they had read about all their lives, and had seen movies attempting to portray, but couldn't describe if they had to. Another soldier on horseback was leading a second procession. Many more guards were assigned to crowd control, and soldiers were whipping and yelling at a lone man carrying a long beam.

"Is that Jesus?" Hudson asked with his eyes wide and mouth agape.

"Yes, that's him."

Jesus, God's only son, and Savior of the world was wearing a crown of thorns and giving his all to carry the crossbeam to his cross.

"That piece of wood must weigh over 100 pounds," mumbled Hudson.

The crowd was in a frenzy trying to inflict pain upon the man making his way through the narrow corridor. Throwing everything they had including stones and trash, it was clear that the people wanted the man dead, yet he continued.

As Jesus passed the two men forced into the situation, they fell to their knees in worship of the God of the universe going through the sacrificial act.

"Lord, please forgive me," yelled Hudson.

"Jesus, I'm not worthy of your sacrifice," Todd followed.

The men were broken before the perfect vision of sacrifice and love. While the crowd continued to yell and jeer, Todd and Hudson just wept.

Their Lord continued his trek through the streets until he was forced to turn a corner and begin the final leg to the place of the skull. When the crowd began to dissipate, the men regained their composure and started to work their way to the small hill outside of the north walls.

"I can't take much more of this," Hudson said to his partner.

"It's almost over, but we haven't seen the worst yet." Todd replied with pain in his voice.

Ten minutes later, the men climbed the hill of Golgotha to see one prisoner already on the cross and Clark being pulled into place.

The base of the cross already vertical and in place was made of a long beam approximately 15 feet high and the thickness of a railroad tie. The crossbeams were resting on the ground where the prisoners were anchored to them before being hoisted up into place by ropes. Once the two beams connected, a soldier would climb a ladder from behind, and lock the large beams together with a metal pin.

The method of execution was not efficient-but reliable. The naked criminals would hang exposed to the elements, without food or water until they died. If the attending soldiers were merciful, they would end the desperate men's misery by putting a sword into their sides or breaking their legs a few days into the ordeal. Many criminals hung for over a week before they went into eternity.

Todd and Hudson were staring at Clark when the cries of another man changed their focus. The screams expressed the fullest extent of pain possible and were coming from Jesus. The men could see one soldier straddling his arm while another hammered a spike into his wrist.

"Aaaahhh," Jesus yelled as the crowd laughed and mocked.

The soldiers changed sides and began to connect his other arm to the beam. Once again, a blood curdling yell beyond comprehension was forced from the man dying for the sin of the world.

The travelers watched the ordeal with tears running down their faces as Jesus' crossbeam began to rise. The surreal site was intensified with the changing of wind direction and the forming of dark clouds in the sky.

Once Jesus' beam was attached, three soldiers went to Jesus' legs. Two men held them in place, while the third hammered the spike through his ankles. The soldiers were surprised when Jesus didn't struggle; instead he willingly allowed them to finish their job so he could begin to complete his plan for redemption.

A scream rang throughout the countryside.

Not feeling that they had done enough to the innocent man, the soldiers completed the scene by scribbling some words on a board and climbing once again behind Jesus' cross. Hudson wasn't an ancient languages scholar like his partner, but knew what the mocking words said.

"Jesus, King of the Jews," the crowd mumbled in several different languages.

The sky grew more red and dark with each passing minute while rain began to fall. The travelers could feel even the earth grieving over the pain of its creator. With the storm brewing, the crowd thinned as people started to leave.

"We need to get to Clark," Hudson said as he heard one of the criminals speak.

"Listen," replied Todd putting a finger up to his lips.

In the moment of silence, while the men were listening for the criminal's words, they noticed several scenes that conflicted with each other. At the foot of Jesus' cross there were a handful of people crying and praying, while twenty feet away, several soldiers fought over a piece of cloth. Mary grieved over the loss of her child, while men fought for his clothes.

Lord, how can you love us so much, thought Hudson?

Looking to his partner, "The criminal said that Jesus ought to save himself if he is the son of God," Todd said translating.

Then from the cross on the other side of Jesus came very broken but understandable Hebrew.

"Wide eyed, Hudson asked, "What's Clark saying? When did he learn Hebrew?"

"Quiet, I can't hear," Todd said, straining his ear through the thunder and increased level of rain. The professor ran closer in an attempt to understand the strained words.

Hudson got caught in a group of people leaving the area, however when he did reach his partner, he found him looking up at Clark in astonishment.

Turning to Hudson, he paraphrased, "He just said that he deserved the consequences of his wrong, but Jesus is innocent. He then asked forgiveness and prayed that Jesus would remember him when he went into his kingdom."

"Has Clark accepted Christ?" asked the agent with amazement.

Todd was about to respond when Jesus began to speak. Following several seconds of thunder and lighting and then a sudden calm, the Savior's words rang throughout the countryside.

"You don't need to translate for me, "He said that today he will be with him in paradise."

The men stood in silence for close to five minutes before Hudson spoke again.

"We need to speak to Clark."

"As long as we move slowly, the soldiers won't try to remove us from the area."

Walking up to the base of Clark's cross, Hudson yelled, "Clark. Clark!"

Todd repeated the call, "Clark, we're sorry that this has happened to you."

The beaten criminal slowly opened his eyes, and looked down at the men who were once his enemies. Slowly and with little breath, he said, "Blackwell, I'm so sorry for what I've done."

Tears began to run again down the agent's face. "I know, Clark, I know."

"I was so wrong. I wanted to murder the true Christ, God's son. If I just would have known him earlier. I wasted my life and have nothing good to show for it."

Even through the hard rain, Todd could tell that the man was crying, and not because of the pain, but because of his wasted years. "Clark, you got it right. God has cleansed your soul. You're going to be in heaven with Jesus. That's a triumph!"

"Ninja…," he smiled weakly, "I don't even know your name," he stopped for several seconds.

"My name is Michael."

While the thunder began to shake the countryside and the wind picked up again, Clark continued, "Clark was an evil person. He sickens me. Call me Michael," he said between breaths.

"Michael, who sent you on this mission? We must go back and stop this from ever happening again."

Michael coughed, and both men moved closer. A lightning strike hit the ground a tenth of a mile away, setting fire to several homes. The men wanted to get out of the elements. "Blackwell, I was bought and paid for by one person. He had me trained, and paid all of my expenses. John Hughes is a very bitter and angry man, and must be stopped. If he knows that I failed, he'll come back and try again."

Todd looked at Hudson, "Do you know who that is?"

"Yes," he said looking at his partner. Craning his head up toward Michael he said, "Michael, a woman's life is at stake. What type of snakes did you use in the house? What could have bitten the woman and rendered her unconscious?"

Michael continued sobbing, "I'm so sorry. Please forgive me. There's no hope for her here." His eyes opened with a small light of hope, "You have to take her forward to our time. They can save her there."

Todd yelled, "What type of snake bit her?"

"It was a Puff Adder. I'm sorry, so sorry."

"Michael, we must go. We're praying for you," said Todd, turning to head down the hill.

"We're praying for you, Michael," Hudson said, looking up at the man one last time. He then looked over at Jesus who was trying to comfort his mother.

Lord, thank You for your sacrifice, and for changing Clark's, I mean Michael's life. From the beginning, you had this whole trip worked out for your glory. You are such a great God! Now please save Aaliyah. Please, Lord," Hudson prayed.

The agent ran after his partner, slipping several times in the thick mud that had been formed within the last hour. The sky was now totally black, except for the lightning which gave the travelers enough illumination to navigate by. With all of their might they ran through the narrow streets, knowing that this would be their last trip through the Ancient City, and to Aaliyah's house.

The final trip to Aaliyah's house took longer than expected for the emotionally drained men. Trees had fallen, homes were on fire, streets were flooded, and the entire population of Jerusalem was frantic looking for safe shelter. The wind, rain and lightning brought down upon the city because of the suffering of the Lord were wreaking havoc throughout the entire area–and the worst was yet to come.

Upon arrival, the men ran inside expecting to find the room filled with people as it had been before, however only two were left: Ophrah and Aaliyah. The elderly woman had stayed by her side and was presently running a cool cloth over Aaliyah's face as she sang gentle lullabies to her unconscious friend.

As the men entered the room, Todd went over to the older caretaker and started to speak to her.

"She says that the others were afraid, and left to take care of their families. She couldn't leave Aaliyah in this condition, saying her breathing has become more labored. Hudson, she doesn't have much more time," he said, hearing the downpour outside increasing.

"What do we do?" the agent replied while several pots fell from a shelf after a large thunder clap. Sitting in a chair, and putting his head in his hands, he continued, "If we leave her here, she dies. However, if we take her with us, who's to say that she lives? She doesn't belong in our time Todd, she belongs here," he paused for several seconds thinking. "What'll it do to our timeline, or this timeline? What if she does live and is the great, great grandmother of some future king?"

"Hudson, we have to take her with us. She'll die here, and she has a future with us. She told me several days ago that our intrusion brightened her life." He looked over and caressed her face. Looking back at his partner he continued, "What did she have before we came? She was an outcast, alone, with no hope and no way out because of the conventions of this society. We can offer her more."

Standing up and pacing, Hudson shot back, "What if she doesn't want to go?" The cloth door flap blew from its mount and fell in a corner across the room. "She's not given a choice. She's unconscious and can't speak for herself. Taking her with us forces her into a society and time that she has no reference for. Who's to say that she'll be able to handle that? Are you willing to make that decision for her?"

Todd grabbed her hand, and with tears running down his cheeks looked at the young woman. "Yes, Hudson, I am. I love her, more than I've ever loved anyone. I don't know how or why, but I do. And it's not because she cared for me after the shooting, and it's not because we're in this crazy scenario together. I love this woman deeply and don't want to live without her." The tears continued.

Hudson moved away from the door opening and out of the rain blowing into the small dwelling. His head ached from all of the physical and emotional abuse, and he needed guidance.

The room began to shake, as small earthquakes rumbled throughout the countryside. Ophrah started to pray as Todd covered Aaliyah's body with his, protecting her from debris falling from the roof.

"Hudson, we must take her. We're the ones who got her into this situation. Let's repay her by giving back her life."

Lighting struck 100 feet from the front door, setting a small tree on fire. The residual thunderclap associated with it was so loud it shook the walls and loosened boards in the roof. Rain cascaded like a waterfall into the once dry room.

"God, I take that as your answer," Hudson said turning to his partner. "Is there anything you need? Because if there is, you better get it now! The three of us need to leave this country before it self destructs. I'd say we have just a short time before Christ dies, and then the real adventure begins."

"Yes, at the instant of his death, the Temple curtain is torn in two, the earth shakes so violently that rocks are split apart, and tombs are opened. The book of Matthew says tombs will be opened and the dead will rise," Todd said with urgency.

"I don't want to be here for that."

"Me neither. Thank you Hudson," Todd said turning to Ophrah.

The little woman started babbling and disagreeing with the professor, however after a minute, she calmed down.

The rain was increasing.

"What did you say?"

Todd responded, "I told her we needed to move Aaliyah to a safer location. I didn't tell her that was over 2000 years into the future." He looked at Aaliyah and then Hudson. "Do we just carry her out of here?"

"I don't think we can hurt her anymore than she is. Let's go."

Taking a blanket that Ophrah offered him, the professor wrapped the delicate woman. He picked her small frame up in his arms and pulled her head next to his shoulder as Hudson stretched the blanket over her face.

"You ready," said Hudson.

"Yes," he said starting to look back at the concern of the older woman. Ophrah was sitting in a corner concerned over her young friend. With a smile, Todd looked back and said, "*Shalom lakhess all teeraoo.*"

"What did you say?" Hudson said pulling his hood over his head and preparing to leave the house.

"I offered her peace and told her to not fear," he said carrying Aaliyah from the relative safety of the house, to the turbulent streets of Jerusalem.

—

Clark hung exposed to the storm, getting weaker by the minute. Each breath was an ordeal for the condemned man. The angle that his arms were attached to the crossbeam and lack of foot support with which to stand made a deep breath impossible, and a shallow one painful.

Even in the worst moment of his life, with certain death within the next few hours, he had peace. Watching his Lord struggling on the next cross, yet still offering compassion had given him new life. The murderer's sins were atoned for, and Jesus was paying the price with his own life.

The cold rain became heavier as lightning flashed all around.

How Clark wished that he could get down from his cross and praise the selfless man, or run from street to street telling everyone of the sacrifice Jesus was making on their behalf. No, his transformation was too late; justice was being served. God had forgiven all of the wrong that he had done, yet the world required a price for his crimes; and that price was his life.

The ground shook, giving the crucified men the feeling that they would plunge from their torturous positions; adding to the terror of the situation.

With the little breath Clark presently had, he yelled, "Jesus, thank you for my life. Thank you for your sacrifice." He coughed several times as pea sized hail began to fall, while the crowd looked in confusion due to the strange language he was speaking.

Wanting to just die and spend eternity with his Savior, his fight for life took over. With his lungs burning for air, he pulled himself back up for another breath and heard Jesus cry out, "*Eli, Eli, lema sabachthani!*"

Clark remembered the words from his early years of Sunday School, *My God, my God, why have you forsaken me*, he thought.

The lightning intensified as the clouds totally blocked the sun, making the day appear to be night. The ground shook violently, causing houses to fall and limestone blocks to move from their places within the mighty Temple Mount wall. The rain increased and got colder as larger hail fell from the sky. The world was starting to come apart.

Clark looked over at Jesus, the wind blew stronger and he saw his Savior's head fall to his chest. The end of a perfect life.

Looking to the heavens, Clark cried out, "Why, God, why," he screamed as the rain covered the tears. "I was not worthy of his life!"

The repentant criminal just stared at Jesus and openly wept. A soldier, frustrated with the time it was taking the men to die, came up and swung a hammer through Clark's shins. He broke both bones on each leg, making it impossible to push up for a breath.

Knowing that his last few seconds were near, the changed man wanted to make sure he went into paradise thanking his Jesus for loving him so deeply. "Thank You, thank You, thank…," he said again, before his eyes dimmed and he left this world.

—

It was only a few tenths of a mile to the opening of the tunnels below the Temple Mount and yet the men struggled for every foot. Rain was falling at monsoon levels while hail the size of golf balls damaged everything it encountered. The wind was blowing consistently at over 40 miles per hour with gusts twice that, as lighting was setting building upon building ablaze and causing thunder that would shatter eardrums. The sun disappeared, and the earth was trembling. Fissures formed throughout the countryside as the world grieved the loss of its creator.

"Hudson, I need help!" cried Todd.

The agent looked a few feet behind to find the professor on his knees in a stream of rapidly moving water, trying to keep Aaliyah from falling from his arms.

"I fell in a ditch. Help me up!" he yelled through the wind as it whistled around a small building.

"Let me give you a break. I can take her!" he screamed, trying to be heard above the chaos of nature and humanity.

"No, I'll carry her. Just help me up!"

Hudson pulled him by the upper arm, and they were once again moving.

People were running from place to place with no true destination in mind; knowing they had to get away from the destruction all around.

Continuing toward the ancient opening, they ran arm in arm. Each needed the physical and emotional strength the other offered. Pressing against the storm, the ragged men looked like the final remnants from an ancient battle. Their comrades had fallen, and determined to finish the fight; they picked themselves up to form another line. These men were resolute in focus and were going to make it; they had been through too much to fail now.

Soaking wet and with biceps burning from Aaliyah's weight, Todd yelled, "There it is!"

Hudson looked through the rain to find the opening covered back with stones. He ran through the mud and started to clear the rocks from the entrance. After 30 seconds, the opening was clear but revealed a problem they never could have imagined.

The agent stood and looked at his partner with panicked eyes. Todd moved around Hudson to see the problem.

"It's filled with water!" the professor yelled. "It's an old water drainage system, I should've expected this. Why wasn't I thinking?"

The opening sat below the base of the Temple wall. Because of its design, it originally filled with water during heavy rains, channeling the fluid to underground reservoirs.

"Hudson, if I remember right, the opening is below the wall line, but just inside, you rise back up. Once we make it under the wall, we should be able to breathe again," he yelled as he huddled against the massive wall through the heavy rain.

"I'll go in to see if you're right."

The agent got on his stomach in the mud and took three quick breaths. On the fourth, he put his head under the water and pushed through the opening. In a second he was gone.

Todd looked at the disordered world; the people running for their lives, the mudslides and buildings falling in upon themselves. He saw the fires burning in the midst of some of the heaviest rains he had ever encountered. As he held his Aaliyah to his chest, the carnage filling his eyes proved that a world without Christ could not exist. The fabric of the universe was held together by its creator, and without him, it would shake itself from its foundation.

His partner resurfaced a minute later. "We have to cross about six feet totally underwater before we're back to breathable space," he yelled climbing from the opening.

The tunic was a great garment for the dry, arid region of Israel, but was not designed to be soaked. Hudson fought the massive amount of cloth as he spoke, "What do you want to do? It's not that far, but it's six feet."

The men stood in the pouring rain. Todd felt the weight of the problem resting in his arms. How could he take the unconscious woman he was doing his best to keep dry under six feet of water?

Lightning hit a building above them on top of the Mount, and the men flinched. Todd knew it was time to move, "Let's hope that because she's unconscious, her breathing has slowed and we can get her through the water between breaths. There isn't anything else we can do."

The men looked at each other and then at Aaliyah. With his hands on his hips and the cold rain beating down, Hudson said, "Let's go. I'll go through to the other side, get several breaths and come back halfway so I can pull her." Looking his partner right in the eyes, he said, "You have the tough job, Todd. You have to force her under the water and push her at me. Can you do it?"

With agony on his face, the professor looked down at the petite young woman and said, "I have to if we're to save her." He looked up.

"Count to 20 slowly once I enter the water. At 20, press her under, and I'll grab her and pull her through."

Hudson patted Todd on the shoulder, got down on his stomach and entered the water.

"One, two, three, four." Todd lowered the woman to the ground as he got down on his knees.

"Five, six, seven, eight." He gently placed Aaliyah's light frame in the water up to her waist.

"Oh, God, I don't want to do this," he said crying as he held her lifeless head in his hands.

"Twelve, thirteen, fourteen, fifteen." He turned her face down as her head fell forward.

"Seventeen, eighteen." Todd looked to the heavens as the rain and hail beat his face. "Lord, please protect her."

"Nineteen." The tears were flowing like the water off of the wall before him.

"Lord, please let Hudson be there; twenty." Todd thrust Aaliyah's head under the water and pushed her forward. Instantaneously, he felt her pull from his arms and she was gone.

Todd looked back over his shoulder one last time to see the carnage and destruction of a world without Christ. Fires were burning amidst great flooding. The earth was trembling and boulders were falling. People were running in a panic while others huddled in corners, hoping to make it through the night.

"If you just knew that you brought this upon yourselves," he said quietly. Then he thought for a second. "No, *we* brought this upon *ourselves*."

Todd looked again at the hole, took a deep breath and disappeared under the muddy water.

Aaliyah was lying on her back next to the light of a flashlight when Todd appeared through the dark water.

He pulled himself from the murky hole, "What's going on?"

"She took in some water and stopped breathing," Hudson barked. Trying to perform chest compressions on the fragile woman was difficult in the small tunnel. "Twenty-five, twenty-six."

"Let me take over the breathing," the professor maneuvered himself to give her a breath of air at count 30. "You sure she isn't breathing?"

"Yep." He pressed her chest. "Twenty-eight."

The professor quickly placed one hand under the unconscious woman's neck and pulled her forehead forward with the other. "Tell me when," he said reluctantly.

"Thirty," Hudson said, rising from his straddled position over her body.

Todd placed his lips over Aaliyah's and forced in two full breaths.

"One." Hudson began again with the compressions.

"How long have you been doing this?" asked Todd.

"One cycle. Sixteen, seventeen, eighteen."

The walls rumbled around them, and several stones fell from the ceiling. Both men instinctively fell forward covering their friend from the falling rocks.

"Oh, Lord, please bring Aaliyah back," cried Todd as he yanked off his soaked outer garment. "Lord, we've been shot, beaten, had bones broken, seen horrific human atrocities, fought snakes, and been through emotional turmoil that can't be described, yet we have honored you all we can," he said, staring at the lifeless form of the young woman he had come to love. "God, we know you can bring her back, and we ask that you do."

"Twenty-five, twenty-six, twenty-seven," Hudson muttered.

"Please, Lord," Todd continued, "we've come too far to lose her now."

"Thirty."

Todd once again pulled her head forward and forced in two breaths. This time a gurgle sound came from deep within her throat.

"Stop," Todd yelled thrusting out a hand as he placed his ear to her mouth.

Hudson stopped the compressions.

"I hear something."

Hudson held his breath. He prayed as his partner leaned over the young woman and placed two fingers on her neck.

An eternity passed.

"Turn her on her side, she has a pulse and is breathing."

The men rolled her over as the water drained from her lungs.

"Thank you, God," Todd cheered as he leaned over the precious woman and kissed her forehead tenderly. Hudson sat back on his heels and breathed a sigh of relief, "Thank you, God." Tears streamed down his cheeks.

A lightning strike just outside the wall brought them back to reality. The thunder was deafening even though they were insulated by over eight feet of stone. "We need to go," they said in unison.

Todd checked the woman's vital signs once again to verify that she was still breathing. Hudson looked on. "She's still alive."

"How are we going to do this?" Hudson asked.

Todd knew what his partner was asking. "It's going to be tough. The only way it's going to work is if I head down the tunnel backwards and pull her while you push."

"Well, let's go. She isn't out of the woods yet," Hudson said pointing the light down their tunnel.

"We'll need to back her into the water a bit so we can turn her down the side tunnel."

Hudson backed into the murky hole and dragged Aaliyah far enough for Todd to squeeze into the side tunnel. Once inside, and with Aaliyah back up to her neck in water, the professor pulled her into the hole with him while Hudson shined the flashlight ahead.

The agent placed his outer garment underneath the young woman to minimize any friction burns that might occur.

The progress was slow but methodical. Todd knew the exact route, so the men made no mistakes in direction. When an obstacle came, they worked as a team and helped their unconscious friend through it.

After an hour of pushing and pulling, Hudson turned off the light. "What are you doing?" barked Todd.

Within several seconds, the men's eyes grew accustomed to the light and started to see a bluish glow up ahead. "I think we made it," Hudson said quickly. "Hurry, pull harder."

Suddenly, the earth shook and both time travelers leaned over Aaliyah. Hudson spoke, "We have to get out of here before the world falls apart." The agent turned the flashlight back on.

The rumbling subsided as the men pulled and pushed, covering the last hundred yards in less than ten minutes.

When the tunnel met the underground cavern that housed the sphere, Todd backed out of the hole and dropped to the floor. Hudson shined his flashlight ahead and saw that the vehicle looked to be in good shape. The earthquakes continued.

"How does it look, Hudson?" asked Todd, picking Aaliyah up under the arms and pulling her from the tunnel.

The agent shined the light once again on the vehicle and spoke, "I think it's fine. Help me out." He thrust his hand through the passage opening.

Todd laid the woman down next to the sphere and ran back over to help his partner. Once out, the earth tumbled beneath them, taking them to the ground with a thud.

"I think our Savior has died, Hudson," the professor yelled, rushing up to cover Aaliyah. "We need to leave!"

The earth shook again, creating a cacophony of noise and fissures in the walls. It looked like the Temple Mount was going to fall in around them.

"Hudson, let's go!" Todd checked her pulse and dodged pieces of rock falling from the ceiling. "Hudson!" he yelled.

The ground rumbled. Out of agitation, the professor looked back to find the agent lying on the floor face down against a large block.

"Oh, no," running to his partner while trying to keep himself upright through the ground swells. "Hudson. Hudson!" He shook the large man as the walls trembled.

Turning Hudson onto his back, he saw a large red mass swelling on his forehead. The professor felt a strong pulse but knew his friend would be unconscious for a while. "Oh, God, how can this be happening? We're so close."

Hudson might have a concussion but would be alright. Aaliyah only had a few hours left.

"Lord, what do I do?" Todd ran to the sphere and tried to raise the canopy, but it wouldn't budge. It was locked down tight.

"How did he get into this thing earlier?" The professor looked the vehicle over and found a square metallic plate on the side; remembering

Hudson placing his hand on the square, Todd did the same. Nothing happened. "Think!"

"It's probably programmed only to Hudson." The man ran over and grabbed his partner by the cloth of his garment. Dragging him over 30 feet, Todd brought him to rest next to the struts holding the fragile piece of equipment above the ground.

Todd pulled up Hudson's arm. It was a good foot from reaching the square panel. "Sorry buddy." He grabbed the man's tunic with one hand and arm with the other. Pulling the agent's upper body several feet up, he placed the unconscious man's hand against the plate, instantly causing a hiss and the upper half of the sphere to rise.

After the smoke cleared, Todd climbed into the cockpit and looked over the panel. "Why didn't I pay more attention when I was in here last time? *The bullet wound didn't help my attention*, he thought.

"I've flown singles, twins, and jets. How much harder can this be?" he muttered to himself. Yet, the flight instructor didn't find horizontal indicators, compasses, and propeller or mixture levers. There were no flap levers, communication devices or transponders. Within the small area he didn't find a yoke or pedals. The professor had given over 1000 hours of flight instruction. This was no aircraft.

The dash consisted of a flat black panel-a glass cockpit-and a square reminiscent of the one on the side of the vehicle. Todd futilely placed his hand over the plate. Nothing happened. He jumped from the vehicle.

The professor picked Aaliyah up in his arms while a boulder fell next to them, and placed her between the two seats of the vehicle. Next, he bent down and tried to lift his friend. The man was dead weight and his first attempt failed.

"God help me." Todd got down and rolled the large man onto his shoulders. He then rose to his knees and pressed him from the floor.

Those years in the gym finally paid off.

While attempting to push his partner into the vehicle, the earth shook again causing him to fall back with his buddy on his shoulders. Luckily, he kept his balance and walked back to the sphere. This time he was able to throw Hudson over the edge of the door and into the pilot's seat. After wrestling with his legs, he buckled him in and took the copilot's seat.

"Okay, how does this thing work?" He placed Hudson's hand over the plate. Immediately, the sphere came to life, and the panel lit up.

From what Todd could tell, the dash consisted of four main areas. The left two quadrants looked to be time specific while the right two were delegated to location. The left side of each half was blinking, showing the professor that they were in the year 32 with a specific coordinate probably indicating the hours, minutes, and seconds of their present location. Just to the right of the seconds number was a negative figure in meters. They were ten meters below sea level. The far right of each side of the dash consisted of solid numbers hopefully indicating where they had come from. The time flashing was the year they'd come from, and the location was the same as the one blinking to its left.

"That would make sense, we left from the Temple Mount," he muttered. "The problem is how do I get it back to Washington? Aaliyah won't make it through the tunnels again, and who knows who might be waiting for us there?"

Todd touched the blinking glass screen referring to time and it came to life, offering him the ability to change the destination year. Placing in the year they left, he pressed enter and the time screen stopped blinking.

"That was easy. Let's see what happens with location."

He pressed the location screen with a similar result. It became accessible but Todd had no idea what coordinates to input. If he keyed in the wrong numbers, they could appear under the Atlantic Ocean. "What now?"

The professor continued to look at the screen. There were several arrows up and down indicating a menu, so he touched the display until he came to a list of coordinates around the world. Every important place on the globe was loaded into memory. Did he want to go to Tienemen Square or Times Square? Mexico City or Greenland; all of the coordinates were there.

Quickly scanning the list, he was hoping to find one destination that would keep the vehicle a secret and yet offer his friends the quickest medical attention. As he moved to the end, he found the perfect spot.

"This should get us noticed," he said while entering the numbers.

Upon inputting the final digits, the time and location panels stopped blinking and a new area of the console lit up. It wanted the professor to lower the canopy, so he pressed the button and the top half began to drop. Once it was mated with the lower section, a final area of the cockpit came to life. The light said execute. He breathed deeply.

The man looked over the console one last time, checking each quadrant and ensuring that everything—from his best knowledge—looked right. Feeling as comfortable as possible in his situation, he looked over at Hudson's belt one last time to make sure it was locked in tight. He checked Aaliyah's pulse, and although weak, she was still alive. Finally, he buckled himself in and cinched the belt down tight.

"God in heaven, let me have programmed this thing right." The ground shook.

"We're in your hands, Lord!"

Todd pressed his head back in the seat and pulled Aaliyah tightly to himself. Stretching his arm across the console, he hesitantly pressed the blinking light, and instantaneously the sphere was gone.

Ten minutes into the early morning meeting, a huge explosion rocked the room. In a flash of light, the two men were thrown face-first against bullet-proof windows.

Military armed security ran in from every possible entry point, surrounding the leaders and dragging them from the scene. Seeing the two men physically shaken, the Marine Colonel shouted, "Get them out of here!" Dense steam filled the space, halting their progress. Finding an exit was becoming impossible in the thick cloud so the security detail dropped their charges to the ground and covered them with their bodies.

A mechanical sound echoed through the small area. "Surround the room, men!" Footsteps were heard shuffling around the perimeter.

Weapons engaged and semi-automatic rifles locked. A small war was about to be wrought on the invisible object in the center of the Oval Office.

Clicking, a thud, then silence.

"Ready your weapons." The Marine spoke quietly now in the stillness.

A troubled voice pierced the dissipating vapor. "Medical help!"

Instantly a man in fatigues tackled the intruder and pressed an M16 to his head. Four others followed suit.

"No, no. My name is Dr. Todd Myers. There are hurt people in the cockpit." His words were forced out as one man lay on his legs while another had his knee in his chest. "Help her or she will…"

"Silence," shouted the soldier still pressing the weapon to his scalp.

The room was beginning to clear. "It's alright." Everyone in the room recognized the President's voice, muffled as it was beneath his human shield. The man looked to his commanding officer who spoke to the world leader. "Sir, we haven't cleared the…"

"Colonel, I'm safe with this man, and am aware of the situation. Now, let me up!"

"Yes, Mr. President. Let him up," he ordered.

"I want this room cleared." He brushed his sleeves and straightened his tie. "Everyone will wait in the west anteroom until this situation is contained. No one is to leave the building, and everyone will be debriefed. Do you understand, Colonel?"

"Yes sir," he replied not recognizing the futuristic machine.

"This is a top-secret vehicle. No one will remember what he has seen here today. Does everyone understand?" yelled the President.

"Yes sir," the room resounded.

Todd tried to speak, but the Marine held his position on his chest.

"Let him up," the President waved.

"Mr. President, a wounded woman is in the sphere," he said with the little breath he could squeeze from his lungs. "She was bitten by a Puff Adder. If she doesn't receive immediate help, she'll die within a few hours. She saved our lives more than once. Please help her." He turned back to the sphere to rescue the woman from her slumped position in the seat.

"Colonel, take the woman to Marine One and have them travel immediately to Walter Reed. Make sure she gets the kind of attention they would give to me," said the President walking forward.

"Yes sir!" He gathered the pale unconscious figure from Todd's arms and left the room.

The man who had been in the room with the President when the sphere had arrived was finally released from his human shield and now sat in a chair near the window. Elbows on his thighs, he bent over and ran shaky fingers through his hair.

The President moved toward the large object in the center of the rotunda. "Dr. Myers, I'm assuming the reason you caused this degree of chaos in the Oval Office was because of the woman's need for medical attention. Is there, perhaps, any other good reason you dumped that top-secret piece of equipment in the most recognized office in the world?"

"Sir, Aaliyah was very close to death. I knew if I dropped the vehicle here, I'd get immediate attention."

"Well, you did get that," barked the President.

"But there's another reason for choosing this location," Hudson said emerging from the vehicle. There was a superficial lump the size of Texas on his head but he was otherwise unharmed.

"Sir you have more problems than a few secret service people staying quiet." "Isn't that right, Senator Hughes?" Hudson turned his attention to the Senator whose eyes bulged from his head in anger and disbelief.

"What do you mean, Hudson?" said the President looking at the troubled Senator.

The agent stood before John Hughes, "John, you failed."

The man began to tremble.

"Explain yourself John," spoke the President, his eyebrows lifted in curiosity.

"It wasn't supposed to end like this. My wife, my daughter . . . supposed to be returned to me . . ." His words came between deep sobs. "I don't understand. I planned. I sacrificed." Tears dropped to the floor, and his body shook with his long-delayed grief.

He raised his reddened eyes to Hudson's. "I never wanted you hurt. You wouldn't leave well enough alone. It can't end like this." He put his face in his hands again and moaned. "My Darlings, you were supposed to come back to me."

Hudson asked, "John, why would Clark's success have meant your wife and daughter would return to you?"

"They were doing his work, and he let them die. If he were killed before establishing his ministry or even just before dying on the cross–forever a martyr to sacrificial good works-my sweet family would have never worked for a cause such as that. They would have lived happy lives instead of sacrificing themselves for others!"

Todd crouched down beside the broken man. "Senator, if your wife and daughter died doing God's work, then they are with him in heaven–a much better place than this earth. They wouldn't want to come back."

He banged his chest once. "I wanted them back!" His head dropped again into his hands.

Hudson continued, "You can't bring your family back, John, but you can see them in the future."

Senator Hughes looked up, "What do you mean?"

Todd spoke. "If you accept Christ, follow him as they did, you will be with your family in heaven when you die."

The Senator stood up and walked toward the fireplace. He tapped the two hundred year old mantle then turned to look at the three men in the room. Uncontrolled hatred burned with a spark of insanity. As he spoke, he lifted his aging finger to the face of each one in turn. "Your Jesus rejected me by taking the only thing in my life that I loved...."

"Jesus didn't take them...," interrupted Todd.

He shouted above Todd's quiet voice. ". . . and because of that, I will *never* accept Christ. I will give my last ounce of energy and last dollar to stop his mission and work." Senator Hughes started to walk toward the men as the President waved in a military guard. "You have not stopped me," he said pointing. "I will have my revenge."

"Take him away," the President whispered to his personal guard. "We'll figure out what to do with him later."

The crazed and broken Senator started to scream, "I will have my revenge. I am not the only one guilty . . ." The guard manhandled him toward the door.

"Get him out of here and silence him," ordered the President.

"Langley," Hughes said yelling at the President, "You know..."

The doors slammed behind the unbelievable scene, and the room went silent. After what seemed like an eternity, Hudson broke the silence. "What are you going to do with him, Mr. President?"

"It's an awkward situation. We can't take John through normal courts because he broke laws that haven't even been created. We might be able to take him before a military court, even though that isn't totally legal," he said pouring himself some Brandy from a snifter in spite of the early hour.

"Anyone else need some?" he asked showing his glass. Both shook their heads no.

Sitting on the front edge of Abraham Lincoln's desk, the President continued, "I imagine that Senator Hughes will have to disappear. We may hide him on some tropical island somewhere." His face was serious but he let out a dour chuckle.

Only a handful of people, other than you know about this thing," he said pointing to the large sphere sitting in the middle of his office, "It must remain a secret."

The professor spoke up, "What are you going to do with the vehicle?"

"We'll mothball it. The world isn't ready for this type of technology; man can't be trusted. In our first use of time travel, we failed." He stopped for a second and walked over to the sphere. "Maybe in the future, we can be more trusted, but not now."

Changing his train of thought, the President continued, "So men, what am I supposed to do now," he laughed looking at the vehicle that was within an inch of the small rotunda within the room. I can't very well hold meetings around it."

The men laughed breaking the stress of the last few minutes.

Responding, Hudson said, "It's your problem, you deal with it."

"That's why the people voted you in, because you're good at diffusing problems," Todd replied.

The President laughed. "Guys, you know we are going to need to spend quite a while together debriefing. You've been through time in top-secret equipment, and what you've seen might benefit the nation. Go home for a few days; then come back ready to talk."

The men looked at each other and nodded.

"Mr. President," Todd said, "what's going to happen to Aaliyah?"

"You said that she saved your lives, is that right?"

"Yes sir, multiple times," Hudson looked at Todd whose worried expression told the depth of his concern.

"It sounds like she's a national hero. We can't really tell the world about her, but we can make her a citizen and give her a position that will, let's say, let her use her expertise." He sipped at his Brandy. "Don't worry Dr. Myers, she will be taken care of," he said with a grin.

"I want to get you men checked out by a doctor." The President stood. "I'm going to have my car take you to Walter Reed where they will look you over and possibly get you some ice for that lump, Hudson," he said putting his hands around their backs and walking them to the door.

Sue Hanover had been the President's assistant for close to twenty years; following him through Congressional seats, Governorships and finally the Presidency. She was placing her purse under her desk and preparing to start the day, when the doors opened revealing two men in first century garb and a large round thing sitting in the center of the Oval Office.

"Sir, what is…has…I mean…where did they…what is that…," the woman said unable to complete a sentence.

"Sue, get these men some proper attire. We'll talk later," he said with a smile.

The President dropped his hands from their shoulders, and they turned to look at him. "Guys, one last question."

"Yes sir," answered Todd.

"What was it like? Going through time. Seeing a culture that disappeared 2000 years ago."

The two men looked at each other in the waiting room of the Oval Office and Hudson breathed deeply—a sigh of relief and complete exhaustion. "Let's just say there isn't enough time to describe it."

As the men were led to a waiting room he answered back. "Well gentlemen, time is something we can now offer in abundance." A small smile played on his lips before he turned back toward his office and shut the door.

EPILOGUE

SATURDAY EVENING, APRIL 18

"You just about ruined everything!" The man swore under his breath as he paced the room. It was late. "I appointed you, encouraged you, supported you! You almost took me down."

The contrite man wrung his hands in his lap.

Pressing his knuckles to his desk he continued. "To get the results we want and the outcome we need, we must go back again–earlier. Now that we know the exact date of his death we can pinpoint precisely the date of his birth. That should be an easier mission."

He sighed heavily. "We go back immediately; there's no time to waste. Do you understand?"

Yes.

"Fine," he said with confidence. "If you would excuse me, I'm late for a program at the Kennedy Center. You know what to do, so get moving," he spoke as he strode out of the room.

Senator John Hughes answered, "Yes, Mr. President."